CONSPIRACY OF ANGELS

COMING SOON FROM MICHELLE BELANGER AND TITAN BOOKS

Harsh Gods
The Resurrection Game

CONSPIRACY OF ANGELS

A NOVEL OF THE SHADOWSIDE

MICHELLE BELANGER

TITAN BOOKS

CONSPIRACY OF ANGELS
Print edition ISBN: 9781783297337
E-book edition ISBN: 9781783297344

Published by Titan Books
A division of Titan Publishing Group Ltd
144 Southwark Street, London SE1 0UP

First edition: October 2015

2 4 6 8 10 9 7 5 3 1

This book is a work of fiction. Names, characters, places and incidents either are products of the author's imagination or are used fictitiously. Any resemblance to actual events or locales or persons, living or dead, is entirely coincidental.

A CIP catalogue record for this title is available
from the British Library.

Printed and bound in the USA.

To the members of the Shadow Syndicate,
who have listened to my stories and shared
with me their own.

1

They were after me. I didn't know who, and I didn't know why, but I had to get away.

There was no other thought.

I fell through darkness till direction lost all meaning. My seizing lungs burned. When I finally breached the surface, I saw water and no shore. Pain chewed my awareness—pain and a wrenching sense of loss like a freshly severed limb. I groped for meaning, but it fled.

I lost count of how many times my head went under. My sodden leather jacket dragged against my shoulders—a dangerous weight. A sick jolt of anxiety stopped me from struggling out of it. The coat was important. I felt it with the same heart-knocking certainty that drove me to outpace my unseen pursuers.

I kept swimming.

I didn't remember reaching land, but came aware of it in stages. Consciousness flickered like an old filmstrip. I hugged a dirty strip of beach, sand clotting my nose. The water lapped my legs. Everything hurt.

A sharp insectile chitter brought me lurching to my knees. I came up swinging blindly, gagged on a shout, then doubled over to vomit about a gallon of the lake. Shakily, I knelt as my breath hitched in my scalded throat, then scrubbed grit and worse from the stubble on my jaw.

That urgent sense of pursuit spurred me to my feet once again. One boot was missing, and the sock on that foot flopped like a dark tongue.

I thought I heard a woman's voice, keening. Trapped.

Whirling at the sound, I hoped to catch sight of her, but I was alone, and the lake—as big as an inland sea—stretched away empty.

Those murky waters surged before me. My vision faltered and for a moment everything dropped away into darkness. The lake became a vast abyss, and nightmares seethed in its depths. The water wasn't water anymore, but a boiling blackness, filled with crimson eyes and gnashing teeth. I loosed an incoherent shout, stumbling backward to put as much distance as possible between myself and the dizzying vision.

I ended up on my ass with my back pressed up against a crumbling wall of shale. When I looked back at the lake, it was just water again, gray and brooding as the leaden skies above.

Keep moving.

Scrambling up the embankment, I kicked away my remaining boot. I'd run barefoot. I didn't care. A scree of stones clattered with the boot to the beach below. The guardrail twisted above me, one section skewed crazily from a collision that left green paint streaked across the metal. Hauling myself over, I bent in the dirt to catch my breath.

My pulse pounded so hard sparkling lights strobed at the edges of my vision. For a moment it seemed like I was going to be sick again. A tractor-trailer whizzed past, snapping me out of it.

The long, smooth stretch of two-lane country highway curved away through rolling farmland. Cornfields edged with autumn-hued trees lay opposite the lake. I couldn't see a house in either direction.

Just my luck.

I needed to catch a ride and get to someplace populated. The urge for a crowd jangled as powerfully as the need to flee.

A few cars sped by, drivers intent on their destinations. I tried flagging them down, but no one stopped. Some lady in a Malibu took one look at me and gunned her motor, swerving as she sped away. I yelled something nasty after her, but really couldn't blame her. I looked like the kind of hitchhiker they wrote about in horror stories—scarecrow-thin, bedraggled, and dressed in black from head to toe.

Doggedly, I kept moving.

It was dark and my feet were getting pretty raw by the time a semi caught me in its headlights and actually slowed. The rig pulled over to the narrow berm, wheels crunching gravel as it came to a halt. I approached the passenger side, trying to look harmless. The driver, a round-bellied man in his middle fifties, leaned over and rolled down the window nearest me. Heavy metal throbbed from the cab.

"You wreck your motorcycle or something?" he asked.

"I don't think so," I hedged, scrubbing at the stubble on my chin.

The man's bushy brows drew together and his right hand dropped to the stick shift. Great. He was ready to drive away, too. I must've looked worse than I felt.

"Look," I said quickly. "I don't know what happened. I woke up half in the lake."

The trucker considered this for a few moments, keen eyes lingering on my face.

"Ah, fuck it," he said with a shrug. "Get in. We're almost to Ashtabula. I'll drop ya off there."

Relieved, I climbed up the passenger side and settled in. My jacket squelched around me. I should have been shivering, but I just felt numb. In the darkness beyond the warm light of the cab, the chittering call of some night-thing raised the hairs on my neck. I slammed the door hurriedly, glad to be able to shut whatever it was away, then shifted my bare feet among the piles of crumpled fast food wrappers on the floor. The trucker's brows shot up when he saw I wasn't wearing any shoes, but he opted not to comment. Instead, he shoved a stubby-fingered hand at me by way of introduction.

"Folks call me Big Bill," he declared. "What's your name, son?"

That was when it hit me.

I didn't have a fucking clue.

2

I half-expected Big Bill to kick me out of his cab when I didn't respond right away. He kept his hand poised stiffly between us, his frown deepening to a scowl.

"Name's only polite, son," he rumbled, "but suit yerself."

To buy some time, I accepted his grubby clasp. The contact felt electric, and my already whirling brain burgeoned with half-formed thoughts and emotions—none of them my own. There was hesitation edging toward suspicion. A rising sense of irritation. The metallic tang of fear. I blinked, fighting to make sense of the onslaught. Instinct told me it was coming from the trucker.

How was that even possible?

"You on something?" Big Bill asked suspiciously, peeling his hand away. He wiped it on his thigh, as if my touch clung unpleasantly to him.

I didn't have an answer, but the unwelcome flood of perceptions cleared as soon as he broke contact. In its absence, my own anxieties surged with renewed intensity—the unsettling sense of pursuit and the staggering realization about my name.

How could I forget my fucking name?

Big Bill put the rig in gear, eyeing me skeptically the entire time. He said nothing further as he pulled back onto the road, so I turned and stared out the window, wrestling my anxious thoughts into some kind of order.

A wallet.

I had to have a wallet. Maybe that was why I'd refused to ditch the coat. Trying not to be obvious, I patted myself down, digging through the pockets of the leather jacket and turning them inside out. Driving gloves, a pen cap, some soggy gum wrappers. Nothing of any use whatsoever. I cursed none too softly.

Bill blasted Metallica and focused on driving.

I found a tiny front pocket with a metal snap rather than a zipper. It looked just big enough to hold a Zippo, or maybe an ID. Something was wedged inside of it—and wedged in tight. My hands were shaking, so it took a couple of tries to finally drag out the thin canvas wallet. It was blue and sealed with Velcro. I tore it open.

Three waterlogged twenties. A platinum card—*go me?*—and a State of Ohio driver's license.

"Zachary Westland," I read, squinting in the dim lighting of the cab.

Nothing.

Not even a flash of recognition.

The photo on the license didn't help. Pale blue eyes peered out at me from a long, narrow face. Gaunt cheeks, a straight nose, and a smooth brow surmounted by a shock of brown hair. It wasn't a bad face, but it might as well have belonged to a stranger.

The address was for an apartment in Cleveland Heights.

"That had to be Lake Erie," I murmured. Big Bill cleared his throat, and I realized I'd used my out-loud voice.

"I'm gonna drop you off at the Pub n' Sub by 531 up here," he announced.

I cast a sidelong glance his way.

"How far are we from Cleveland?"

"'Bout sixty miles," he said. "You can catch Route 20 or I-90 from 11. They'll both take you into the city."

"You're not headed that way?"

Big Bill fixed me with a steely glare. "Son, you're getting out soon as we're in East Ashtabula, and that's all I'm gonna say on the matter." To punctuate this, he cranked the music even louder. 'Enter Sandman' thundered through the cab. As dark as this stretch of country lane was, it really felt like we were heading off to never-never land.

With Big Bill brooding beside me, I dug through the rest of the wallet, searching for anything that might loosen my stubborn memory. There was a conceal carry permit, which I hid immediately, an insurance card declaring coverage on both a Buick and a motorcycle, and a business card for what looked like a nightclub. On the back of the business card, there was something scribbled in blue ink. I didn't think it was my handwriting.

55 and Marginal—2

All of it was meaningless to me.

We passed a gas station that was already closed for the night, and pulled in next door onto a gravel lot. There was a long, squat building that looked more suited to be a machine shop than a bar. A brightly lit sign with garish green and yellow lettering declared it the Pub N' Sub.

"Here's your stop," my reluctant Good Samaritan announced. He put the rig in park and folded his arms across his chest, scowling.

"Thanks, man," I said, and was relieved when he didn't extend his hand again. I wasn't sure what had happened when we shook the first time, but I didn't want to repeat the experience. I swung down from the cab, and he started pulling away almost as soon as my feet were on the gravel.

I stood blinking in the harsh glare of the floodlights mounted on the roof of the single-story bar. The wide lot held two semis, half a dozen mud-spattered pickups, and a few bikes out front. A couple of neon signs in the windows let me know I could get fresh eats and cold beer—except the "E" in "Eats" flickered dully, making the sign read, "Fresh ats." I pondered the nature of a "fresh at" while I tried to figure out my next move.

I had an address. It was safe to assume that's where I lived, but with no car and no shoes, the sixty miles to Cleveland might as well have been six million. Maybe I could use the phone and call a cab.

Throwing my slightly less sodden leather jacket over my shoulder, I picked my way across to the entrance of the pub, the gravel sharp and painful against the raw pads of my feet. The wind kicked up, scattering dried leaves across my path. If it was cold, I didn't feel it. From about ten paces out I could hear the muffled strains of country music, and I drew up short when I spied a predictable sign on the door:

No Shirt. No Shoes.
No Service.

To which was appended in less-regular red letters, *No Shit*.

"Really not my fucking day." I sighed, then shook my head and went in anyway. The worst they could do was throw me out, right?

3

I opened the door to a sensory assault—fryer grease, cigarette smoke, stale sweat and even staler beer. Half a dozen old TVs were mounted at various angles over the bar and seating area. The pictures flickered unsteadily and not a single one had the same color balance. Loud country music blared from the speakers, completely drowning out anything coming over the TVs—and yet none of the TVs were on mute, adding a dull, insensible hum to the chaos. The bass of the speakers completely swallowed the treble, so what little I could hear of the lyrics came out garbled at best.

Considering it was country, maybe that was a mercy.

I flinched as—for an instant—it seemed as if the patrons of the bar were shouting, all at once. There were about ten of them, and the cacophony drowned even the din of the music and TVs, then abruptly receded as I realized almost no one's mouth was moving. Most of the guys just sat morosely, staring into their beers. The bartender looked up as I hesitated near the door.

He was big, not as tall as I was, but broader again by half. I figured he had about fifty pounds on me, and little of that was fat. He had a hair net beneath which a snowy sweep of ponytail started about halfway back on his scalp. Of all things, he had a beard net, too, covering a plume of white and gray long enough to make a Tolkien dwarf envious. As he regarded me, his ice-chip eyes went ten degrees chillier.

"Sign's there fer a reason," he grunted in a basso voice that cut easily through the noise.

I was still trying to work out why I'd heard voices. Was I hallucinating?

"If I had shoes, I'd be wearing them," I shot back. "Look, I just need the pay phone... and change for a twenty." I approached the bar, holding out one of my soggy bills. From the look of his stained and greasy apron, he was also the cook. He squinted down at the damp and crumpled money, then took in the whole of my appearance.

"The heck happened to you?" he grunted.

Wish I knew, I thought, but I just shrugged. Out loud I answered, "Bad day. I don't imagine cabs come all the way out here?"

He quirked an eyebrow at me. It was one of those old-guy eyebrows where a couple of the hairs had gone wild and grew three times as long as any of the others. They stuck out from the middle like curling antennae.

"From where?"

"Cleveland?" I asked hopefully.

A few of the patrons stole sideways glances at me and snorted over their beers. The bartender let out a bellowing laugh.

"You're kidding, right?"

It was worth a shot.

That left me with the business card. Glossy black, it had "Heaven" stamped on it in stylish silver lettering. The phone number and address were in red. I had no idea how or even *if* it pertained to me. At least there was a number I could call. That was somewhere to start.

"Is there a hotel nearby?" I asked glumly, just in case Heaven didn't pan out.

"Roadway Express 'bout a mile the other side of town," he offered.

"If you've got their number, I'll take that, too."

Shaking his head, the bartender grabbed something bulky from under the register and chucked it. I caught the phone book with a speed and accuracy that surprised even me, snapping my left hand up and seeming to pluck the unwieldy tome from mid-air. I paused, staring at this. Half a dozen of the bar's patrons were staring now, too. Whispers surged, threatening to swell into shouting again. I closed my eyes against the sensation, fighting for order in my own head.

"Uh… thanks," I muttered a little weakly. I tucked the phone book under one arm and did my best to look inconspicuous. At six foot three and covered in lake muck, it wasn't happening.

Still shaking his head and muttering to himself, the fellow counted out my change and set the money on the bar. I scooped up the bills and quarters, pointedly avoiding touching his hand. Biker Santa jerked his thumb toward an alcove which, according to the battered tin sign tacked above it, also led to the "Used Beer Department."

"Phone's back there," he said, then he abruptly turned around and ignored me.

The pay phone was clunky and ancient, but I hadn't expected anything less. In this age of ubiquitous cell phones, I was just happy the bar hadn't ripped the thing out and replaced it with some flashy gambling machine.

It was dented on one side, some of the paint scraped down to the metal. I ran a finger over one of the dents curiously, then froze as I got that electric feeling again. Something blossomed in my mind—not just thoughts this time, but whole images. They came in rapid flashes, like a stop-motion film, each scene super-saturated with emotion. A man in a pale shirt and a cowboy hat pacing on the phone—this phone. A woman on the other end—and somehow I could see her, too. She was seated on a couch with a hideous floral print, a box of tissues open on the coffee table before her. She had a black eye and raw bruises across her jaw and chin.

There were scrapes on his knuckles from breaking two of her teeth. He rubbed the raw, infected skin while he argued.

She was breaking up with him. He couldn't yell loud enough to berate her, wanted to hit her even then, but she was miles away.

He had a thumper dangling from his belt—something shaped like a mini-baseball bat used to test the tires on his truck. I couldn't say how, but I knew the nature of the little tool in an instant. Red in the face and raging, he grabbed the thumper and beat it repeatedly against the side of the phone. Then he was screaming into the receiver that she couldn't do this to him, that he would show her, he would make her pay.

Through hiccupping sobs, she said no more—she wouldn't let him hurt her anymore.

That was when she grabbed the gun sitting next to the box of tissues. When she closed her lips around the muzzle, the blast nearly drove me to my knees. With a hoarse cry, I tore my hand away from the side of the pay phone. It felt like I was going to vomit again, and my pulse hammered painfully in my head. I tried to breathe through it, acutely aware of the feel of eyes on my back.

What the hell? Was this some kind of vision? If it was, what was I supposed to do with it—run out and stop her? I didn't recognize either the woman or the man. Maybe it was something that had already happened. Yet it was so immediate—I could still taste the metal of the gun.

Clenching my teeth against the echo of the gunshot, I tried to get a grip on myself. There wasn't anything I could do for anyone, not in my current state—even if what I'd just seen was real. I closed my eyes and counted my breaths until my heart resumed a steadier pace. I had to get my own shit sorted out.

Picking up the business end of the phone, I started feeding it quarters. With trembling fingers, I punched in the number for Heaven. I needed answers. With luck, they would be on the other end of the line.

4

No one picked up. I counted to ten, gritting my teeth tighter with each ring. It didn't even go to an answering machine.

I was tempted to revisit the abuse to the phone, only with my fist instead of a thumper. Knowing how little that would accomplish, I took a deep, steadying breath. Still, I hung up the phone with such force that it made the internal bell *ding*. The coin return vomited quarters and they cascaded onto the floor. I could feel eyes on me from the bar again and I just put my back to them.

After collecting the change, I leaned over the little shelf next to the phone, gripping my head with both hands. All the weird shit spinning around in my brain made it hard to think.

I was just about to call the Roadway Express and ask about a room when something prompted me to try the number for Heaven again. Nothing so clear as a vision. Just a feeling.

Couldn't hurt. I had the quarters.

The line started ringing. I pressed the phone to my ear, irritably pacing the short distance its cord allowed, looking everywhere but at the people who were glaring at me. The flickering television screens caught my eye, if only for a few moments each. A football match. A poker game—which somehow was a sport now. Local news. World news. Hockey.

By the fifth ring, I was ready to give up on the hunch and just call it a night. Sure, I was going to have to walk at least another mile to the damned hotel, but at the end of that walk there was a hot shower and a soft bed waiting for me—assuming the platinum card in my wallet was legit.

Abruptly, the monotone ring cut short and the throb of very loud, oontzy dance music spilled from the other end. Then there was a muffled voice, lilting and female.

"Club Heaven. Can I help you?"

I opened my mouth and went totally blank. What was I going to say?

Hi, this is your friendly neighborhood amnesiac. I'm lost in East Bumfuck and seeing all kinds of weird shit. Come pick me up, please.

Sure, that would work.

Stammering a bit, I managed, "Uh, this is Zachary. Zachary Westland?" The name still felt foreign on my tongue.

She was silent on the other end, though the pounding music never ceased. I started to worry that she hadn't heard me clearly.

"Hello?" I prompted.

Pitching her voice a little louder, she repeated, "Can I help you?"

"It's Zachary Westland," I said a little more firmly.

"Are you calling about a special event?" the woman asked. She sounded bored. Then I heard a male voice and her giggled response. The pulse of the music suddenly grew muted, as if she'd cupped her hand over the phone. There was the dim exchange of voices, hers and the man's. None of the words translated, but there was enough vocal inflection to guess that they were—at the very least—flirting.

I scowled, whirling around in the alcove on the short leash of the phone cord.

That's when I saw it. My face—or at least a reasonable approximation of the face in the driver's license. It was a police sketch. Of course, considering the kind of day I was having, what else could it have been?

The reception on the TV was terrible, lines marching up the screen and flickering spastically. At the bottom, a little ticker-style announcement scrolled along.

...wanted for questioning in the Rockefeller Park shooting. Consider armed and dangerous. Notify police immediately. It was followed with a hotline number, as well as a code for texts.

"Shit," I breathed and nearly dropped the handset.

A brassy-haired woman sitting at the end of the bar followed my gaze, then did a double take. Her gaudily painted lips opened to make a little "O" of surprise. The sketch was replaced with an innocuous image of a park—nothing but some leafless trees and a statue of what looked for all the world like Mahatma Gandhi. The woman squinted, trying to follow the scrolling letters as the warning repeated across the bottom of the screen.

A sick cocktail of anxiety and fear roiled in my gut.

Not good. Not good at all.

The music on the other end of the phone came through clearly all of a sudden.

"I'm sorry," the girl said, a little breathlessly. "Were you calling about a special event?" A throaty purr beneath her words replaced the boredom.

"Zachary Westland," I repeated automatically, as if the name were a talisman, but my real attention was on the woman with the bad dye-job as she debated what to do.

Considered armed and dangerous. Notify police immediately.

"Sir, this is Club Heaven. We're open from ten pm till three am Thursday through Sunday. We do special events weekdays..." She droned on, reciting from memory. The brassy-haired woman bent to retrieve a mammoth purse from the floor beside her stool. Digging around frantically in its depths, she pulled out a cell phone and retreated to a quieter corner of the building.

"Oh, fuck me running," I complained.

The girl on the other end of the phone thought I was swearing at her. She cursed right back, her voice rising stridently.

"Look, you stupid bastard, we don't have a Zachary Westland on staff. Ask a real question or get off my goddamned phone—*hey*!" This last came out as an indignant squeak. There were sounds like a mild struggle over the handset, then another voice came across the line.

"*Zaquiel?* Is that you? Why on earth are you calling this line?" It was the male, no longer murmuring. He spoke in a clear, mellifluous tone, words clipped with a subtle accent that I couldn't quite place.

The name lanced through me like lightning. Images flooded my head, jumbled and incoherent. The only thing I made out with any clarity was the thunderous music of hundreds of voices raised in perfect song. Beautiful and agonizing, it hit me like a punch to the gut. I struggled to recover, and at the same time, I saw the woman snap a picture of me with her cell.

Damn, damn, damn!

"Gotta go," I said hastily, hanging up the phone and snagging my coat in one swift movement. Then I headed for the door as quickly as I could without attracting any further attention. I kept Ms. Bad Dye Job in sight out of the corner of my eye. She was talking rapidly and urgently on her phone as I slipped out to the parking lot.

It wasn't like I had anywhere to go. No getaway car. Not even a good pair of running shoes.

Fuck my life.

5

I stood on the small patch of concrete that seemed to serve the Pub n' Sub as a patio in warmer weather, wracking my brain for what to do. I scanned the night, looking for flashes of blue and red. Nothing so far, but with the way my luck was running, that wasn't going to last.

My gaze fell to the three bikes parked in front of the bar. According to the card in my wallet, I was insured to drive a motorcycle. Did that mean I knew how to steal one? At least I wouldn't have to break into it, like I would a car. Of course, these three were right out front, in full view of the windows. There were about ten guys in there, not counting Biker Santa of the beard net, and some of them were as big as he was. None of them seemed kindly disposed toward my person, and I didn't think their opinions of me would improve if they caught me stealing one of their bikes.

Catching some angry yokel's bullet struck me as a pretty rotten way to die.

That was when I spied the tarp. Sun-bleached and

covered in a fine layer of dust, almost the same color as the dead stalks of corn lining the field behind the bar. Crabgrass and Queen Anne's Lace had grown thick around the bottom edges, dried to a yellow tangle now that summer had come and gone. The bike beneath the tarp hadn't moved in a while, tucked halfway behind the building, but it was out of sight of both the road and the front windows.

"Best chance you got," I muttered, shrugging into my damp leather and trotting along the thin strip of concrete that hugged the side wall. I whipped off the tarp, scattering a wave of dust, seeds, and field spiders. It was a beautiful old Harley, the casing over its gas tank a deep, rich red. Betting it belonged to Biker Santa, I honestly felt bad at the thought of stealing it. It looked like something from the late '70s or early '80s, but was in pristine condition.

Someone loved this bike.

Still, I needed wheels, and fast.

"I'll get it back to him," I promised myself, and I meant it, too. Which made me wonder about the police bulletin. Armed and dangerous. Seriously? I was agonizing over a motorcycle. "Feel bad once you've managed to steal it," I chided myself.

Disengaging the stand and trying to ignore the spiders underfoot, I swung my leg over the bike and settled onto the seat. I was a little too tall for the thing, and if I managed to get it going, I was risking the loss of my toes by riding barefoot, but I gripped the handlebars tightly, getting a feel for the controls.

As soon as I did, I was inundated with impressions—

riding with someone clinging to my back, the welcome warmth of her nearness eclipsing even the exhilaration of the open road. Younger times, the days spent riding and the nights spent tangled together, often under the open stars. Then a crushing sense of absence. Impossible to ride the bike without wrestling with her ghost. Revisiting it to polish and care for it every anniversary, then mournfully returning the tarp. A sense of loss so sharp, there was no surcease.

"Not my feelings, not my feelings," I whispered, fiercely willing the emotions away. In that instant, there was no denying what they were—psychic impressions of some sort. I wanted to ask Biker Santa about his wife—if they had ridden together, and how long ago she had died.

Yet I already knew the answers.

Gripping the handlebars that somehow still held cherished memories of his long-dead lady, I fought to focus on the here-and-now. Dried-out strands of crabgrass rasped against my ankle. It took all of about thirty seconds for me to realize that I didn't know the first thing about how to steal a motorcycle.

Sirens wailed in the distance.

"Dammit!" I snarled. It was a kick-start bike, so I tried forcing it into neutral and rolling forward as I jammed my foot down on the starter. With the way my feet were chewed up from walking, that hurt about as much as I thought it would. The pain was hardly a deterrent, though. I did it a second time and fiercely willed the thing to go.

The engine growled to life.

Astonished, I gaped at the controls. Down the road, the sirens blared ever closer, overpowering the pulse of the engine.

"Not the time for questions," I mumbled.

Readjusting my grip on the handlebars, I pulled out of the lot just in time to see a bunch of guys spilling out of the front of the bar. They were led by Biker Santa. His face was scarlet as he aimed a shotgun at me, and he wasn't the least bit jolly. Police lights flashed against the buildings south of the pub and the sirens ratcheted up to a deafening wail. My bad luck was holding. The cop cars were effectively cutting me off from the direction I needed to go.

"Move now, think later," I snarled, then swung the growling bike around and sped into the cornfield behind the bar.

6

Riding a motorcycle through a cornfield without protective gear is a recipe for pain. Doing it while *barefoot* ranks right up there with rappelling down razor wire or wrestling a rabid porcupine. I was cruising for a Darwin Award. Add in the after-effects of weird psychic visions, pursuit by the local authorities, and being chased by a pack of gun-toting bikers, and my day was rapidly approaching nightmare status.

Somehow I managed to lose them.

More astonishing than that, I managed to find a road. It was little more than a narrow strip of asphalt running between whispering fields of dried corn, but it headed in the right direction. I leaned forward on the Harley, rocketing along as fast as I dared on the lonely country lane. Once in a while I passed houses, but they were all an acre back or more, their lights shaping dim constellations in an otherwise starless night.

I continued like that for several miles, keeping an eye out for any cross street that was bigger than a driveway.

Finally I came to Route 20. Given that this was the first intersection that had a stoplight, albeit a blinking one, it had to be a major road for this lonely corner of the Buckeye State. Swinging right, I followed 20 for a while as the clusters of houses became more frequent.

Up ahead, fields and houses gave way to a wide and brightly lit expanse of asphalt. A monolithic building sat back from the road, squat and unattractive. From the look and size of it, I first thought it was an institution. As I drew closer, however, I spied the fluorescent lights spilling out from glass shop windows and automatic doors. A strip of navy-blue signage running across the entire upper portion of the building declared it to be a Wal-Mart. There were perhaps sixteen cars in the parking lot.

Though desolate, it looked open.

I slowed as I approached the turn-off, mentally tallying the remainder of my cash. If the police were looking for me, I didn't dare use that platinum card in my wallet, however tempting it might be to procure a fresh set of clothes. But I needed footwear badly. I probably had enough cash to get a cheap but serviceable pair of boots, some socks, and maybe even a package of bandages. My feet were pretty chewed up at this point, so cramming them into boots wasn't really a delightful prospect.

Still, it was better than the alternative. I was lucky so far to have only scrapes and blisters, and if things were cheap enough, I might even have some money left over to feed the gas tank. Biker Santa had seen fit to keep it topped off, so that wasn't yet a priority.

I pulled up to the front of the store and started to

park. Then I realized there was a serious flaw in my plan. Dumb luck and desperation were the only things that had got the Harley running in the first place, so I didn't dare turn it off.

"Well, crap," I muttered to myself, glancing around the lot. No one in sight. Empty fields stretching to either side. "Not much choice," I observed with a shrug. Then I coasted up to a display at the front of the building.

Dying mums in battered plastic containers sat beside a boldly lettered sign proclaiming them "On Sale." I maneuvered the motorcycle close to the half-dead flowers and set the kickstand, leaving the vintage machine idling in neutral. The area was brightly lit, and I hoped this would have the effect of deterring potential thieves, rather than calling attention to the unattended bike. Reluctantly stepping away from it, I cast a glance heavenward.

"If you've got any mercy at all, let this thing be here when I get back."

Regarding the mute expanse of the sky, I was overcome with a near-crushing awareness that nothing up there was listening to me. I blinked with the force of it, tearing my eyes away from the reflective bellies of the clouds. Mercifully, the feeling passed. Swiping at some of the cornfield detritus still lingering on my jacket and in my hair, I scowled.

"Boots now," I told myself. "Existential meltdown later." I padded into the store, leaving russet smears on the tile as I went.

Management was going to love me.

As it turned out, I didn't have to worry. No one I encountered was out to win any beauty pageants.

There were three solitary souls browsing the aisles, and if I'd been clean-shaven and less rumpled, I would have stood out more. I kept my head down anyway, and headed for the footwear section.

Looking over a rack of reasonably sturdy work boots—"Prices Slashed! Now only 29.95!"—I realized that I had no idea what size I wore. The amnesia thing was really starting to get on my nerves.

I yanked off what was left of my socks and studied my poor abused feet. *Probably a twelve.* I had long, thin toes to match my long, thin fingers, so maybe it was more like a thirteen. I grabbed a three-pack of athletic socks and tore a pair from the plastic. Looking around for sales associates or security cameras, I eased my feet into the fresh socks, then started trying on boots.

After three attempts I got the right size, or at least close enough. I laced up the boots, grabbed the box and the remaining socks, and carried them over toward the single open register. No one looked twice, not even the gaunt-faced fellow wearing deer-hunter orange who was walking in circles near the housewares, muttering to himself about elephant guns.

I *so* didn't want to know.

At the counter, the bleary-eyed girl with a torn-out eyebrow piercing held up the empty shoebox and shook it at me.

"I gotta scan the boots for you to buy them." She almost touched my hand and I jerked back. She gaped at me like a carp.

"That's too bad," I said impatiently. "I'm wearing them. That's why I brought the box."

"But the box is empty," she argued.

"That's because I'm wearing them!" I said again. We went round and round like this for a couple of minutes, and it felt like being caught in the loop of some old comedy, only it didn't feel at all funny. I gritted my teeth, resisting the urge to reach over the counter and shake her.

Elephant-gun man began wandering toward the register, and he looked way too interested in our conversation.

"Look," I said, trying to keep my voice down, "I wrecked my boots out in the mud. I got socks here and I got boots. The boots came in that box, which has a bar code. All you have to do is scan the fucking bar code. I just want to pay and get out of here."

Frowning, she set the empty box down and picked up the three-pack of athletic socks. She poked at the ragged edges where I'd torn open the packaging. "This is already open. You wanna go back and get a new one?"

I felt my eye twitch.

"It's fine," I managed. "Just scan it, and scan that box. I'm buying the box, too."

Looking at me like I was the one with the mental deficiency, she took her little gun and ran the laser scanner over the bar codes. I shoved money at her before she finished ringing up the total, which made her pause again and almost lose track of what she was doing. With agonizing care she slipped both the empty shoebox and the opened package of socks into a thin plastic bag. Only then did she take my money and cash me out.

I fought the urge to grab the package and bolt from the store, instead forcing myself to walk slowly back to the entrance. I thought a series of very unkind things about her parents as I pulled the socks from the bag on my way out of the store. I tossed the bag into a nearby trash bin, stuffing the two extra pairs of socks into an inner pocket of my jacket.

The Harley still rested next to the bedraggled mums, its engine humming softly.

"Thank goodness for small favors," I muttered, then swung back onto the motorcycle and resumed my trip toward Cleveland, now about 35 miles away. Then all I had to do was find a club I didn't remember in a city whose streets were forgotten to me, as well.

7

Once I got onto I-90, it took me straight into the city. As I drove through the eastern suburbs, the highway split off into a bewildering number of alternate freeways. I followed my instincts, surrendering to the feel of what seemed right, and by eleven-thirty I was within sight of the Cleveland skyline.

The skyscrapers were lit from below with candy-colored floods of red, blue, and gold. Gleaming lights illuminated the downtown bridges as well, making the art deco giants flanking their arches come ominously to life.

A wealth of apparently random facts spun through my brain—the foibles of the Van Sweringen brothers, pride in native son Bob Hope, and rueful memories of J.D. Rockefeller's cutthroat tactics. I found myself wondering about my curiously selective amnesia. Everything was poignantly familiar. I knew the shape of the Terminal Tower, the tales of the Detroit Avenue Bridge, the fervor sports-minded locals held for the stadium that was home of the Cleveland Tribe.

As long I didn't think too hard about it, I knew where every street led. I took the exit that funneled me down a winding path from the overpass to the Flats. I found myself on River Road, got routed around a drawbridge that was undergoing repairs, passed the Nautica stage, then drew up short at a sleek black sign with familiar silver letters.

HEAVEN

Parking was ten dollars in the attached lot. All too conscious of my dwindling funds, I decided to take my chances and leave the Harley on the street. That proved to be an adventure. Although no special event seemed to be going on at the Nautica or anywhere else in the Flats, cars crowded nose-to-bumper, tires half up on the worn and shallow curbs. Listing pylons twined with thick, weathered chains blocked access to one side street after another, till I found myself again at the bank of the river.

A great, rusting monolith rose to one side, its purpose lost to the city's industrial past. The broad, oily expanse of the Cuyahoga drank the light from the crumbling bridges arching above it, their reflections dragged mercilessly into its muddy depths.

There was a parking space right near the river's edge, but I wanted no part of those still, brooding waters. Choking on shapeless memories I could neither ignore nor divine, I guided the old Harley deeper into the tangle of one-way streets and back alleys, dodging potholes big enough to swallow the front tire. I finally found a space a good several blocks from Heaven. The lone streetlight at the corner had been shot out. At that point, I didn't care.

Setting the kickstand I reluctantly cut the engine. If I was lucky, Club Heaven would give up the answers that I needed, and I'd be able to make a discreet call pointing the authorities to Biker Santa's cherished ride.

I oriented myself in the direction of the club and started walking. A gusting wind carried the stench of the river, thick and ripe and fishy. The scent dredged half-formed images from my hindbrain—none of them clear enough to hold onto, but they spiked my anxious pulse nevertheless.

It didn't help that this corner of the Flats was questionable at best. I passed a pair of seedy-looking characters slouching along in baggy pants and oversized hoodies. They stared too long at me as I strode past, and the feel of their eyes made my skin crawl in a way I couldn't really justify. I kept my head down and tried to ignore them.

A shrill, chittering cry rang piercingly through the street and I froze, overcome with the irrational fear that some terrible creature had followed me all the way from Ashtabula. Once I convinced my legs to move again, I quickened my pace, faltering when I heard the scrape of a shoe against the cracked and uneven sidewalk behind me.

The ruffians staggered along in shuffling pursuit, glassy eyes fixed on everything and nothing at once. Shadows swirled thickly around them, clinging to their backs like living things. The minute I turned and spotted them, they charged forward, mouths agape.

One of them pulled a gun.

That cry came again, and I could have sworn it issued from his throat. I knew it wasn't possible—nothing human could make that sound—but I didn't care. I vaulted over the hood of a car parked beside me, sprinting across a dark and narrow side street. The neon sign of a bar burned on the corner, less than a block away. I headed toward the light.

From the frenzied slap of feet against pavement, they were right on my heels. At least they weren't shooting—yet. As I pelted around the corner toward the bar, I ran right in the path of oncoming headlights. The vehicle was already slowing to a stop at the intersection, but I still hip-checked its grill, rolling onto the hood and nearly kissing the windshield.

It was a cop car. I got an up close and personal look at the startled faces of the driver and his partner. The older guy behind the wheel just gaped at me. The younger woman in the passenger seat yelled something, her dark features shifting swiftly from shock to fury. I slid off the hood and was already charging down the sidewalk before the cruiser came to a complete halt. Visions of the news bulletin flashed through my head and I sped away, certain the cops would come at me shooting.

By then the thugs had run headlong into the side of the vehicle like they didn't know they could go around it. They jostled alongside it, thumping their palms against the hood.

I didn't ask questions. There wasn't any time. I had no interest in being caught by either the hoodie gang or the police, so I just thanked whatever power was responsible for finally throwing me a break. I tore off down an alley, leaving the cops to contend with the two delinquents.

After I'd gone a couple of blocks, a shot rang out, and then another. I ducked reflexively beside a dumpster. Shrill cries echoed through the night—they hardly sounded human. Suddenly my lucky break didn't seem very lucky—at least not for the cops. I hesitated in my hiding spot, and almost turned back, but what was I going to do? Charge in unarmed?

I'd get shot or arrested.

Probably both.

Shouts again. It made more sense to run, but I couldn't let it go. Cautiously, I doubled back toward the bar, hugging the shadows and moving as stealthily as my gangly six-foot-something frame would allow. My hands tingled like they were wrapped around live wires. Restlessly, I shook the sensation from my fingers, but it clung like ants swarming the wrong side of my skin.

The officers were standing over two lifeless bodies.

"What the hell were they thinking?" the lady cop said. "They saw our guns. Why didn't they stop?" She still held her service piece trained on the dead men, her African complexion gray with shock. One of the corpses twitched, and she nearly squeezed off another round.

"Drugged up, from the look of it," her partner grumbled. "Sometimes it's shoot or get shot, Maggie." He toed one of the fallen forms, kicking a gun out of its now limp hand. He looked up and scanned the alley. "What happened with that other one—the guy we hit?"

I pressed myself deep inside a doorway, ducking my head low. It was time to go. The minute he turned back toward the cruiser, I fled, tracing my way between windowless warehouses till I came once more to Club Heaven.

No matter how I tried, I couldn't quite shake the expression on the lady cop's face. It looked like she hadn't had to kill anyone before. Maybe there had been a way to avoid it. Maybe if I'd stayed and faced the thugs myself, things would have played out differently.

But that was stupid, and I was wanted. Pleading amnesia wouldn't make that go away.

As I approached the massive brick warehouse that was home to Club Heaven, I smoothed back my wind-torn hair and tried to shake some of the tension out of my shoulders. No sense going in looking like I was spoiling for a fight.

It was close to midnight, and Heaven was in full swing. Big double doors were propped open beneath an awning of blood-red vinyl. Pulsing electronica spilled into the night. A bull-necked doorman stood nearby, his thick arms not so much folded as resting on his broad chest. Despite the hour he wore sunglasses, and his meaty jaw was given definition by a dark and meticulously trimmed goatee. His head appeared to be shaved down to the scalp underneath a black leather top hat that had a pair of steampunk goggles perched atop its brim.

He shifted his weight almost imperceptibly as I approached. I dug out my wallet and retrieved my ID, holding it at the ready. I knew the drill.

"How much?" I asked, hoping the few crumpled bills I had left would cover entry.

The doorman barely spared my license a passing glance.

"Fifteen," he said automatically. I searched his face for any hint of recognition, but he had the bouncer glare down, regarding me stonily from behind the shades.

"All right." I handed him a ten and a five, noting glumly that this just left me with a couple of singles. "Hey, dumb question, but..." For a moment I faltered—but what did I have to lose? "Do I come here often?"

The guy gave me a curious look, dark brows furrowing over the sunglasses. Then he shrugged.

"I'm new, man." He waved the cash away, gesturing further into the club. "Pay the girl when you see her."

"Um, right," I said. "I still need the ID?" He shook his head, so I put it back in my wallet, which I wedged into the back left pocket of my jeans. Then I dove into the riot of sound and shadow that was the interior of the club.

Dim red bulbs cast a sepulchral gloom over the entryway, and a kind of privacy wall made it necessary to step left or right. The ceiling of the club yawned cavernously above it, black except for intermittent strobes of light. Another thick-necked bouncer-type leaned against the left-hand side of the wall, his hand resting idly on a velvet rope strung across that entrance. I took the other path toward a short counter with a cash register. A curtained archway rose beyond. The heavy red velvet drapes vibrated in the stultifying thunder of the bass.

A girl sat behind the counter, the Asian lift to her eyes highlighted by heavy black eyeliner and shimmering smears of red and gold. Her face was powdered bone-white and the natural shape of her lips was obscured by a small, stylized black heart painted over them. The heart made her look as if she was constantly puckered up for a kiss.

Her black and gold-streaked hair was swept up in a severe knot, with an asymmetrical fan of it sticking out to one side, the ends coated so heavily in styling gel that they might as well have been spikes of black glass. A red lacquered chopstick topped with a tiny skull-shaped bead angled through her hair. A matching skull dangled from the lobe of the opposing ear.

"Fifteen dollars, please," she said with an air of crushing boredom. I recognized her voice immediately and gawked for a moment, struggling for something to say. She fixed her gaze on me, blinking once. As I continued to hesitate, a little crease of irritation formed between her penciled brows.

"Um, I'm Zachary Westland?" I offered.

The flat ophidian cast to those eyes never faltered, but her brows went up just a touch.

"Oh," she said. Her gaze slid from me to the curtain, and for a moment she seemed to be peering through it. "He's expecting you," she said. "Up in the Sanctuary." She didn't bother to explain who, or what that was—just gestured vaguely toward the curtained door.

"Uh, thanks," I managed. I held the ten and five out to her, but she shook her head.

"Family's always free," she said.

Family?

Chewing on that interesting morsel, I ducked through the curtain.

My eyes had no time to adjust—lasers burst forth in a

brilliant cascade, dazzling as they reflected off a massive disco ball suspended over the dance floor. Black walls, black floor, and black-clad people blended into a mass of writhing shadows punctuated by stuttering strobes. Before the lasers exploded in another scintillating display, a stampede of unexpected sensations ran roughshod through my mind—faces, visions, colors, and a host of conflicting emotions enervating beyond tolerance.

I hit the floor without any conscious awareness of it, dragging the velvet curtain down on top of me. In my fading vision, times and styles blurred together in a jumble. Goths and flappers and sleek-suited toughs all danced cheek to cheek with the same frenetic air of desperate indulgence.

I had no idea if any of it was real.

My last scrap of awareness flashed with galvanizing imagery—so vivid, it felt as if I'd been thrust into a movie. A place like this, rife with hunger, decadence, and sex. Not a club. More like a temple—halls of carved stone, impossibly old. Tall, gaunt men with grim expressions stormed the place, tearing down tapestries and toppling columns. Clad in rough-spun tunics, they held near-identical expressions and carried strangely curved bronze blades.

Driving half-naked revelers before them, they spared none who resisted. All were tainted, all were judged—but the real goal was the abomination perched at the heart of the nest.

He sat amidst the trappings of some sort of shrine, poison-green eyes glinting from beneath a thick fringe of lashes. He looked human, but his mouth was fanged.

Overwhelmed by sheer numbers, he hissed and spat curses as they dragged him from his throne. A thin bone stylus carved the sentence across his forehead in curving letters of gleaming blood. They held him, wrist and ankle, wiry limbs splayed and straining.

There was no room for mercy.

At a sign from the leader, bronze blades flashed through pale flesh. The creature's throat fountained crimson. The final dagger punched under his ribs, curving upward to seek his heart. His oath resounded on a gurgling breath.

"I'll repay you for this, brother. You and all your tribe."

I stared down at the crumpled form.

It was my hand wrapped around the killing blade.

8

"Zaquiel!"

The name dredged me from a sea of uneasy visions. Nothing but scraps accompanied me to the surface, mostly vague intimations of bloodshed and struggle. I still felt the shape and heft of the curved bronze dagger, my fingers curling as if I could carry it with me to the waking world. I clenched my fist until the feeling went away. I wasn't sure what to make of that dream... memory... whatever it was, but the vivid way it clung to my thoughts unsettled me.

I'll repay you for this, brother.

I blinked up at a spacious room, fighting to focus on the here-and-now. Everything within the scope of my vision was black—black leather couches, black painted walls, black tiles on the floor. That alone suggested that I was still inside the club. Even the doors and ceiling had been given a coat of matte black paint. Spatters of silver randomly speckled the ceiling and walls, as if some budding Jackson Pollack had been called in to decorate.

The brief dots and arcs of shine were the only things to break up the unremitting monochrome of the décor.

The music of the club still throbbed, albeit distantly. Wherever we were, however, the soundproofing was impressive.

There was someone standing over me, and when I got a good look at him I thought I might still be dreaming. He was decked out in a dark red suit and matching red tie worn over a sleek black dress shirt that could only have been silk. The suit made him look like an escapee from a Tim Burton remake of *The Untouchables*. All he needed was a fedora over his flowing, ebon mane.

He peered down at me with eyes the color of a tropical cove. They were such an intense shade of azure they seemed as surreal as his outrageous suit.

"What's the matter with you?" he demanded. His vaguely accented voice was rich and mellifluous. There was no mistaking it. This was the man from the phone call.

I started to respond, but nothing English came out. Panic gripped me then—was that aphasia? Maybe I had brain damage, and amnesia was just the start. I flailed, struggling to get up, but the man pressed long-fingered hands against my shoulders, holding me prone.

"Zaquiel, please," he said. "There's no call for that. Calm down and explain yourself."

He leaned over me, his thick, straight hair swinging forward to partially obscure his narrow face. I caught the pale curve of cheekbone, an aquiline nose, and those deep and soul-searching eyes. Something about his features seemed familiar—hauntingly so—but I was too muddled to place it.

Licking dry lips, I croaked, "Something's wrong." My voice was rough, but at least this time it was intelligible.

"Well, obviously," he responded dryly. "Otherwise you wouldn't have come back here so soon. She's still furious with you, you know."

Images weltered in my mind—a woman with warm, olive skin and hair like a cascade of midnight. He couldn't mean her. She was trapped... somewhere. A tiny space, curved windowless walls—the knowledge fluttered just on the periphery of consciousness. I tried to grab it, but it skittered like mercury, leaving a heart-wrenching echo of loss. I needed to help her. I didn't even know who she was.

"Who's furious?" I murmured.

"Saliriel, of course," he sneered. "You don't insult a decimus so thoroughly without expecting consequences. Things aren't as lax with us as with your tribe." Then, far more gently, he asked, "Can you stand?" He extended his hand and I took it without thought.

That was a mistake.

The minute I touched bare skin, I was seized with a chaos of impressions—lust and blood and naked flesh. The woman at the counter, her lips parted for a kiss. Someone bound, leather straps biting into creamy skin. Other impressions, thankfully too brief to adequately process.

A yawning emptiness opened under my ribs so intense it stole my breath. I jerked away as if he'd burned me, then sat huddled around that gnawing sensation of hunger. It wouldn't go away. If anything, it got worse.

He stared mutely at his pale fingers for the space of

a heartbeat, then his porcelain-perfect features twisted into a ferocious mask.

"How dare you!" he spat. "I'm not some mortal whose thoughts you riffle at a whim. Me, of all your brothers? Maybe Saliriel's right, and you *have* taken leave of your senses." The hot metal of his anger pierced like a blade through my mind.

Brothers? A tidal surge of images battered my reason—shattered stones in the temple and those hateful, poison-green eyes. *You and all your tribe.* I pressed my hands to my head, desperate to block it out, but it just sucked me down further until I couldn't distinguish memory, reality, vision, or dream.

Somewhere in the midst of this Red Suit realized I hadn't been attacking him.

"Zaquiel?" he murmured, sounding vaguely contrite. "Please tell me what's wrong."

I felt more than saw his hand extend toward my shoulder, and twisted away, pressing myself into the corner of the couch.

"Don't touch me," I snarled.

His hand still poised, he said, "All right, but I need to know what's going on. You're not even supposed to be here. You know that."

"I don't know anything," I hissed through gritted teeth. I still held my hands clamped over my ears and probably looked ridiculous—like a kid trying to hide from the bogeyman by covering his eyes. Yet I couldn't help it. My brain was a roiling maelstrom, filled with things that weren't my own. The emptiness where my own thoughts should be—memories, knowledge, anything—gaped like a chasm.

"Well, that's a problem," Red Suit murmured. "Vikram, go talk to Alice and the ones who found him. See if he was attacked."

It took me a minute to realize he was talking to someone. A big guy, almost as broad across the shoulders as I was long in the legs, stood beside a second door set into the far wall. The door was black and his suit was black, effectively rendering both of them invisible. He was lively as a gargoyle, his face an expressionless mask.

"Go on," the man in the red suit said with a curt gesture. "I'll make sure no one goes into the back rooms."

With a grunt that barely counted as even a monosyllable, the bouncer obeyed. For the brief moment that he opened the door, the music that flooded into the room was so loud it seemed to possess both substance and weight. It was too much, and I cringed. Thankfully, the sound returned to a muted rumble as soon as the door swung shut behind him.

Red Suit turned back to me. "You're wide open," he said. "No cowl, no shields. No wonder you're a mess."

"Good of you to notice," I grumbled. I was fighting to relax. It was a losing battle.

"Look at me," Red Suit responded, gesturing to his unearthly blue eyes. "Just like your lessons. Focus on me first. You have to close it down, like clenching a fist." He held his hand out and for a moment I thought he was going to try to touch me again, but he just curled his slender fingers into a tight ball. He repeated the gesture, murmuring encouragingly.

"Come on. You have more discipline than this."

His whole aspect and manner changed and he seemed oddly paternal. He didn't look that much older than me—younger, if I was being honest—but it stirred some vague memory. Like I was a boy, and he was teaching me. I didn't question it. His voice, rhythmic and soothing, guided me back to myself.

"Clenching a fist," I repeated.

I followed his example and made a physical fist, trying to match my thoughts to the gesture. I held so tight, my nails bit little half-moons into my palm. The psychic noise receded by degrees, though that gnawing ache in my chest lingered. With effort, I blocked that out as well, though every once in a while it surged back into awareness.

"That's it," he murmured. "Clear your thoughts. Better?"

I considered it, then nodded.

He dropped his hand and resumed his previous manner—stiff, formal, with the vaguest hint of reproach. I wasn't sure which was the mask. Tenting his fingers, he paced a little, nervously looking me up and down. The Italian heels on his expensive shoes clicked smartly against the tiles, and for a while it was the loudest noise in the room. After a nerve-wracking eternity, he spoke.

"All right then. Care to tell me what this is all about?"

I didn't even know where to start.

"Zaquiel?" he prompted.

The name no longer gobsmacked me like it had the first time he'd said it over the phone, but the syllables still felt like they vibrated my damned molecules.

"Why do you keep calling me that?" I wondered.

"Every time you say it, I feel something, here." I gestured to that spot under my ribs where the hollow sensation still ached.

"Of course you feel it. It's your name."

"But my driver's license says Zachary," I insisted. I almost pulled it out to show him.

The color drained from Red Suit's cheeks—which was quite a feat, since he was already two shades short of looking like a corpse. Then his expression grew canny.

"This isn't a joke, is it, or some ploy to see her again?" he asked cautiously. "You know she had no answer the last time, Anakim. That's not going to change."

I didn't recognize the word, but hearing it on his lips like that stirred white-hot fury in me.

"I don't even know who you're fucking talking about!" I all but shouted at him.

"Oh, Zaquiel," he breathed. I fought not to react as the word shuddered through me. "What have you gotten into this time?"

9

Red Suit offered me a hand up. Still seething over nothing I could identify, I stared at it like it was a viper.

Then I hauled myself to my feet—albeit a little shakily. I kept my left fist clenched, determined to prevent any further psychic incidents. I was seriously over them. Red Suit hesitated for a moment, appearing to decide whether or not he was offended. He turned smartly on his heel and headed toward the second door—not the one that led out to the main floor, but the one the bouncer had been guarding.

From the way Red Suit shouldered it open, I gathered that it had some real heft to it. There was music here, too, but it was different from the pulse-pounding rhythms of the dance floor, although it was still some variety of electronica. It played from speakers set into the black-painted ceiling, and was turned low enough that I had to focus to catch anything more than a sense of cycling rhythms and ethereal female vocals. It had a hypnotic quality to it, and pitched this low the lyrics were essentially subliminal.

The theme of the décor continued from the little antechamber—neo-Gothic with a touch of the post-apocalyptic. The ceiling and walls were black, although the little flecks of silver were absent back here. Immediately past the door was an alcove, and this was set apart from the rest of the hallway by a privacy screen fashioned from chain-link fencing.

The floors were covered in a tile that tried to mimic black marble, but mostly ended up looking streaked and dingy. Little runners of carpet were arranged every eight to ten feet down the hall, their deep crimson pile breaking up the unrelieved black. The deep red of the area rugs was echoed by the trim around the doors—and there were a lot of doors. We were pretty much in a long, narrow hallway lined with them. It was as if we'd crossed from Club Heaven to Hotel Hell.

The doors themselves were painted black, and each sported a silver number about three inches high. Like the fire door we just came through, they all seemed to be made of metal beneath the paint. There were windows alongside most of the doors, and it took me a moment to realize that these windows didn't look out anywhere. Instead, they opened into the little rooms. All of them seemed outfitted with red velvet curtains—set up on the opposite side. In most cases these were closed, but a few of them stood open, revealing the rooms within.

All it took was one peek through the red-curtained windows to figure what Club Heaven really was about. The only thing that surprised me was that not all of the little rooms were done up in black.

Each was tricked out in the latest bondage equipment. A couple were even occupied. One seemed dark and empty until a sudden burst of fire dazzled my eyes. The lone, brilliant flash illuminated the figures of a shirtless man and a naked woman. The focal point of the fire, she threw her head back—laughing, not screaming—as the flames danced and then burnt out on her bare skin. The soundproofing here was impressive—I may as well have been watching a silent movie.

"Don't start," Red Suit said automatically when he noticed me staring. He shot me an unhappy look before striding down the hall.

"Start what?" I asked, jogging along after him.

"One of your odious little tirades," he said with a dismissive wave. "I know you don't approve of the way my tribe does things, but we don't care about your approval. The last of the Blood Wars is far behind us. I don't want to hear it."

"Uh..." I said, looking to a room on my right long enough to see a scene that involved a woman and needles. Lots and lots of needles. Considering the profusion of needles, there was very little blood. I had a momentary instinct to rush in and rescue her. There was no way she was a willing participant in that, was there? I clenched my fist tighter, trying to read her body language through something that didn't involve psychic juju. She actually looked dreamy rather than distressed. Had they drugged her?

Red Suit must have caught my expression as I hesitated at the door. He stopped and pointedly cleared his throat.

"I'm not joking," he warned, waggling a finger my way. "We leave our tribes behind when we deal, you and I. I've never judged you, brother."

Brother. That was the second time he'd called me that. The girl out front had mentioned family, but after the vision in the club, those words came with very mixed feelings.

I tore myself away from the unnerving scene in the bondage suite and met Red Suit's cerulean gaze. "What do you mean by that?"

"Our tribes or our arrangement?" he inquired stiffly.

"No, 'brother'," I said. I'd need answers on the other things, eventually, but for the moment I felt driven on the topic of family. "Do you mean that literally? Are we related?"

Red Suit seemed flustered by the question. "You really don't remember anything," he marveled. After a moment he took off down the hall without offering a response.

I lengthened my stride, easily pacing him. The hall split off and he turned abruptly to the left, barely looking where he was going. He had the air of someone who could navigate this rabbit warren blindfolded if it was necessary. Me, I wasn't even sure I could find my way back to the main door, and we hadn't gone that far.

"Hey," I called. I went so far as to grab his shoulder, hoping that the cloth of his suit would shield me from unwanted psychic input. He stopped long enough to shrug off my hand.

"Don't do that," he said irritably.

"Then talk to me," I insisted. "I mean, you kind of look like me, now that I think about it, but who the hell dressed you growing up? I don't think I'd be caught dead in a suit like that."

Red Suit pinched the bridge of his nose. "Your mouth never stops running, yet I'm always amazed at how little you say."

"Hey!" I objected.

"Should I remind you now that you started it?"

I scowled a bit, but didn't answer him.

"Besides," he added, smoothing down the lapels of the obviously expensive jacket. "I'm rather fond of my suit. The things you wear..." he added with a dismissive gesture that seemed eloquently to condemn the whole of modern fashion, "That half hide of cow? T-shirts emblazoned with what you think are witty slogans? You look like a vagrant... or a scoundrel."

I glanced unhappily down at my water-stained leather, the thin T-shirt beneath, and the wrinkled, faded jeans. Considering the day I'd had, none of them were exactly clean, and yet I felt a need to defend them.

"I like this jacket," I objected, "and clothes like this stand up to a lot. How'd you think that fancy suit of yours would have managed a dip in Lake Erie?" I left out the wild escape through the cornfield and my most recent dash through the grimy back alleys of the Flats. Dodging cops was getting to be a theme.

Red Suit flipped his hair. "Why on earth would you swim in Lake Erie at this time of year?" he inquired with disdain.

"To get away from the cops, maybe," I ventured. "There's some kind of APB out for me. Do I look armed and dangerous to you?"

An inscrutable expression tracked across his features. "Always," he murmured.

"What the hell is *that* supposed to mean?" I demanded.

He pulled away from me, refusing to elaborate, no matter how I hounded him. I gave it up. We proceeded in silence for another couple of twists and turns through the dimly lit maze. Finally, he drew up in front of one of the black doors. This one had no number, and there was no voyeur-friendly window opening onto the room beyond. Red Suit laid a hand on my shoulder in a gesture that seemed cautionary, affectionate, and patronizing all at once.

"Remember," he said, pitching his voice low, "when you speak to Saliriel, don't slip and use any male pronouns. She still hasn't forgiven you for the last time you were here."

"Last time?" I asked.

"You're really not joking, are you?"

"Why would I joke about something like this?" I cried.

"A respectful tone will serve you better," he suggested. At my look of outrage, he laid a quelling hand on my shoulder. Lowering his voice conspiratorially, he added, "And if you recall nothing else my brother, know that I am your ally here."

"Mmmkay," I responded skeptically. "So when do I start getting answers?"

He withdrew his hand quickly. I didn't miss the fact that for a moment he couldn't meet my eyes.

"Whenever my Decimus Saliriel decides you deserve them."

10

Saliriel, as it turned out, was the mother of all drag queens. At least, that's how it looked to me. He—or she, rather—was conservatively six foot six, but stood significantly taller thanks to a pair of candy apple red platform heels that added at least another five inches to her towering, slender form. The heels had the effect of making her already long legs look like they went on for miles.

Like Red Suit, she had porcelain-pale skin with nary a blemish. Her pallor was heightened by the fact that she wore almost exclusively white—white fishnets, a white vinyl mini, and a matching white halter with a red vinyl cross stretched between sizably enhanced breasts—*hello nurse?* Her wild mane of hair was a bright platinum blond with pink streaks and what looked like tinsel woven in, so that as the light caught it, lone strands here and there glittered in shiny metallic bursts.

Her eyes were a green so pale they were almost yellow—not the green from the vision, I noted with irrational relief—and her bright blend of gold, silver, and white eye shadow only served to heighten the cat-like effect. Her full, pouting lips were painted a pale, opalescent pink that looked like it was looted from the inside of a conch shell.

When Red Suit ushered me through the door, Saliriel utterly dominated the room. She had a force of personality that was palpable. It didn't hurt that she stood towering over two collared slaves—a man and a woman, both naked—and their posture was that of total submission. The set of her shoulders, the angle at which she lifted her pointed little chin, bespoke an authority that brooked no resistance.

The room wasn't huge, but it seemed spacious because it was nearly empty of furniture. As with the rest of the club, floor, walls, and ceiling were black, but four blocky columns were painted the same dark red as the trim out in the hall. These stood two apiece on either side, creating a visual line that drew the eye to an elaborate throne of crushed red velvet. It stood on a raised dais against the far wall. There seemed to be another door tucked in the corner behind the throne, but aside from a few restraints on the walls, the rest of the space was bare.

Saliriel stood out like some vinyl-clad version of the White Queen, her pale, slender limbs and long platinum hair Barbie-doll perfect and unreal. She turned her leonine gaze on me, and I noted two things from her expression.

One, she recognized me.

Two, she wasn't pleased that I was here.

"Oh, really, sibling?" she sighed in a well-trained contralto. "It's only been two days. Do you have nothing to occupy yourself besides badgering me?"

Sibling? My brain actually hiccupped for a moment as I tried to process this news. Me, Red Suit, and now Ru Paul's long-lost white sister—we were related? I could see it, kind of, in the nose and the jawline, but seriously? I wondered what Mom and Dad were like.

"He says he doesn't remember anything," Red Suit offered in the silence that followed. "He stumbled in here and collapsed. No shields. No cowl."

Saliriel heard this, and the edge of her mouth twitched, but otherwise she refused to acknowledge that Red Suit had spoken. Her cat-like eyes guarded, she paid the two naked people at her feet just as little mind. For their part, they kept their gaze on the floor, apparently inured to such treatment. I had to fight down a rising urge to tear their leashes from her manicured hand. People weren't for being owned.

Still, I was the guest here. Red Suit had made that clear enough.

Saliriel seemed to read the tension in my shoulders and take a subtle pleasure in it. With exaggerated disdain, the leggy giantess dropped the leashes then strode languidly in my direction. She balanced on the stilettos with such practiced ease that she might as well have been floating. She stopped a few feet in front of me, crossing her lightly muscled arms just beneath her breasts. This had the effect of lifting the surgically augmented D-cups, which were already pretty hard to ignore. It seemed like a practiced and habitual gesture.

Otherwise it was really creepy, considering the fact that she had just declared herself my sister.

She drew herself up to her full height. "And tell us, Remy," she said. "Why should we believe such a thing? On Tuesday, it was pacts with cacodaimons, and this time—what will it be? Some forbidden amulet, lost on the lake? Wild conspiracies to herald a new war? This is Cleveland, dear brother. It's not all that interesting."

Even though she started out talking to Red Suit—Remy—her gaze remained on me. Her attention pressed like a palpable weight against the barriers in my mind. Instinctively I shoved it away, clenching my fist so hard the knuckles cracked.

"I didn't come here to play games," I snarled.

Remy sucked a hissing breath, but Saliriel didn't give him a chance to add anything to the discussion. She walked a slow circuit around me.

"Oh, but it's all about games, my dear sibling." Her sharp heels ticked against the tiles like the second hand of a clock. "Games and favors—it's all we have left, really. So did you come to play with me, Anakim?"

The word from her lips nearly sent me into a blind rage. It wasn't the term itself, but how she said it—like it was something filthy.

"Stop calling me that," I growled.

She smirked, eyes flicking to Remy. "I thought you had no memory," she purred. "Why would it bother you, if that were true?" She completed her circuit around me, hungry cat eyes searching my own. With a motion almost too swift to track, her pale hand shot out and she plucked at my jacket. "You stand before a decimus of the Nephilim. Take that unlovely thing off. I wish to see you without your armor."

I surprised myself by matching her speed, slapping her hand away as soon as it landed. I wasn't gentle about it. Her pretty pink lips skinned back in a snarl and she hissed at me like she really was half-cat. All my smart-ass comments died in my throat, because I finally saw her teeth.

Pearl-perfect and flawless, they looked normal except for the two delicately pointed canines that extended almost half again as long as the rest. I stared openly, trying to see some sign of prosthetics or anything that could help it make sense. Yet the impossible teeth continued to look like a very natural part of her unnatural smile.

Saliriel had fangs. *Real* fangs.

My thoughts tumbled back through the earlier vision, and I almost lost my grip on the mental control Remy had so patiently taught me. The creatures were real. I was standing in front of one—and it had called me brother.

I ran my tongue quickly over the insides of my own teeth, just in case I had missed an important detail like, say, *fangs*, since dragging myself out of Lake Erie. Nothing. It didn't seem as if I would terrify my dentist any time soon, and I found myself letting loose a breath I didn't realize I'd been holding.

"Do not presume to touch me," Saliriel bellowed. "You have no standing within my tribe."

"You touched me first, bitch."

It was out of my mouth before I could think better of it.

The giantess in white vinyl responded with a string of expletives, most of which seemed concerned with my preferential sexual activities and diseased, incestuous goats. As she spat her venom, she stormed around the room in an exaggerated show of fury, shiny red heels striking the tiles with a sound worthy of gunfire. When her steps brought her toward them, the two collared slaves withdrew obsequiously to a back corner of the room.

While she ranted, Remy leaned his head close to mine, pitching his voice low.

"Why do you always have to bait her?"

"How should I know?" I shot back. "I don't even remember her."

Saliriel rounded on us both.

"Silence! You, especially, Remiel." She gave him a look that could have curdled milk, and for all I knew, it would have. He faltered back a step and dropped his eyes to the ground, seeming almost as subservient as the naked slaves. The long, smooth curtain of his hair swept forward, obscuring his face. Saliriel then turned her furious gaze on me, and I surprised myself by meeting it without flinching. This only made her angrier.

She stopped in the middle of the room, fangs bared and nostrils flaring. Color had risen to her cheeks and a flush was visible across the naked expanse of flesh above her cleavage, running from one prominent collarbone to the other. Her eyes flashed yellow fire and there was no mistaking it.

They were glowing.

"You dare to enter my personal domain and accost

me with insults." No longer yelling, this quieter tone carried a deadlier weight. "I am a decimus of the Nephilim, and only the primus stands above me. I know rank holds no meaning for your pathetic tribe, but *here* it is currency. While you are under my roof, you will respect me. If I ask you to approach me naked and on your knees, you will do so because it is my whim. And if you are unwilling to do that, I will happily eject you as I did earlier this week. Are we clear, Anakim?"

"Crystal," I spat.

I was done—done with all the bullshit about ranks and tribes and other things that made no sense to me, done with the way she treated the other people in the room like they were lower than furniture, done with her holier-than-thou attitude. I turned on my heel and headed for the door. There had to be some other place I could go for answers.

I glanced to Remy before I left, but he was still staring down at the tips of his crocodile-skin shoes. From his words in the hallway, I knew he was sympathetic to my plight, and I honestly felt bad for the guy. But if he wasn't going to stick up for me, there was no sense in me hanging around. I started to say something—I owed him a thanks at least for helping me get the visions under control—but I never got that far.

The doors to the private chamber burst open and Vikram, the bouncer, charged in. The seam of his tailored suit was torn at one shoulder and there was a spatter of blood across the lower portion of his face. His eyes looked huge and shocky, and then I realized the blood was everywhere. It covered the entire front of his suit, slick and still pumping against the dark fabric.

Saliriel opened her mouth—no doubt to spew some scathing reprimand—then she, too, noticed the blood. Her nostrils flared.

"They're out there shooting people," he managed. He gulped air, and it didn't sound right, gurgling faintly. "They're shooting people in the club."

"Who?" Remy demanded. The bouncer turned wild eyes on my brother. When he answered, it sounded as if he didn't quite believe it himself.

"Police."

11

A shrill, chittering cry followed the words of the bouncer. All the hairs prickled on my scalp—I'd been pursued by that terrible sound all night. A moment later, a phlegmy voice sounded.

"Police. Freeze!" A middle-aged officer lumbered into view—the cop from the cruiser. There was a ragged wound on the side of his throat and his uniform was sticky with blood. There was no question that he was dead. Unhindered by this fact, he lifted his gun and opened fire, shooting the bouncer twice in the back. A gout of crimson erupted from the man's mouth and he went down choking.

The blast of the gun was incredibly loud in the small space, and all the shouting that followed it seemed muffled by comparison.

Remy whirled toward the sound of the gunfire, then dashed to the far left of the room with a speed I could barely track. The cop tottered in the doorway, bringing his weapon around with unstable hands. His partner staggered into view. She opened her mouth and loosed that cry of whatever had been stalking me all night. I had no idea what had happened to the two of them, but instinct clamored that it was tied to those delinquents I'd led straight to their cruiser. But the cops had shot them. Had the dead men gotten back up to attack the officers? The possibility turned my guts to water.

Behind me, Saliriel roared angrily.

"What have you brought to my house, Anakim?"

My brain stuttered over the possibilities. The barrel of the gun, which looked enormous from my perspective, swung toward me. The arm of the police officer jerked spastically, and this was the only thing that saved me from being uncomfortably ventilated along with the bouncer. Like Remy, I skittered to the far side of the room, ducking behind one of the columns and moving faster than seemed natural. I didn't question it. It got me out of the way of the damned gun.

"Fuck my life," I gasped. "Zombie cops and vampire drag queens."

"Police! Freeze!" the guy cop roared again, but it came out mushier than before, as if it was an effort for him to speak at all. From his blank expression, I doubted he had any understanding of the words. He moved more like a puppet than a person.

Then I saw what was pulling his strings.

In some way that wasn't physical, I saw a shadow so black it seemed to drink up the light. It clung to his shoulders and back. Something that might have served it for a head was curled over the dead officer's balding pate. For the space of a few heartbeats, I thought I was seeing things—but then it looked at me, and I knew with a certainty as nauseating as it was absolute that this nightmare-creature was aware that I had noticed it. It turned its impossible eyes to notice me right back.

Black and completely featureless, it was like a living shadow shaped vaguely like a manta ray. The only thing shining from the light-swallowing depths of its form were two glaring eyes of murderous red, and then I swore I saw it flash a razor-edged smile, all glittering silver and death.

As I gawked at his rider, the cop squeezed off another round from his gun. With me absent from the space I had previously occupied, the gun was aimed at Saliriel, but her two collared slaves had sprung to life from the back of the room the minute a threat was imminent. Naked as they were, their response wasn't to scream in terror or run for their lives. Instead, they threw themselves in front of my towering sibling, shielding her pale, leggy form as much as they could with their own bodies.

Her male slave took the bullet. It was a lucky shot—or really unlucky, depending on how you looked at it. It caught him in the face, just over one cheekbone. His eye and the entire side of his head exploded in a spray of bone, brains, and blood. Saliriel and the naked woman were painted with it.

The woman seemed too stunned to do more than stand there blinking. Saliriel howled with fury, gore dripping from her shiny white vinyl. Her voice held such raw, animal power that I expected the ceiling tiles to rattle with it. And then, despite the clinging arms of her female companion, Saliriel did the unexpected—she launched herself at the gun-toting attackers, snarling something in a language that certainly wasn't English. It communicated her intentions all the same.

The second cop—the young black woman who had looked so stricken at shooting my pursuer—shambled around her partner, gun at the ready. One side of her face was a bruised and bloody mess and I saw purpling handprints around her throat—as if someone had seized her by the neck and pounded her head against some unforgiving surface. In saving my own skin, I had left both these people to die.

The certainty of it paralyzed me.

The same kind of dark shadow-form clung to her back. It had something like arms, but they were thrust *into* her, working her limbs like a puppet. I felt a stomach-churning sense of wrongness as it twitched and wriggled to make her body respond. This one seemed to be having more trouble, probably because of the head trauma, and the shot from the lady cop's gun went wild, burying itself in the far wall.

Saliriel dodged left and right, a blond-maned blur. Both cops swung their guns unsteadily, trying to keep a bead on her, but she was too fast for their zombified nervous systems. In another moment she leapt over the fallen bouncer, practically crawling up the front of the older cop's body. She wrapped her legs around his midsection and snatched at his gun, the rhinestones in her manicure flashing. I had a sudden thought of her breaking a nail, and cackled madly. Pressed against the wall beside me, I felt more than I heard Remy hiss my name—not Zachary. The other one.

That snapped me out of it, though I couldn't shake the icy feeling that those horrible shadow-rays were looking at me.

"What *are* they?" I choked.

"Zombies," Remy whispered. "Something has to be riding them."

"Yeah. I see that. What the fuck are they?"

Saliriel's bellow thundered through the room as she wrestled with the dead officer. She disarmed the older cop almost literally, wrenching the weapon from his hand with such force that both bones of his forearm snapped wetly. His hand went limp and he flailed at her. She slashed at his eyes, forcing him to the ground under her weight.

The lady cop tried for Saliriel again but instead fired into her partner. This didn't seem to bother him much, and he kept smacking at Saliriel with his useless limb.

The naked woman who served Saliriel recovered from the shock of getting covered with her male counterpart's gray matter. She ran to her mistress's side, then grabbed the gun from where it had clattered across the tiles and, reasonably, tried to deal with the female officer by shooting her in the head.

It was pretty much a point-blank shot. The collared submissive knew how to handle a firearm. Her stance was good and she gripped the pistol in both hands, anticipating the recoil even as she pulled down on the trigger. She caught the lady cop neatly between the eyes. The back of the woman's head exploded in a shower of gore. I clapped my hands over my ears, uselessly striving to drown out the ringing.

Remy shook me urgently. “Tell me what you can see.”

I looked up in time to watch the thing atop the female officer struggle in the wake of the headshot. The body still stood, despite taking a bullet in the face. The inky black shadow writhed and twisted madly.

At first I thought it was in pain—then I realized that it was shoving bits of itself deeper inside of her, like it was grabbing fistfuls of her nerves and yanking them like strings. There seemed to be too much damage for any kind of fine-tuned control now that a whole section of her brain was missing. Her gun hand spasmed, sending a wild shot into the floor, and then the fingers started to go slack.

“Shadows,” I said quickly. “Stuck to the back of them. You can’t see them?”

“No, but I’m not Anakim.”

I frowned at that. “At some point you’re going to tell me what all these damned words mean.” Then, “You seriously can’t see that shit?”

Saliriel pounded the male officer into a pulp on the floor and I heard his rider scream in frustration. It was the sound of nightmares. The naked woman fired another round into the lady cop, and her rider also shrieked in fury, if not in pain. I twitched as the unreal sound clawed against the insides of my skull.

“There’s… smudges. Something behind them,” Remy replied, squinting. Whatever he was doing, it made his eyes flash with unearthly blue fire. Then he made a frustrated noise. “I can’t see them like you can. Tell me what’s happening,” he urged.

After the second bullet, the rider lost nearly all

control over the lady cop. With a final, last-ditch effort, it did something that made no sense at first. Awkwardly, it made her drop the gun, sending the weapon sliding over the floor toward the throne-end of the room. I stared, unable to respond to my brother as I watched the shadow-thing shuck itself out of the lady cop.

She crumpled to the ground like a cast-off suit of clothes, and then it did the unthinkable. It slithered darkly across the floor, hugging its belly along the tiles. It had more limbs than I could have imagined and reminded me of a fat black centipede crossed with a hooded cobra. It followed the path of the cast-off gun, and too late I realized what it was really after.

A fresh host.

"It's on the move," I breathed and tried not to bring up any of the food I hadn't eaten all day. The thing paused between the slave and the dead bouncer, its sort-of head questing with little feelers around the two corpses. Then it seemed to make a decision and dove for its target.

Remy reached over and grabbed my shoulder. He shook me once, firmly, locking his unearthly blue eyes on mine.

"Brother, if you never believe a word I say again, believe this now. If you can see them, you can hurt them. That's what you do."

"How?" I gasped.

Like a fashionable, ebon-haired Yoda, he replied, "Don't think. Just do." Then he shoved me toward the fallen bouncer even as the body started to twitch. Thereafter, he launched himself toward Saliriel, joining the fight at last. Belatedly I realized that he hadn't been cowering with me in the corner out of fear. He had stayed there to watch over me.

Setting that thought aside to consider later, I charged the short distance across the room to the coiling, horrible thing that only I could see.

12

The shadow-ray-centipede-thing responded with a furious hiss. The fact that I was the only one in the room who could hear it—aside from the other creepy-crawly—made the sound that much more unnerving.

The creature flashed scarlet eyes and its Exacto-blade smile at me, then thrust its head deep into the dead bouncer. The black, squirming length of it pressed up against his back, going flat like a tapeworm. The body twitched disgustingly as it fought to take control of his nervous system, and the bit that served it for a face quested deep within the dead man's skull. I stared, momentarily stunned to inaction as I saw its steely grin ghosting through his slack, gray features.

The bouncer's eyes snapped open, and for an instant they were its eyes—red, malevolent, and impossible. Writhing against his back as it worked his nerves from within, it brought the dead bouncer ponderously to his feet. His right hand, still trembling unsteadily, began to reach for the nearby gun. I didn't waste time waiting for him to grab it.

I rushed it, yelling.

Well, maybe not yelling, exactly.

It was more like... singing.

If a voice could be raised in song that was all fury and destruction, my throat opened up and this sound poured out. I felt it reverberate from the very bottom of my chest, filling my head till my teeth rattled. It electrified me in ways I could neither name nor pause to understand in that adrenaline-kissed instant. I bellowed something like, "*Zhaaaaaaaah!*" and the end of it cut off in a guttural huff that was as much a curse as a challenge.

Just as instinctive was the motion of my hands. I brought them up as if I held twin versions of that curved bronze blade. The weapons weren't a dream this time—they coalesced from power and light as if shaped by the purity of my will. I could see the white-blue glow of them on the edges of my vision, and I knew with a certainty as inexplicable as it was absolute that the syllables pouring from my throat honed and focused these weapons. In the few heartbeats it took to close the space between the dead bouncer and me, the glow of light exploded to a brilliant cascade.

With a second shout tearing up from my chest, I slashed ferociously at the shadow-rider's face. The light streamed forth. It passed harmlessly through the flesh of the dead man, but tore into the writhing form of the shadow. I cackled wildly as I realized that I wielded what amounted to truncated lightsabers.

The rider shrieked under my onslaught, the brilliant power tearing whole chunks from its blacker-than-black form. Baring its teeth and keening with both pain and rage, the thing launched its host at me, dead fists flailing. I took a blow to the jaw, but shook it off, then dodged the second strike with that faster-than-seemed-right movement. In the midst of the barrage I somehow had the presence of mind to kick the gun with a backwards sweep of one leg, sending it spinning far to the other side of the room.

After the initial strike, I found I had to pause, take a breath, and gather my focus before the weapons once again coalesced. I could feel a hollow tugging in the center of my chest, breathless and hot.

I pinned the dead bouncer against the big square pillar so I could concentrate on the thing working his body. We were twined so close, the dead man snapped his teeth at my throat. Instinctively, I struck out with... *something*... on that side of my body. I caught a glow of light in my peripheral vision, softer than what was gathering in my hands. Like the blades, it didn't seem physical, exactly—just a wall of force that slammed up from behind my shoulder to strike the bouncer in the side of the face.

It didn't phase the zombie much, but the shadow-rider reacted as if I'd broadsided it with a two-by-four. I felt the impact as if I'd shoulder-checked the thing, but with something that wasn't precisely my shoulder. My brain refused to process it in that moment, stuttering past the unlikely bits to keep me in the fight.

Eye to eye with the rider, it shrilled its fury, spearing me with a look of utter hate.

"I don't like you either, asshole," I snarled, loosing

another volley of power. I shouted the same two reverberant syllables right into its face.

"*Zhaaaa-kiaaaaalll!*"

I'm not sure when I realized it was my name.

The thing went slack, slipping within the dead man's flesh. I was out of juice and gasping with effort. Before the abomination could escape, I reached out and seized it in one hand. Shock robbed the strength from my grip. The whole of the creature was cold in a way that sucked the heat from my skin.

A part of my brain back-pedaled in horror at too many things to count—the slick rubbery texture of its flesh, the fact that I had my hand wrapped around something that wasn't physically there, the nerveless chill that prickled like teeth all the way up my arm. A searing weight spread across my back in defiance of the cold. Tied to something wild and electric just behind me, it tugged a little painfully at muscles running down either side of my spine.

When I flexed those muscles, it felt as if nothing could stand against me.

Battle lust surged through me, finding vent in another shout. I yanked the creature through the dead bouncer. Its long whip of a tail coiled spastically and its many filament-like appendages scrabbled at my face and hands. The end of each felt sharp as a cat's claw. My skin welted wherever its legs struck.

Ignoring the pain, I hoisted it and stepped away from the dead man. He crumpled to the floor in an untidy tangle of limbs, his head striking the tiles with such a rotten-melon sound that I was grateful he was already a corpse. The rider hissed and gnashed in a bid to intimidate, but instinct and adrenaline bulwarked my will. I snarled a rapid patter of syllables. Intent, rather than meaning, blossomed somewhere deep in my mind. The only translation I had was *unmaking*. With that intent clamoring through me, I gripped the inky shadow and let my other hand fall like a hammer against what must have been its heart.

I struck the blow with a nimbus of energy and the shadow-rider exploded like a mass of black jelly. The particles clung to my skin, cold at first, and then gone.

The other shadow-rider loosed a defiant shriek that ended with that self-same chittering call that had pursued me from the lake. In the periphery of my vision, Saliriel and Remy held the male officer pinned. He bucked against Saliriel as she knelt on his chest, teeth snapping for her flesh.

Then he went perfectly still.

Even as I calculated the odds that the rider had opted to go for another body, I heard shouting. Two voices, running down the hall. Then one of the same voices erupted from the dead bouncer at my feet. I stared wildly at him until I realized the voice had come from a walkie-talkie clipped to his belt.

Two of the black-suited security staff pushed urgently into the room, and instantly the rider from the dead male cop darted out the door between them. With an inarticulate shout, I dove after it, leaping over bodies, almost trampling Saliriel and shouldering roughly past the two bouncers. I was dimly aware of someone—two someones, in fact—yelling my name, but I didn't stop.

All my focus narrowed to the nameless horror escaping down black halls.

I was done being hunted. I planned to end the thing.

The shadow-creature shimmied away like a panicked centipede, careening from side to side and running halfway up the walls as it went. It seemed only partly bound by the laws of gravity, and I half-expected it to run *through* the walls. As it came to one of the right-angle turns, it seemed to have the same idea, because rather than turning, it attempted to charge straight ahead.

It crashed face-first into the masonry, recovered messily, then scrambled to make the turn and keep ahead of me. Its little mishap allowed me to gain a few feet in my pursuit, and I lengthened my stride, pushing myself even harder. I started to compensate for the turn three steps ahead of it, reaching out with my right hand to steady myself, then pushing off once I was around the bend.

One of the occupants of a side room took this most inopportune time to investigate all the ruckus. He stuck his head out into the hallway, looking curiously up and down. His door opened inward, or I'd have crashed headlong into it. As it was, I practically had to slam myself into the opposite wall to avoid shoulder-checking his face.

I raced past him, snarling for him to get back inside. The shadow-rider continued to lead me on a not-so-merry chase, every once in a while diving at one of the walls as if to test whether or not it was solid. I had no idea why something that seemed to be a spirit couldn't just jig right through, but then, I also had no clue as to why I could see it in the first place.

As we ran, I gathered a nimbus of blue-white energy around my hands. We arrived at the little foyer with its chain-link privacy screen and heavy black fire door. The door was wide open, dented a little where either the fleeing bouncer, the zombie police officers, or perhaps both had charged past. The rider zipped through, and I pelted after it just a few steps behind.

And then we were back in the room with the couches. The shadow-rider created a nightmare-shaped patch of negative space against the silver spatters that decorated the otherwise black walls. Having learned physics the hard way, it cautiously slunk toward the door that led to the main dance floor. I thought I'd finally got lucky—this one appeared to be closed.

We both saw it at the same time. The door stood slightly ajar, held that way by some obstruction close to the floor.

I charged forward, striving to get a grip on the rider, but it was a few heartbeats quicker. It dove at the space between the door and its frame and did this freaky cartoon-like maneuver, flattening itself and zipping at right angles through the crack. I made a last-ditch effort to seize its whip-like tail, but managed to over-balance myself. Before I could crash bodily into the door, I caught myself with my right hand, slamming my palm against the wall. There was a concussive sensation as the nimbus of blue-white energy I'd gathered dispersed upon impact.

I looked down, dazzled and blinking, and saw what was jamming the door.

It was a hand, delicate and feminine. Slender fingers tipped with stylish red and black polish curled lifelessly toward the ceiling, a little splash of blood cupped in the palm.

Shit.

Not wasting a moment more, I threw open the door—and was driven instantly to my knees.

13

Chaos. The main floor of the club exploded in sensory chaos.

The bastion of order Remy had helped me build in my mind crumbled in the face of it. There were lights and colors everywhere, jagged geometric patterns in harsh reds and ugly browns flooding the interior of the club. It took me a few moments to realize that what I was seeing wasn't really there—at least not in a physical sense. The shock and terror of the crowd hung upon the space, visible to me as shapes and colors. If the rider was there at all, I had lost it in the riot of perceptions.

The music had stopped. In its auditory vacuum was a constant anxious murmur punctuated by the staccato bark of security staff. No one was actually screaming, though the echo of screams surged against my mind. I could hear the gunshots, too, as if the violent scene replayed on some level perceptible only to me. My nails bit deeply into my palm as I struggled to focus.

Tables and chairs were overturned in the wake of the

assault, and the massive disco ball had been shot down. It rested in a scattering of mirrored tiles, three broken bodies flung to the floor around it in various attitudes of sudden death. Dark stains spread around the corpses.

On the floor before me lay the prone form of the Asian woman who had been running the cash register. It was her hand that had blocked the door. Her backless top revealed an intricate tattoo of Shiva Nataraja. Two gunshot wounds blossomed on either side of her spine, obliterating portions of the ink work. I stared, wondering stupidly why the rider had passed over this and the other fresh corpses.

Remy finally caught up with me. He seized my shoulder, but then his grip went slack.

"Oh, no," he said, his voice low. "Not Alice."

Without another word, he shoved me aside. Dropping to one knee, he rolled her over, running delicate fingers along the curve of her jaw. His long fall of glossy black hair swept forward, so it was impossible to see his face. That didn't shield me from his pain. Jagged blues and reds strobed from him. Blinking hard, I struggled to focus on purely flesh-and-blood perceptions.

I failed, and saw what looked like ghostly wings rising from Remy's back. They were as red as his suit and shimmered insubstantially. Had they been real, I would have been standing half inside one of them. I took a step back just in case, then jammed the heels of my hands against my eyes in a futile effort to banish the impossible perceptions.

The sharp rapport of stiletto heels echoed down the corridor to my right. Saliriel. She argued with one of the bouncers as she strode purposely our way.

"Why didn't you shoot them the instant they pulled their guns inside the club?"

"But, ma'am, they're cops," the bouncer insisted. "You don't shoot cops."

"Idiot!" She snapped witheringly. "You couldn't tell they were dead already?"

"But, ma'am—"

Flesh striking flesh resounded from the corridor. "No excuses," she hissed. "You shoot anyone who's shooting at you first. Worry about explaining things once it's over. Honestly, it's a miracle your species has survived with such piss-poor powers of reasoning."

"Yes, ma'am," he replied. They stopped a couple of feet behind us.

"Remy! Zack!" Saliriel barked. "What do you think you're doing?" Raw as I felt, the sheer volume of her words registered as physical pain. Then she focused on the bouncer again.

"You," she snarled, backhanding him again before she gestured toward the door. "Move! Find out who sent those shooters. As for you, sibling," she said, fixing me with a disdainful sneer as the bouncer hustled to carry out her orders, "I want an explanation of what went on in my throne room, and then I want you out of my club. For good."

I opened my mouth to speak, then faltered as whatever was trying to come out still didn't feel like any language I thought I should have known. I took a deep breath.

"Shadows," I said. "There were shadows."

Saliriel's eyes narrowed. "Shadows? Explain yourself."

I shrugged. "Shadow-riders. They were puppeting the corpses. I don't know what they were. They were just... *wrong*."

Saliriel spat threateningly, "Don't start spinning tales about cacodaimons. I didn't buy it the last time, and I don't believe it now."

"Cocademons?" I muttered, stumbling over the strange word.

Rolling her eyes at me, Saliriel addressed my sibling. "Remy, what did you see?" she demanded.

He pulled Alice into the room so the bouncer could close the door behind him. At least it blocked out some of the chaos from the club. Heedless of the bloodstains seeping onto his expensive suit, he sat up against the wall, cradling the dead girl in his lap. When he spoke, his usually crisp and cultured tone was rough with grief.

"You know I don't see as well as he can, Decimus."

"But you saw something," Saliriel pursued.

"After he pointed it out, yes. Like a dark smudge on the air. Sal," he said, looking up from Alice momentarily. Unshed tears shone in his eyes, but underscoring his sorrow was another emotion—it might have been fear. "I think he's right. Cacodaimons—"

She cut him off brusquely, fury bringing gold fire to her eyes. "No," she growled. "I'll not have you contributing to the madness. There's another explanation."

"Whatever they were, they were here for me," I said with no small measure of guilt. "I'd been dodging them all night. I just didn't realize it."

"And you led them here?" Saliriel demanded.

"I didn't know what I was seeing!" I shouted. I felt helpless, and it was pissing me off. I scrubbed restlessly at my stubbled jaw, muttering, "Fuck me running."

"You are nothing but trouble, Anakim," Saliriel declared, slapping my chest. It was a half-hearted blow at best, and my leather jacket absorbed most of it, but it still made me bristle. I raised my hand to warn her off. We weren't going to do this again. She balled her fists and glowered for a moment. Then she whirled on her heel and stormed to the other side of the room. Without looking over her shoulder at either of us, she cried, "Remy, leave that and get him out of my club before anything else comes after him."

Slowly, Remy got to his feet. His long fall of hair still partially obscured his face, but not so much that I didn't see the stricken look in his eyes.

"Her name was Alice," he said in a deadly quiet voice.

Back still to us, Saliriel threw her hands up in an exaggerated gesture and stomped off to her throne room.

"Get him out!" she shouted from the other side of the dented door.

I cast a withering glance of my own after Saliriel's retreating form.

"What a fucking bitch."

14

Remy didn't look happy about it, but he left Alice behind. Head down and all business, he hustled me past the chain-link partition to another fire door. Opening this, he ushered me into a back hallway almost identical to the first one.

There were fewer doors here and no peep-show windows. A cloying scent of industrial cleaner hung heavily on the air. He strode swiftly ahead of me, Italian heels clicking sharply on the black marbleized tiles. I had to jog to keep up.

My brother stared at his toes as he walked, long hair obscuring most of his pale features. From the set of his shoulders, he wasn't in the mood to talk, and I really couldn't blame him, but as he navigated the dimly lit back corridor I saw my last chance for answers slipping away.

"Hey," I said, grabbing him by the shoulder.

"Don't," he said icily.

I tightened my grip and he twisted away.

"Don't touch me!" he snapped, enunciating each word crisply around wickedly pointed fangs. So it wasn't just Saliriel.

"Got the memo," I gasped, my hand still half-raised between us. We fell into awkward silence.

"Your power is spilling everywhere," he muttered with a note of apology. "I'm far too raw for it right now." Then he resumed his course down the hall. I took several long strides, hurrying again to catch up. I was careful to keep my hands to myself.

"I still need answers, you know," I pressed. "The police are after me. I have no idea why, and if things like those... cocademons show up again, what the hell am I supposed to do?"

"You'll fight them," he responded without pausing. "Cacodaimons, spirits—that's what you do. Obviously some part of you remembers."

"Yeah, but *why*?" I persisted as we turned sharply down a side hall. "And why would they follow me all the way from the lake? Tell me something useful, goddammit!"

"God has nothing to do with any of this," he shot back bitterly. "If He ever did, He left his post ages ago. It's just the lunatics running the asylum, now."

A sound from the direction of the club proper made us both draw up short.

"More gunshots?" I asked.

Remy cocked his head, listening intently.

"Too muffled to be certain." The sound came again. Remy's eyes flew wide. "Someone breaking down a door. That's never good." Grabbing me by the arm, he rushed us at an inhuman pace toward a set of stairs at the end of the hall. "You need to be out of here," he said. "Now."

The stairs were choked with shadows, the lone, naked bulb at the bottom a useless, shattered stump in its socket. The only light came from an Exit sign and the muted LED screen of a security pad mounted beside the door. Remy strode confidently through the dark, but I slowed considerably. On the steep flight of concrete steps I struggled not to trip over my size thirteens. At the bottom, he started digging in his pockets, frowning.

"Don't tell me I left it," he murmured.

I thought I heard another rumbling crash from the depths of the club. I had a vision of black-clad SWAT cops pouring through the doorway at the top of the stairs, riot shields and rifles at the ready. The image had everything to do with the state of my nerves and wasn't the least bit psychic in nature. At least, that's what I insisted to myself so I didn't scream at Remy as he frantically patted down his suit.

"There you are," he muttered triumphantly, withdrawing a security swipe-card fixed to a small set of keys. He slid the card through the mounted security unit and punched in a code.

"So this is it," I said over his shoulder. "Nothing useful. Just fend for myself?"

Holding the door slightly open, Remy turned to me and sighed. His features were a mixture of irritation and regret—or at least something that I interpreted as regret.

"I'll make it quick, so pay attention."

"You say that like I normally don't," I responded.

Remy glared.

"OK, OK," I said, holding up my hands. "I'm all ears."

He nodded, then said, "You're Anakim. That's your tribe, like mine is Nephilim. You can walk between the realms of flesh and spirit—the Shadowside. Otherwise we're essentially the same thing."

"I'm not a fucking vampire," I said out of reflex.

He actually slapped me across the face. I was too stunned to do anything but gape.

"I know you're not this stupid," he said testily. "And you have to do something about those wings. With everything spilling out like that, things on the Shadowside are going to home in on you like a beacon. Moths to a flame."

He couldn't have stunned me more with another slap. Instinctively, I flexed muscles that could not possibly exist, feeling that familiar burn down either side of my spine.

"Wings?" I gasped.

Sirens rose and fell in the distance, drawing nearer to the club. Remy made an impatient sound.

"Pull them tight to your body. Then hide them with a cowl. It's like a veil of energy, meant to obscure. Think about it and I suspect you'll do it naturally. If not..." He shrugged.

"Do you have any idea how crazy this sounds?"

Remy fixed me with another piercing glare. "You asked me to help you. Don't turn around and argue about it. Now," he added, opening the door a little wider and pointing, "the front of the club is that way. Don't go that way."

"I'm amnesiac, not an idiot," I responded bitterly.

"An improvement, then."

It was my turn to glare. "Funny," I growled. "Now what else can you tell me?"

He shook his head. "I've wasted enough time already. Saliriel will be missing me. But," he added, an odd expression flickering across his features. He clamped down on it pretty quickly, but it left me with conflicted feelings of guilt and nostalgia. He fished in his pockets. "Here," he said, holding out his hand.

When I extended my own hand, he dropped two things into my open palm. The first was a set of keys. The second was a fat roll of cash. I examined the keys curiously. They had a small clear plastic fob, like the kind that comes on the keys to a rental car, but instead of make, model, and year, the little slip of paper inside the fob had a Lakewood address written in neat, tiny lettering, along with a random string of numbers.

I arched a brow quizzically.

"One of my safe houses," he explained. "I think there's about three hundred cash in that roll. You may not remember the circumstances, but I hold fast to my oath."

"Oath?"

He chewed his lip, practically vibrating with some unspoken inner conflict. "If I were smart, I would turn your loss of memory to my advantage and ask that you release me right now… but that wouldn't be fair." He said it in a rush, more to himself than to me.

"What are you even talking about?" I demanded. The wail of sirens grew closer.

"I gave my word, and such things are binding. Good luck, Zaquiel." It was a dismissal. He practically shoved me onto the empty street.

I stared at the keys and cash in my open palm.

He started to close the door. I shoved my foot in the way.

"Gave your word for what?"

Remy paused, his face half lost in the shadows of the nearly lightless stairwell. "To help save you the way you saved me," he said, voice barely a whisper. "Now get out of here, before you get yourself killed again."

He toed my foot out of the way and pulled the door shut with a metallic *click*. It didn't even have a handle on this side. Standing alone in the darkened alley behind the club, I could just make out the chatter of police radios and walkies drifting on the air from the front of the building. Cleveland's blue brigade had arrived in force. I *definitely* wasn't going that way.

Closing my fist around the keys and wad of cash, I stared at the boarded-up windows and graffitied walls of the warehouses across the street, feeling more lost than I had waking up on the edge of Lake Erie.

15

Taking the long way back to where I'd parked the stolen Harley, I made certain there were several blocks of buildings between the police and me. This part of the Flats was a desolate testament to urban decay. Sagging chain link edged condemned lots filled with rusted husks of metal, and the sidewalk jutted at weird angles, exposing old bricks beneath.

The scenery matched my mood. I couldn't stop brooding over all of the dead—Alice, the officers, the naked slave, Vikram the bouncer. There were others gunned down inside the club, and all of it because of me. For a moment, I considered turning myself in to the police, but I had a feeling that wouldn't be safe.

For them.

I passed beneath a derelict bridge crusted almost completely white with pigeon droppings and finally turned toward the street that, with luck, still hosted my ride. I thrust my fists deep into the pockets of my jacket as I went, trying to concentrate on what Remy described as a "cowl." I wasn't even certain I believed in the parts the cowl was supposedly masking.

"Hey, flyboy," a throaty female voice called from the sidewalk. "Why won't you return my calls?"

I was so wound up in my thoughts that I probably would have walked right past her, had she not spoken. As it was, her words stopped me dead. I gawked for several moments, uncertain how to respond.

She stood next to a teal Sebring convertible with Illinois plates. Despite the chill of the weather, the ragtop was down. She had her arms crossed beneath ample breasts, while one curvaceous hip rested jauntily against the passenger side door. She was perhaps five and a half feet tall with her boots on, wearing a pantsuit of midnight blue. Her dark red hair was long and loose, falling in wild waves around her face to tumble halfway down her back. She wore no jewelry that I could see, and her olive skin was clear and softly tanned.

Even in the jaundiced light of the streetlamps she was stunningly beautiful, but her storm-gray eyes glittered with fury as she regarded me.

I glanced nervously around the street. Red and blue police lights stuttered between the empty buildings on the left, flashing against the windows of the parked cars as more cruisers sped toward Club Heaven. The stolen Harley sat half a dozen spaces beyond the Sebring, and for a moment I debated running for it. Not that I could reliably start it.

"Um... do I know you?" I asked.

"Dammit, Zack." She stamped her foot, the heel of her sleek leather boot loud against the pavement. "Don't play dumb with me. You know I hate your stupid games."

"You and everyone else," I muttered. With her waves of dark red hair and thunderhead gray eyes, she was fiercely beautiful. Glowering at me in that moment, however, she just seemed fierce. I couldn't tell if she was a good guy, a bad guy, or an angry ex-girlfriend. With my luck, it was the latter. They were usually the worst.

She shifted her hip on the door of the car, readjusting her arms—and everything above them. From the thin camisole and breezy pantsuit she was wearing, she should have been cold, but she didn't look it. Not that I was looking.

Well, I was trying not to look.

"I drove all the way from Joliet the minute I got your voice mail," she complained. "Then I spent the rest of the day looking for your sorry ass. The least you could've done was answer my calls, Anakim—or did you kill your phone again?"

Anakim. So she knew about that.

Angry ex-girlfriend was probably off the list.

"Seriously, lady. I don't know what you're talking about."

She made a disgusted noise, then pulled out her cell phone. Setting it to speaker, she held it up in my direction. My own voice spoke urgently at me.

"Hope this is still your number, Lil. They have your sister. Not sure what's going on, but the Nephilim are involved. I'm going to try to get her back. Hope I don't disappear like the others... Gotta go."

"Lailah," I breathed. The name came to me on a sudden tidal wave of emotion—fury, urgency, a cutting sense of loss. She was the one with the pleading eyes and the flowing, midnight hair. The trapped one. "She's in trouble," I said and felt it thunderously.

"Of course she's in trouble," the woman spat. "She got tangled up with you."

I wanted to argue her point, but a lingering sense of guilt rose from the muddied depths of my memory. The meaning behind the sensation tantalized just beyond my reach. I ground my teeth in frustration, overwhelmed with the urge to hit something.

"Can I hear that again?" I asked, making a grab for the phone.

She slapped my hand away. I half-expected a barrage of psychic images from the contact, but my mind's eye seemed blind to her. Not that I was complaining.

"You don't touch my phone," she snarled. "Now where is she? Where's Lailah?"

I struggled to catch anything else that crashed to the surface along with the name, but it was like trying to pluck fish from the ocean. It was all too slippery. I held my hands out a little helplessly.

"I don't know."

The woman's gray eyes flashed. "You better start talking, Anarch. Anything happens to her, I hold you responsible."

"Anarch? What?" I said. That was a new one.

More sirens wailed in the distance.

"I really need to get out of here," I said, taking a few steps away from her shiny green convertible. "I can't help anyone if I'm in jail."

She put her hands on her hips and maneuvered in front of me.

"You're not skating away that easily," she declared. "Not till I get some answers. What were you doing with the Voluptuous Ones just now? Is she in there? If she's in there, cops or no cops, I'll go in and tear the place apart."

"Lady, have you been paying attention? I don't know you, and I don't remember your sister." I glanced back in the direction of Club Heaven as someone shouted orders through a loudspeaker. "Dammit. Could we discuss this somewhere that won't be crawling with cops in the next five minutes?"

The woman narrowed her eyes. "With your friends on the force, what are you so worried about?"

"Friends?" I scoffed. "That's not likely."

"What kind of shit-pot did you stir? Sal doesn't normally call the police. It's bad for business." With undisguised satisfaction, she added, "I'd pay good money to see the look on the old bastard's face about now."

"People died."

She gave me a weird look. "So?"

"What the hell is *wrong* with you?" I demanded. Exasperated, I said, "Look, I woke up half in the lake. I don't remember shit, and I've got cops and cocademons trying to track me down. I don't have time to argue with you."

"Cacodaimons? You can't be serious."

I tried to step around her again to make a break for the motorcycle, but she just matched me movement for movement. Her little chin jutted.

"Explanations," she snarled. "Now."

I threw my hands up. "That's what Remy called them. I don't know what the fuck they were aside from hella-creepy," I said with a shudder. "Nothing should crawl into dead things and make them get up and walk around again."

She studied me, frowning. The full weight of her gray-eyed gaze bore down.

"Those things don't come out of the deep places where they live," she murmured.

"Tell that to all the dead people in the club," I replied.

She considered a few moments more, then gave a dismissive toss of her wild hair.

"It can't have been cacodaimons," she said. "Besides, whatever they were, they can't have you until you help me find my sister. Get in the car."

"Just a damned minute," I said. "How do I know I can trust you?"

She was halfway around to the driver's side, keys in hand.

"You don't," she replied curtly. "Now get in."

16

She slipped behind the wheel and keyed the ignition, leaving the top down. The engine came to life, purring like a happy little tiger cub after a bloody meal. She smiled at the sound, actually patting the dashboard like someone from a different era might stroke the neck of a favored steed.

Despite her claim of having road-tripped from Joliet, the car was pristinely clean—there wasn't even a stray travel mug in the cup holder. The only thing that struck me as messy was a curious profusion of beaded and pewter charms dangling from the rear-view mirror. They looked like they had been dug out of the bargain bin of a New Age shop, and were wholly at odds with the sleek elegance of both the woman and her vehicle. Maybe she'd slaughtered a wild gang of hippies on her way out to Cleveland, and these were her trophies. I couldn't figure it, but something about the pendants with their frayed hemp and leather cords kept drawing my eye.

Before putting the Sebring into gear, she fussed with

her cell phone, fixing it to a hands-free cradle on the dash between us. I adjusted the seat to give myself more legroom.

"I don't even know your name," I said awkwardly.

"Lillee," she replied without looking up from the glowing screen of the smartphone. She set it to a map function, backtracking to a previously entered address.

"So... Lil," I said. "Like in the message."

"That's what you call me, genius," she said. "You still at the old address?" she asked, glancing up briefly from the smartphone. "Down near Coventry?"

I blinked stupidly at her.

She made an irritated noise. "Just give me your wallet."

Too stunned to argue, I complied. She flipped it open, glanced at my driver's license, then handed it wordlessly back to me. I shifted on the leather seat enough to slip it back into my pocket.

"I'm not sure we should go to my place," I objected. "There's a police bulletin out for me."

"Police bulletin? You really stepped in it. They know your name yet?"

I peered in the direction of the flashing lights. "Maybe not." I closed my hand around Remy's keys in my jacket pocket, briefly debating if we should go to the safe house—but I wasn't sure how safe I was with her... not yet.

"If they don't have your name, they won't be at your place," she said, "and I want to get there before anyone else does. Knowing you, you've got notes and files of whatever you and Lailah were working on, scattered all over the place."

That sounded right, but I still wasn't certain it was a good idea. That sense of pursuit loomed in my mind. People were looking for me and I had a feeling they had more than coca... *caco*daimons at their disposal.

"But—"

She cut me off with an irritated gesture. "No buts. My car, my rules. We're going to your place. Unless you want me to drop you off with the cops over there?" she asked with a nasty smirk.

"You wouldn't dare!" I said.

"Try me," she shot back.

We locked eyes for a few tense moments as I mentally tallied all the reasons I should just get out of her car and try for the Harley. Yet that had been my voice on her phone. I'd reached out to her before everything went south. And Lailah—whose name I couldn't even call to mind without feeling a poignant stab of regret—Lailah was her sister.

Lil had a stake in this as much as I did.

"Fine." I sighed. I shoved Remy's keys deeper into my pocket and stretched against the bucket seat.

"Good boy," she cooed. "Now put this on." She grabbed one of the charms from the rear-view mirror, unthreading it from the rest. The various pendants jangled musically against one another as she tore it free. I stared at the little pewter half-mask she thrust into my hand.

"Is this from *Phantom of the Opera*?" I asked, genuinely puzzled.

"Just put it on. There's no point in making things easy on them—whoever they are."

I turned the curious little item around in my fingers.

"You want me to wear this around my neck or something?"

"No, Einstein, I want you to clip it to your pretty brown hair," she shot back. "Of course I want you to wear it. The sooner you put it on, the sooner we can get moving. Your cowl sucks, and I'm not going to run the risk of anyone tracking you like I did."

"Wait, you *tracked* me?"

She rolled her eyes, reached over, and snatched the necklace. Then she more or less lassoed me with its cord. It got stuck on one of my ears, but she was relentless.

"What the hell, lady?" I demanded once she had it on me.

"That'll do for now," she muttered. I moved to take it off, and quick as lightning, she reached over and slapped my hand like I was a toddler about to put something dangerous in my mouth. "Don't fuss with it," she scolded. "The shield's delicate. I had to throw all of those together on the fly before I came out here. Didn't know what I was wading into."

"So this is some kind of magic charm?"

"What else would it be?" she responded so matter-of-factly that I decided it was foolish to argue.

She put the car in gear and whipped onto the street, maneuvering through the one-ways that led up and out of the Flats. I leaned my head on the neck rest, the wind rushing against my face. It felt weird against the growth of whiskers. Clearly, I was used to a cleaner shave.

At length she spoke again.

"You don't remember anything?" she asked.

She didn't seem to mind the November chill any more than I did, and actually had a smile playing round her full, red lips as she lifted her face to the breeze. The way her thick waves of russet hair whipped around her face reminded me of snakes. Of course, for all I knew, I was sitting next to the real-life Medusa. I wouldn't have found it shocking at that point. Not after everything else that had occurred.

"I can tell you everything you never wanted to know about the Terminal Tower," I said bitterly, "but when I woke up, I didn't even remember my name."

She made a thoughtful sound. "Any idea what happened to you?"

"Not a fucking clue. I went to Heaven to get answers. They were supremely unhelpful."

Lil snorted. "You never get straight answers out of the Nephilim. Especially not Sal. Machiavelli's an amateur by comparison."

"Remy seemed decent."

She fell conspicuously silent, pecking at the steering wheel with her long red nails. She muttered something to herself and it didn't sound like English. Even so, it niggled things in some back portion of my brain.

"What is that?" I asked, canting my head at her.

"What's what?" she responded, turning left on a red light once she saw no one coming in the opposite direction.

"That language. I heard Sal speaking it earlier."

She gawked at me, swerving as she nearly missed the entrance ramp to the highway.

"Mother's tears, Zack—you forgot that, too?" She turned her concentration briefly back to the road while I gripped the edge of the seat. "No wonder you didn't have a cowl up. Probably had no idea you needed one."

"Bingo," I replied bitterly. "Give the lady a prize."

She whipped the car around the sharply curved entrance ramp and I was glad of my seatbelt.

"I told Lailah she shouldn't come back to Cleveland," Lil growled. "She had a good thing going at the Oriental Institute back in Chicago. But no... you had to lure her to your museum." She shifted gears and gunned the motor as she merged with traffic. "She should have known better, Zack. You shit trouble on a daily basis."

With all that had happened, I couldn't really argue. I hadn't been in the city for more than a couple of hours, and already there was a bloody trail of bodies in my wake. Even without the cacodaimons, my life seemed complicated at best.

I looked down at my hands where they rested against my knees. I turned them over, clenching my long, thin fingers into fists. There were scars along the knuckles, pale but unmistakable. These hands had been in a lot of fights. The echo of those twin blades tingled against my palms. When I'd ended the cacodaimon—or whatever it was—I'd felt fierce exhilaration. Battle lust.

I was capable of killing. I had probably killed before. I just hoped it was for a good cause.

Suddenly overwhelmed by a crushing melancholy, I gazed out at the passing cityscape. The wind was cold and crisp, but my awareness of the chill was distant at best. There was just the rush and the rhythm of the open air and the constant sensation as it buffeted my face. It was actually kind of soothing.

Lil urged the sporty convertible up to ninety and the streetlamps streaked by with hypnotic regularity. I adjusted the seat again, stretching out as much as my long legs would allow. This was the first chance I'd gotten to relax since waking up on the shore of the lake—unless you counted passing out at the club. Dimly, I heard Lil talking to me, but it was increasingly difficult to make out her words. I closed my eyes for just a moment…

17

"Hey, Sleeping Beauty. Rise and shine."

I had a moment of panic where I thought I was suspended between darkness and void, the sound of churning water mingling with the rhythm of great wings. A dark figure pursued me, wearing an amulet with a stone like a burning eye. He extended fingers wreathed in tendrils of pure night.

Snapping from the nightmare with a start, I managed not to shout. Flailing a bit, I smacked my hand against the roof of the car. The top was up. The last thing I remembered, we were zipping along I-90 and the top was still down.

Self-consciously I wiped drool from the side of my mouth. "I fell asleep?" I asked thickly.

"Passed out, more like." Lil chuckled. "Whatever you got up to at Club Heaven wore you out. Have you slept or eaten anything in the past twenty-four hours?" she asked. "You look like hell."

She leaned in close, keen gray eyes studying my face,

and it was hard not to notice her very rich, very feminine smell—all spice, vanilla, and musk. I jerked away, pressing my shoulder against the rolled-up passenger-side window.

"When did you put the top up?" I asked.

A sly curl touched her lips as she noticed my discomfort. "I stopped at a gas station before we hit Coventry," she replied. Settling back behind the wheel of the car, she flipped open the mirror on the visor and ran her fingers through her long, russet mane. "As much as I love to feel the wind in my hair, driving around Ohio with the top down in November isn't exactly subtle. I wanted to attract as little attention as possible while I cased your place."

I peered out at the four-lane divided street. We were parallel parked near a three-way intersection. A traffic light blinked in the distance, swaying a little in the wind. That part of the road was well lit, with a drug store on one side and what looked to be a repurposed movie theater across from it. The cross street ran down a short incline, leading to high-end storefronts. Lights shone in only some of the windows. At this hour, everything was closed. Behind us, residential buildings—mostly apartments and townhouses—stretched away into the night.

"I wanted to be sure no one else was watching the place. I've driven around a couple times while you snored." Wryly, she added, "You were loud as fuck. If I didn't think you needed the rest, I'd have smacked you awake."

"Gee, you're sweet," I responded, scrubbing grit out of my eyes.

"Oh, that's me," she said with a throaty laugh. "Sugar and spice." Then her expression turned serious again. "So what went down at Sal's latest den of iniquity?"

I wasn't sure how much I should tell her.

"How do you know Sal?" I asked.

She made a sour face.

"Oh, we go way back."

I thought about checking her for fangs, too, but with her warm, bronzed complexion she didn't seem the type. Also, if I got anywhere near those full, red lips, I was pretty certain she would bite—fangs or no fangs.

"Spit it out, Anakim," she said, eyeing my expression.

I rubbed the heels of my hands against my forehead.

"Give me a minute. I'm still working through all this *Constantine* shit."

"Get used to it. Everyone you know is a monster," she said flatly, and she wasn't joking. I took a careful breath, not wanting to reveal how much that unnerved me.

"So what are you?" I asked, trying to sound casual about it.

She fixed me with her lucid, stormy glare. "I'm your worst fucking nightmare, if we don't find my sister. Now tell me what happened at the club. If we figure out what's after you, it will help me track its source."

"I said it already. Cacodaimons."

Irritably, she shook her head. "I call bullshit. Those things don't come crawling out just to follow someone around."

"But Remy said—"

She cut me off with a sneer. "Don't tell me what he said. Tell me what you saw."

I thought back to those adrenaline-kissed moments at Heaven. The whole experience came flooding back and I realized I could call it up as vividly as one of my visions. My hands buzzed with recollected power, and I could almost feel the blades.

"Shadows," I breathed. At that, the words spilled out of me. My eyes were closed, but I hardly noticed. The replay in my mind's eye eclipsed everything. "Inky black, invertebrate. Sharp teeth, hideous eyes. Long whipping tails and all these little arms. They rode on the corpses, worked them like puppets. I was the only one who could see them."

Lil fell silent beside me in the car. When I opened my eyes, she was staring out the driver's-side window. Little hairs stood up along the tanned length of her forearm.

"Lil?" I prompted.

She puffed her cheeks, releasing a shaky breath. "Those sound like cacodaimons all right. What the hell did you and Lailah get into?"

"I guess we should go check my apartment and find out." I reached for the door, ready to open it to the night. Lil seized my arm, dragging me to a halt.

"Isn't that your car?" she hissed.

"How the hell should I know?"

I followed where she gestured. In the apartment building across from us, an old gray Buick was backing onto the street. I should have been trying to stare at the driver, but instead I got side tracked by the bumper stickers. One had a *Battlestar Galactica* insignia. The other showed a familiar blue police box with a wibbly wobbly proclamation on the nature of time.

"Pretty sure that's yours," Lil replied. "I can smell the geek from here."

I frowned at the single working tail light of the retreating vehicle. The Buick had seen better days.

"Remind me why I drive a car older than most college students?"

She ignored me, grumbling, "This complicates things." She released my arm, shoving it off the divider between us. Flipping open the armrest, she revealed a white leather clutch-purse tucked inside. She dug around in the purse and took out—no joke—a little pearl-handled Derringer.

"Holy crap," I muttered.

"All right," she said, oblivious to my shock at seeing the gun. "We wait a couple of minutes to make sure he doesn't come back. Then we head in."

"Do you always pack heat?" I wondered—and maybe my voice quavered just a little.

She made a disgusted noise. "Stop being a pussy. It's not like I'm going to shoot you." She paused, then added, "Unless you piss me off."

From the steely glint in her eyes, I wasn't entirely certain she was joking.

18

Lillee got out of the car and gestured for me to follow. I still wasn't convinced I should trust her, let alone follow her into a darkened apartment building while she was carrying a firearm.

"Are you coming, Zack? Where's your Kimber?"

"My what?" I asked.

"Your gun, you idiot."

"What part of 'nothing but the clothes on my back' did you miss, lady?"

"So there's no chance you've got keys to this place."

"Nope," I responded, holding out open and very empty hands.

She muttered a curse, then thumbed a button on her key fob to pop the trunk. Tucking the Derringer at the small of her back and adjusting her blazer over it, she went and rummaged around. She pulled out a device the approximate shape and size of an electric drill, then she grabbed a camel-brown overcoat and draped it across one arm, tucking the hand tool under it.

"What else you got back there?" I asked, craning my neck to see over the lid of the trunk. "A James Bond Do-It-Yourself Spy Kit?"

She chuckled despite herself, using her free hand to shut the trunk as quietly as possible. "The trunk of a lady's car is a lot like the contents of her purse. Mysterious to menfolk like yourself, and intended to remain that way."

She began striding smartly toward the other side of the street. She'd parked so close to the car in front that there was barely enough room for me to fit through. By the time I jigged past, Lil was already halfway across, but I easily caught up to her.

"Seriously, Lil. What if you get caught with that thing stowed in your trunk? Isn't it illegal or something?"

She laughed openly at this. It was a warm throaty sound and she only remembered we were trying to be quiet about halfway through. Stopping with one foot on the curb in front of my apartment, she turned to me.

"On the rare occasions that I have been pulled over, I have never, *ever* gotten a ticket. No one has asked to look inside my... *trunk*."

As if to elaborate, she pitched her shoulders forward ever so slightly, tilting her cleavage into full view. Then she lifted her storm-gray eyes to mine, regarding me from under her thick nest of lashes. With a coy tilt of her head, she gave me her best come-hither. That warm spice and vanilla scent rolled off of her, and her very female-ness seemed like a palpable force clawing at me.

"I bet that works on all the lady cops," I choked.

Lil batted her lashes and it felt like the temperature

of the chilly fall night rose to something measurable in Kelvin. I took a judicious step back, even though my body was screaming that closer would be better—and much more fun. Lil eyed me for a few moments, the curl to her lips unmistakable.

On the other hand, maybe it does, I thought.

"Uh, ladies first," I said with an awkward and exaggerated bow.

"Always," she replied primly, and continued toward the apartment building. I made sure she got a head start, then followed cautiously behind. It was a good bet Lil put the fatal back in *femme fatale*.

As it turned out, we didn't need the lock-pick gun. The door sagged partly open. I nudged it the rest of the way with one elbow, moved into the living room, then automatically reached for the light switch on the inside. A brass pole lamp leaning across a pile of books flickered once then burned out with a sizzling pop. All the other lamps in the room were similarly toppled.

"Perfect," I grumbled.

Lil was still in the outside hallway, checking to see if we were alone. I took several more steps into the mostly darkened room, trying to assess the chaos. It was a nice apartment, as such things go—or at least, it looked like it might have been nice before the hurricane blew through.

The living room had a central tiled area in front of an inviting stone fireplace. An overstuffed couch and matching loveseat had been arranged in front of the hearth. The couch was tipped on its back, cushions scattered and upholstery slashed. Bookcases that had once lined the walls were toppled to the floor, their contents spilling everywhere. Picture frames had been torn from the walls and tossed haphazardly among the piles of books. The desk and filing cabinet tucked in one corner had been thoroughly ransacked, drifts of papers spilling from manila folders everywhere.

A conspicuously empty section on the desk suggested that it had once been home to a computer.

Lillee whistled sharply. "Jeez, Zack. I knew you were a bachelor, but this is excessive even for you."

I glared over my shoulder. "Very funny. The place has been tossed."

"No shit," she said, carefully stepping around the scattered piles. She toed one of the books that lay open, pages torn by a hasty hand. "They were hot to get their mitts on something."

"Yeah," I responded glumly, "and I've got to figure out what they wanted, when I don't even remember what I owned."

"You got gloves?" she asked. She set the lock-picking gun on a clear patch of beige carpet, fished in her purse, then produced a pair of blue nitrile gloves. Slipping one on, she gingerly picked up one of the picture frames. Glass tinkled as she shook little slivers onto the rug. Her delicately plucked brows went up and she made a little "hrm" sound in the back of her throat. "I didn't know you were still a collector," she observed.

"Let me see that." I reached out and took it from her. She started to object, but I shook my head firmly, making a sweeping gesture with my free hand. "My place, remember? My prints are all over."

"Good point," she said, and she relinquished the frame.

Moving to the front windows where a patch of light shone from a nearby streetlamp, I squinted down at the picture in my hand. I wasn't sure what I'd been expecting, but it certainly wasn't this. The roughly nine-by-twelve frame housed not a picture nor a photo, but the page of a book. It was very old, with a stylized drop capital, florid calligraphy, and an illuminated panel at the top. The rich pigments of the illumination took on a dark and velvety texture in the weak spill of light, accented with the unmistakable glint of gold leaf. The parchment had a rich and creamy texture, glowing with a depth you just didn't get with ordinary paper.

"It's from a psaltery," I muttered. "Latin—probably thirteenth, maybe early fourteenth century. France, I think." I looked around the room again, taking things in with a new set of eyes. There were more framed pages. "I study this stuff," I said, and almost remembered it. I tried to catch more, but it slipped my grasp. For a moment, I considered unclenching that fist in my head and seeing what impressions I might pick up from the place, but I still didn't have a handle on those powers. I really didn't want to end up twitching on the floor—especially not around Lil.

So I went for a more conventional approach, digging through the untidy piles of books and reading the spines. Lil didn't move from her relatively clear spot just inside the entrance. With her gray-eyed gaze, she watched me curiously.

"*Ancient Near Eastern Languages*," I read. "*A History of Sumer, Babylon, and Akkad*." I grabbed the next one. "*Ugaritic Culture and Its Impact on the*

Abrahamic Faith." And the next one. "*Sons of Ur: the Sumerian Roots of the Book of the Watchers.*" Pretty soon, I stood in the midst of a growing pile of thick, obscure tomes, only some of which were in English. "I study this!" I declared with mounting excitement.

"Well, of course you do," Lil purred, "but you cheat. You spoke most of those languages back in the day."

I dropped the book I was holding and goggled at her.

"Uh, Lil," I said, "that was like, six thousand years ago."

"So?" she asked archly. "You're immortal. Don't tell me you forgot that, too." At that I flashed back to my very first memories of the night.

Struggling to keep my head above water.

Swimming, then face-down in the sand.

Coughing up lake water.

Wondering why I hadn't drowned. *What if I did?*

"Six thousand years?"

The other vision came surging back. Ancient temple. Rough spun tunics. Bronze—*not iron*—blades. It had felt like a memory, but how long ago had it been? My head felt too full and I sat down heavily, scattering books.

"What the hell, Zack?" Lil cried.

Then she did the most humane thing I'd seen out of her since our introduction in the Flats. She sidestepped the piles of books and knelt down by me, reaching a comforting hand toward my shoulder. All I could do was flinch away.

"Don't fucking touch me!" I cried.

She scowled, but kept her hands to herself. Perching in front of me, she easily balanced on the balls of her feet.

"All right, then," she said, "but you need to get a grip."

I pressed the palms of my hands against my eyes, trying to breathe through the panic.

"Just don't talk about the weird shit right now, OK?" I muttered. "This is a lot to take in."

"Fine." She smirked. "I won't even tell you you're being a pussy. How's that?" she added with a sarcastic grin.

I glared at her and actually took a swing in her direction. I didn't intend to hit her too hard—just cuff her on the shoulder for being such a snot. She saw it coming and nimbly danced away, laughing in her maddeningly sexy way. I tried to scramble after her, but between the books and my size thirteen boots I got all tangled up on myself. Tumbling onto the nearest upended bookcase, I smacked my elbow and very nearly whacked my chin.

After such an impressive display, I felt my ego swell. Though maybe it was my elbow. I lay nose to nose with a Starbuck action figure flung atop one of the framed pieces of manuscript. Lamely, I tried to recall why Starbuck was a woman with a bitching blonde bob—when my eyes focused on the framed piece beneath the figure.

It was caught under a half-toppled bookcase. I wasn't even sure what I was looking at, but every fiber of my being clamored that it was important.

"I got it," I said, reaching for the frame.

"You got it all right." Lil laughed, wiping tears from her eyes. "Showed that bookcase who's boss."

"No," I snarled as I pulled the picture frame free. "I found something they missed."

Lil was standing over me as quick as that. She peered down at the framed vellum page in my hands.

"All right. What is it?"

The answer poured from my lips before I could think about it. "This is an illustration from the *Celestial Hierarchy* of Pseudo-Dionysius the Areopagite. Venice. Fifteenth century."

"I'll take your word for it," she said a little skeptically.

I gestured with mounting excitement as my knowledge of the piece came flooding back. "See these three circles, twined together? They represent the three tiers of heavenly hierarchies—and the three circles inside each of them are the three choirs, or orders, assigned to each tier."

Holy crap, I thought. I'd actually remembered something.

"It's pretty much just circles and funky letters, Zack. Compared to some of the others, with the gold and all, this piece is kind of dull."

"That's not the point," I grumbled. "I think I picked this one because it's not flashy. It's just black ink. Easy enough to reproduce something that doesn't stick out."

She leaned closer, squinting at the illustration, and made an irritated little noise in the back of her throat. "You're going to have to spell it out for me. All that Latin and angel stuff is your gig, not mine."

"The ring of numbers just inside each of those big circles," I said, tapping the glass. "Those aren't supposed to be there. *None* of those numbers are. It's a code."

She frowned, shook her head and wandered over to the front window, looking up and down the street.

"Great," she said without bothering to turn back. "So what does it say?"

I looked back down at the carefully inserted rings of numbers. The surge of elation crashed suddenly back to reality.

"I have no fucking clue."

She smacked her forehead with a groan.

"Mother's tears," she said.

"I'll figure it out," I insisted.

"Sure—once it's no longer useful." She waved with an impatient gesture. "Make it portable. I don't think we should stay here much longer. Morning traffic's starting up, and if there's a police bulletin out for you, we can't count on this place staying off the radar forever."

I began removing the vellum sheet from its gilded frame. As I got the glass and matting off, a small white envelope fell out from behind the cardboard. I wasn't sure why, but I glanced over to see whether or not Lil noticed. She was leaning on the sill, a crease of worry marring her brow as she tracked some car or another on its journey down the street. I snatched up the unmarked envelope and stowed it in the interior pocket of my jacket. With the extra socks from Wal-Mart, it was getting kind of crowded in there.

"Hey, Lil," I said, rolling the antique vellum and looking around for a poster tube or something. I settled on the empty tube from a roll of paper towels. The edges poked out, but it was better than nothing. "At least let me grab some clean clothes."

"Sure," she said distractedly, "but make it quick."

I headed for a short hallway leading away from the living room. The bathroom door was partly open, and I was reminded of yet another thing I hadn't done all day, in addition to sleep and eating. An extra minute or two wasn't going to kill me—assuming *anything* could kill me. I cast the thought from my head almost as soon as it manifested.

Basic needs now, weird shit later.

I flicked the light on, did my business, then paused in front of the mirror to wash my hands. It was the first time I'd really had a chance to look at myself, and Lil was right. I looked terrible. Abrasions scabbed my jaw underneath at least a day's worth of stubble. A little cut crusted above one eyebrow. The bruises didn't hurt as much as I thought they should. Maybe there were upsides to being immortal.

As I tried to comb my tangled hair into some uniform direction, I caught sight of half a dozen grays scattered among the brown. Briefly, I wondered if immortals were supposed to get gray. If it was about not aging, then I wasn't doing a very good job. Not that I looked bad or anything, but there were laugh lines around my eyes and a kind of starkness to my jaw that I took for another sign of wear and tear.

Gazing into the pale blue eyes that peered out of the mirror at me, I could see the resemblance to Remy, if not Saliriel. With that thought in mind, I checked my teeth, still feeling peculiarly paranoid. They were neither perfectly straight nor perfectly white. As I grimaced at myself, I even spied a couple of fillings back in the molars. As far as I could tell, I looked like your average, thirty-something guy.

"Zack?" Lil called back from the front room. There was an edge of impatience to her voice that reminded me of my mother. Which was a curious thought. Did winged immortals even *have* mothers?

"Hang on!" I called back, grabbing a little brown leather travel case from the back of the toilet. I snatched up a razor, comb, and toothbrush. There were two in the cup. One was purple, one was blue. I took the blue one, instinctively knowing it was mine—which left me wondering about the other one. Still pondering it, I flipped off the light and slipped back to the apartment's single bedroom.

Whoever had turned the place upside down hadn't spared anything here. Even the mattress was slashed. I dropped the leather jacket onto the disaster of a bed and shucked out of the clothes I'd worn for who knew how long. Sand cascaded everywhere when I pulled the T-shirt off, and I tried not to think about how badly I wanted a shower.

Donning a fresh T-shirt and jeans, I managed only to feel slightly cleaner. Riffling through upended drawers, I snagged a couple changes of clothes. Across the dresser lay a T-shirt emblazoned with a memo from Grand Moff Tarkin, reminding all storm troopers to report for mandatory target practice at 0600 hours. Rushed as I was, it still brought a grin. I packed it.

Every article of clothing I owned seemed like it was black or some other dark shade, with the lone exception of a heather-gray hooded sweatshirt. It had a college logo emblazoned across the front.

CASE WESTERN
RESERVE UNIVERSITY

When I picked up the sweatshirt, something tumbled to the floor—a little black-lace bra. That certainly didn't belong to me. Seized with an overwhelming impulse, I rushed to the dresser, searching among the shattered bits of broken mirror. Receipts, business cards, other junk—then I found what I was looking for. A little strip of images, done up like they'd been taken in one of those old-fashioned photo booths, but it was laser-printer slick—a modern photo. Torn at the bottom, half the images were gone. The first two remained with gut-wrenching clarity.

Against a generic background, my face smiled out at me, wearing a goofy expression I probably thought was funny at the time. Beside me, looking only slightly more serious, was the black-haired woman who'd haunted me in visions. Her skin and features placed her heritage somewhere in the Middle East. She carried the warmth and exoticism of those lands in her knowing smile and arresting gaze.

Lailah.

The bra, the toothbrush, and now this.

I dropped onto the edge of the ruined bed trying to remember how to breathe.

"Dammit, Zack, we don't have all night!" Lil cried, storming down the hall to retrieve me. She stopped in the doorway when she saw the stricken look on my face.

I wetted too-dry lips.

"You didn't tell me..." I began. "You didn't say I was involved with her."

Lil's gaze flicked from the lacey undergarment to the torn photo held loosely in my hand.

"She never said you were."

Lil had carried a book back with her—the one with the torn pages. She tossed it next to me onto the bed. "Pack that. It's the only one they damaged. I want to know why. The damned thing's in French." I didn't even look at it. Wordlessly, I shoved it in with the rolled-up T-shirts and jeans.

Lil lingered awkwardly in the door. "With Lailah—does it make a difference if you can't remember?" she asked.

My throat suddenly felt too tight. I swept off of the bed and finished stuffing clothes into the backpack. There was a pair of engineer boots in the corner of the wrecked closet, and I traded up from the cheap shit kickers I'd bought at Wal-Mart. Finally I trusted myself to speak again.

"Yeah. It makes a fucking difference."

I grabbed my jacket and turned to go, nearly crushing the cordless phone underfoot. It had fallen from the nightstand and lay half under the bed. It looked like something transported from the wrong decade, a digital answering machine built into its base. I froze when a tinny voice announced a date and time stamp. They hadn't erased the messages.

"*Tuesday, twelve fifty-two A.M.*"

My voice, breathless. "*They're safe. I'm on the run, though. One of those bastards chased me all the way through Rockefeller Park. Some kid saw the shoot-out. Get ahold of Bobby before that turns into a real clusterfuck.*"

Traffic sounds in the distance and a loud click as I hung up. That explained the police bulletin. I wondered who Bobby was. The answering machine didn't give me time to ponder for long.

"*Tuesday, two-forty-six* A.M."

"*Lailah. If you're there, pick up. Don't go back tonight. The Nephilim have anchors all over. They're watching the place.*"

I didn't have a fucking clue what an anchor was, but my voice made it sound urgent. The computerized records-keeper made her inexorable advance to the next message.

"*Tuesday, three-thirty-five* A.M."

My voice again, desperate. "*Lailah? Lailah, pick up! Your cell's going straight to voicemail.*" There was a pause and the wind gusted over the mic. "*Lailah? Fuck!*"

I'd practically been yelling into the phone. The answering machine continued to play.

"*Thursday, four-twenty-five* A.M."

A male voice, flat and uninflected said, "*Lake View, nine* A.M. *The angel. You know the one.*"

Something about the voice or what it reminded me of made all the hairs stand up on my arms. I had no conscious recognition, however. The guy sounded almost as robotic as the automated voice reciting the time and date stamp. The only thing that stood out was a curious twang to his a's.

His message was the last.

A suffocating silence fell over the room. Lil asked, "Do you know who that was?"

"Nope," I replied. My pulse thundered. I didn't want to subject myself to the messages again, especially not the ones where I was calling for Lailah. Still, I steeled myself and hit play. I listened carefully for anything that might offer more information. I could hear cars in the background in each of mine. So I'd been on the move, probably on a cell. In the final message, background noise was conspicuously empty. Not even an echo, like the speaker stood in some soundproofed room.

"You think he's talking about Lake View Cemetery?" Lil asked.

I shrugged. "I guess."

"At least we have a timeline," she observed. "Now let's get the hell out of here."

I nodded, the voice of the stranger still rattling uneasily in my head. Before I left, I yanked the wire from the phone and erased everything.

19

We fled to a diner near Ford and Mayfield called Egg Hedz. I wasn't keen on being someplace so public, but Lil insisted it was safer with people around us, and we needed somewhere to sit and go over what we'd found. She ignored my concerns about the police bulletin, insisting people would only take notice if I acted like I had something to hide. Easy for her to say—she wasn't the one who'd been spotted in a shoot-out only a few blocks away.

The little greasy spoon was busier than expected, probably because it was so close to University Circle, but we managed to score a booth tucked far away in the back. Despite my clamoring nerves, no one looked twice at us. All the customers seemed to be students from Case Western too intent on scarfing down some breakfast to bother paying attention to anything beyond their smartphones. Few of them bothered looking up from the devices, rapidly tapping out texts or scrolling through their social media and newsfeeds.

"So what do we have?" Lil asked.

I shoveled the last of my "Barn Buster" omelet into my mouth and hastily chewed. "A whole lot of nothing if I can't decode that cipher," I admitted.

Lil scowled into her coffee. "Assuming it's relevant to any of this."

"No," I objected, gesturing with the fork. "It's important. I know that much. I just can't tell you how."

"Then you'd better get cracking. What about that meeting at Lake View?"

I shrugged. "No clue. Not even sure I got that message before I ended up in the lake." Neither of us brought up the issue of the shooting, though it nagged in the back of my thoughts. Who was Bobby and what had I been doing to get chased? Had a shoot-out been my only option?

Lil made a frustrated noise, bringing my thoughts back to the present. "Give me something, Anakim. I'm tired of chasing shadows."

"Let me grab some paper," I grumbled. Casting a quick glance around the diner to be sure no one was looking, I reached over to the empty booth across from us and snagged a clean place mat and roll of silverware. Focusing on clearing the space in front of me, I unrolled the silverware, using the spare napkin to wipe off any crumbs and grease that had collected on the table. Then I dug the roll with the manuscript page out of the backpack, holding my hand out to Lil.

"What?" she asked.

"A pen. I need one. Do you carry pens in your purse or is it just for your little peashooter?"

She shot me an unhappy look, but grabbed her clutch-purse and began to dig through its contents. Cigarettes, a lighter, a tube of lipstick, and a compact all appeared on the table in front of her, followed swiftly by a tin of breath mints and another pair of nitrile gloves.

"You didn't tell me you were carrying around a portable hole," I commented as a tube of mascara and yet another compact emerged from the purse. "Does that thing *have* a bottom?"

"Here's your pen," she said curtly. As soon as she handed it off to me, she focused on the collection of make-up and personal effects spread out on her side of the table. One by one, the items disappeared back into the little purse. It was like watching a magic trick in reverse. Had a live dove suddenly fluttered from the purse's depths, I wouldn't have been surprised.

"It's a TARDIS," I muttered. "That explains everything."

"Oh, shut up," she grumbled. "I'm going to the ladies' room. Don't do anything stupid while I'm gone."

I barely acknowledged her. Now that I had a clean workspace, I carefully unrolled the sheet of antique vellum. There was a scent and feel to the page that stirred memories deep in the back of my mind, but I couldn't waste time with them. Instead, I spread the sheet out and began studying the three rings of numbers added to the design. On a corner of the place mat, I began arranging the numbers in a couple of different orders to see what patterns might emerge.

The more I worked, the more frustrated I got.

There were too many to be a lock combination or a

routing number. Latitude and longitude didn't fit. I tried adding them a couple of different ways, but that netted me nothing but more numbers, none of which seemed significant. I even checked to see if they were part of a Fibonacci sequence, marveling that I even remembered what the hell that was.

Somewhere in the midst of all my mad calculations, Lil came back from the ladies' room. She took her seat across from me, waved the waitress over for a refill on both our coffees, and watched in silence as I worked.

"I need something to do instead of just sitting here," she complained.

I glanced up from the page, rolling my neck until it popped. "You could look up the book you threw at me. You have a smartphone."

"I don't know French," she replied with a grimace.

"I probably do." I dredged the book from the backpack. It had an old leather cover with damage on the spine. The author and title were stamped in worn gold leaf. "*Le Pillage de l'Egypte par Napoléon*," I read, then translated for her, "Napoleon's Plunder of Egypt." I flipped to the title page. "The author is Henri Charles de Garmeaux. Published 1809. It's number 15 of 100 copies. Shit. They jacked up a super-rare book. I hope they had a good reason," I said with a frown. I set the book on the table between us, nudging it over to Lil. "It's a long shot, but maybe it's in some digital collection you can run a search engine through. Just see what we're missing between pages 197 and 202."

"Sure… whatever," she grumbled, then half-heartedly tapped the information into her browser.

I bent back over the cipher, but the puzzling strings of numbers still didn't fit anything that made sense. Stretching in the booth, I tried a different vantage point, turning the manuscript page first sideways then upside down. I stopped short of folding the antique vellum to see if there was some physical key to the code.

"No luck?" Lil wondered.

"It's right in front of me. I just need to get my brain in gear."

"Well, I'm not finding shit," she said, shifting around in her seat to tuck her legs under herself. Taking small, careful sips from her steaming coffee, she looked out across the crowded restaurant, eyes gliding vigilantly from one patron to the next.

"I'll take a look when I'm done," I said, and I went back over the Latin of the diagram, hoping the key was in the original text. "*Prim ternari ordo*," I read, "The first order: *Seraphin*, *Cherubi*, *Throni*. Ugh," I added with a grimace. "It's all names of the orders of angels, but it's in that mangled Church Latin. It should be *Seraphim* and *Cherubim*. Thrones should be *Ophanim*. The original words are Hebrew, after all."

Lil rolled her eyes, muttering, "Thank you, Captain Wikipedia."

I didn't really hear her. It finally hit me. I hunched back over the page, jotting letters and numbers with feverish intensity.

"Got something?" she inquired, lazing halfway across the booth on her side.

"Hebrew," I said excitedly. "In Hebrew, every letter is a number. All these numbers. They're really letters. I just need to switch them to their Hebrew counterparts then back to English to see what they say."

"Sure. You do that. How long?"

"Give me a few minutes. Hebrew's basically solid consonants. I just hope I was using the Hebrew to disguise something in English, otherwise this is really going to suck. Could you look up angels in Lake View?"

"No," she said flatly.

I frowned at her.

"Do you have any idea how many angels are in that cemetery?" she demanded. "I'd have more luck tying a leash around your neck and letting you run through it like a bloodhound."

"Oh, hell no," I responded.

She smirked nastily, as if enjoying the image she had conjured. "If you don't crack that cipher, it's *exactly* what I'll do."

After about ten minutes of transcription, I had a set of three phrases—one for each of the diagram's rings. Even so, I wasn't sure if they helped me or not. They read like telegrams from the *Twilight Zone*.

Anakesiel and lieutenants bound.

Neferkariel's eye in Dorimiel's hand.

Gandhi guards my brothers.

I double-checked my number–letter substitutions, wondering if I'd gotten everything right. Then I looked up at Lil.

"Anakesiel. Neferkariel. Dorimiel—those have to be names, right?"

She reacted so violently, she nearly upended her coffee. As it was, some of the steaming fluid splashed from her cup, landing perilously close to the antique page. With that quicker-than-human speed, I jerked the precious piece of vellum out of harm's way. My dubious ally practically stood up on her seat in her effort to slam her hand down over the piece of scratch paper where I'd written the names.

"Have you gone *crazy*?" she demanded. From the expression on her face, I was tempted to ask the same of her, but for the moment, I was too stunned to speak. I just sat there, protectively holding up the sheet of the *Celestial Hierarchy*.

"You almost got coffee on it."

She stared at me as if I had grown a second head, and that head was reciting Esperanto love sonnets about goats. She fisted her hand around the scratch sheet, crumpling it as she pulled it away from me.

"Hey! That's important work you're destroying."

"What were you thinking, intoning those names?" she growled.

"What is this, fucking *Beetlejuice*?" I responded.

"You make endless pop culture references no one else understands," she complained. "Why can't you remember anything useful? Names have power. You can use them to summon, banish, and bind. You don't speak names like that lightly."

The waitress chose that moment to come over, ostensibly to refresh our coffees, but most likely to make it clear she was keeping an eye on us. She looked rather pointedly at the check on the table. Neither Lil nor myself had put down any cash. We both clammed up and I hoped desperately the waitress hadn't caught last night's news. As soon as she walked away, I gave Lil a sour look.

"You think I'm stupid?" I growled. "Fine. Explain it to me."

She folded the scratch sheet over and over with sharp, meticulous gestures, and dropped her voice nearly to a hiss. "Those are names of the primae. At least two of them—leaders of the Nephilim and the Anakim. Dorimiel is four syllables, so he has to be a decimus."

"Four syllables is a decimus?" I wondered. "Like Saliriel? Why four?"

"I don't fucking know. That's just how it works. With you guys, your name is your power. Each syllable is like a spell. Speaking the name, even writing it, calls a little of the power up."

"So you're afraid they're going to hear me?" I scoffed.

She clenched the tightly folded paper against her palm. "Let's just say I've learned to be cautious."

"So, the Anakim primus—if it says he's bound—"

"It says he's *what*?" she squawked, hurriedly unfolding the repurposed place mat and smoothing it out on the table before her. Her glinting gray eyes flew over my scribbled transliterations. Her olive skin grew waxy. "Are you sure you got this right?" she demanded.

"If the names are right, then the rest is right," I said. "Not that it makes much sense. I mean, eyes in hands? Isn't that a little *Pan's Labyrinth*? And Gandhi? Don't tell me *he's* still running around. Maybe I was delirious when I wrote it."

"If you wrote your code in code, I'm going to kick you," she promised.

I held my hands up helplessly. Lil scowled and picked at the crumpled edge of the paper.

"The first line seems clear enough. If someone managed to bind the Anakim primus and his lieutenants, then it's war," she said, adding, "If you dragged Lailah into another fucking war, I am *never* going to forgive you."

"Another one?" I asked. "How many have there been?"

"Someone's counting?" she demanded. With an exasperated snarl, she explained, "It's all you people do. One tribe goes after another tribe because they don't like the way they're doing things. They bloody the other guys' noses, so of course, vengeance must be had. You know what a war among immortals amounts to? It's a glorified circle-jerk. I kill you, you come back and kill me—we go round and round. It accomplishes exactly *squat*." By the time she finished, she was practically spitting out the words.

I opened my mouth to respond, but she was really on a tear, color rising to her cheeks. A couple of the college students glanced curiously our way.

"Your tribe's the worst of all," she continued. "You think you're the fucking purity police—like you've got a right to judge anything that isn't mortal. I don't know how many times you've passed 'judgment' on the Voluptuous Ones." She said it sneeringly, and actually used air quotes. "What you should be doing is your job—patrolling the boundaries, but no. It's just crusade after crusade."

An angry tirade rose to the back of my throat. I wanted to bellow that she was wrong, that we had a right and a *purpose* for our actions. The words "sacred duty" blazoned in my mind. Snippets of the vision from Club Heaven rose unbidden in memory, and I was back in the temple filled with writhing, naked revelers, hunting the fanged priesthood at the heart of it all.

And there *was* an end to war. I got a little more of the memory. Killing him wasn't the last thing we did. There was some kind of prison sentence connected with those letters scribed upon his skin. That little bone stylus had been the key. My pulse sped with the force of the recollection, but it cut off, leaving my hands to throb with the memory of heavy bronze blades.

This wasn't getting us any closer to saving Lailah. I closed my eyes, trying to shove the thoughts and their attendant emotions aside.

"Yeah, that's right," Lil chided. "Think about it for once. You're no better than the rest of us, flyboy."

Lil's features locked in a grim smirk. She was baiting me—and enjoying it. I didn't think it was a good idea. Half-glimpsed memories continued roiling just beneath the surface of my conscious mind, stirring turbulent emotions. My hands were shaking. I balled my fists until the only thing I could feel was the ache of nails digging into my palms. If I stopped, a tidal surge of fury would sweep away all reason.

"We're done discussing this," I muttered. I swiftly rolled the manuscript page, grabbed my backpack, and escaped to the rear of the restaurant.

20

It probably wasn't the most mature way of ducking out of the argument, but I locked myself in the bathroom. Egg Hedz's men's room was a single person affair, which suited me perfectly. I dropped the backpack onto the floor, then leaned over the sink, splashing water on my face. I could almost see the memories stirring in the depths of my pale eyes—a shapeless march of phantom images bereft of sense but blazing with emotion. My pulse raced as my adrenaline rose—immediately answered by a twinge over my heart. It didn't hurt exactly.

It just felt... empty.

Something wasn't right.

The pain—or non-pain, really—came again, stealing my breath. I slipped out of my leather, hanging it up on the hook. Then I stood in front of the mirror and hiked up my T-shirt until I could get a good look.

Five neat, oblong-bruises shone darkly against my pale chest. I hadn't noticed them earlier. They were spaced in a curious arc across my sternum. The rich purpling under the skin suggested recent bruising. The chest hair was missing over each of them—not burned away, but simply absent.

The shape and the pattern of these five bruises—four spaced out from one another in a loose arc and one a little further down—left me feeling unsettled. As I ran my fingers over them, pressing for tender areas, I realized why. I laid the tip of my right index finger over the first of the four top marks. It fit almost perfectly. With a little contorting on my part, I managed to twist my arm around so I could match all five marks up to the splayed fingers of my right hand, plus my thumb. Though I had a wide span with my fingers, I had to stretch a little to match the pattern on my chest. The hand that left these marks was a little larger than my own, then—a fact which was impressive by itself.

I stared at the mirror for several long moments, trying to work out both why and how someone would leave bruises over my heart with the tips of their fingers. Considering some of the wild things I'd witnessed over the course of the night, the idea of someone marking me didn't seem beyond the realm of possibility, but it did make me wonder.

What else had been done?

Maybe there was more to see and I just wasn't looking with the right eyes.

"Clenched fist," I murmured to myself, recalling Remy's rushed lesson. I held out one hand, matching motion with intention. Only this time, I slowly uncurled that force of psychic perception.

It was awkward, trying to do it in the mirror. My

irritating monkey brain offered up at least half a dozen reasons for why I probably wasn't going to see anything at all. I closed my eyes, willing myself to relax and "just do," as Remy had counseled.

When I looked back to the mirror, nothing had changed, but my gaze was drawn to the stupid little half-mask dangling from its cord just below my throat. Frustrated, I reached up and yanked the charm off, stuffing it in the pocket of my jeans. Lil could squawk over it later. Right now I didn't need masks or amulets or whatever, interfering with what I wanted to see. Still holding my shirt up awkwardly above the bruises, I looked back to my reflection in the mirror.

The first thing I noticed was the wings.

They arced up and out behind me, the ghostly outline of them glowing with pale filaments of energy. The color was blue-white, just like the power I had wielded against the shadow-rider in combat at the club. That had been bright, almost blinding. The wings, however, were a softer, steadier glow. They didn't look feathered exactly, but they weren't leathery bat wings either. They had their own unique shape and form, like nothing I'd seen in nature. There was visible structure and musculature, all of it rimmed with—or completely comprised of—light.

If I'd had any doubt left, this settled it.

Angels.

I flexed muscles that weren't strictly physical and watched the wings shift in response. Once I got past the impossibility of it, I thrilled with exultation. I had fucking *wings.*

How cool is that?

I couldn't help playing. I stretched and flexed them, watching as they spread out behind me—to the point where they intersected with and extended through the bathroom walls. That was a weird sensation, and it was even stranger to see. Then I tried to think of the cowl Remy had described, tucking them tight against my back and imagining a shimmering veil of energy settling over them. Not shimmering, though, I reminded myself.

Lackluster.

Unremarkable.

A non-color that perceptions should skitter past. As I tried to envision this, the only thing that came to mind was a Romulan cloaking device. I chuckled at the insanity of it, then decided to roll with it, and watched my image ripple slightly—then the wings were gone. Or almost gone. I could just barely make out a hint of the energetic structures tucked tight against me. It felt cramped somehow, and a little stifling, but I could live with it.

So much for needing Lil's little mask.

Given her tirade about my people earlier, I didn't think I wanted to be wearing anything she made for me anyway. She might have answers, but there was going to be a price every step of the way.

With that thought, I turned my attention to the bruising on my chest—and was almost violently sick in the bathroom sink. Looking at them with my altered perception, the marks didn't look so much like bruises as they did ragged holes in my skin. Like patches of pure void, they bored to the core of me. I jerked my hand away on instinct, afraid that if I touched them now, my fingers would sink endlessly into their depths. That would completely unhinge me.

I looked away.

Then I pulled the shirt back down, tucking it in hurriedly. For several moments, I stood there, feeling sick and scared. My instincts clamored that the marks were tied to my loss of memory. Even as I thought it, a recollected flash galvanized me—a green-eyed figure lifting a hideous, shadow-wreathed hand. Searing pain. Dark water. Falling.

I knew those eyes. They belonged to the ancient master of the temple, in that vision of judgment and murder. Aside from those two snippets, however, nothing else broke through the haze of my amnesia. I slammed my knuckles against the sink. I had so many pieces of the puzzle. They had to fit together somehow.

With a rush of urgency, I started digging around in my jacket for the white envelope. I hadn't wanted to open it in front of Lil, but maybe it was the key that would make everything else fall into place.

Before I could find it in the inner pocket of my jacket, however, Lil was outside, pounding on the door.

"Zack! We've got company!"

21

Hurriedly, I zipped my biker jacket, tightening the buckle that fitted it against my waist. It felt like I was girding for battle. Hadn't Sal called it my armor? I took some comfort from that.

Slinging the backpack over one shoulder, I flipped the lock. Once I opened the door, Lil moved to press herself against the opposite wall, hunkering down and eyeing someone—or something—out in the restaurant. With one hand, she held the leather clutch-purse tight to her chest. The other hand was mostly inside of it, gripping the Derringer. She seemed genuinely spooked, which wasn't an expression that looked familiar on her.

I edged cautiously into the hall. Maybe it was because of how I'd opened my vision in front of the mirror a few moments before, but I had a stronger sense of the people gathered out in the rest of the diner. Thinking about it, everything seemed clearer and less muddled in my head. So the little charm Lil had tossed round my neck in the car had been hiding me, but also blocking my senses. I grimaced, getting really angry with her, but then pushed it aside.

Bigger fish to fry.

Amidst the sense of idle chatter and stress about exams, I could feel something sinister moving among the booths. Once I leaned to get a look around the corner, my attention snapped right to him. A little on the short side, with a paunch, he was wearing a Cleveland Indians jacket and a matching ball cap. He had a beard that looked like it hadn't been trimmed in a few days, black, streaked on either side of his chin with gray.

Aside from the scraggly beard, he didn't look particularly unkempt or dirty. The jacket was leather, now that I got a good look at it, and those things were expensive. This wasn't some drugged-up delinquent—but a cacodaimon still rode him.

I remembered how the other riders had noticed once I caught sight of them, so I tried to keep him just on the edge of my peripheral vision. I noted two things that left me feeling increasingly unsettled. One, his movements were smooth and easy. The rider was having no trouble at all interfacing with the guy's nervous system. Two—and I wasn't sure if this was a good or a bad thing—Ballcap appeared to be very much alive.

Then I realized that he wasn't alone.

There were two others standing by the cash register—a man and a woman, both early thirties. If not for the scarlet-eyed shadows leering just above their heads, I might have mistaken them for a married couple stopping for a bite to eat on their way to work.

"Three," Lil breathed. She stood just this side of the

corner, back against the wall, her stance loose and wary. "I don't believe it."

I concentrated on Romulan cloaking devices and fought not to stare at the things, keeping my voice low.

"They won't try anything in the restaurant, will they?"

"If they haven't yet, then probably not," she replied. She never took her eyes off the one circling among the booths. I didn't have to look up to know he was getting closer. She made an impatient sound halfway between a huff and curse. "I've never seen them act like this."

"How are they acting that's different?" I asked. Shifting the weight of the backpack, I stepped away from the corner and ducked down. Given my height, I was more likely to be spotted than her.

Lil hunkered down a little more herself, shoulders tense, her left hand ready to pull the dainty gun from the handbag at the first sign of trouble. Her gray eyes shone brightly as she tracked the rider moving our way.

"Purposeful," she said. "Organized. Cacodaimons are creatures of chaos. It's in the name."

"I told you," I whispered. "Someone's sending them after me."

"No one should be able to do that," she objected. "They're not bloodhounds. Orders go against their basic nature."

"Try telling them that," I said, still edging away from the main section of the diner. I turned to see how much farther I had to go before I couldn't back up any more. The hallway jogged to the right. Just around the corner was a fire door. The bar across the door was covered in a bright, reflective sticker.

WARNING: ALARM WILL SOUND

I hissed to get Lillee's attention, motioning her toward me. She gave an irritated little shake of her head, but didn't look my way.

"Door," I whispered urgently.

That did it. Without really turning away from the front of the diner, she slid back along the wall, side-stepping carefully on the balls of her feet so the heels of her boots didn't click against the tile.

"You move like a chick in a cop movie," I observed.

"This isn't a movie, Zack. Eyes front, or the bad guys get you," she hissed. Twitching the Derringer in my direction, she added, "Call me a chick again and you won't have to worry about the bad guys."

I pointed at the fire door.

"Shoot me once we're clear, hunh?"

She looked grimly down at the warning. "Let's hope it leads somewhere useful, because the minute we open that door, they'll be after us."

"I'm not facing them out in the diner," I insisted. "No way I'm dragging all those college kids into this crazy shit. Enough people have died because of me."

She rolled her eyes. "Bleeding mother. You pick this moment to develop a martyr complex?"

I didn't give her time to argue. "Count of three," I said. Then, without counting even as far as one, I opened the door and charged outside.

"Count of three my ass!" she snarled after me, but most of it was drowned in the squeal of the alarm. I was ten feet down the back alley at that point and she had to hustle to keep up with my long strides.

Ballcap must've been right at the front of the hallway when we went through because he pelted out the door close behind. The rider on his back lifted its head above his, spreading its cobra-like hood. Baring its teeth as he ran, it made a chittering sound that hit me on such a visceral level I almost broke my stride. Lil was right behind me and the minute I faltered, I felt her hand on my back, urging me on.

"Can you hear that?" I gasped, my breath starting to come hard and fast as we raced to the mouth of the alley.

"Yes," she said through gritted teeth. "Now *move*!"

The alley opened onto a little side street running behind the bank of buildings housing the diner and other shops. The street was barely more than an alley itself, cluttered with garbage cans and piles of trash. To our left in a large stretch of gravel were the tracks for Cleveland's answer to streetcars—the Rapid Transit. Across the tracks I could see rows of little houses tucked away behind sagging privacy fences.

I thought about dashing across the tracks, then seemed to recall something about them being electrified—or maybe that was an urban legend. Either way, the gravel drop-off from the narrow side street was uninvitingly steep and featured a rather intimidating fence tipped with barbed wire.

That made it kind of a non-option, really, but I didn't like the other alternatives, either. All I saw ahead of us were trash cans, dumpsters, and the back ends of buildings.

"Hey, Lil, I killed one of these things back at the club," I panted.

"And...?"

"So should we stop? Face him?" I leaped over a fallen trash can even as Lil jogged left to avoid it.

"One, maybe. Three?" she responded. "Besides, I think he has a—"

She didn't finish. Gunfire exploded behind us and a bullet whined off the bricks just above my head.

"Yeah," I acknowledged, starting to weave back and forth to make myself harder to hit. "That complicates things." So far, the cacodaimon seemed to be a terrible shot.

There was another alley up ahead, among the buildings to our right. The Rapid Transit tracks stretched opposite its mouth, creating a wide span devoid of cover between us and the houses across the way. Parked outside the alley was a big metal dumpster. I didn't know where the alley came out, but our current path was little more than a long open corridor running beside the tracks. There was nothing we could put between Ballcap's gun and our backs.

"Lil," I called, hoping she caught my gesture. Then I jigged around the dumpster, pausing just long enough to get an idea of how far back Ballcap was. *Not far enough*. I charged off into the alley just as he was taking aim in the vicinity of my head.

The buildings on either side were tall enough to cast the narrow little alley in a cloying pall of shadow at this early hour of the day. I wasn't complaining. Unless Ballcap had blacklight-vision, courtesy of the nightmare on his back, lower lighting meant we were harder to see and harder to hit—especially since we were both wearing dark colors.

The alley in ended in a wall.

Shit.

"Good work," Lil said, hunching behind a spill of boxes and readying the Derringer.

"Sarcasm not helping here," I grumbled, trying to hide my six foot three frame behind the same tumble of trash. I shrugged off the backpack and shoved it against the wall, trying to give us a little more space.

"Hunh?" she responded, genuinely puzzled. "You found a crossing. This is perfect. I'll shoot the body, you hop over to the Shadowside and face the rider on its own turf."

"Which would be great if I had a clue what you were talking about," I said. Ballcap's footfalls were already coming at us from the other end of the alley.

"OK, Captain Amnesia," Lil said through gritted teeth. "Here's how this will go down. I've got two shots, but he has to be close. Once he's distracted, grab the rider. I don't care from which side. Just take it out."

I tried not to cackle madly at the thought of a bullet wound as a distraction. Instead, I focused on my sense of the other half of reality. It would come naturally, I told myself, just like at the club. Charge in and react. Don't overthink.

In front of me, Lil shivered and I knew it couldn't have been with the cold.

"Mother's tears, Zaquiel," she said under her breath. "If he didn't know we were down here already..."

"You could feel that?" I whispered stupidly.

"*Duh.*"

And then he was on us. Lil sprang into motion,

standing up from her crouched position and firing the Derringer. The little pistol went "pop, pop" as opposed to "bang, bang," but he was close enough that the end result was more or less the same. She planted the first shot in his throat. The second she aimed at his balls.

I reminded myself never to piss her off.

Ballcap staggered back, and while her initial bullet was going to be fatal in the long run, it was the second shot that drove him to his knees. I didn't blame him. Hell, I almost felt sorry for the poor bastard—but not for long. The rider started shrieking and yanking around inside of him, making his muscles work despite the pain and imminent death. He hadn't dropped his gun yet, and I could see the rider trying frantically to get that arm to work.

Managing that burst of speed thing, I closed the space between us in what felt like an eye blink. In the course of that transit, there was a vague ripping sensation, like I tore through the very air in front of me. It drove all the breath from my lungs. The shadows in the alley grew suddenly starker, and the sounds of the city fell away.

I didn't stop to wonder at the abrupt transition, because the cacodaimon was right there, hissing bare inches from my face. I shouted the syllables of my name so forcefully that the rider staggered back from it. I took that hesitation to dive in. The blades leapt to life in my hands, less solid this time, but still burning fiercely. I slashed madly at the thing, and it shrieked its fury.

As it writhed within him, Ballcap jigged and flailed as if he gripped a live wire. Somehow his gun passed right through me. I didn't stop to wonder how or why as I grappled with his rider.

Behind me, Lil was doing something that made all the hairs on the back of my neck stand up. I hoped it was something helpful to me and dangerous to the cacodaimon, but I had no guarantee. I started to call up my power again, finding it harder this time to burn so brightly. I shouted in the thing's face once more, willing myself to obliterate it. It didn't explode into a million pieces of dark, but it did go slack and uncoil from Ballcap's failing body.

I seized and wrestled with its shockingly cold form, and then it did the unexpected. Instead of trying vainly to get Ballcap's broken body to work, the thing jumped ship entirely. That long, sectioned tail whipped free to wind all the way down my legs. Bitter waves of numbness cascaded in its wake. The wicked little scythes at the ends of its spindly appendages slashed furiously, scoring hits on my hands and face—although they seemed to be deflected by the thick leather of my biker jacket.

Armor indeed.

The blades sputtered, so I let them wink out, then dug both my hands into the neck of the thing. I held its razor-toothed maw just inches from my face as it gnashed viciously, trying to get a taste of me. Its gleaming red eyes looked like two bloody wounds slashed into the night of its form, and as it glared at me, malevolent intentions pressed like a weight against my mind. It made that awful chittering sound again, and then—unthinkably—it spoke.

"*Eeeeaaaattttyyyooouuuu, sssskkkky-bbbooorrnnn! Eeaaatttt yyyoouurrrr ffacceee!*" it hissed.

Buzzing insects and shrieks of tortured metal converged

in that eldritch sound. It unnerved me so thoroughly that I stumbled back beneath the rider's weight, losing my footing enough that I fell to my knees. My immortality was still a question, but I had a sinking feeling that if the monstrosity started chewing on me, I was going to end up dead in an unpleasant and very final way.

Just as what little I remembered of my life started flashing before my eyes, there came an unexpected and deafening roar from Lil's direction. I didn't have time enough to be shocked by it, because less than a heartbeat later something muscled, tawny, and very big leapt at the cacodaimon. I got an up close and personal view of bright pink gums and long, ivory teeth as a huge cat came out of nowhere and clamped its vise-like jaws down on the back of the rider's neck.

The only good thing about being body-slammed by a cat as big as me was that it had the effect of shaking my grip loose from the rider, or else I might have lost a couple of fingers as the feline bit down on the cacodaimon. Very effectively distracted, the rider convulsed, whipping its tail off of me and grappling with the new attacker.

As it unwound itself, the rider also detached half a dozen little legs it had managed to sink into my numbed thighs. I experienced a gut-twisting stab of nausea as I watched them slip out of me.

The walls of the blind alley reverberated with the coughing roar of the big cat as it struggled with its quarry. I sat on my ass on the damp and filthy pavement, vaguely aware that the only reason I wasn't flat on my back was because of my wings. They were as physical as the rest of me, which didn't seem right. Everything around me had grown strange. Taking a shaky breath, I tried getting back to my feet.

Lil appeared and passed right in front of me, looking like a ghost in an impressionist painting—I could see her, but not clearly. There was this slow, floaty quality to her movements, and all the colors around her were streaking. Her lightly tanned skin glowed as if lit from within, and her stormy gray eyes scintillated like twin alien stars. Her hair streamed out in rich red waves, curling on the air like the fronds of some exotic undersea flora.

Other shapes moved around her, coiling at the edges of her hair or twining around the flowing legs of her midnight silk pantsuit. Vulpine, feline, winged and scaled, I saw hints of countless animal faces, but mostly, I saw their eyes.

At least one of them winked at me.

Lil turned her head as if following the gaze of the animal. Then she was speaking, but her words and mouth didn't line up properly, the sound and action stuttering out of joint.

"Step out," she said, echoing strangely. "...'s not good... in too long."

I reached out to touch her, and couldn't. It wasn't that my hand ghosted through her, like it had with Ballcap. I was half expecting it to. Instead, I got this unpleasant electric tingle in my fingers, the closer they got to where she stood. The further I tried to press into the wash of light and color spilling around her, the more resistance I felt.

It hurt.

She must have felt something as well, because as I extended my hand closer to her aura, marveling in spite of the pain, her head snapped around and she stared right at me. Well, mostly right at me. Her gaze was off by a few inches.

"…'m serious!" she called. All of the animal faces shifting in and out of her energy turned wild eyes on me. As one, they loosed a warning growl—a sound that was much clearer than her voice. Taking the hint, I pulled my hand away and tried once more to get to my feet. My legs were a little less shaky this time, as the clinging cold of the cacodaimon faded.

Shifting my wings for balance, I finally managed to get into an upright position, reaching out to the wall to steady myself. The bricks weren't right, feeling squishy somehow. Rather than trying to get a clear look, I simply pulled my hand away. I wiped it on my jeans.

The space of the alley loomed dark around me, far too dark for the time of day. Jagged portions of night and shadow angled unevenly upon one another, each caught in a perspective skewed and strange. As I tried to adapt to the sensations, I stumbled over something. It was a dead woman. She lay scattered in pieces on this end of the alley. Her decapitated head had fetched up against the wall at a mostly upright angle, and her eyes gazed up at me, as if they were pleading.

Only a heartbeat later, she was standing there whole, and then she was running from the mouth of the alley to that same spot. She flickered again, and now she was struggling with another figure, indistinct and featureless, like an imperfect projection.

The whole scene flickered again…

And then the alley was empty.

Memories. I was looking at memories burned so deeply into the space that they had substance and weight. The events replayed continuously, flickering against themselves. I was somehow standing on top of them and in them at the same time.

I couldn't shake the intelligence in the woman's eyes, though. She wasn't simply an echo. She seemed like a real person trapped in that awful moment where another human being had stalked her, violated her, then tried to erase her very person-ness by hacking her to pieces.

So I looked away. I had to. Each time she flickered through the space, she stared at me as if she expected me to do something—yet I had no idea how to help.

Then I had bigger things to worry about. A chillingly familiar sound echoed from the mouth of the alley. There was an answering hiss a short distance away. Cacodaimons. The other two lurched into view, one just behind the other. On this side of reality, they cast shadows that were darker yet, their blacker-than-black forms both sharper and more intense. The bodies they rode were little more than husks—dull and hollow and not worthy of attention.

Abruptly light began to spill from the arcs of my wings, hissing against the darkness. Before I could even think about it, I was running full tilt down the alley toward the newcomers. Shrilling my name, I called the blue-white fire to my hands, and though I was aware of a painful tugging sensation at my very core, the power came—and it came in force.

The heat and brilliance coalesced into the wickedly curved blades and I closed my hands around their comforting weight. Fueled by a terrible fury, I gave the riders no quarter. I slashed them with single-minded purpose, gravely wounding one even as the other tried latching onto my shoulders. I felt searing pinpricks of cold at the back of my neck and the base of one wing, but most of its burrowing appendages scrabbled uselessly against the jacket's thick leather.

With the first one down and dispersing, I turned my attention to the other, reaching backward to pull it off while at the same time flailing with both wings. All of my perceptions narrowed to the fight with my prey. The cowardly thing turned tail and attempted to flee. Determined not to lose it, I launched myself after the scurrying shadow just as it whipped out of the alley.

Then I learned that the wings weren't merely for show. With a massive down stroke I leapt and caught up to the rider, all in one swift motion, driving both blades into its back and pinning it to the ground. It shrieked and writhed, and I slashed the knives down and outward, yanking them through the meatiest portion of its form.

With a final agonized hiss, the cacodaimon dissolved into so much black goo.

A coughing roar drew my attention from the kill. The big cat trotted up behind me, causing me to pull back. It chuffed once, then bumped its head against my hip as a rumbling sound somewhere between a growl and a purr poured from deep within its throat. Its jaws were flecked with an oily black substance that seemed to drink in what little light was present in this not-quite physical space.

My diamond-edged fury swiftly fading, I turned to meet the creature's eyes. It lifted its head as if to acknowledge me, then shouldered me aside and began to *eat* the cacodaimon. I swallowed thickly, trying desperately not to imagine what one of those horrors might taste like.

The big cat didn't seem to care, however. It hunkered down over the kill and tore great gobbets of dark flesh with its powerful jaws, swallowing them hungrily. At least that explained why the cat hadn't joined my fight with the other two.

It had stopped to eat the first one.

22

This still left me with a problem, and it was a big one. I didn't know how to get back to the flesh-and-blood world.

At least I knew where Lil was waiting. Amidst all of the shadows crowding this place, it was hard to miss her glow. So I headed in her direction. It was slow going, however. Had I really chased the cacodaimon that far?

As I moved, aches flared to life all over. In the middle of combat, I'd ignored the various stings and blows. Now there was no denying the pain dished out by my adversaries. Points on my hands, legs, neck, and wings all throbbed unpleasantly, and an answering pulse pounded in my head. If this was what victory felt like, I really didn't want to try defeat.

I tottered as I fought to stay upright, each step costing me more than the last. My wings hung like weights against my back, and the thundering pain in my head progressed to the point where all I had was tunnel vision. Only a pinprick of sight remained, edged with pulsing patterns of light and void.

It was my name that pulled me out of it.

Not Zachary. The other one.

Lillee leaned over me as I lay blinking up at clouds backlit by early morning sunshine. I think she might have slapped my face a few times, though if she had, I'd hardly felt it.

"Get up!" she demanded, jerking on my wrists. "What were you thinking, staying in there so long?"

Groggily, I let her try to hoist my lanky frame. Getting up. Getting up was good. Getting up meant I wasn't dead.

As Lil wrestled me into a sitting position, I started feeling as if I could breathe again. My vision cleared by degrees, though my arms and legs were still watery with over-exertion. It felt like I had run a marathon. Scratch that. It felt as if I had run a *marathon* of marathons. Finally I lurched shakily to my feet, then waved Lil off, doubling over and holding my gut.

"Sick," I announced, then proved it by tossing my breakfast all over the pavement. Lil danced nimbly away from the splash zone, guarding the polished leather of her expensive boots.

"Serves you right," she said. "Crossing into the Shadowside is like deep-sea diving. You can't stay down indefinitely. Why didn't you come out when I told you to?"

"Didn't know how," I croaked, scrubbing at my mouth, my other hand on the wall to steady me. Then I gestured at the two crumpled forms at the mouth of the alley. "Plus, cacodaimons."

"Yeah, about that..." Lil responded, glancing significantly at the two bodies.

They were twitching. More like convulsing. Pinkish-gray sludge seeped from their noses and the corners of their eyes. Seeing it, I almost threw up again, only this time there was nothing left to spew.

"What the hell's going on with them?" I managed.

"Something that shouldn't be happening," she murmured quietly. "This whole thing—it's not right."

I watched with mounting horror as the two well-dressed business people who had played host to the cacodaimons thrashed and jigged in the dirt. Their mouths were working to form words, yet nothing but gibberish came out. The sound swiftly degraded to an awful keening as unnerving as the insectile call of the cacodaimons themselves.

"Can't we help them?" I asked.

"You see that goo leaking out of their ears?" she said. "That's what left of their brains. Their nervous systems are mush. They must have been ridden for two or three weeks for that to happen."

I stared at the two, unable to find words.

"I told you, cacodaimons are pure chaos—the antithesis of form," she continued. "You know the line, about 'the darkness upon the face of the deep'? Cacodaimons are what was here before. They don't fit, and when they crawl in, they tear apart anything they touch."

She shouldered my backpack and started walking.

"There's a reason there's a Shadowside and a skinside,

Zack. If things like the cacodaimons manage to slink out of their holes, they have to hijack a body in order to interact. Generally, though, for them to even *touch* a vessel like that, the host already has to be broken." She frowned, and stepped around the two convulsing forms with the air of someone avoiding nasty road kill. "These really don't look the type. I don't know what the hell is going on here, but we have got to go."

"But they're not dead yet," I objected. "We can't just leave them like this."

"Yes, we can. They'll be dead soon enough." She produced a folding knife from somewhere on her person and held it up, the blade gleaming despite the shadows. With a wolfish grin, she asked, "Unless you want me to put them out of their misery."

For a moment I didn't know what to say.

"What the hell is wrong with you?" I demanded.

She gave a careless toss of her head that sent her russet curls cascading down her back. She started walking away—then stopped once she realized I wasn't following. Her eyes flicked restlessly around, peering across the train tracks to the run-down houses on the other side.

Looking for witnesses.

Ignoring her, I knelt unsteadily next to the two seizing bodies. Neither of them could have been much more than thirty. The woman wore a wedding ring—I wondered if she had a family. Her kids couldn't be very old.

"Oh, come on, Zack," Lil growled. "The police are going to be here any minute now, and there might be more cacodaimons lurking around. There shouldn't be, but given what's happened here, we can't count on any of the rules."

As I leaned over the woman, her lids snapped open, and I jumped. Her eyes were filled with blood, sightless and twitching. She spasmed so hard that her whole body arced up. Her collar pulled back and I caught sight of marks on her throat. They looked like fingerprints, deeply bruised, and they looked fresh.

My eyes flew to the man.

The marks were there, too, on his temple, under his ear, behind his jaw. If I didn't know what I was looking at, I might have mistaken them for birthmarks.

"Lil?" I called, stumbling backward. "You said for cacodaimons to ride someone the person had to be broken?"

She grunted, still vigilant.

"That's the way it works with living people, anyway—drug addicts, crazies. Fresh corpses are easier. They're already empty." Then she started to leave.

I pressed a hand to the space above my heart where wells of void tunneled through my being.

Empty. I had a little taste of that.

I gazed one last time at the fallen couple. Whoever they were, they'd been gone the instant those marks were seared upon their skin. There was no helping them. So I hauled myself to my feet, and caught up with Lil.

23

She took the long way around to her car, and I nearly didn't make it. I'd exhausted myself with that trip through the Shadowside.

Lil started talking about getting a room at a hotel. She wanted a nap and a shower, and thought we'd both be better off after a little rest. I couldn't have agreed more, but I didn't like the idea of bunking with someone who had cheerfully offered to slit the throats of a couple of innocents.

So I pulled the keys from my pocket and rattled off the address printed on the insert in the fob. When we arrived, she eyed the place suspiciously from the street, almost as if she was trying to remember why it annoyed her. I didn't tell her it was Remy's safe house until we were standing on the porch.

If looks could kill...

As safe houses went, I was expecting something less ostentatious than a three-story Queen Anne, but maybe that wouldn't have been Remy's style. There was nothing small or subtle about the rambling old Victorian. Painted a heather gray that looked suspiciously close to lavender, it had white gingerbread wainscoting and an honest-to-God turret. If this was Remy's guest house, I wondered what the heck his real digs looked like.

"Remy gave you the keys?" she spat. "*Remiel?* We wouldn't be here if I'd known this was where we were headed."

I just glowered back at her, so far beyond exhausted that I didn't care whose keys opened the lock, as long as a hot shower and a bed lay beyond the door.

"Stuff it," I growled. "So far, he's the only person who's gone out of his way to help me."

"Don't mistake enlightened self-interest for charity," she responded, planting her feet and making a grab for the keys. "Let me list the reasons this is a bad idea." She held up her hand and started counting off fingers. "Remy is Saliriel's bitch. There is no point at which Saliriel can be trusted. Your message connects the Nephilim to Lailah's disappearance. Remy and Saliriel are both what? Nephilim," she answered before I could speak. "And if that little cipher of yours is accurate, your tribes are at war. Again. Now I'm out of fingers. Got it?" She looked at me as if I were an idiot.

"Look, Lil," I said, dodging as she tried again for the keys, "I'm filthy. I'm tired, and I hurt all over. All I want is a shower, a nap, and a little privacy. There must be somewhere you need to be for the next couple of hours—one that doesn't involve hovering over me."

Giving up on the keys, Lil switched to blocking my path. It was kind of comical, really, considering she was almost a full foot shorter than me. She fixed me with a withering glare, but by this point, I'd endured so many of those from her, I'd become immune, and was consumed with a single-minded purpose—to find a shower.

"Get out of my way."

"You look like hell, Zachary," she said flatly.

"Thanks for noticing," I replied.

"You're tired and worn-out, and that's precisely why you need me. If you won't listen to reason and go to a hotel, then I'm coming in with you. After that stint in the Shadowside, if you don't recharge your batteries soon, you'll be no good to anyone," she said, "but you need someone watching your back, *especially* in a house owned by one of the Nephilim."

"I'm not so sure that someone should be you," I responded. Wearily, I hefted my backpack and tried to push past her, but she pressed herself very close to the front of my body and did that shoulder maneuver that practically spilled her cleavage out of her top. She cranked up the charm, till she smelled like sex on a stick. That's how I knew I was really exhausted. I got a noseful of her spice and vanilla musk—and I simply didn't care. Her sex appeal only irritated me more.

"Seriously," I said. "Get out of my way. *Now*."

I said it with a little more force than I'd intended, but maybe that was a good thing. She tried staring me down for a few moments longer, then relented.

"You get your ass killed, and I'm hunting you down through your next six incarnations, just to kill you again," she warned. I was too tired even to ask. "I'll go chase down a few leads I may have, then I'll be back here by seven. Make sure you're ready."

Half a dozen responses leapt to my lips, none of them kind. And as much as I wanted that shower, I waited till she was at least halfway to the car before I put the key in the lock. Once I was through the door, I threw the deadbolt behind me

The interior of the house was all dark woods and deep colors. Heavy curtains cloaked all the windows—though that didn't come as a surprise, really. Between the décor and the antiques, I felt as if I had stepped onto a movie set for *The Great Gatsby*.

Then the security system started chirping.

Just my luck.

I turned around, expecting to see a little keypad mounted by the door. There was nothing of the sort—even though that's where the sound was coming from. It might have been my shredded nerves, but it seemed as if the beeps were getting louder with each passing moment. As the sound escalated, my eyes finally locked onto a decorative wooden box mounted at about shoulder height to the left of the door. The spectral glow of LEDs was just barely visible through the spaces of its ornate filigree.

I flipped the thing open, revealing a very modern-looking keypad with a message in scrolling green digital letters that prompted, "Alarm... code?" over and over again.

The LED screen continued to prompt me to enter the code while the chirping sounds grew louder and more insistent. I had a sinking feeling that once the chirps reached a certain pitch, the system would send signals along to the police or some private company.

Wracking my sluggish brain, I tried to recall whether Remy had mentioned anything about a code, back in the stairwell. No, despite the cloak-and-dagger feel of that entire conversation, nothing about alarms or codes had come up.

Dammit.

I fisted my hand around the house keys till they dug painfully into my palm. Maybe if I booked out the front door, I could catch Lillee and we could drive away before the police came. I hated the idea, though—I'd never hear the end of her gloating. There had to be another way.

Glancing down at the fob of the keys I white-knuckled, I saw it—a six-digit number written neatly on the last line of the little insert. Hoping beyond hope, I punched it into the keypad. My hand trembled, and I tried vainly to swallow the panic I felt welling up from my chest. Each key I punched merely added to the incessant beeps. Then I hit the final number in the code.

Silence. Blessed silence.

A moment later, the LEDs prompted me to arm the system. Alongside the number pad on the security interface were three big buttons. A green one stamped YES, a yellow one stamped NO, and a bright red one stamped with EMRGY. I pressed the green button and armed the system.

Then I turned and really took in the luxury of Remy's impeccably decorated home. With all the dark wood paneling and heavy antique furniture, there was a kind of unassailable weight to the space around me. Instinctively, I knew the security system wasn't the only protection on the place. Cacodaimons and anything else from the Shadowside would have a hard time violating this sanctum.

Feeling truly safe for the first time since dragging myself out of Erie, I headed off to find the shower, moving with the single-minded purpose of Ponce de Leon seeking the Fountain of Youth.

24

After the shower, I found a massive four-poster bed and climbed in, wearing only my jeans. Unfortunately, I did not find sleep. I almost did—and then my brain did that thing that brains often do when they're far too stressed. It fixed on something important that had otherwise slipped my mind.

The white envelope.

Nerves jangling, I jerked awake. I tried lying back down, tried rolling over, but my mind raced mercilessly. Projected on the insides of my eyelids, I watched a tedious replay of the envelope tumbling from behind the page from the *Celestial Hierarchy*. It repeated again and again. The image came complete with a full-body memory of the guilt and anxiety I'd experienced as I pocketed the item while Lil wasn't looking. My stomach went sour and my head began to throb.

"Fuck it," I grumbled irritably. Apparently I didn't need Lillee around to argue. I even argued with myself.

Swinging my legs out of the bed, I felt around for the

rest of my clothes. My jacket, boots, socks, and shirt were piled in a messy heap beside the bed. I grabbed the jacket and started digging through the pockets, but I couldn't find the little envelope. With a mounting sense of anxiety, I renewed my search, pulling out the wadded-up socks and tossing them onto the floor.

Still nothing.

That wasn't right. There were two deep interior pockets in the biker jacket. I'd slipped the envelope into the left one. I was sure of it. With the way the jacket zipped tight against my chest, it couldn't have fallen out.

Could it?

Working my long fingers down to the very bottom of the interior pocket, I felt along the seam—and discovered a hole. Forcing my fingers through the tear in the seam, I ripped it further, then for several anxious heartbeats dug around in the lining of the jacket. There was something hard and thin at the very bottom—a pen or pencil, half-buried against a seam. I jammed my finger against the pointy end, recoiling a bit at how sharp it was.

Finally my fingertips brushed an edge of paper. I couldn't get my thumb around it, so I tried trapping it between my first and second fingers. It took a little finagling, but I finally pulled the damned thing free.

Hastily, I tore it open. I didn't know what I was expecting, but the Holy Grail didn't tumble into my lap. Actually, for a moment, I was afraid the envelope was empty and that I had worked myself up over nothing. Then I shook out a little rectangle of paper. It bore two rows of neat print. The first line was a URL for something called "Crash Protect." It was long and contained a lot of digits. The second line looked like it might be a user ID.

Silent_War.

Well, that's ominous.

There was no way I was going to sleep now, so I got up and padded across the plush carpet in search of Remy's office. The door was slightly ajar and I could just see the gloss of the darkened computer screen through the opening. The little work space was starkly modern in contrast with the retro-politan feel of the rest of the house. I slipped inside, dropping the leather jacket beside the computer chair. Then I hesitated.

Using a strange computer to access a site I wanted to keep secret carried some hefty risks. Privacy mode was never as private as anyone thought, and even if I purged the browser history, there were temp files and audit logs with which to contend. I still didn't know how far I could trust Remy. Then curiosity overruled my sense of caution, and I turned the thing on anyway.

"Crash Protect" turned out to be an online service that offered secure storage and redundancy for important files. The multi-digit extension of the URL took me directly to a log-in screen for what I assumed was "my" account. I entered the Silent_War ID and then stared blankly at the password entry field. I glanced back to the little slip of paper. No password. Not even the hint of one.

Well, that figures. Why should my luck change now?

I frowned at the screen, wracking my brain before daring to try anything. It was hard to come up with passwords when I barely remembered my life. There didn't seem to be any character limit, and a little notice under the entry field reminded me that all passwords were case sensitive.

Just to make things easy.

Given where I'd stashed the envelope, I considered *CelestialHierarchy*. After a moment's hesitation I tried it, only to be routed back to the log-in screen, now with an error message. *Great.* Trying to think like the person my apartment suggested I must be, I ventured the Latin version of the title—*DeCoelestiHierarchia*. That seemed clever enough.

The screen went blank for a second, getting my hopes up. Then it reloaded onto the log-in screen again.

No dice.

Remembering both the action figure and the bumper sticker on my wayward vehicle, I attempted several variations of Starbuck and *Battlestar Galactica*. All this netted me was a message in bold red letters on the top of the log-in screen, warning me that the security protocol was in place, and lock-out would occur after three more failed attempts.

Crap.

Taking a couple of deep breaths, I shifted in the desk chair and thought hard. The envelope was stored with the *Celestial Hierarchy* page. They had to be related in some way. Mentally, I went back over the names hidden in the alphanumeric code on the antique illustration. Feeling like I was onto something, I tried one of them. The page reloaded, only now it warned me that lock-out would occur after *two* more tries.

I fought not to smash anything.

Taking a moment to shake the tension out of my hands, I let my fingers move on instinct. Then I typed in my name. Not Zachary, but *Zaquiel.*

Denied.

I shouted a barely coherent string of curses at the screen and it flickered as if in response to my tirade. I had one more try.

My mind racing, I did a quick number-letter substitution in my head using the same system as the cipher. Then, with my final attempt, I typed in the resulting number string, followed by the name in English. As an after-thought, I added a tilda at the end.

The page reloaded. I stared at a blank white screen for what seemed like a small eternity. As the page resolved itself, I half-expected to be greeted with flashing red letters announcing full security lock-down.

But it worked.

A new screen appeared. There were three folder icons, each with a little green bar next to it indicating the percentage of storage space taken up by the files inside. The folders were labeled "History," "Anakim," and "Nephilim."

This was it.

Considering how little I remembered, I opted to open "History" first. Inside was a large PDF file. Still jittery from the down-to-the-wire quest for the password, I double-clicked and waited impatiently for the file to load.

It was an eBook, sort of. Cobbled together by me. The title page read "The History of the Watchers." Below this was my legal name, and further down was a range of dates, which appeared to show how long I'd been working on the project. The start date was nearly fifteen years ago. The end date was only last year. Long-term research, then—or maybe just a personal obsession.

Personal obsession, I decided after skimming a few pages.

The sprawling document read like some gene-splicing experiment between the Bible and the Brothers Grimm. Earth-bound angels, warring tribes, and ancient icons buried away for humanity's own good. One page discussing the "Five Accursed Nations" linked Anakim to anarchists. The Nephilim were called "Voluptuous Ones." Gibburim and Rephaim were names supplied for other tribes. Conflicting terms were given for a fifth.

Such conflicts and outright contradictions peppered the document. There was scan after scan of material, some texts in English, some in Latin, others in languages more exotic still. I could read all of it—even when I had no clue what letters glimmered on the screen.

That's a useful super-power, I mused.

Judging from the typeset of the reproductions, most of the scanned works were very old. It looked like I'd made copies of the pages, then scribbled all over the margins, finally scanning them into this massive PDF. It was too much to digest in one sitting, and the contradictory claims offered little but frustration. Even my notes in the margins argued with themselves.

This is what I'm missing sleep over, I thought bitterly. Irritated, I closed out of the "History" folder. I almost clicked out of the whole thing. What had I expected to find, anyway? All my answers tucked neatly in one place? Fat chance that would happen.

Not the way my luck was running.

I hovered over the mouse button, deliberating. Swallowing against a sudden tang of adrenaline, I clicked the file labeled "Anakim."

This was the heart of the "Silent_War." Dossiers on scores of Anakim spread before me. Out of about a hundred names, more than half of them—including the primus—were labeled "missing." The files were exhaustive, tracking individuals over the centuries. There were painted portraits, countless aliases, places of residence noted in sequential order, even scans of old documents from more than a dozen different countries. All the faces were eerily similar. Not identical, exactly, but the "family" resemblance was unmistakable, even in the old portraiture.

Every entry supplied birth and death dates, followed by what could only be *rebirth* dates. Sequential immortality. I tried wrapping my head around the concept, but in my current state, it fit poorly. The files showed a pretty clear cycle—a cycle abruptly truncated in every Anakim marked as missing. Most of their dates cut off in the 1800s, though a few made it to the twentieth century.

"We're time lords without the TARDIS," I muttered.

If I understood it all correctly, my tribe didn't live forever, but if we died, we came back. Except for when we didn't. So what was happening to the other Anakim to take them out of the game?

I thought about my own situation. Immortality didn't mean much if you couldn't remember all those other lives. Maybe the missing ones weren't dead, just empty.

Everything they knew stripped away.

That was a bleak consideration.

I clicked open the folder for the Nephilim. Maybe the answers were there. I looked for names from the cipher, clicking the primus first.

Go big or go home.

It contained a single JPG—no aliases, no birth or death certificates, no other notes. The picture file opened to reveal a bas-relief that was Old Kingdom Egyptian, clearly a part of some museum's collection. The lone figure in the artwork wore a pendant with an elaborate Eye of Horus. Among the hieroglyphs carved alongside the figure, I had circled one cartouche. Scribbled to the side of the cartouche was my translation of the name: *Nefer-Ka*. Beneath that, in quotes, I'd written, "Beautiful Soul." It wasn't much of a stretch to go from Nefer-Ka to Neferkariel. I wondered if "Beautiful Soul" was just another way of saying "Voluptuous One."

"Still doesn't tell me shit to sort this mess," I muttered. I clicked out and went for Dorimiel. The cipher said *Neferkariel's Eye in Dorimiel's hand*. Hopefully, the file could explain.

I opened to a list of names—Darren Harrow, Dorian Hartleigh, Dean McCormick. All were file names attached to JPGs. I clicked the picture files, advancing rapidly through each. An oil painting, a portrait in miniature, a water-damaged photo in black and white. My sight skittered off the images as recollected visions surged within my mind—that blasphemous temple and its fanged abomination. Vengeance sworn even as I drove home my blades.

Stripped of every other memory, I would still know those eyes.

You and all your tribe.

Now I knew his name.

Mouthing the threat of his words, I memorized every iteration of Dorimiel's face. New York in the 1920s—that was the photo. The miniature hailed from Napoleonic France. The oldest was the oil painting. Eighteenth-century England. Nothing at all suggested the ancient temple from my vision, nor any connection to the missing Anakim, but certainty shivered through me, chilling and absolute. Other memories started welling to the surface, but they were abortive and incomplete. Water. The chittering of cacodaimons. Lailah's name in ancient letters, carved on a clay surface with a pale length of bone.

That gnawing not-pain burned within the marks upon my chest. Each hammer-stroke of my pulse sent it singing through my skin. With unsteady fingers, I closed out of the folder, hiding Dorimiel from view. I stared at the screen blankly, struggling to quash the sick waves of fear threatening even now to pull my thoughts into some darkness I shrank to perceive. I ticked my eyes away from the names on the folders, seeing but not seeing the data in the other fields—type, size, modification date. All the letters smeared.

My pulse leapt again, vision focusing abruptly on the dates.

None of the files for the Nephilim had been altered in the past three months.

None—except Saliriel's.

I clicked on the folder. The entire file had been wiped at noon yesterday.

While my short hairs tried crawling up the back of my scalp, a sound in the hallway made me jump to my feet so suddenly that I sent the computer chair crashing to the floor. In the strained silence following its explosive clatter, I distinctly heard someone—or some*thing*—moving out in the hall. Standing there bare-chested and in nothing but my jeans, I prepared to defend myself. I called power to my hands. At least, I tried to.

Instead of a brilliant coalescence of light, it looked more like I was holding damp sparklers. The blue-white energy sputtered weakly, and I quickly discovered that maintaining even that sad show of strength made something in my chest feel unpleasantly hot and tight.

Even so, I braced myself. It wouldn't be pretty, but if I was going to go down, I wasn't going down without a fight.

25

The door to the computer room swung open, and I moved to launch myself at the intruder. A shout formed in my throat as I began invoking the power of my name—then I nearly choked on it when I saw Remy.

"Goodness," he exclaimed, taking half a step back. "A little jumpy, aren't we?"

"Shit," I breathed. "You ever think about knocking?"

An ironic smile tugged at his pale lips. "My house, remember?"

I shook the power out of my hands and picked the chair up, flopping down onto it.

"Yeah, well, I'm kind of tense right now," I said, sagging with exhaustion. Even that pathetic show had left me feeling spent. I needed to get some sleep, and damned soon.

"So I see," he observed archly, "but at least you look less like a vagrant." He pushed the door the rest of the way open, leaning a shoulder against the jamb. His long fall of hair was pulled back in a neat braid and he wore unrelieved black from head to foot—jacket, slacks, shirt, and tie. A hat that matched his suit and looked suspiciously like a fedora was tucked lightly in the crook of one arm, a newspaper folded beneath it. "I was in the neighborhood making funeral arrangements with Alice's parents. I thought I'd drop in and check on you." With a tilt of his head, he added, "You seem awfully pale, Zaquiel. Have you been feeding properly?"

"Hunh?" I grunted, grinding the heels of my palms into my eyes. I'd been staring at the computer screen too long. Absently, I said, "I've tried eating. Can't seem to keep anything down, what with bouncing around the Shadowside and everything."

"No, I mean—" he started, then cut himself short. I looked up in the intervening silence to see a mortified expression cross his face. "Oh," he breathed. "You don't understand, do you?"

"Understand what?"

"Where the power comes from," he replied delicately.

I shrugged. "I still don't remember everything clearly. I mean, I've worked out most of the details. I focus it with my name, there's this kind of inner fire, then I'm moving between two halves of reality. Sometimes I can step through completely," I added with an unconscious shiver, as I recalled how close I came to getting stuck just that morning.

He shook his head. "No, that's not what I mean. Just look at you. It's obvious. You've been throwing it out there—rather copiously, I might add—but you haven't replenished anything, have you?" It came out as an accusation, but his bright blue eyes shone with genuine concern.

"What the hell are you talking about?"

"You need to take some back in." He seemed to be struggling with a concept he either couldn't put into words or was reluctant to do so.

"Remy, what does that mean, exactly?"

"Take it in, Zaquiel," he said with a quirk of one brow. "From people. You take it from people."

"Now wait just a damned minute," I said. I'd have gotten in his face if I'd felt like I could stand without falling over. Instead, I settled for gesturing angrily from the relative comfort of the chair. "I'm not the vampire in this room, Remy. I'm Anakim. You said it yourself—I'm not like you."

His preternaturally blue eyes glittered coldly.

"In light of your current predicament, I'll set aside the fact that you're insulting me under my own roof. While it's true that we are *not* of the same tribe, it's equally true that we both rely on people—each in our own way. Mine is a little more obvious, yes, but if you're going to cast aspersions, you had best consider how they apply to you."

I started to tell him where to stuff his aspersions, but felt so shitty that I didn't even bother.

"All of us?" I asked instead.

He nodded. "In one fashion or another. For you, it's the pulse of a crowd, the little currents left behind everywhere the mortals move. You can take it more directly with a touch, though."

Self-consciously, my hand strayed to cover the livid bruises on my bare chest. I'd been blaming Dorimiel for that, but he was Nephilim. Wouldn't he have just bitten me?

"So you're saying I can grab people, and suck the life out of them with my bare hands." The very thought made me grimace.

Remy threw his head back and laughed, exposing his delicately pointed canines.

"Nothing quite so dramatic, Zaquiel," he said when he'd recovered.

So who—or what—had left the marks on me, and on the couple in the alleyway? Had Dorimiel learned a new trick over the centuries? I fell silent, and it quickly got awkward. After a few moments of that, Remy pulled out the newspaper that was tucked under his arm.

"I owe you an apology, Zaquiel."

"Oh? What for?"

He held the paper out to me, folded to an inner page. I took it and looked. My own face stared back at me—and it wasn't a police sketch. Standing next to me was a woman, and she looked way better than I did in a suit. The caption read, "Two Missing. Former CWRU Professor Zachary Westland and Dr. Lailah Ganjavi."

"What's this?" I asked.

"It's the museum incident you came into the club shouting about—not yesterday. The last time—Tuesday. The article was buried in a back section of the *Plain Dealer*." He scowled. "There's no way we could have known. I swear to you. There were no reports on this until today."

"When did it happen?"

"Monday. Just as you claimed."

Lailah's face stared out from the photo, beautiful and accusing.

"This makes no damned sense," I said, slamming the newspaper onto the desk. "This says I went missing that night, along with Lailah. We both know that's not true. And there's nothing about the Rockefeller Park shooting. How can I be a missing person *and* wanted for murder?"

Remy's brows ticked a notch. "Are you talking about the police bulletin you mentioned at Heaven last night? You didn't say it was for murder."

I faltered, uncertain how much I should share. *Fuck it*, I thought. Remy's eyes tracked my face, as if reading the thoughts as they played out. He shifted slightly at the door, leaning once more against the jamb.

"I left messages for Lailah at my apartment," I admitted. "One about the shooting. I didn't say murder, exactly, but I sounded guilty as hell. Is that what I do? Shoot people that get in my way?"

"Not every time," Remy responded. His tone was light-hearted. I found no humor in it.

Venting a wordless growl of frustration, I smacked the desk. The crack of my palm against the polished wood echoed through the room.

"Whatever you did, the incident at Rockefeller is easily handled," Remy soothed. "I'm surprised the sketch made it as far as the television. Your people are getting sloppy."

"My people?" I opened my mouth to launch an argument, then remembered the rest of the message on the answering machine. I'd mentioned someone named Bobby, exactly as if I'd expected him to run damage control on the shooting. I thought uneasily about Lil's shocked expression when I'd objected to her proposed mercy killing of the battered couple in the alley. What kind of guy was I?

"Read the article," Remy suggested gently. "Perhaps it will jog your stubborn memory." With exaggerated nonchalance, he fussed with his hat—it was, indeed, a fedora.

With an irritable huff, I reclaimed the paper.

"Two guards dead, another in the hospital," I murmured unhappily.

"Head trauma," Remy confirmed. "I made some inquiries. He's not waking up any time soon. Otherwise I'd suggest that we go question him." He paused, and then added, "This woman, Dr. Lailah Ganjavi. Odd that you've never mentioned her. It's clear from the article she was your colleague at the museum. Is she why you quit Case to work with the art recovery agency?"

I thought back to the things at my apartment—the photos, the toothbrush, the bra.

"I think we were dating," I said.

Remiel made no attempt to hide his surprise. "Even stranger, then, that you said nothing about her when you barged into the club on Tuesday. The only thing you concerned yourself with at the time were the demon jars you accused our tribe of stealing."

"Demon jars?" I choked.

"Oh, come on, it's right there—second paragraph from the end."

I skipped ahead, frowning. "According to this, they were forgeries—early 1800s," I replied. "Why would anyone steal bogus artifacts?"

"You know better, Anarch," Remy said pointedly, and he leaned in. "You were keeping demon jars at the museum. Why didn't you share that information before the break-in?"

"I don't remember, and you know it," I said. He gave me a significant look, like there was more I should be saying. "Come on, Remy," I continued. "Demon jars? Don't tell me they had real demons in them. Unless you mean the cacodaimons…"

Remy looked disappointed. Then the stern line of his brow softened.

"No, when you came to see Saliriel on Tuesday, you insisted that the cacodaimons had been sent *into* the museum. Two of them in fact, and you claimed they were working with the Nephilim who also broke in." He sniffed. "It's an impossible allegiance. That's why we were so… disinclined to believe you."

"What are you saying?" I countered. "That no Nephilim would ever attempt a museum heist?"

Remiel bristled. "No, that we would never work with the cacodaimons."

We locked eyes again. I was the first to look away—this was getting us nowhere. I read back through the article, but it didn't have much else to offer.

"Cacodaimons, forged demon jars, and thieves dumb enough to steal them," I said. "Something's not adding up. And why would they take Lai… Dr. Ganjavi, and leave me?" I rubbed my eyes, grumbling, "Dammit. Why can't I remember?"

"You're not thinking clearly," Remy prompted. "You'd do better if you took care of a few basic needs."

"That again?" The idea repulsed me.

But Remy wasn't giving up. "Get dressed. There's a great little Italian place down the street," he said. "We'll catch dinner, and I'll walk you through it. Just like old times."

I stared at him without moving. "You know I've got the police after me—right?"

He sighed with the air of a martyr. "If you're so bent out of shape over it, I can have my people handle it. I could call Roarke right now."

He reached for his cell phone, pausing with his thumb over the call button. I watched him warily. I had no idea what such a favor might cost me.

"No," I said.

Remy piqued a brow but after a moment, he tucked the phone back into his suit. With a little sniff, he said, "Well. Tell me if you change your mind—but you shouldn't have to worry at the restaurant," he assured, plopping his fedora atop his head. "If the local Dons can eat there, I'm certain you will pass unremarked."

I opened my mouth to respond, then clapped it shut again.

Remiel knew the local Mafiosos.

Why the hell would that surprise me?

"For the record, I don't think it's a good idea."

"Have you got a better one?" Remy inquired. "What are you accomplishing here, playing computer games?"

I turned back to the computer. Crash Protect had gone into some kind of inactive mode, leaving a screen that looked suspiciously like *Plants vs. Zombies*.

"Hunh," I grunted as a manically grinning daisy

swallowed a shambling green monster. "What the hell—I'm kind of hungry anyway. Give me just a sec," I said, then I purged the browser history.

It isn't paranoia if they're really out to get you, right?

26

It was almost five thirty on a Friday, so the restaurant was thronging with people, and from Remy's expression, this was just what he wanted. As we wove our way to the hostess stand, he slipped off his John Lennon-style sunglasses, stowing them in the inside pocket of his suit jacket. Then he greeted the hostess with a winning smile that somehow managed to hide his unnaturally pointed canines. I was guessing that he practiced.

"The usual table open, Maria?" he asked, nodding toward a back corner of the restaurant.

The petite brunette practically swooned as he held her in his cerulean gaze. I did my best not to roll my eyes while he flirted effortlessly.

"Of course, Mr. Broussard," she tittered with a little bob of her head. "Right this way." Maria scooped up two menus and conveyed us briskly to a cozy back table set up for two. There was a crowd of people in the lobby, still clutching their pagers, and they glared at us as we passed.

Remy took a seat, gesturing for me to do the same.

Maria laid out our menus, then hovered blushing near my brother. He dismissed her with such courtesy, she seemed flattered to be walking away.

"I still think this is a bad idea," I grumbled. "Everyone's staring."

"Relax," he responded, feigning interest in the menu. "They're only staring because you're uncomfortable. Besides, I know the owner—or at least, his grandfather. This is a safe place. People know to respect certain rules." With practiced nonchalance, he added, "You should take advantage of the crowd in here."

I looked around, feeling squirmingly uncomfortable. Not to mention under-dressed. Remy looked right at home in his sleek black suit. Me in jeans and a biker jacket, not so much.

"Yeah, about that..." I hedged. "I'm not really sure how I feel about this whole 'feeding' thing. It seems really... awkward, and kind of wrong."

Remy sighed wearily, eyes gliding among the various couples and families. "It's like you're fifteen all over again," he murmured.

I wasn't sure what to say to that, so I glanced over the menu, trying not to go into sticker shock at the prices. Most of these dinners cost more than my boots—the good ones.

Holy shit.

Wistfully, he continued. "It does bring back some pleasant memories, though. I rather miss the days when you called me Uncle Remy. Things were so much less complicated then—at least between the two of us," he amended.

"Uncle Remy?" I repeated incredulously. "I thought you were my brother."

"So I am," he said, and he chuckled. "But we've had an arrangement, you and I, at least these past few times, and I always start out older than you."

"Arrangement?" I asked, genuinely curious.

He nodded, "Ever since that business in Providence. What was it, a hundred and fifty years ago? Maybe a hundred and sixty," he murmured with an elegant wave of a hand. "So hard to keep track."

"Hey," I objected. "Johnny Amnesia here, remember? You've got to use small words, and stop talking about ancient history like it happened yesterday. I'm out of the loop."

He pressed his pale lips together in a pensive expression that wasn't quite a frown.

"All right," he agreed, "but I wish we knew what happened to you, so we could remedy it. Memory is rather... integral... to your sense of self." After a pause he added, "If you don't mind my saying so, it's a little difficult seeing you like this. At the club, I almost didn't believe it. To tell the truth, I don't know how you're managing."

That stopped me for a minute.

I tried to tell myself that the sudden stinging at the backs of my eyes was just the perfume rolling off of an octogenarian two tables over. I wasn't about to start feeling sorry for myself. I didn't have time for that shit. Taking a deep breath, I answered as firmly as I could manage.

"I don't need your pity, Remy. I need answers. So start with this arrangement thing. You said the 'past few times.' I think I'm beginning to see what you mean, but spell it out, OK?"

A waitress came over to bring us water and a basket

of warm dinner rolls. She could have been Maria's older sister, and given the family-owned vibe of the swanky little bistro, she probably was. Remy dazzled her with his carefully revealed smile, murmuring something about needing more time with the menu. Then he waited till she was well out of earshot.

"We're all immortal," he said succinctly, making a point of meeting my eyes. "Surely you've figured that out by now." He waited for me to nod, then went on. "But each of us—each of the tribes, I should say—has a different method to cleave our immortal souls to vessels of flesh. Given the ties to the blood, mine's not appropriate to polite dinner conversation." He flashed me an almost apologetic grin, this time showing enough teeth to expose his pointy canines, albeit briefly.

"Got the memo," I muttered.

"Well, you die and get born the old-fashioned way. Believe me, I find that thoroughly unsettling. Infancy? Diapers?" He shuddered dramatically.

I tried not to glare as I waited for him to go on.

"Well, while the Nephilim stay together in our proper ranks and order, the Anakim are scattered. They have been for a while now. There's no structure, no support for you as you start over, and begin remembering." His expression spoke of disapproval. "It doesn't all come right away to you, either. You need guidance."

There was a huge gulf between "scattered" and "missing," but this wasn't the time to bring it up.

"So you're my Ben Kenobi," I supplied.

His brow furrowed. "Is that from the movie with the starships, and the pointy-eared fellow?"

I groaned.

"You made me watch it with you," he said helpfully. "Claimed it would curb some of my anachronisms, through immersion in popular culture."

"Clearly it didn't work," I muttered. "Moving right along..."

"Right," he said, yet a slight crinkling of the laugh lines around his eyes suggested that he might have been making fun of himself. "There's not much to explain beyond that, really. Each time around, I help to confirm your memories, and help you get a handle on the things you can do."

"Like stepping through to the Shadowside?" I asked.

He nodded. "And one of the most important lessons involves how to take the power that you need." He glanced again at the dinner crowd. "In our own ways, we all rely on humanity."

I frowned at this, still unwilling to tackle that issue.

"Is there anything you get out of this arrangement of ours? I mean, don't take this the wrong way, but you don't strike me as the kind of guy who helps someone out of the goodness of his heart."

Remy crinkled the edges of his menu, regarding me icily.

"Don't presume to judge what is good in me, brother," he responded with a quiet fury.

Well that *touched a nerve*, I thought, then I redirected my attention to my own menu. "Sorry," I muttered. "Didn't mean it that way."

He gave a little exhalation that wasn't quite a sigh.

"I'll believe you," he murmured, "for the moment—

but if you must know, I made a vow to you about a century and a half ago. You've not released me from it yet."

I looked back up, studying his bloodless features. "You say that like maybe I should've done so by now," I observed cautiously.

It was his turn to shift awkwardly in his seat. In the tense silence that followed, something else occurred to me.

"Wait a minute," I said. "How do you even find me? I mean, don't I end up some place different each time? And I can't possibly look the same."

Remy loosed a nervous chuckle, clearly relieved at the change of topic.

"Oh, you'd be surprised how much influence the spirit has over the flesh. Certain traits always come through. However," he added, "I never need to look for you. Without fail, once you reach your teenage years, you find me. It probably helps that I've lived here in Cleveland since 1883. Or was it '82?" His gaze grew distant as he debated with himself.

I fought to picture my fifteen-year-old self seeking out a vampire as a sensei. Pat Morita with fangs. What kind of excuse had I cooked up to explain *that* to my parents?

"This is too fucking weird," I said, rubbing my temples.

"I wish you would watch your language in public." He wasn't joking. "Now pick something out on the menu. We're going to be sitting here for a while."

He motioned for the waitress.

27

It wasn't as hard as I thought it would be, though I still wasn't convinced that it was right.

Remy guided me into opening my senses—unclenching that fist in my mind. Control was tricky at first. If I opened things too much, it felt like everyone was shouting, just like that first time I'd walked into the Pub n' Sub. It was easy to get overwhelmed by the resulting barrage.

If I held my senses open just enough, though, I could feel everyone around me—not their thoughts, exactly, but the constant, thrumming buzz of their existence. Power came off of every living human, whether they were aware of it or not, and before long I could see it drifting in subtle currents on the air, like a mist rising from hot pavement after a cool rain.

When I looked deeper, the currents of power were punctuated with color, and sometimes texture—all of which seemed tied to emotion. The octogenarian two tables over was having a birthday celebration with what looked like three generations of her family gathered round. Bright yellows and greens leapt out among them in flashes. The lady herself gave off waves of contented warm colors—muted shades of orange, mostly. I couldn't be sure if there was a set meaning for each of the colors, or if the shades were influenced by my own expectations.

Deciding it was too complicated a topic to ponder just then, I let myself relax into the process. The rigatoni I'd ordered sat largely untouched.

Guided by Remy, I pulled wisps of the shimmering stuff into myself. At first it took an effort of will, but before long it was just like breathing. I could feel it warming me all the way down to the tips of my wings. Actually, that was a downside—it was nearly impossible to concentrate on pulling power, while simultaneously maintaining my cowl.

On the upside, I felt worlds better—clear-headed, focused, and strong. Even better, despite my initial trepidations, it didn't seem to be hurting anyone. Remy watched me closely as he cut tiny forkfuls of his veal picatta, a curiously intense expression making his eyes glitter.

"Be careful not to focus too much on any one person," he murmured, gesturing discreetly with his fork, pointing in the direction of a well-dressed older man who seemed to be on a date with a woman nearly half his age.

I felt a hint of panic.

The steely-haired gent's eyes were fixed on me, and he wore an expression of bewildered offense.

"They might not know exactly what they're feeling,

but some of them will notice you, regardless," Remy explained. "Their responses can be... unpredictable."

There was an awkward moment where the stranger and I accidentally locked eyes. He met my gaze with an open challenge, and I looked away as quickly as possible—but not before I got a detailed impression of exactly how passionate he felt about the young lady.

"Now you tell me," I grumbled. "Thanks a lot."

"Actually, I was waiting for it to happen," Remy said. "If there's one thing I've learned about you over the years, brother, it's the fact that you never take my word for anything. You always have to learn things the hard way."

I shot him a withering look.

But I couldn't argue the point.

"How can you tell what I'm doing, anyway?" I asked after a while. "I mean, back at the club, you couldn't see the cacodaimons—not clearly, at least—and Saliriel didn't seem to see them at all."

Remy nodded, taking a sip of his wine. He held it in his mouth for a few moments, relishing the flavor.

"Despite our common origins, we're not all alike," he responded. "While it's true that most of the Nephilim's powers lie with the flesh and the blood, we're not entirely insensible to the perceptions you Anakim enjoy. I've always had a talent for that, and you've helped me to hone it over the years. And while I can't cross into the Shadowside like you do, I understand most of the mechanics—on a basic level, at least."

"Does that help you teach me when I come back from the dead?" I asked, still struggling to wrap my head around the idea.

"To some degree," he acknowledged after another sip of his wine. "Though it gives me an edge in other things, as well."

What those things were, he didn't elaborate, and I didn't think it would be useful to press him on it. Instead, my thoughts drifted to the disturbing files stored in my "Silent_War" account.

"So you said the Anakim were scattered," I said, as casually as I could muster. "What do you mean by that?"

"Just what it implies," he said with a shrug. "Your primus is… an elusive fellow. Elusive and, I daresay, a little eccentric."

I narrowed my eyes. "Eccentric how?"

"Anakesiel always hated structure and hierarchy—saw it as some kind of yoke beneath which we all toil," Remy explained. His eyes grew unfocused for a moment, and he wore an expression I was beginning to associate with his more distant recollections. "Before the Blood Wars, he did away with the Anakim's structure entirely. Put you all on equal footing—at least ostensibly," he added with a disdainful wave. "Try as he might, he couldn't stop being primus any more than he could change his Name. Hierarchy is etched into what we are."

When he said Name, I could hear the capital. So they were as important as Lil had implied.

"Blood Wars," I echoed. "You mentioned those at Club Heaven."

Remy's blue eyes grew guarded. "You don't want me talking of the Blood Wars, sibling," he said. A note of warning edged his voice.

I pushed food around on my plate, debating the

wisdom of pressing him anyway.

"Were those the only wars?" I ventured.

"No," Remy said distantly, "but they were the last of the great wars among our kind."

That you know of, I thought, trying to hide my frown. Suddenly, Remy pushed his meal away, abandoning even his wine.

"It's best to avoid such unpleasantness," he said, and he sighed. "Suffice that even the primae agreed they had gone too far. When the tribes convened on the slopes of Mount Hermon, all of the primae swore to bury their symbols of power, as a show of good faith."

Some of that was familiar from my history file. Guess it wasn't a fairy tale after all.

"So everyone was there," I said. "Anakesiel? His lieutenants?"

Remy gave me an odd look. "The Covenant of the Six wouldn't have accomplished much if Anakesiel hadn't relinquished his icon, along with everyone else," he said carefully.

The names of the missing Anakim scrolled unbidden through my mind.

"Have you seen them since then?"

Something in my expression must have tipped him off, because he cocked his head at me, his eyes suddenly canny.

"Is there something you're not telling me on this matter, sibling?" he asked, reclaiming his wine but not taking a drink.

I stared for several long moments at the plate of rigatoni next to my half-finished bowl of soup, debating how much I could safely explain. In spite of his allegiance to Saliriel, I wanted to trust Remy. He wasn't exactly the bravest soul, but he had proven—at least to me—that he was kind.

"What do you know of a decimus named Dorimiel? I think he's Nephilim."

Remy quirked an eyebrow, that guarded expression never leaving his pale features.

"I can't say I remember him well," he replied. "He was gone for a very long time."

"Gone?" I persisted. "What do you mean gone? I thought we were all immortal."

Remiel swirled the dark liquid in his glass. "Zaquiel, sibling—our past is complicated," he said without meeting my eyes. "And as much as you dislike my people, your own committed atrocities, as well, claiming they were executed in the name of—"

He was cut short when a throaty female voice broke over the casual chatter of the other diners.

"Zack! What the hell are you doing here?"

Shit!

At the sound of my name I jumped, and probably looked as guilty as a kid caught torturing the family hamster. Lil stood glowering two tables away, hands on her hips, her gray eyes threatening a storm. Everyone in the restaurant was staring at her, but she didn't appear to care.

During the hours she'd been away, she had changed clothes. Her new ensemble consisted of a lapis-hued blazer, a scoop-necked beige camisole, and khaki cargo pants that hugged her curves. I wasn't sure how, but she had a gift for making business-casual look almost pornographic.

Remy nearly dropped his wine.

"Lilianna?!?" he gasped. Then he hissed accusingly at me, "You didn't tell me you were working with the Lady of Beasts!"

28

"It's Lillee now," she corrected, and she didn't seem to share Remy's discomfort.

He didn't respond, and there was an awkward silence. The patrons continued to stare, from the octogenarian on down.

"So I guess I don't need to make introductions?" I offered. As I did, Lil dragged a chair from an empty table and made herself comfortable. Remy looked mortified, his gaze darting around the restaurant. I wasn't sure someone so pale could blush, but he was certainly working on it.

"Oh, come on, Remiel," Lil said with a smirk of satisfaction. "Not even a 'hello, how are you?' Is that any way to treat your wife?"

Hell of a time to be taking a drink.

I nearly shot water through my nose.

"Wife?" I choked.

"Ex-wife," Remy corrected swiftly.

"Guess who introduced us?" Lil asked, flashing me

a grin like the baring of teeth.

"Why am I glad I don't remember?" I muttered. After another significant glance my way, Lil blessedly turned her storm-gray gaze back to Remy.

"I don't recall signing any papers," she purred.

"One of us was dead," he gritted. "I think that counts."

She rolled her eyes. "Details."

"Zaquiel, why?" he cried, pointedly trying to ignore Lil as she leaned in closer and plucked a morsel of veal from his plate. She popped it into her mouth and chewed with undisguised relish.

"Always did have good taste," she said.

"Um, she followed me home?" I quipped, unable to stop myself.

Remy made a disgusted noise and started to rise from the table. He tossed his wadded-up napkin onto his plate, snarling angrily.

"I will not subject myself to this. I—"

Lil cut him short, "Yeah, that's right. Go rush off, now that you've had a chance to play the dutiful sibling, and pick his brain. That's just your style."

He paused, halfway between standing and sitting. "I resent that."

"Of course you do," she spat. "Doesn't mean it's not true."

"Lilianna!"

"Lillee," she corrected again.

"All right, *Lillee*. I don't know why you have such a low opinion of me—"

"Maybe it's all the times you've double-crossed me when the chips were down," she suggested with a snarl.

"You're over-looking, I believe, all of the times you betrayed me."

"You say that like survival's a bad thing," she purred. "I had my reasons. You, on the other hand, just jumped whenever Sal told you to. It's not the same."

"So, you two know each other?" I said, determined not to be left out. "Great. Remy here thought we should go out to dinner, just us guys, talk about that article in the paper, and other stuff..." *Like feeding*, I thought, though I couldn't bring myself to say it out loud.

Remy wavered, but sat back down—though not before releasing his most put-upon sigh.

"You saw the article then," Lil replied. "That's one of the things that turned up while I was out. Still don't know squat about that meeting at Lake View, but there is something I need you to take a look at. Just not in front of *him*." She jerked a thumb toward my brother.

"I'm flattered you think so highly of me, that you would withhold information," Remy huffed. "I have to wonder, though—what is *your* interest in the events at the museum?"

Lil shot him a withering look. "My interest," she replied acerbically, "is in whatever my sister was studying, and how it got her kidnapped."

"Your sister?" Remy responded, his eyes still cautious. "Which one?"

There are more of them? I thought. If they were all like Lil, then two seemed to be plenty. Any more might tip the cosmic scale of snark. More importantly, I wondered how much information the "Lady of Beasts" had been holding back.

"Lailah," she answered after a moment's hesitation.

"Dr. Ganjavi," he said, pressing his palm against his forehead. "I should have known. When did you reconnect with the Lady of Shades?" He directed this last to me.

While I fumbled for some response, Lil smacked my arm with the back of her hand. "What are you waiting for?" she demanded. "We need to get to the museum."

I just stared. "You're joking, right?"

"You don't think the article covered everything, do you?" she shot back a little too loudly. "All that fuss over forgeries? There's more to it—there *has* to be—and we won't know what till you go and check out your office." She locked eyes with me. "Unless you have a better idea."

Mindful of the people still staring, I lowered my voice. I was, after all, still wanted by the police, mob-friendly establishment or not.

"And how exactly do you propose that we get into a closed museum," I hissed, "less than a week after a major break-in?" She gave me a look that made me feel like a particularly thick-headed pet.

"You walk in, of course."

I practically tore my hair.

"Have you been listening to *anything* I say?"

Remiel had been watching in silence.

"She means from the Shadowside," he interjected.

Lil jerked a thumb. "What he said."

"Whose side are you on, anyway?" I demanded of Remiel, and he pouted a little.

"Whichever side helps resolve what happened to you, sibling. And despite any, ah, bad blood between us," he added, as I winced at the unintentional pun, "if Lil's sister is missing, that can't be good."

"Like you care," she grumbled.

He sighed, shaking his head sadly. "You know, Lilianna, I am not as heartless as you seem to think."

She glowered at him, and if lightning had flashed behind the thunderclouds that were her eyes, I wouldn't have been shocked.

"Don't pretend to know what I think, Nephilim," she growled, and it made me think of the big cat. "Now why don't you go scurry off to your master, and make your report?"

Remy ground his teeth, but didn't reply. The waitress headed for our table, carrying a dessert tray. She took one look at our expressions and did an about-face.

"We both know who you work for, Remiel," Lil spat. "Zack, why did you even give this spineless bloodsucker the time of day? What made you think you could trust him? You know the Nephilim are tangled up in this."

Remiel's whole face darkened and his eyes glittered with an inhuman light. When next he managed to speak, his voice was quiet, but each word carried a thunderous weight.

"I will not bear your insults, woman."

"Then bear this," she retorted, grabbing her phone. With a triumphant air, she played back the voicemail. My voice came out, tinny and urgent.

"*Hope this is still your number, Lil. They have your sister. Not sure what's going on, but the Nephilim are involved. I'm going to try to get her back. Hope I don't disappear like the others... Gotta go.*"

Remiel stared at the smartphone for several moments, but Lil didn't bother to repeat the message.

"Zaquiel?" he asked, confused.

I shrugged. "I don't know. It's my voice, but I don't remember leaving the message."

"Maybe you were mistaken?" he replied hopefully.

As gently as possible, I said, "You said yourself that I came into the club Tuesday, accusing Saliriel of sending people to rob the museum. I knew they were Nephilim. They might not have been *her* people, but wouldn't I have recognized them as Nephilim?" I wasn't sure about that, but I was fishing.

"You also said there were cacodaimons," Remy reminded, "working together with them. That doesn't happen."

"What about the ones that came after me at Heaven?" I insisted.

"We don't know for certain they were after you. They just came in shooting," he said. "We're by the lake. Every once in a while a gate opens up, and they make it to the shore." He didn't sound convinced.

"Oh, they were after him, all right," Lil chimed in. "I didn't believe it either, until I saw the ones this morning."

"There were more?" Remy gasped. He struggled to keep his voice low. "There has to be a logical explanation."

"Someone's sending them after me," I insisted. Lil talked over me.

"One or two I could chalk up to chance," she replied. "They slink out of Lake Michigan back home now and then, too, and while Erie's shallow by comparison, it's still deep enough where a couple might get through. But we're talking—what—five total, maybe more?

Something funny's going on."

"There is nothing funny about the unmakers," Remy responded hollowly.

"I don't get why this is so hard. It's the one thing that's obvious to me. Somebody's calling the shots with those creepy-crawlies, and he's hot to have them eat me."

Lil made a dismissive gesture, shaking her red curls at me. "I'm not sure someone can actually be directing them. How could they? But if this swarm ties back to the Nephilim, Saliriel would know."

Remy gave her a wounded look.

"Come on, Remy," she said. She snagged another bite of veal. "Do you really think Sal doesn't have a clue? Not bloody likely. He's got his fingers in more pies than Sweeney Todd."

"She," Remy corrected automatically.

"Hunh?" Lil responded.

"*She*," Remiel stated. "Saliriel is a woman now."

Lil nearly choked. "What? When the hell did that happen?"

Remy refused to respond, pale nostrils flaring.

"Whatever." Lil made a rude gesture. "Whether he's wearing a suit or a skirt, Sal's a lying sack of shit making some kind of power play. Just like old times. The only thing surprising is that you're still working for him. Or her. *It*, maybe," she snarled, throwing up her hands in frustration. It sounded rude, even to me.

With quiet urgency, Remiel said, "Our hierarchies are inescapable. I cannot disobey my decimus." Anger, indignation, and regret all vied for dominance on his features.

"Yeah, that's what you said the last time," she complained. "Guess who ended up dead? It's not like I'm bitter or anything."

I shifted in my seat. This was getting us nowhere.

"You know what would be great about now?" I asked no one in particular, though plenty of people around us were staring. "The check. Yeah, the check, and getting the hell out of here. That would be stellar."

"Not my problem." Lil shrugged. "Why don't we just go, and he can settle up."

"No, I'm coming with you," Remy said firmly. He withdrew a billfold from his pocket, dropping a handful of twenties onto the table.

"Like hell you are," Lil shot back. She grabbed me by the sleeve, tugging. "Zack and I need to have a little chat, and not with you around, *husband*." Coming from her lips, the word was an insult.

"*Ex*-husband," he responded quickly. "And I wasn't asking for your permission." He turned to me. "Zaquiel, you have no memory, so you have no idea how dangerous she can be." He tilted his head toward his… wife. "You need someone who's on your side, before she drags you into things you cannot possibly comprehend."

"Seems fair," I said, eyeing Lil and daring her to argue.

"You don't seriously think you can trust him?"

"I don't seriously think I can trust you, either," I replied, "but I've been running around with you since yesterday. So what do you say? It's both or neither. Take your pick."

"Fine," they said in unison.

29

They argued like an old married couple. Of course, they *were* an old married couple. At least in some incarnation.

"We're taking my car," Lil declared, storming ahead of us into the parking lot.

"There's more space in my Lexus," Remy replied automatically. "Some of us have to think about legroom, you know."

Lil whirled around, hands on her hips. "You are so not driving. I bet you still drive like somebody's grandfather."

"I'm a very safe driver," he objected. "I have a perfect record."

"Just proving my point," she snorted.

"We're taking this one," I said, pointing to the Sebring.

They turned as one, regarding me with nearly identical expressions of incredulity.

"Why?" they asked.

Like that wasn't creepy.

"It's closer. People are staring, and I don't want to

listen to you two argue anymore," I responded irritably.

Lil shot Remy a grin of pure triumph, then hit the clicker on her key fob. For a moment, Remy looked as if he was going to try to open her door for her, out of sheer habit. He stopped himself, stepping around to the front passenger door.

On the way he ogled her backside.

Really wishing I could unsee that, I folded myself into the back seat behind Lil, hoping I could get her to move her seat up. Remy had a point. Most cars weren't made for people more than six feet tall. I couldn't imagine what it was like for Saliriel, especially with those crazy heels she wore.

Lil hit the ignition, threw the sporty convertible into gear, and peeled out of the lot, swinging onto Clifton at what felt like twenty miles above the speed limit. Remy cursed, belatedly strapping on his seat belt.

"She has that effect on me, too," I muttered, chuckling at his expense.

White-knuckling the armrest, Remy asked, "Why are we getting onto the highway?"

"We're hitting the art museum, remember, dear?" she replied sweetly, gunning the motor as she caught the ramp and merged with traffic.

"You can take Detroit the whole way over. There's no need to get on 90."

"And deal with stoplights at every intersection?" She scowled at him like he was crazy. Good to know those looks weren't reserved just for me.

"Mile for mile, it's shorter," he said.

"Mile for mile, it's slower," she replied.

He scowled. "Fine."

"Fine," she echoed mockingly with a toss of her head.

"Would you kids settle down up there?" I demanded. "A freaking carful of immortals, and *I* feel like the adult? It's just wrong."

That shocked them into silence, at least for the moment. When he wasn't holding on for dear life, Remy drummed his fingers restlessly, and Lil did that maddening thing with her nails, pecking incessantly at the steering wheel.

The peace was short-lived.

"You're taking him to the *Thinker*, right?" Remy said, twitching perceptibly as Lil crossed three lanes of traffic to get around a semi with its hazards on.

"Why the *Thinker*?" she asked, blissfully oblivious to the blaring of horns in her wake.

"It's the closest crossing to the museum proper," he replied.

"Really?" Lil pecked harder at the steering wheel as she pondered this. "I was going to swing down MLK to Rockefeller Park. There's one by the Cultural Gardens, isn't there? Or am I remembering it wrong?"

"Rockefeller Park? How close is that to the museum?" I asked. But Remy talked over me.

"Are you trying to get my brother killed?"

"No," she said defensively. "Not really. At least, not this time."

"Then think about it," he said. "Rockefeller Park to the museum—that's a lot of ground to cover, once he's on the Shadowside. In his current state—"

"Hello!" I said, reaching up and waving a hand

between them. "Right here, you know—unless the back seat's an invisible dimension, and no one thought to tell me about it."

Ignoring my outburst, Lil glanced over at Remy.

"The *Thinker*?" she said.

"Or what's left of it," he replied, "after the terrorists tried to blow it up."

"Terrorists?" Lil muttered. "Like on 9/11?"

"Don't be ridiculous." Remy laughed with an elegant gesture of his hand. "It was that group calling themselves the Weathermen, back in the '70s."

"Kind of missed the '70s," she responded. "Still dead, you know."

"Oh," Remy murmured. "I thought you were just avoiding me."

Lil made an aggravated noise. "It's not always about you, Remington."

I nearly died choking.

"*Remington?*"

"Please don't call me that," he said, glowering at her.

"You're still calling me Lilianna," she chided.

That shut him up, and he just looked out the window, sulking. We squealed around another curve, and I took the opportunity to try again.

"This *Addams Family* reunion is entertaining and all," I said, "but when you two are done arguing over ancient history, could you fill me in on what you think I'm supposed to be doing?"

Lil looked up at me through the rear-view mirror. Eye contact. *Holy crap*. We were in the same dimension, after all.

"Just slip in through the Shadowside," she said, as if it was obvious. "Find your office, or whatever space they had you working in, and grab all the files you can. Piece of cake."

"If you need help finding your way," Remy said, "you can just ask Terael."

"Terael?" I echoed.

"Our local Rephaim," he responded mildly.

Lil almost swerved into the next lane.

"There's a Rephaim in the museum?" she choked.

"Of course, when he's not out on tour," Remy replied. "Surely you knew that. He's been there since the '30s. The Wades kept him in their mansion, up until they donated him."

Lil seemed genuinely rattled. "Wild horses couldn't drag me into that museum now," she breathed.

"Is there anything I should know about this Rephaim?" I asked cautiously, looking from Remy to Lil and back again.

"Only that they're bat-shit crazy—every last one of them," Lil said. "*Scary* crazy," she added with quiet emphasis.

Remy frowned at her, fluttering his hand.

"I wouldn't say that. Eccentric, perhaps." He turned to catch my eye, explaining, "He just has a very different perspective on things. If you were working in the museum, he must like you. He hasn't let me set foot in the place since 1970, when I made an unfriendly comment about the extension they were adding. Apparently, I insulted him, and he doesn't forgive easily."

"Right," I said skeptically. "But if he's in there a lot, he might know something about the break-in."

Remy made a thoughtful noise. "Now that you mention it, yes, he should know a great deal. He has a bird's-eye view of the interior."

"Good luck getting him to make sense," Lil grumbled under her breath.

I glared at each of them in turn, irritated at the things they weren't telling me. Either they withheld information as some kind of power trip, or it simply didn't occur to them that I needed to know these things. Either way, it was pissing me off.

"All right," I muttered, letting it go for the moment. "I'll jump off that bridge when I come to it. How am I getting in? Back in the alley, the walls were just as solid on the Shadowside as they are in the real world. I can't just poof through them like Casper, you know—or can I?"

"Some of them are solid, yes," Remy allowed. "It has to do with the age of the building, and the collective perception of humanity."

"Of course… that makes perfect sense," I said, rolling my eyes. "If you're trying to clarify, you'll need to try harder, or—*fuck*!"

With a muttered curse, Lil whipped the car across two lanes of traffic to catch an exit. Remy and I did our best to remain upright. It was like being on the command deck of the *Enterprise* during a red alert. The charms dangling from the rear-view mirror swung wildly, smacking into the windshield with a sound like castanets.

When we were relatively stable again, she shot me a glance in the mirror.

"It's easy, Zack. People come and go through the

main doors every day. That wears a path in the energy. The doors should have no substance at this point—they're just part of the current. Get yourself caught in the current, and you'll be swept inside."

That sounded like something I could work with.

"So, there is no door, and there is no spoon," I muttered, knowing they wouldn't get it. At that point I didn't really care.

It meant something to me.

"Just remember," Remy cautioned. "You can't linger on the other side forever. It costs you power, and your power is your life. Wear yourself out, and you won't have the strength to return."

"Almost found that out the hard way," I muttered, feeling a cold stab of fear in my gut.

"This is natural to you," he added encouragingly. "Don't think too hard about it, and it will come on its own. I have faith in you, brother."

I sighed, leaning my head back on the seat and staring at the ragtop of the car, fervently wishing I could say the same thing.

30

We turned off Euclid and parked the car on East Boulevard, then walked past the lagoon to the oldest portion of the Cleveland Museum of Art. The reflecting pool lay still and dark, like a mirror of black glass turned up to the vault of the sky. The gardens were devoid of flowers and all the trees stood stark and bare. Here and there, statues dotted the lawn, many placed to mislead the eye so that it seemed the gardens were alive with lovers, dancers, and children at play, even at this late hour.

Aside from the statues, we were alone. Not even the ducks and swans that made the lagoon their home in warmer months chose to winter here.

Sticking to the shadows whenever possible, we climbed the steps leading to the original entrance. The perfectly manicured lawns gave way to paving stones and concrete. We passed more statuary, a massive fountain drained to protect it over the harsh Ohio winter, and then the central piece of this promenade—the hunched and hulking form of Rodin's *Thinker*.

We could see the damage as we approached—portions along the statue's base winged up and out where an explosion had turned the bronze to shrapnel. It had nearly obliterated the figure's foot, like a still life with violence captured in the very substance of the metal.

I could feel the crossing as we drew near. It manifested first as a kind of unsettled quality to the air. As we approached the tear between the two aspects of reality, my senses grew sharper, requiring no effort on my part. Around me, the character of the gardens shifted. Some of the shadows deepened, and these seemed to take on a kind of weight that they had lacked before.

Other parts of the garden became easier to see, not because the darkness lifted exactly, but rather because the darkness became visible. All of this had little to do with my physical senses. Things were thinner here, or perhaps more entangled, allowing Shadowside and skinside to intermingle.

This was the pull that had drawn me to the blind alley. There it had been subliminal. This time I was conscious of it.

"Why here?" I wondered aloud.

"You mean the bombing?" Remy asked, his eyes gliding appreciatively over the statue. He actually winced as he surveyed the damage. "It was the '70s," he said with a shrug. "The mortals did crazy things all the time—still do, more than ever. I've learned not to question it."

"No, not that," I said. "I'm talking about the crossing."

"Oh, that?" he said absently. "It's tied to the explosion, as well. Strong emotions. Traumatic events. These all can break down the barriers between the spaces. The terrorist attack was a perfect example."

"Boom, new crossing," Lil supplied helpfully. "In this case, literally."

Suddenly I flashed on the flickering images of the dismembered woman in the alley.

"What about murder?" I asked.

"Oh, that would do it," Lil responded—a little too eagerly, I thought. "Especially something really vicious. Crimes of passion, or torture. Something long, drawn-out and inventive—that would really ramp up the emotions, and leave a stain on the space. You could even do it on purpose, if you wanted to make one."

She was practically grinning as she talked about it. There was nothing sultry or attractive in the expression, just a kind of naked bloodlust that I didn't really want to ponder. I folded my arms across my chest, taking comfort in the thick leather of the biker jacket.

Remy lifted a brow at this.

"You can't be cold. Are you stalling?"

"Kind of nervous," I admitted.

"Well, get over it," Lil said flatly.

It wasn't an answer I liked, but I really couldn't argue. So I stretched a bit, shaking out my hands. They tingled all the way up to my elbows. While it wasn't exactly painful, it wasn't a pleasant sensation either. After a while, it started feeling itchy on the wrong side of my skin.

I mused that I probably looked like a runner, about to

do a marathon—then recalled how I'd felt after coming back out of the Shadowside, earlier that morning. The marathon comparison was pretty apt. This was going to push the limits of my endurance. At least I'd had a chance to recharge my batteries.

"All right," I said, taking a step toward the *Thinker*. "Here goes nothing." With that, I willed myself to move from the flesh-and-blood world to that realm Lil and Remy called the Shadowside.

"We'll be waiting here for you," Remy said, his vaguely accented words already taking on a hollow and echoey quality.

It happened almost before I realized it. There was an initial sensation of pressure that stole my breath and made my ears pop. Then I was through, as if I'd pushed past a curtain. Suddenly everything appeared in shades of gray, with hints of color blooming here and there.

In front of me, the *Thinker* was caught in a state of perpetual explosion. The fire punctuated the soft monochrome, and even that was washed-out. Then it flickered, and was intact again, brooding upon its pedestal. In the next instant the pedestal was empty, with indistinct figures scurrying about, maneuvering the massive bronze casting atop its display. It was like the murder in the alley. Different snapshots of time jumbled over one another, vying for which was on top.

Echoes of people moved around the statue, but they were just blurry smudges on the space—the memory of passing crowds. Mostly the statue shimmered between sitting there and shattering.

Weird.

Past the *Thinker*, the museum itself was an even stranger sight to behold. Multiple versions and extensions of the building angled together in the space, some appearing more solid than the others. It was as if someone had taken pictures from the different stages of the museum's construction, cut them out, then pasted them on top of one another in a Cubist collage. The clearest was the 1916 original—its white marble façade and towering columns a soft gray on this side.

"Tick tock," I muttered to myself, and I started to move.

As I walked along the promenade, the memories of people ghosted past, silent and insubstantial. At best they were fingerprints left behind by the passage of the living, though in the strongest of the echoes it was almost possible to get a snippet of a thought or a face. None of it lingered, however, and the echoes of different events constantly jostled, rearranging on top of one another.

As Lil had pointed out, the repetitive movements of people on the flesh-and-blood side created currents in the Shadowside. The river of remembered footsteps parted around the *Thinker,* moving out toward the lagoon on one side, and in toward the museum on the other. The stream running toward the museum was the strongest, and I allowed it to guide my steps. It approached the main doors, but echoes of past construction flickered to life, blocking the old 1916 entrance. I veered sharply right, dodging the rise of partially imprinted walls as they faded in and out on the Shadowside. I followed the flow as it swept around the east side of the building.

It was darker over there, clustered with memories

of old trees. My instincts suddenly jangling, I moved forward with caution.

It was a good thing I did. I wasn't alone.

Nothing jumped out to threaten me—not yet—but oddly shaped things slipped in and out among the shadows. Not cacodaimons. Apparently, there were other denizens of the dark on this side of things. At least one of these proved to be the wan specter of a little girl. Her prim ringlets and dainty white pinafore, all faded to a uniform gray, tied her to a bygone era. She stepped out from behind a massive oak that held more substance than she did, regarding me in silence with big, soulful eyes.

Not quite sure what else to do, I raised one hand and wiggled my fingers in what I hoped was a friendly wave. She continued to stare a few moments longer, then turned away.

"Another angel," she muttered as she disappeared into the towering echo of remembered trees. She sounded almost bored.

Belatedly I realized that the transit had torn my cowl away. My wings were still tucked tight against my back, but they shone softly, trailing glimmers of blue-white power in my wake. That was when I realized how bright and colorful I appeared in comparison to everything else around me.

Subtlety was right out.

Keeping a wary eye on whatever else was moving within the ghostly arbor, I continued toward the eastern entrance which, I hoped, would be accessible. It seemed farther away than it should have been. I hadn't been keeping track of how long I'd spent on this side—frankly, it was hard to do. Surrounded by past echoes, the very concept of time held a vague and distant quality. Still, the pressure of the space bore down on me, and while I wasn't exactly sweating with effort, the strain increased the longer I moved through the shadowy realm.

Spotting the glassed-in entryway that led into the museum on this side, I finally got to witness first-hand what Lil had tried to describe. There was the vaguest suggestion of doors along the entrance, but they blurred beneath the stream of perpetual images passing in and out of them. The closer I got, that well-established current exerted a pull that became impossible to ignore.

"Resistance is futile," I muttered to myself, though in my head the words were spoken by a Borg with Patrick Stewart's face. Chuckling a little at my own random geekdom, I surrendered to the flow.

And then I was inside.

31

Words erupted from everywhere and nowhere, resonating with a crushing intensity.

Do you miss the music as much as I do, brother? I have not heard it since we came.

Instinctively, I clapped my hands over my ears to block out the eerie and atonal sound, even as the voice came again, beamed directly into my brain.

Have you brought our brothers back? Have you learned to set them free?

It wouldn't have been so bad if the thoughts didn't feel as if they were coming from inside of me. It wasn't just words, either. Everything was layered with sense and feel and meaning, in an overwhelmingly nuanced way. All of it felt somehow twisted and bleak. Alien emotions flooded my mind with every contact, as profound as they were painful—desolation, solitude, and a brittle, attenuated longing.

If thoughts were a sea, these could drown me.

"Terael?" I croaked. I spoke out loud, if only to

establish a boundary between my voice and the thing resonating in my head. "I'm looking for a woman named Lailah." Then I added, "Dr. Lailah Ganjavi."

Ignoring my question, the voice continued.

Kessiel came to ask forgiveness, for the slight he paid to me. Three doves he slaughtered in the offering-place, to pay for the loss of my servants. Three doves, two guardians. The numbers calculate favorably.

"Terael, can you hear me?"

Of course I hear you, Zaquiel. You stand in my domain. Although I am diminished in this time and place, I still can hear and see.

I was beginning to understand why Lil refused to come into the museum. The Rephaim's thoughts thundered in my mind in a jarring and unnatural way. Terael's presence lent an added pressure to the space, and I felt it wearing me down quickly. I wasn't sure how much longer I could—or should—remain in the Shadowside.

Yet I still needed some idea of where to go—and a way to get there without bringing the entire Cleveland police force down on my head.

"Terael, I need your help," I said. Even speaking was an effort. "There was a break-in the other day—"

Kessiel I forgive, for he has paid in blood. All who come to worship now give only coin. I long for life spilled sweetly on the altars.

That was the second time he'd mentioned Kessiel. The pervasive feel of Terael's thought-speak made it hard to concentrate, so it took me a moment to parse the implications.

"Terael," I asked urgently. "Is Kessiel... is he here now?"

He has been granted access to the guarded inner sanctums. The bells and red eyes slumber, as the space obeys my will.

It was beginning to make sense, the way this strange sibling perceived the world. Maybe it was how his mind surged against my own. Images and concepts came clinging with each word. The museum was his temple, its guards and curators his servants. He assumed the daily visitors came to offer worship—and perhaps some of them did, after a fashion.

A deeper knowledge of this sibling carried on the tide of his thoughts. The Rephaim were tied to idols, like the Nephilim were tied to blood. Somewhere within the museum there was a statue that served to house my sibling's soul—and somehow, from that statue, his influence spread throughout the building.

"Bells, red eyes," I muttered, struggling to comprehend. "Terael, have you shut down the alarms? Is that what you mean?"

As I have done for you often, on the nights when secret things must move within my sanctum.

I didn't have time to ponder the implications of that. Instead, I dropped my hold on whatever allowed me to shadow-walk through the spirit realm, and took a step back into ordinary space.

Sight, sound, color and sensation all slammed into me with the force of air suddenly filling a vacuum. The whisper of the ventilation. The electric buzz of computers banked behind the greeting station. Red light spilling from the exit signs, dim under any other circumstance but almost blinding now in contrast to the non-light from whence I'd come.

There was a smell, too—sharp, coppery and wet.

Not three feet away stood a donation box crafted of Lucite and brushed metal. A pattern of gleaming droplets beaded in an arc across its front. On the tiles of the floor, a crimson splash of blood shone stark against the white of the marble.

Piled untidily in the middle were three crumpled little bodies, chests gaping redly, the gray pinions of their wings clotted in the blood. Three doves sacrificed at the foot of the donation box.

"Now that's old school," I muttered, stepping carefully around the mess. The newspapers were going to have a field day when they heard about it in the morning.

"Terael, where is Kessiel?" I said to the air.

He stands in that domain I have carved for you as a sign of our mutual respect, beyond the halls of service, in the cells of study and repair.

Heard from the flesh-and-blood side of reality, Terael's voice-thoughts weren't quite as paralyzing, but they were still damned creepy.

"Let me guess," I said with a grimace. "He's taking my things."

I have forbidden him to touch the statuary or the stones. Nothing precious may he have. He has not earned that right.

"What's he doing right now?" I asked. "Can you tell me?"

A box of lights he seeks, and paper things once stored away. His thrumming mind brushed mine, wavering. *Have I erred, my brother?*

"Damn, damn, damn!" I breathed. With the desperate hope that I'd miss any guards who might be doing their rounds, I hurried down a nearby flight of stairs. If my instincts ran true, there would be a stretch of classrooms and lecture halls, and if I hung a left from that, I'd be moving in the direction of back offices and conservator labs.

But my memories were out of date. I ended up at a bank of doors leading to a parking garage. Rubbing my temples, I wracked the fried mess of meat and synapses that was my brain.

"Terael," I called, looking up as if he somehow hovered above me. I knew he didn't, but I had to look somewhere. "I don't know my way around. Where should I go?"

Have you taken new flesh so soon, that your memory has fled? It seems only days since you were here, a grown man and whole.

"Look, it's hard to explain," I said, trying not to let the "whole" bit get to me. "I just don't remember, OK? Can you tell me left or right?"

In answer, my mind flooded—not with words, but with images almost too quick to absorb. It wasn't directions so much as a download of place-knowledge burned directly into my brain. Reeling a little, I turned and started walking. Different portions of the halls looked suddenly familiar, and I followed the spatial awareness Terael had gifted to me.

You are wounded, brother, Terael observed as I strode quickly through the darkened halls. The voice was gentler this time, less numbingly omnipresent.

"Yeah," I said. It kind of hurt to admit.

What war between the tribes erupts beyond my walls, that Nefer-Ka has marked you so?

That stopped me cold.

I stood there, shivering as adrenaline banged around my nervous system with nowhere useful yet to go. When I managed to speak, the tremor made it to my voice.

"What did you say?"

Terael took me literally and repeated his previous statement, word-for-word—or thought-for-thought, as the case may be. I reminded myself that he was a non-human intelligence, stuck inside a statue for more years than I probably cared to consider. He couldn't possibly be expected to think in a normal way, so I rephrased the question, choosing my words carefully.

"What do you mean when you say I bear the mark of Nefer-Ka?"

The holes you bear above your heart, my brother. If not Nefer-Ka, then one of his chosen. Yet the Eye of Nefer-Ka must be buried and lost to the sands. He stood on the mountain and swore the oath, as did all the firsts of our tribes. Such things are binding.

"His eye?" I asked with sudden urgency. "Nefer-Ka is the Nephilim primus, right? What do you know about 'Neferkariel's Eye'?"

In days long passed, each Primus shaped an icon, his power thus to share with those who were his heralds.

Icons again. Buried symbols of power, Remy had said. And here I'd dismissed that stuff in my patchwork PDF.

Terael paused and I felt a quavering touch, like fingers made of smoke trailing against my skin. A heartbeat later, the Rephaim recoiled within my mind, nearly blinding me with a burst of animal terror.

Scenes of death and warfare cascaded through my mind in a stupefying jumble before he sufficiently recovered to frame comprehensible words. Though he had no lungs, he sounded breathless.

You bear the Stylus. Two Icons unearthed. The wars have come to us again.

Stylus? My thoughts flashed unbidden to my own memories of war—visions of the temple, that thin bone tool etching lines of pain across Dorimiel's brow. Writing his sentence.

A pen.

A pen lay buried in the lining of my coat. I'd felt it when I'd retrieved the envelope. With nerveless fingers, I dug through the hole in the pocket. When I connected with the hard length tucked against the seam, Terael's terror of the object spasmed in my mind.

I withdrew a carved and yellowed length of bone not much longer than a No. 2 pencil. One end was shaped into a wedge. The other tapered down to a wicked point. Scrimshaw symbols spiraled along its length, elegant and fearsome as striking cobras.

The Stylus of Anak. Please, brother, please, do not take it up. We have left the wars behind us, traded blood for simpler ways.

"Anak," I breathed. My tongue moved thickly in a mouth stone-dry with shock. "You mean Anakesiel, don't you? This is the icon of the Anakim primus."

The Holocaust of the Idols, all the burning shapes and shadows in the wretched Hinome valley—so many Names bound and shattered. My brother, please, do not take us there again. Terael was genuinely panicked, words, emotions, and images spilling in such a riptide through my head that I had to cling to my own thoughts, or else get swept away.

"I'm not going to use it," I cried. "I don't even know why I have it."

But if I had it—it was a good bet Dorimiel had the Eye. That was what the cipher had been telling me.

"The Eye of Nefer-Ka," I said. My heart thrashed desperately against my ribs. "Tell me, Terael. What does it do?"

It took him several moments to settle down.

As the Stylus breaks and binds, the Eye swallows memory and power. It drinks it with a touch. All the skills of Nefer-Ka are gifted to those who pay the blood.

Understanding blossomed as he brushed minds with me. I struggled to frame a response, but Terael's panic surged again.

They swore, they swore! It rang like a clarion in my head.

"I need to be very clear on this," I said. I touched the hollow ache above my heart. "You're telling me that someone can use the Nephilim icon to take memories away."

Not merely take, but to devour, so the knowledge feeds the one who eats it.

White-hot fury blazed within me, till all my thoughts were fire. I had stood in Sal's throne room, practically spelling out an attack with the Nephilim icon, while she and Remy pretended it was nothing.

Lil was right—and Remy was as bad as Saliriel. They were all involved. How the hell else could two of the fucking icons of the primae be rattling around right under their noses?

I was being played.

"Is Kessiel one of the Nephilim?" I growled. I already knew the answer.

In a tiny voice—or what served him as a voice—Terael answered.

Yes.

I wrapped my fingers around the Stylus as the item whispered promises of power. *Breaking and binding, hunh?* It would be so easy—but what was the cost? Forbidden artifacts were usually forbidden for a reason.

Shaking with emotion, I pulled open the inside pocket of my leather jacket. With an effort of will, I slipped the ornate stylus of yellowed bone back against the inner seam. Best to forget about it completely. With luck, no one would be able to sense its presence the way Terael had while he connected with me.

"Is that pulse-sucker still in my office?" I demanded.

He gathers those things for which he came. Terael's mind-speak came across as pensive, bewildered even. I caught images of the Stylus flashing intermittently through his thoughts.

"I wasn't kidding," I assured him. "I'm not going to use it. I don't know how I got it, and I don't think I want it, but you keep your mouth shut about it, OK?"

I keep many of your secrets. I will swear it on my Name.

"Just keep Kessiel from leaving till I get there," I responded. "He's going to explain a few things."

Heedless of the threat of guards now, I shouted my power till my hands danced with blue-white flames. While Terael's place-knowledge still sizzled in my brain, I sprinted through the warren of back halls.

There would be hell to pay.

32

There was only one back office with lights on. In a fury, I kicked the door wide. It opened onto a space that was larger than I expected—part office, part lab, judging by the furniture.

On the far side of the room, a man with a long blond ponytail leaned over the drawers of a filing cabinet, yanking out photos and papers and stuffing them into a canvas messenger bag. He was at least my height, maybe a little taller. With his distressed jeans and stylish button-down shirt, he looked less like a robber and more like a model for some trendy men's cologne.

The way he jumped when I kicked the door open, he wasn't expecting anyone to disturb his larcenous search, though he recovered quickly enough.

"You!" he cried in a voice eerily reminiscent of Remiel's. Baring his fangs theatrically, he pulled out a gun. I did that preternatural speed trick and threw myself behind a big metal desk situated at the end of the room. As I crouched there trying to determine my next move, I reminded myself to find that Kimber Lil had mentioned, and reacquaint myself with its use. It sucked dodging bullets without the luxury of being able to return fire.

At least he wasn't shooting yet.

"Kessiel, I presume?" I called from behind the desk.

"I didn't believe it when they said you'd survived that leap from the ship. We've made a game of searching for you, you know," he taunted.

"I'm flattered. Really."

In answer, he put a few bullets into the desk—as if they were punctuation. It wasn't fair. The gun had a silencer, so I barely heard it when he squeezed off a shot. The sound of the bullet smashing into the metal was louder than the little cough it made exiting the chamber.

Kessiel took a few casual steps—no hurry—and moved to flank me. Keeping my body low, I darted from behind the desk, heading for a long, freestanding counter with heavy cabinetry underneath. There were two of them, arranged parallel to one another in the approximate middle of the lab, both covered with equipment, sorting bins, and other important-looking clutter.

He squeezed off another shot and it smashed into the wall just over my shoulder. He wasn't even aiming.

"You having fun putting holes in my office?" I called out. "You're a worse shot than most storm troopers."

"I'm not supposed to kill you, Anakim," he sneered, "but that doesn't mean I can't hurt you. So why don't you save us both some pain and tell me where you stashed the things you stole? We'll start with the easy answers.

"Where are the demon jars?"

That threw me for a loop. Last I'd checked, I was the researcher, not the crook.

"What makes you think I'd tell you?" I replied.

"You know, he can give your woman a jar of her own, even without the Stylus," Kessiel said. "He's swallowed enough of your tribe for that. It's only a matter of time before we recover it. Cooperate now, and he'll consider her release."

He wasn't even pretending to be sincere.

Realization flashed bright as a magnesium flare. The demon jars were soul prisons—not just for demons. For anything. That's why Remy had been offended that I'd kept their presence a secret. There was no telling what—or who—was in them.

"Fuck you, fang-face!" I shouted.

"Give us the location of the jars you found, and perhaps he'll leave you enough of a mind so you don't shit yourself." Then he added, "There are worse things than death, Anakim. He'll bind you both and feed you to the darkness in the depths of the lake."

Another bullet whined past me, closer this time. I duck-walked down the length of the counter, relying on my psychic impressions to keep track of my opponent. The bullets were a serious problem. The minute he stopped fucking around, I was going to get shot. I needed to get my hands on his gun, but if I was going to do that, I had to get the drop on him. I started to call power to my hands.

The air of the room crackled around me, reminiscent of a crossing. My racing thoughts flashed to Terael's statement about giving me my own domain in "his" museum. I had an idea now what he'd meant, and it gave me a plan.

Even if I pulled it off, it was going to hurt.

"Alive doesn't mean it has to be pretty, Anakim," Kessiel said. "He can rip the information from your screaming wreck, as long as you still have a pulse—and I'll watch."

Stalling, I asked, "Isn't sucking my gray matter against some kind of peace treaty? I thought there were oaths and things, after the Blood Wars."

Again Kessiel laughed, reminding me of every bad Bond villain.

"There are loopholes in any oath. Only the primae swore. You didn't think items of such power could stay buried forever, did you?" He planted another lazy bullet into the wall. "Your whole tribe has earned a reckoning, Anakim. One by one, he'll swallow your memories, your powers, and every dream you've ever held dear."

"Yeah, yeah. Mr. Ooky-Spooky and the Eye of Nefer-Ka," I taunted, using the sarcasm to deflect my own bitter terror. I listened for another cough from the silencer. Once it came, I jumped up from behind the counter—then stepped straight into the Shadowside.

It was just like I thought. The entire room was a crossing. I whispered a silent thanks to Terael, even as the rapid transition tore the breath from my lungs. Slamming through that hard and fast was about as painful as I'd expected it to be. I stumbled, but managed to stay upright and maintain my momentum.

The space went dark around me and all the angles grew strange. Most of the furniture disappeared, as it didn't seem to exist on this side. Maybe it was too recent. The room itself seemed larger, as well, and while the differences were minor, I did my best to keep track of them. They were important for what I was attempting.

On this side, I had wings. Functional wings. All it took was a jump, paired with one powerful down stroke, and I closed the distance between us, overshooting just enough to place myself behind Kessiel. I strained to keep track of where the filing cabinets were located so I didn't run the risk of reappearing inside one of them. I had no idea if that could happen, or what it might feel like if it did, but I was reasonably certain I didn't want to find out.

As with Lil in the alley, I could perceive Kessiel from this side of things. The Nephilim shimmered imperfectly through the veil, a pulsing red mist in a vaguely human shape, with dimmer parts of it arcing out in wings.

I was seeing his blood—his blood and his power.

I didn't take the time to contemplate the nauseating truth of that. Instead, preparing myself for a jarring re-entry, I pivoted in the space behind him and slammed myself back through.

I was rewarded with an instant headache and lancing fire through all my limbs. I pushed through the pain, reaching around from behind to seize the gun. Kessiel snapped his head back into my nose, but I buried my face against his shoulder. I had one hand on the slide, but he kept control of the grip. I dug the fingers of my other hand hard into the tendons on the underside of his wrist.

He tried twisting away, and we grappled. A shot went

off, burying itself into one of the counters.

He was stronger than me, which only figured. As a vampire, he had an automatic edge—faster, stronger, more fashionably inclined. I danced back a few steps before he could seize hold of me and really make things difficult, but I got the gun out of his hands. The pistol skidded halfway across the room, coming to rest underneath the metal desk. He didn't go for it.

Instead, he turned to face me.

"Hand-to-hand?" he spat. "Are you really that stupid?"

"Just shut up and fight, you over-dressed bastard."

"I'll swallow what's left of you myself," he replied. Then he lunged at me, fangs bared.

I tried dodging but was half a second too slow. He slammed into me and, with a leg sweep, sent me sprawling. I recovered quickly, but not quickly enough. He pressed his advantage, working to pin me up against the counter. I could feel his breath hot along my throat.

Not good.

I landed a few quick rabbit punches into his gut, twisting away, but he was just as lithe and spindly as me. He tackled me again, clinging with a strength I couldn't hope to match. *Damned vampires.* He got me down a second time. I dug for his eyes, shoving hard with both thumbs. That at least got him to back the fuck off.

This wasn't quite going the way I'd hoped. I edged away a few steps, struggling to regain my breath. It hitched in my throat in the next moment as Terael thundered through my head.

I wish no disrespect, brother, but I can feel your

distress through the walls. Do you need my assistance?

Desperately I shouted, "Assist away!"

I was trying to get a leg up to kick at Kessiel—belly, groin, any soft spot would do. In the next moment, the lights flickered and the sprinklers came on. The sudden downpour of water, though harmless, shocked the Nephilim enough to let me land the blow and squirm away. I scrabbled backward on the now-slick floor, finding my back against the big metal desk.

Kessiel shook himself, scowling up at the sheeting water and cursing Terael. The Rephaim must have cursed right back, because for a moment, Kessiel wobbled, gripping his head. I didn't envy him that.

It was just enough time for me to pull the gun out from under the desk. I was too rattled to aim, so my first shot went wild and just grazed his arm. This only made him angry. I steadied my shoulders against the solid metal of the desk, then slowly exhaled as I pulled down on the trigger a second time.

I caught him above the left eye. I wasn't sure how to kill an immortal-angel-vampire, or even if it could be done, but I figured a bullet in the brain would ruin anyone's day.

The little 9mm from his Beretta didn't leave much of a hole going in. With the silencer, it didn't pack the same kind of punch. There was no backspatter, so the bullet didn't make it back out, either. I hoped it was rattling around in his brainpan, making a real mess of his gray matter.

Kessiel's stonewashed blue eyes rolled back in his head, and he went down like a sack of rusty hammers.

33

Once Kessiel was on the floor, Terael cut the sprinklers, though he left all but the emergency lights off.

Gingerly, I approached the body.

"Did I kill him?"

You cannot kill immortals, brother. Killing the body is merely an inconvenience to the soul.

I stood dripping over Kessiel's crumpled form, aiming the gun down at him just as a precaution. I didn't ride the trigger, but I was rattled enough, I came real close. Experimentally, I nudged the Nephilim's shoulder with the toe of my boot.

"Looks pretty inconvenienced to me," I muttered.

That was when his head whipped around and he sank his fangs into the meat of my calf. He hugged my legs and it was all I could do to not drop the gun. I shouted something that wasn't remotely related to English, wildly jerking away from him, but Kessiel had a firm grip for a guy I'd just shot in the head.

The tile floor was slick with water, and my feet went out from under me. I wasn't landing on my ass a third time in this fucking fight. I caught myself on the counter, sending conservator tools and papers everywhere as I floundered. Kessiel dragged himself up the front of my body and slapped the gun away.

"Brave and feeble Anakim," he snarled, my blood still painting his lips. He swiped the blood away with the back of one hand, like his latte had come with a little too much foam.

Instinct kicked in. Instead of the gun, I wrapped my fingers around raw power, dredging it forth with the syllables of my name. The twin blades leapt to life and I slammed them into the center of his body mass, bellowing my defiance.

The spirit-blades didn't cut his flesh, but they sure knocked the wind out of him. I pivoted away, looking around for the gun. I didn't see it anywhere, so I hit him again with the scintillating power, landing a wicked slash across his throat. No physical wound opened up, but he reacted as if he felt one.

I lashed out again. This time he got his arms up, catching the blows with his wrists. He winced each time I connected. I kept at it, and soon he was the one sprawled on the counter.

I slammed a burning blade deep into one of his shoulders as he struggled to lever himself up. He flailed. Most of the strength seemed to go out of that arm.

"Who's feeble now, asshole?" I growled.

He went for me with his other arm and I speared it, too, driving the shining weapon between the bones of his forearm. The blades weren't technically physical, but they still held him pinned. I boggled at the physics of it—or metaphysics, maybe. With Kessiel spread like a dissection project across the top of the counter, I leaned bodily against him, trapping his legs before he could start kicking.

"I'm not some specter you can banish with spirit-fire," he hissed.

"It still looks like you're hurting," I said. "So maybe now I get some answers."

Kessiel strained against me. I pushed back, twisting the blades. Muscles corded on his neck and his face grew red. Then he fell back, and went limp.

"Fuck you," he said wearily. "I just have to wait."

"Expecting someone?" I asked.

"You'll exhaust yourself soon enough," he spat. "Or didn't he leave you enough of your brain to remember that?"

That might have been a bluff, but soon as he mentioned it, I realized I could feel that familiar burn just under my ribs. My arms tingled. With effort, I maintained the blades' cohesion.

"Where's Lailah?" I demanded, ignoring the painful thrum in my fingers.

He smirked "On a boat."

"Where, you asshole?"

"Lake Erie." He was grinning. I wanted to smash in his fangs. I twisted the blades till his grin became more of a rictus.

"Stop fucking with me!" I yelled.

"You got there once, and you couldn't save her. Are

you fool enough to try it again?" he taunted.

"Is that why I met with your people at Lake View? To arrange some kind of exchange?" It was nothing but desperate conjecture, but throw enough shit on a window and eventually something will stick. From the avid shift in his expression, I knew I had made a mistake.

"Is that how you got on our ship?" he murmured.

As I scrabbled for some flippant answer, his mostly free arm spasmed. Half a dozen items—lab equipment and restoration tools—clattered from the counter. I thought it was unintentional, then he brought that hand up. His fingers were closed around something. It looked like a carpet knife.

He took a swipe at my throat.

Zaquiel?

"Not now, Terael!" I let go of the blade at Kessiel's shoulder. It dissipated as soon as I did, but I managed to catch his wrist while the nimbus of power still clung to my fingers. Given the way he twitched, it had to burn, but I couldn't wrest the weapon from him without both hands. We continued to grapple. With my daggers out of him, his strength started to come back. I had to be quick.

His back was still bowed over the counter, his legs mostly pinned. I drove a knee hard into his groin, and that hurt him as much as it would any other guy. His grip slackened just enough for me to get control of the wicked little tool. The handle was wood, with a half-moon blade maybe three inches long. I couldn't imagine what it was used for, if not mayhem.

I wrapped my hand around it, calling power without a second thought. Blue-white flames danced along the metal and I was reminded briefly of a very different blade in a long-fallen temple. With a ferocious cry, I thrust it up and under his ribs, angling instinctively for the heart.

There was more than one way to stake a vampire.

Kessiel loosed an ear-splitting wail, then arched backward, blood gouting from his mouth.

"Heal that, bitch," I spat, and I smashed my knee in his junk again for good measure. Kessiel slid to the floor and began convulsing dramatically. His heels danced against the tiles, then he curled up in a partial fetal position. Blood oozed from his mouth to spread in lazy ribbons through the water puddling all over the floor.

Now he is inconvenienced, Terael said helpfully. *Step clear, for thus begins his reclaiming.*

"His what?" I asked out loud, taking half a step back out of sheer reflex. That's when I realized blood wasn't just coming from his mouth. It pooled up in his eyes, dripping like tears down the sides of his face. Blood poured from his nose, even his ears. Pretty soon it seemed to be seeping from his very pores, dark stains spreading across his fashionable clothes like he was some expensively dressed Ebola victim.

The blood wove like scarlet ribbons in the pool of water beneath him, only it didn't disperse in the water like normal blood should. Instead, it retained shape and cohesion, extending beyond the body like the questing tendrils of some alien plant.

"Uh, Terael?" I choked, staggering away from the fallen vampire. "What's happening?"

It is his reclaiming. He recalls himself to his mortal anchors.

Anchor. I'd heard that word before—the message on the answering machine. I still didn't know what it meant. I took another halting step back.

There was no denying it now. The crimson streamers of blood weren't flowing out of the body so much as they were writhing, as if they had sense and will of their own. I was reminded of half a dozen horror movies, most of which ended with the world being taken over by some semi-sentient blob. Feeling my gorge rise thickly, I backed away from the bleeding corpse until I banged my leg into the open drawer of the filing cabinet.

The Nephilim are tied to their blood, my sibling. Just as they can empty their mortal vessels, so too may they fill them. They feed them blood and power so they can reclaim them, should their own flesh be destroyed.

"By reclaiming, you mean take over—like possession?" I knew I needed to deal with the stuff in the filing cabinet, but I couldn't tear my eyes away from the gruesome spectacle unfolding in front of me.

Of course, my sibling. The best anchor is chosen, though sometimes it is merely the closest—and then they merge, spirit to flesh.

"That is beyond creepy," I breathed.

The tendrils seemed to have reached the limit of their cohesion, and something like a red mist rose from the blood and the body alike. It shimmered in the dim light of the back office, and it wasn't a strictly physical thing. I was watching the play of his power as it escaped from the physical substance, crossing into the Shadowside. It dispersed into what looked like clouds of faintly gleaming red particles, then faded entirely from fleshly sight.

I wondered briefly whether I would still be able to see the questing crimson stream floating through the space of the Shadowside, then decided that I had no desire whatsoever to put that to the test. Here in the physical world, almost all evidence of the blood was gone, evaporated alongside Kessiel's power. His clothes were still stained with it, but those stains looked weeks old, faded to brown and cracklingly dry. There was some powdery residue floating in the water on the floor, but that, too, had gone the rust-brown of old blood.

His body looked sunken and strange, more like a mummy than a minutes-old corpse. The only part of him that appeared at all like it had when I first confronted him was his thick blond ponytail. Compared to everything else, the vibrant plume of yellow hair looked wrong.

His mortal remains must be hidden from view, unless you wish my guardians to discover them.

I was still so riveted by the spectacle of Kessiel's corpse that the thunderous sound of Terael's thoughts in my brain practically made me jump out of my skin.

"You still have guards here?" I wondered incredulously. "How did they not hear that fight just now?"

I lull them to sleep and send them good dreams, though I can only occupy their little minds for so long. You must act swiftly, my sibling.

"Uh, yeah," I said, tearing my eyes away from the desiccated corpse and remembering what I originally came for. The sprinklers had done a number on the files in the open drawer, and the canvas messenger bag sitting on the desk was similarly soaked. Fortunately, everything Kessiel had managed to stuff inside the bag seemed dry enough.

Thumbing through the wet hanging folders, I looked for anything he might have missed, but it seemed like all the important stuff was already in the bag—copies of notes, entry logs, and a stack of glossy black-and-white photographs.

Curious, I pulled one of the photos out, squinting at it in the low light of the office. In the image there appeared a simple earthenware vessel, a little stained on one side but otherwise quite plain. The mouth of the jar was sealed with a cork, and the cork was fixed in place with pitch. On top of the pitch was a waxen seal. A sigil of some sort was pressed into it, the intertwining geometric symbols just visible from the angle of the picture. Along the side of the jar ran another set of symbols, scored directly into the clay.

They weren't random symbols. They included a name—a name I'd first read in the *Celestial Hierarchy* cipher.

Anakesiel.

The cipher said he was bound, along with his lieutenants. In my "Silent_War" file, he was labeled as missing. Now I had the proof of it. He hadn't just retired. The Anakim primus had been given the genie treatment.

I didn't want to believe it, but I probably had the tool that was responsible, hidden away in the lining of my biker jacket. Had I stolen the Stylus aboard Dorimiel's ship? That would explain swimming across Lake Erie without ditching the water-logged leather. The icon would have been a little obvious, stuffed in my back pocket.

"Terael?" I said. My pulse thundered in my ears, keeping time with my racing thoughts. I needed confirmation. "What—*who* was in the jars? Do you know?"

Our brother Anakesiel and others of your tribe, Zaquiel. Unfairly locked away these many years.

"Fuck me running," I swore.

Confused, Terael offered commentary on the anatomical improbability of such an action.

I continued flipping through the reference photos, still hardly able to credit what I was seeing. There were four jars in all, and they each bore angel names. I got a flash of memory—more tactile than visual. The heft of a vessel, clay rough against my palm. The sound it made as it clattered against the others when I stuffed them into the front of my jacket. A sense of urgency that made my breath catch in my throat.

"I stole the jars," I said to no one in particular. "Kessiel was right. I stole them."

I hadn't asked it as a question, but my disembodied sibling felt the need to agree. His thought-speak echoed in my mind, the sing-song tone cutting through the hammering of my heart.

You fled with them when the Unmakers violated my domain, to hide them away until such time they could safely be freed.

"Why didn't I just let them out?" I wondered, stuffing the photos back into the messenger bag and slinging it over my shoulder.

The key to binding lies with him that committed the act. Within the sigil hides the words. Speak the phrase to set them free. You and the Lady of Shades worked to discover his name, so better to divine his methodology.

"Well, I know the bastard's name now," I said. "I'll just have to get him to cough up the phrase. You don't happen to know where I put the jars, do you?"

The Lady of Shades fought so you could flee, but one of the Unmakers pursued. He chased you out beyond my domain. Past these walls I cannot see.

"All the way to Rockefeller Park, I bet. That's how we got separated," I muttered, "and then they took her. Dammit."

My guardians awaken shortly, brother. I cannot hide your space from their minds for so long.

Tick-tock, then. I glanced down at the crumpled form of the dead vampire. I was going to have to do something about that, and it wasn't going to be pretty.

34

As it turned out, I could strip and joint a dead vampire in under ten minutes. With Kessiel all dry and bloodless, it wasn't as messy as I expected, and I had a feeling I had done it before.

Probably not something to put on a resume.

With the exception of his slick leather cowboy boots, Kessiel and his blood-stained clothing fit neatly into a faded green military rucksack, which I found after rummaging around in a cabinet alongside the big metal desk. Judging from the *Dr. Who* and *Battlestar Galactica* patches sewn all over the front, it was a safe bet the pack belonged to me, so I didn't feel guilty for repurposing it. Only the thigh bones poked conspicuously out of the top.

I left the boots in the cabinet, and hoped no one would think to investigate them too closely. Then I collected the 9mm Beretta and spent casings—at least all the ones I could find. After removing the silencer, I tucked everything into the inside pockets of my biker jacket along with two spare magazines I'd found in Kessiel's clothes. It made the lines of the jacket hang all wrong, but between the messenger bag and the rucksack full of dead vampire, I was seriously running out of hands.

I had no idea what the museum guards were going to make of the fresh bullet holes all over my office. Then again, they were going to have to puzzle out the three bloody doves, as well. Given their unscheduled nap, courtesy of the local Rephaim, maybe they'd just sweep it all under the rug

Not likely, I mused ruefully.

Before I headed out, I asked Terael to put the sprinklers back on, and to leave them like that till one of the guards checked the office. He didn't like the idea, but he complied, citing respect for my domain. It would make a mess in the workspace, but it would also wash away the last traces of dead vampire. I hoped.

Considering the visibility of Kessiel's thigh bones, I didn't want to risk running into anyone on my way out, so I slipped into the Shadowside. Stepping through to the other side of reality was still a little jarring, but it grew easier each time, and this particular crossing didn't feel like a typical nexus of violence and death. I wanted to ask the Rephaim about that, but would have to save the questions for later—Kessiel had already cost me enough time.

I stomped purposefully through the shadowy realm on my way back to the *Thinker*, wondering whether it was my imagination, or if Kessiel's bones were becoming heavier. I was tempted to examine them as the rucksack jostled uncomfortably between my shoulder and my wing, then thought better of it. Given the bizarre way things tended to look in that twilight realm, I wasn't sure I was up for what I might find.

My mind turned to the demon jars, the Nephilim, and the various attacks on my person. The more I thought about them, the angrier I got—especially at Remy. Even if he didn't know about the icon, he had to know that the Nephilim primus could steal memories. Saliriel I could see covering her ass by making lies of omission...

But Remy had pretended to care.

Two-faced bastard.

By the time I came within sight of the *Thinker*, I was so worked up that my wings were leaving blue-white trails in the Shadowside. Good thing I'd given up on subtle.

Peering through the watery veil between the two halves of reality, I could just make out the forms of Lil and Remy as they waited near the statue. They were both unmistakable, each in a distinct way. Lil had that incandescent glow about her, with all the animal faces clustering near her energy. I expected them to turn wary eyes on me, but they were all focused on the figure standing next to her.

If Remy appeared to them the same way he appeared to me, I couldn't blame them. He looked just like Kessiel—a gleaming blood-red shadow with the intimation of wings.

Their voices carried across to the Shadowside, hollow and incomplete.

"...'s been too long... help, maybe?" That was Remiel, fussing as usual.

"...'s a big boy... care of himself..." came Lil's phlegmatic response.

"...such... 'mpossible woman..." he huffed.

As mad as I was at Remy, I didn't realize exactly *how* mad until I saw him like that. I sort of lost it.

With one swift movement, I stepped from the Shadowside, tossed both the rucksack and the messenger bag to the ground, then seized the vampire by the shoulders of his over-priced suit. I swung him around to face me.

"You smarmy, simpering *sonofabitch*!" I cried.

Then I smashed my fist into his face. I caught him right in the mouth, cutting my knuckles and his lip. Remiel was too shocked to do anything but stumble backward, blinking.

"Tell me you didn't know about it," I bellowed, grabbing him by the lapels. I threw him up against the base of the *Thinker*, lifting him with a strength I barely realized I possessed. "Go ahead. Lie again to my fucking face!"

As Remy worked to muster a response, Lil grabbed my elbow and tried to yank me away.

"What the hell, Zack?" she cried.

I shrugged her off, rattling him till his head knocked against the base of the heavy bronze figure. Remy struggled feebly, but he didn't strike back—just stared with that unearthly blue gaze.

"Zaquiel!" Lil shouted, smacking my arm with the back of her hand. She didn't hit hard enough for me to really feel it through the leather of the biker jacket, but the way she intoned my name sure got my attention.

I faltered just enough to set Remiel back down on his feet. Clenching my fists till my knuckles cracked, I seriously considered popping him again. Remy turned and spat blood onto the ground, pulling a handkerchief from his breast pocket to wipe the rest off of his face. His lip already seemed to be healing. Lucky bastard. No wonder Kessiel didn't stay down, even with a bullet in his head. They healed almost as fast as Wolverine.

"What's gotten into you?" Remy demanded.

"Your tribe aren't just bloodsuckers. You fucking eat memories," I growled accusingly. "You didn't think that was important enough to mention?"

My brother locked eyes with me, his expression hurt in a way that had little to do with the cut on his lip.

"Zaquiel, it's not like that," he stammered. "I—"

"You what?" I yelled, lunging at him. "Didn't want to disobey your hierarchy? Or maybe you didn't want me knowing the ugly truth?"

"I... didn't think it was relevant to your situation," he murmured half-heartedly.

Slamming the heels of my hands against his chest, I drove him backward into the *Thinker* again.

"Didn't think it was *relevant*?" I roared. "Who are you protecting? Saliriel? Your primus? Does it even matter, so long as I'm too ignorant to figure things out?"

"Zaquiel!" Remy pleaded.

"OK, that's it," Lil snapped. She reached up from behind me, looping her arms through my elbows. Pivoting sharply, she twisted my upper body one way while sweeping my long legs out from under me in the opposite direction. There was a moment where I thought I heard the purring growl of a great cat, and felt a pressure like massive paws bearing down upon my chest, but it all happened too quickly to be certain.

Then, before I could say boo about it, Lil had me pinned on my side, practically kissing the pavement.

"We are *not* doing this," she said firmly, one elbow driving the side of my face against the concrete. "Not out here. Not right now. You want to scream at him, you do it in the car, where we won't attract attention. Got it?"

"Bastard's been lying to me this whole time," I objected, thrashing.

"Oh, like I didn't tell you that before you dragged him along?" she responded. "Cry me a river."

Standing over me, a desperately pained expression on his face, Remy said, "I have not lied. I don't know why you're so angry at me, brother."

I was almost calming down, but that just set me off again. I struggled against her grip, spitting curses in that long-dead language I couldn't master with conscious thought. Something way heavier than a five-foot-four redhead pressed me into the concrete. If I closed my eyes, I could see the lioness lying on me, her paw casually resting on the side of my face.

"Get a fucking grip," Lil demanded.

"Dammit, Lil," I objected. "Let go already."

"If I let you up, are you going to be a good boy, and stop hitting the vampire?"

Under any other circumstances, that comment might have had me laughing, but I just couldn't let it go. I strained against her, but she continued holding me prone as if it cost her no effort at all.

"I was attacked by one of the Nephilim," I snarled.

"That's how I lost my memory. Your fucking primus can steal power and memories—and you didn't think that was relevant to my situation?"

"How can it be?" he sputtered. "Our primus is on the other side of the world, Zaquiel. He's never set foot in the United States—not even when they were colonies."

"So he sent a decimus to do his dirty work!"

Remy crouched down so he could look at me, eye-to-eye. "Only the primus could take from you in that way," he said with a patient, wounded sincerity, "and even he swore never to do so, as part of the *Covenant of the Six*. That was twenty-five hundred years ago, Zaquiel. A decimus couldn't do that. Not to one of our own."

"Oh, yeah?" I demanded. "What if he had the E—"

Lil slammed her hand over my mouth. I bit down on her fingers, and she ground her hips against me.

"Tease," she purred.

Remy's brows shot up, though it was impossible to tell if he was reacting to Lil's salacious comment, or because he'd guessed the word she'd made me swallow.

"You can get up if you shut up," the Lady of Beasts promised sweetly. She leaned close to my ear, so the breath of each word sent shivers down to my toes.

My head whirled with the scent of spice and vanilla and the warm pressure of her curves. I tried clinging to my anger, but the blazing fury I'd harbored for Remy was rapidly being transmuted into a different sort of heat. I knew she was using some trick on me—and boy, was it working. Before I started acting out the images of passion spilling through my head, I nodded against her hand.

"Good boy," she cooed, peeling back her fingers, one by one.

As soon as I had breathing room, I tried to speak before she could react.

"Neferkar—"

Lil grabbed a handful of hair at the back of my head, whipped my face around at a less than comfortable angle, and devoured the rest of my statement with a kiss. My tenuous hold on rational thought fell before the silken pressure of her tongue. Twisting beneath her, I reached up to bury my hands in her hair, but she shifted to keep me pinned, scissoring her legs through my own.

Never relinquishing her grip, she broke the kiss off slowly, leaving me gulping air. Her gray eyes were fixed on mine, but all I could focus on was the little Cupid's bow at the center of her full, red lips.

Carefully, she shaped the words, "Mum on the icon." Then she hauled me up till I was sitting with my back against the pedestal. Too dazed to marvel at her strength, I scrubbed at my mouth while my brain stripped a few more gears. I could still feel the touch of her lips lingering against my own.

Remy just stared.

"What was that for?" I choked.

Lil gave me a look.

"But," I sputtered, pointing to Remy. "My brother. You're married."

"*Were* married," he corrected softly.

Lil laughed, tossing her wild locks of red. "Like that's ever stopped any of you."

I looked to Remy for confirmation, while I struggled

to get hold of myself. My pulse throbbed everywhere Lil had touched me—and at least one place she hadn't reached. I knew she'd whammied me, but that didn't help to quell the very visceral reaction.

Remy found the nightscape stretching above us intensely captivating. He took a few discreet steps away, feigning disinterest in my plight. Lil took that moment to shove her smartphone at me.

"Don't share this information," she warned.

I was still stuck. "You kissed me. What about Lailah?"

"Some things sisters always share," she replied with the grin of a cat picking canary feathers from its teeth. "And look, you're not arguing anymore. So get a move on. We're too obvious out here."

I squinted down at the phone. She had it on its dimmest setting, and I could just make out what was on the screen. A PDF file—the missing pages of the French book. I glanced up at her as I started getting to my feet. She gave me that look again and laid a finger against her lips, urging silence, but the sight of them brought back all the sensations. It nearly put me on my knees.

"You play dirty," I complained. I slipped the phone into my pocket while Remy still wasn't looking.

"Dirty would have been grabbing that polearm you're packing," she replied sweetly.

Remiel choked and tried covering it with a cough.

"Sure. Laugh it up, fang-face," I said. "You still have some explaining to do."

"Not until we're out of here," Lil warned. She bent down and hefted the backpack full of Kessiel. She didn't even look twice at the round knobs of the femurs sticking out of it. I grabbed the nearby messenger bag and started riffling inside for the damning photos of the demon jars.

"Car," Lil ordered. "Now." And she started walking.

"When she gets like this, it's useless to argue with her," Remy whispered.

"Not helping," I snarled.

Remy offered me one of his very Gallic shrugs.

I chewed my cheeks, struggling to drive the smell of musk and vanilla from my head. It seemed to cling to everything.

35

I called shotgun. Unfortunately, neither of them seemed to understand what that meant. Lil froze for instant, scanning the trees for an actual shooter. The street was empty at this hour—not even a stray cat skulked among the cars parked along the curb.

"That means you get into the back seat, Remy," I explained.

He shrugged without comment, the heels of his shoes clicking smartly on the pavement as we crossed East Boulevard. Lil thumbed her key fob and the lights on the Sebring flashed twice. Then the engine started up. *Fancy.* She shifted the rucksack on her shoulder, letting Remy pull ahead of her.

"Who's the dead guy?" she asked. She kept her voice low as my sibling ducked into the car.

"Kessiel," I replied.

"Nephilim?"

I nodded. We stopped walking about ten feet away

from the convertible. Lil waited for Remy to shut the door after getting in.

"His ears are good. He can probably still hear us," she breathed. It was so quiet, she might have been talking to herself.

"Why all cloak and dagger?"

"When you see those missing pages, you'll understand," she answered, "but I think you know already. It's back in play, isn't it?"

I started to respond, but she made a cutting motion at her neck. "Not where he might hear you. He finds out, then Sal finds out, and that would be bad for everyone. Why do you think I interrupted you back there?"

"You kissed me," I objected.

"And?" she responded. "You didn't like it?"

"No—I mean—that's not the point," I fumbled. "You did it just to shut me up."

"Of course I did." She laughed. "Doesn't mean it wasn't fun." With a smug look, she started walking again. I tried not to stare at the way her hips swayed, the rucksack bouncing jauntily. I failed. She opened Remy's door and shoved the over-stuffed bag of bones into his lap. She made sure she bent in my direction while she did it.

"Do something with this," she said curtly.

He blinked, frowning at the bag.

"Are those human femurs?"

"Depends on what you consider human," she replied, then she slammed the door shut on him, and got in on the driver's side.

I stepped around and slid into the passenger seat. Lil

sat behind the wheel of the car doing that maddening thing with her nails. Remy had eased the bag full of Kessiel onto the seat beside him. He didn't look too happy about it, and I didn't offer him a chance to ask me questions. I had other things on my mind.

Reaching into the messenger bag, I pulled out the photos and all but shoved them at him. He took them wordlessly and sat for a few minutes, slowly poring over the images.

"I'm not sure what I'm looking at," he murmured at length.

There was a streetlamp not three car lengths away, and with his night vision, I knew he wasn't having trouble seeing. Irritably, I twisted around to check which one he was holding.

"Those are reference photos from my office," I explained. "They're the demon jars the *Plain Dealer* was talking about."

He frowned, delicate brows drawing together. "Yes, but this writing, Zaquiel—"

I cut him off. "What, you can't read it?"

"I can read it without difficulty," he retorted. "That's the problem."

"Then stop pretending you're shocked by it. That's exactly who it says it is." "But it can't be," he objected.

"Why not?" I demanded.

"For the same reason that none of the Nephilim could be responsible for your amnesia, Zaquiel."

"Enlighten me," I shot back.

Remy made an irritated sound, twitching the photo. "Only your tribe can bind someone like this, and only the primus can bind souls as complex as ours. He can't be in a jar himself. It's a paradox."

"So you're saying no one else could learn how to do that? I've taught you a few things about the Shadowside. You said it yourself."

"That's different," Remy objected. "What you propose is impossible—especially after the Covenant of the Six."

"What if you sucked the power to do it right out of my soul?"

Lil cleared her throat warningly. I was too close to what she wanted me keeping from Remiel.

"Again, impossible," he cried.

"I need to know where we're going," Lil broke in. "Maybe you could take a look at my *phone* and enter the address for me, Zack."

"Hunh?" I responded. "Oh, sure..." I pulled out the little device and glanced over it while Remy continued to frown at the photos. He was acting like, if he stared at them hard enough, the names on them might change. Lil regarded me out of the corner of her eye, pecking at the steering wheel the whole time. I gritted my teeth and tried to block out the nerve-shredding sound.

She'd tracked down the missing pages from de Garmeaux's book. They contained sketches of items from an archaeological dig originally funded by an Englishman, then seized by Napoleon on his infamous jaunt through Egypt, back in the late 1700s. My eyes were drawn to one particular name—Dorian Hartleigh. It couldn't have been coincidence.

Dorimiel.

I angled the phone toward the passenger-side window,

scrolling swiftly through the PDF. My thumb froze above a sketch of one of the treasures. My stomach dropped like a runaway elevator.

It was an Eye of Horus—but not just any Eye of Horus. Central to the eye was a thick, dark stone. It looked as if the pendant had been shaped to accommodate the slightly oblong chunk of rock, not the other way around. The sketch was black and white, but in my mind's eye, that stone burned a dark and bloody red. I didn't need anyone to tell me what I was looking at.

The Eye of Nefer-Ka.

With nerveless fingers, I shoved the phone back at Lil. She gave me a look. I gave her one right back. I turned to say something to Remiel—which, for the record, didn't have anything to do with the icon, but Lil misunderstood. She raised her hand, ready to smack me the minute I opened my mouth.

Remy chose that moment to pass the reference photos back to me.

"I understand now why you're so upset," he began, holding the images poised between us. He glanced pointedly to Lil, adding, "And why Lilianna is trying so hard to shut you up about it, but I assure you, I knew nothing of these things."

Beside me, Lil ground her teeth, her features locked in a furious scowl. She didn't even bother to correct her name.

Remy tapped the topmost image with a gleaming, manicured nail. It was the jar with Anakesiel.

"If he is really in here," he said in barely a murmur, "there is only one way it could have happened. It's unthinkable, but no other conclusion makes sense.

Someone uncovered the icon of the Anakim primus, and they used it to bind the man himself. I didn't think such a thing was even possible."

Shit. Now we were in territory I didn't want to make common knowledge. One icon on the table was bad enough.

"Uh—why does it have to be the Stylus?" I stammered. "There are other Icons out there. Your tribe has something that can steal powers, right?"

Lil shot me a speculative look—then jabbed her elbow into my ribs. At least it wasn't the side with the gun. Remiel piqued a brow at this exchange, but opted not to comment.

"I'm not sitting here and swapping theories all night," she complained. "Lailah's still out there somewhere—or did you two forget? My sister's in trouble because of your shit."

"Dorimiel has her out on a boat," I answered. I rubbed my side, feeling both annoyed and contrite.

"Dorimiel again?" Remy wondered. "Is that why you were asking about him at dinner?"

"Don't feign ignorance," I demanded. "He's behind this whole damned thing."

Remy scowled and fussed with the end of his braid. "We don't keep close tabs on one another. Not outside of our own hierarchies—and besides, Dorimiel was gone for such a long time."

"That's what you said at dinner."

"Shall I spell it out for you? He was bound," Remy stated flatly. "As a consequence of the last of the Blood Wars. You throw accusations at me right and left,

Zaquiel, but the members of your tribe are hardly blameless. That includes you," he added with quiet heat.

I thought back to the murderous scene in the temple and shut my mouth.

"Tell me you at least have the location of the boat," Lil said.

"Nope," I admitted glumly. "Kessiel was more interested in dying than revealing the master plan."

"Oh," Remy responded, poking the bag of bones on the seat beside him. "So that's who this is."

"He started it," I shot back.

Lil smacked her hands against the steering wheel, hard. "If you two don't stop fucking around," she shouted, "I'm going to drive this car right into the lake. Get me something I can use to help my sister!"

"What about Saliriel?" Remy offered.

Lil emitted a strangled sound of wordless rage.

"Are you nuts?" I demanded.

Undeterred, Remy persisted. "This is her territory. If Dorimiel is responsible for these events, she is the local decimus. She needs to know of these things."

"That was my fucking point," I snarled. "She has to know what's going on. How can she *not* know?"

"Zaquiel. She is not as bad as you think," Remy objected, shooting me that wounded expression that was beginning to irritate the hell out of me. I was tempted to smash it right off of his face. I clenched my fist so tightly the cuts on my knuckles reopened. My sibling inhaled sharply.

He could probably smell the blood.

"If Saliriel was a part of this, do you think I wouldn't

know?" he asked. His clipped and proper accent grew thicker the more defensive he got. "What you are claiming is no less than a conspiracy, brother. It could easily re-ignite the Blood Wars. Saliriel *must* be informed."

Lil sneered at him in the rear-view mirror. "Remy—dear heart—if your naïveté didn't get people killed so often, it would almost be charming."

"Lilianna—"

"Don't 'Lilianna' me. Do you seriously believe Saliriel is in the dark about any of this? If anything, he's cheek to jowl with Dorimiel, orchestrating the whole conspiracy."

"She," Remy corrected quietly. "Allow her that much, please."

"Fuck that!" Lil pounded the steering wheel again, growling in frustration. "You're impossible!"

My thoughts strayed to tattered memories of Dorimiel and the Eye of Nefer-Ka. The marks he'd left above my heart twinged—though maybe that was just a memory, too. Was it possible to feel an absence of being?

"Let's do it," I said.

"Do what?" Lil squawked.

"Let's go see Saliriel," I said. "Confront her directly, now that we have more information. The worst she can do is throw us out."

Lil barked a bitter laugh. "You've forgotten a hell of a lot if you think that's the worst Sal can do."

"I'll talk to her," Remy promised.

Lil glowered at the both of us. A muscle ticked in her cheek as she clenched her jaw.

"Fine," she grumbled. She turned to Remy. "You'll talk to her. Then what? You'll cave the minute she tells you to. I've played that tune before, Remington," she spat. "I know how it ends."

"This is different," he protested.

"Oh?" she demanded with a little toss of her head. "And how is it different?"

With quiet vehemence, he said, "This involves family."

Lil ground her teeth, snarling furiously, "At least I know where I rate." Then she gunned the motor and tore onto the street.

36

Lil took a circuitous route to the Flats, navigating a maze of backstreets that had me feeling irreparably lost after the first five minutes. A strict edict of silence reigned in the car as she raced down one-way streets and whipped around curves. She didn't even do that restless thing with her nails—just gritted her teeth and choked us in a smothering pall of unspoken fury.

Maybe it was Lil's mood, but I thought the city had a post-apocalyptic feel at this hour. Sure, it was close to two in the morning, but in any other city we would have passed at least a little foot traffic—vagrants, restless teens, locals stumbling home from the bars—something. It was a Friday night. Instead, the streets we drove were empty, with the exception of parked cars mutely lining the curbs.

When we got to Club Heaven, the lot was nearly deserted. This only underscored the impression that it was a zombie apocalypse version of Cleveland. I half-expected to see shambling hordes of walking dead lumbering across the empty lot, dragging themselves from the depths of dumpsters, sewers, and derelict factories.

The thought stopped being funny once I remembered the other night.

There were a few beat-up trucks near the door of the club, a couple of them with logos for industrial repair and construction companies. They would have been more at home at a redneck bar.

"Oh, damn," Remiel muttered as we pulled up to the empty lot. "The repairs were scheduled for tonight. I forgot entirely. Saliriel will be furious."

"It sucks to be you," Lil muttered. She swung the car in a sudden arc, wheels spitting loose gravel. Then she skidded to a halt. "Everybody out."

She unwound several of the pendants from the mess of charms hung from the rear-view mirror, wordlessly shoving them into her pockets. Tucking her little white clutch-purse primly under one arm, she stepped out of the car, tapping the heel of her Versace boot as she waited.

Remy and I exchanged glances, each daring the other to ask her about the charms. Neither of us was willing to risk it. Before I slammed the door behind me, I grabbed the rucksack full of Kessiel and tucked one of the reference photos into my jacket. Remy frowned a bit as I hefted the sack of dead vampire, but he didn't try to stop me. He headed toward the entrance of the club.

Lil and I followed mutely along.

The double doors of Club Heaven appeared locked up tight. As we approached the awning, I could just spy a makeshift sign tacked to the door with electrical tape.

REPAIRS TONIGHT.
HEAVEN IS CLOSED.

I wondered if anyone else appreciated the irony.

Remy pulled out a ring of keys. Despite the *Mission: Impossible* complexity of the security on the back exit, the front door was relatively prosaic. He fussed with a deadbolt, then held the door open for us.

"Let me do the talking," he urged.

Lil muttered snidely, "Whatever you say, dear."

The minute we were through the doors, I was reminded why places like Club Heaven were almost never seen with all of their lights on. In the harsh overhead halogens, everything looked dirty and worn. The paint job on the partition was half-assed at best, with huge swaths that were so sparse it was possible to see the original industrial green that lay beneath. The curtains draped across the far wall turned out not to be velvet, but faded, cheap velour. They were covered with cigarette burns and other, less-identifiable stains. Most of the acoustic tiles on the ceiling were warped and sagging, and several were missing entirely.

I glanced at the floor, and quickly looked away.

Instead of throbbing electronica, the sound of hammers and power-tools spilled from the interior of the club. For a few moments there was just the productive rhythm of construction, then Saliriel's voice cut shrilly above the noise, shouting orders and reprimands with equal fervor.

"At least we know somebody's home," I muttered.

Remy pulled ahead, stepping around the corner of the

front partition. I followed along, noticing that he stopped where the cash register stood, a bittersweet expression playing across his features. Hell, even I was thinking about poor Alice, and I'd only known the girl briefly.

It made me wonder how many others had died the other night, as the cacodaimons searched for me. I wasn't sure I really wanted to hear the final head count. It was a testament to Saliriel's pull with the Cleveland police that the club was even free to start making repairs. Most places would still be closed off after an incident like that, tied up in lawsuits and red tape.

I steeled myself before I walked any further, envisioning that fist clenched tightly in my mind. I could already feel impressions plucking at me—a sense of panic, the ghostly echoes of gunfire and screams. Now wasn't the time to go all *Dead Zone* on the place. I shoved those senses to a back corner of my mind. The impressions retreated, though I still caught flickers on the periphery.

The curtain I'd pulled down on top of myself was gone, so once we passed the cash register, we had a clear view of the interior of the club. All the blood and debris had been cleared away, and an antiseptic scent hung heavily upon the air.

My sibling, the gender-bending beauty queen, stood near the center of the dance floor, overseeing the replacement of the disco ball. Her outfit was far more conservative than the previous night, and might have even passed for business casual in the outside world—low-cut V-neck, bolero jacket, a little pencil skirt and three-inch pumps—all in shades of light beige and a pink so pale it might as well have been white.

Her tinseled blonde hair was swept back from her face and pulled into a loose ponytail. This starkly accented her aristocratic features, especially the sharp sweep of her high cheekbones. It occurred to me that she looked a little like Glenn Close, though I wasn't sure the actress would appreciate the comparison.

A couple of workers stood nearby, one on a ladder operating the pulley system that lifted the huge mirrored ball into place. Another was replacing a panel of wood on one of the bars. Two bullet holes scarred the damaged section propped beside him. A trio of other guys was off in the back, repairing a railing. Among the workers, I recognized at least one of the bouncers from the night before. Out of uniform, he wore jeans and an old T-shirt with a faded Nine Inch Nails logo. It actually made him look beefier than the black-on-black monkey suit. I wondered briefly if he was on steroids, or if his excessive musculature had a creepier explanation. Terael's conversation about Nephilim feeding blood to their "anchors" rattled uneasily around in my head.

As Remiel stepped into the club proper, Saliriel looked up and called out sharply.

"Where the hell have you been?"

He rocked back as if her voice held weight and force. Then again, to him, it probably did.

"Decimus," he said, once he recovered a bit. "There are some things you need to be made aware of."

She took a step forward, lips parted to respond—and then she caught sight of me. For an instant, she studied my features with an air that seemed unusually calculating, even for Sal. A heartbeat later, the look was lost to her customary hauteur.

"Ah, Remy, you've brought your favorite stray," she mused. "How many times are you going to make me throw you out this week, Zaquiel?"

I was working on a witty comeback when Lil strode up behind me. The Lady of Beasts made a show of taking in the whole of the Saliriel's appearance, a nasty smirk on her face.

"What is *she* doing here?" Saliriel demanded, voice cracking.

"Nice to see you, too, Sal," Lil purred. "That's an interesting look for you."

Saliriel sputtered, too incensed for words. Lil's smirk curled into a full-on Cheshire grin. No mirth glinted in the steel of her eyes.

The workers in the back paused to look in our direction. Their power drills fell silent and they murmured uneasily amongst themselves. After a moment, they resumed their labor with the mien of people struggling to seem invisible.

The bouncer in the band shirt had a very different reaction. He set his tools down carefully by the bar and stepped closer to Sal. The way he stared at us, a strip search would have been less invasive.

"Please, let me explain, Decimus," Remy said quickly.

"Oh, you had better," Sal snapped.

Remy winced but forged ahead. "Zaquiel wasn't lying. The theft at the museum happened. They released news of it earlier today, and Zaquiel retrieved some evidence suggestive of a very serious issue."

"I'm listening," Saliriel said.

Remy wetted his lips, glancing our way for support. Lil wouldn't even look at him. She just kept staring at Sal, like she expected the decimus to turn into a bat, or perhaps a great white serpent. Puffing out a breath, Remiel continued.

"What do you recall of the one called Kessiel?" he said. "He was apparently seeking to steal from the museum tonight."

"Kessiel?" Saliriel said absently, and she tapped a manicured nail against a collagen-plump lip. "Why should I recall someone else's foot-soldier?"

I snorted. "Here," I said. "Let me jog your memory." I slid the rucksack off my shoulder and dragged Kessiel's skull out by its long blond ponytail. I grimaced at his shriveled features, then chucked the head at Saliriel's feet. The bouncer tensed as it clattered across the floor. It came to rest against the toe of Saliriel's shoe.

Remiel's eyes flew wide when he saw the grisly trophy.

Even Lil did a face palm.

"I can't believe you just did that," she muttered.

"What is this?" Saliriel demanded. She minced back from the head, recognition slowly gelling on her features. NIN guy kept his gaze fixed on my hands, veins cording in his neck. The bouncer working on the disco ball stopped what he was doing and backed slowly down the ladder. He wore an unbuttoned bowling shirt over his dark tee, and I was fairly certain the shirt concealed a gun.

"Want me to make him gone, Sal?" he asked, a belligerent set to his shoulders. His deep voice held very little inflection—but there was a distinctive twang to his a's. Lil and I exchanged startled glances. We had both heard that voice before. This was the man who had spoken on my answering machine—about the mysterious rendezvous at Lake View.

I clenched my left hand. It was that or start swinging at people. Lil had been right all along. Sal was neck-deep in this shit.

"Which angel was it, Sal?" I demanded, choking past the rising fury. "You know, in Lake View Cemetery." I couldn't keep the threat out of my tone. Both bouncers moved with purposeful steps to shield their mistress, creating a wall of human muscle between us and Saliriel. Bowling shirt guy didn't have his gun out yet, but his right hand hovered near the small of his back.

The workers in the back picked up their tools and found something else to do, as far on the other side of the club as they could manage. I almost felt sorry for them.

With languorous grace, Saliriel bent at the knees and retrieved the skull. She rose just as slowly, smoothing her skirt with one hand while the other gently cupped the desiccated head. Kessiel's shriveled lips skinned back from his teeth, gratuitously displaying the fangs.

"You killed him," she observed coldly. "There will be repercussions for this, Zaquiel."

"You should answer the question, Sal," Lil demanded. She had gone very, very still, her little purse tucked casually under one arm.

"Don't speak," Saliriel spat. "I don't take orders from you."

"Lake View? What are you two talking about?" Remy whispered. He looked anxious and perplexed, and with all his hair pulled back in the braid, he didn't have an easy way to hide it.

"Sal knows," I answered, speaking more to the decimus than to my brother. "I've got a feeling Sal knows lots of things about this mess."

Again I caught a flash of that intensely calculated look from Sal. Yellow fire glimmered in the depths of her eyes, and I wondered what the decimus was trying to see.

"You have proof of this incident at the museum?" she inquired. She toyed with Kessiel's head, turning it to face me. "More than a corpse, I hope."

I nodded.

Pressing her sculpted lips together, she said, "Show it to me." With a poisonous look toward Lil, she added, "In private."

Then she tossed the skull with its bright plume of hair casually to one of her bodyguards—the one without the concealed firearm, I noted. He caught it without hesitation, tucking it in the crook of one elbow with the air of a man who was accustomed to handling random bits of corpses.

"See to it that this disappears," she ordered.

I wondered idly if minions got time and a half for disposing of bodies. Sal turned abruptly on her heel and started walking toward the back of the club.

Lil made a hissing sound of displeasure.

"Don't do it Zack. That's how she gets you. Divide and conquer." To Sal, she yelled defiantly, "Anything you need to say, you can say in front of all of us."

Witheringly, Sal called back, "You present your case to me in private or not at all, Anakim. Remy, please calm the Lady of Beasts. I don't want to have to clean up after another fight. We just got the blood out of the tiles."

Lil snarled her displeasure, a threat clear in every line of her face. The bouncers both reacted, rising onto the balls of their feet. They faced off with the petite redhead, and I didn't think they'd be bested with a smile and a flash of cleavage.

"Still as uncivilized as the beasts you command? Please," Sal sighed. "Boys, restrain her if she becomes a problem, and put on a little music to entertain our guests. Perhaps some VNV Nation. If I recall, Zaquiel's fond of *Beloved*." She delivered the order with an exaggerated flick of the hand.

"Get back here, bitch," Lil growled. "You might get away with pushing Remy around, but you have no authority over one of the Anakim. Zack—you don't have to go with her." She twined the fingers of her left hand in an oddly geometric position.

The tang of generic disinfectant suddenly gave way to a wholly different scent—hot sun, warm earth, and dry, dusty grass. The lioness ghosted to life beside her. The beast wriggled her haunches, ready to pounce at the slightest provocation.

"Back off," warned the heavy in the NIN tee. He didn't seem to see the lioness, but he clearly knew that something was up.

"Give me a reason," Lil snarled.

"Lilianna, please," Remy whispered desperately. Turning to me, he said, "Zaquiel, you've been in here twice this week seeking help from Saliriel. Isn't this what you wanted?"

"Zack, seriously," Lil hissed between her teeth. "This is a bad idea."

The lioness chuffed once and started pacing. Her gleaming gold eyes tracked Saliriel as she continued toward the far end of the club.

"Sal doesn't boss me around," I agreed, "But neither do you, Lil. This is my call." I eased the backpack onto the floor, not wanting to rile the bouncers any further. Then I turned to my brother.

"If this goes south for any reason, you do everything in your power to help Lil find her sister, you hear me?" I demanded. "I might not remember, but Lailah was special to me, too."

His gaze flicked between me and the naked knobs of Kessiel's thigh bones. He couldn't bring himself to look at Lil. Wordlessly, he nodded.

With a deep breath—and wondering whether I'd taken leave of my senses—I stepped through the living gate of Sal's two muscle-bound attendants. Then I followed the towering figure of the Nephilim decimus as she strode toward the soundproofed back rooms.

37

"We had a deal, Anakim," Saliriel snapped.

We faced off tensely in the silver-spattered room. I hovered near the back, avoiding the psychic stain where Alice's death was blazoned across the threshold. Sal had her arms folded under her breasts in that disturbingly provocative gesture while she leaned a hip against the arm of one of the leather couches. I'd expected a lot of things to happen once the door swung shut, but this wasn't one of them.

"It might help if I remembered any of it," I countered.

"Yes, well," she sniffed. "I have to accept that you're not faking."

"Why the fuck would I fake this shit?" I demanded.

"The power that the Eye holds is very alluring, especially for someone with your checkered past. I couldn't rule out a double-cross," she said, her yellow cat-eyes fixed on my own. Pointedly, she added, "I still don't."

Words failed me. My mind raced through the events of the past forty-eight hours—the cacodaimons, the cipher, the insanity at the museum. Lailah.

"You need to tell me what the hell is going on, right the fuck now," I hissed.

She shifted her weight till she was sitting fully on the arm of the couch, legs primly crossed at the ankles. She balanced with a shoulder against the wall.

"Like I said, we had a deal," she repeated. "I give you the means. You confirm that the Eye is back in play. I got you to that ship once, Anakim. I didn't expect you to fail. You're normally more efficient than that."

I wanted to smash the disapproving look right off her face. Instead, I pressed my palms hard against my temples. There were so many scenarios whirling in my head. I didn't know which way to jump.

"And Remy?" I asked. "He in on it?"

Saliriel stood so swiftly I didn't even see her move. One minute she was lounging on the arm of the couch, the next, she had me by the shoulder. Her long fingers vised into the leather of my jacket as she spun me around.

"You tell him *nothing*," she hissed. Her face was inches from my own.

"Back off," I said and shoved.

To my surprise, she let me. Crossing her arms again, she started pacing. Her heels ticked like a metronome against the tiled floor.

"The icon must remain a secret," she said with quiet intensity. "From everyone."

I watched her as she moved, trying to get a read on her body language. I'd grown accustomed to a certain level of flounce from Sal. Back here, however, all of that was missing. Lil's many warnings clamored in my head. How much of Sal's demeanor was genuine? I was tempted to drop some of my shields, to sense my sibling on that other level, but the pressure from Alice's death bore down on me even though I was standing at the far end of the room. I wasn't certain I had the control yet to block out one while sensing the other.

"So all that posturing and denial the other night—that was for Remy's benefit?" I wondered.

"In part," she allowed, "but as I said before, I thought you might be bluffing. The attack that followed in your wake? You work with spirits. You could have set that up." She grimaced unhappily. "And it would be just like you to use my resources, then keep the goods for yourself."

"That's not like me at all!" I objected.

Her pale yellow eyes locked onto mine.

"Are you so certain of that?"

I couldn't respond. What did I have for an answer? All that was left to me were ragged memories of the man I once was—and if I was being honest, I wasn't certain that man was exactly a saint. I leaned wearily against the back wall, my wings ghosting out of the room.

"All right," I acknowledged. "Forget that. You don't trust me, I don't trust you. We're even," I said. "But if you wanted to keep it secret, why bring me in on it at all?"

The edges of her plump, pink lips curled into a delighted smile. I had a sinking feeling that the proverbial scorpion once wore a smile like that—right before it stung the equally proverbial frog.

"My dear Zaquiel," she answered, "you were the one who told me the Eye might have been recovered."

I blinked. "I did?"

"That meeting, Thursday morning. Lake View Cemetery," she prompted. "I set a time and a place to hear your offer."

"What offer?"

"You promised to wipe a certain file in exchange for passage to Dorimiel's vessel."

"How did you even know about those files?" I choked.

Saliriel's smile widened, exposing her fangs. "Because I am very good at this game, brother... and you are extremely predictable."

I stood there and quietly fumed, reminding myself that she could be making all of this up—and with my ravaged memory, I had no sure way of knowing better. So I waited for her to continue.

"With your typical blundering boorishness, however, you failed to comprehend why I would refuse to act directly against another decimus of my tribe."

"Is that a fancy way of saying you told me no?" I asked.

Saliriel laughed once, a harsh, dry sound. "Not exactly, Anakim—simply that I required more incentive to risk my own neck for a single missing woman. Transporting one of your kind across the water, so you could infiltrate my sibling's ship? Treasonous. So you brought up the matter of the Eye, insisting that Dorimiel was a threat to us both."

"And I was willing to hand over the Eye to you, just like that," I scoffed. "Not likely."

She arched a perfectly plucked brow. "And why not? I'm a decimus of the Nephilim. I've handled it before. I know its powers—and its price."

"No," I insisted.

Her painted lips curled in a feral grin. "Yet you brought pages torn from an obscure archaeological text in French, to prove to me that Dorimiel had acquired the Eye," she purred. "Do you recall that book, or did he take that from you, too?"

I struggled to process all this new information, reconciling it with what I already knew. Was Sal lying? Of course she was—her lips were moving—yet some of it rang true. So I tried poking holes in anything that struck me as inconsistent.

"How did you *not* know?" I asked.

"Hrm?" Sal responded.

"The Eye," I insisted. "It's an ancient Icon that belongs to *your* primus, and it's in the hands of another decimus. Someone from *your* tribe. If you're so good at this game, how did you not know?"

The smug expression faltered.

"I wish I had an answer," she responded, "but if Dorimiel truly uncovered the Eye during that expedition—and we must accept the possibility, given what's happened to you—then he has been extremely... discreet about it. I would have expected him to flaunt such power."

At no point did she mention the Stylus. I filed that away for later—I needed every advantage to keep on top of her game.

"He has kept his secrets well," she observed, and the wily quirk of her lips returned by degrees. "But this works in our favor."

"Your favor, you mean," I said bitterly. It still didn't sit right. "Why the hell did you meet with me

Thursday morning, anyway? I heard how things went down Tuesday, when I first came to you for help. What changed your mind?"

"Let's be clear," she snapped. "Tuesday night you didn't come here looking for help, Zaquiel. You came in here to accuse me of attacking you and your precious museum. Even Remy lost his temper—and that should tell you something," she added with a sneer.

"Fine. I'm an asshole," I responded. "Which makes Thursday even more confusing."

She sighed. "Wednesday night Dorimiel sent one of his people to speak with me." With a sniff of disdain, she continued. "That was the first I learned they were out on my lake. They had been there nearly three weeks, and hadn't even had the courtesy to email me."

I bit back a smart-assed comment. Sal was as delusional in her own way as Terael, who thought the museum was his own private temple.

"So what—Dorimiel's lackey just copped to breaking into the museum?"

"Actually, he asked for my help in retrieving some things he felt belonged rightfully to his decimus." There was a sudden edge to her voice, switchblade sharp and directed at me. Eyes agleam with yellow fire, she said, "You'd never told me what was stolen, Zaquiel. Which of my people are bound in those things?"

"Your people?"

"I read the papers today," she spat. "That's why Remy's so agitated about this now, isn't it? You were keeping demon jars—soul prisons—and all were made within the last two centuries. You neglected to mention that very salient detail," she growled, and she started pacing again. This time her heels struck the floor like she intended to pound straight through it.

"Who were they, Zaquiel? And how did your tribe manage to circumvent the strictures laid out in the Covenant of the Six, in order to lock more of us away? Anakesiel couldn't do it—he'd sworn as surely as my own primus to never use those skills on any of our brethren. Never again."

"Whoa. Hold on," I said, showing my palms. "You think *my* tribe's responsible for the jars?" That confirmed it—she knew nothing about the Stylus.

She whirled on me. "Of course your tribe. Who *else* but your tribe? Anakesiel and the rest of you and your endless judgments—those sanctimonious atrocities should have ended with the Blood Wars."

Slipping a hand into my leather jacket, I pulled out the photo I had tucked away. Wordlessly, I held it out to her. She sneered at it and hesitated, as if expecting some trick.

"All our cards on the table," I said. It was a lie—but for once, a convincing one.

She leaned a little closer, peering at the letters pressed into the clay.

"This is an image of one of the stolen jars?"

"It is," I responded.

Sal snatched the photo from me, incredulity twisting her features.

"Haniel?" she read. "But this is one of the Anakim."

I'd made certain to leave the image of Anakesiel's jar under the seat in Lil's Sebring. Remy would tell her about that one, sooner or later, but the longer I could deflect her from asking about the Stylus, the better.

"Surprise," I said.

38

"Time's up, Zack!"

That was Lil's voice. She yelled so stridently from the other room that the words actually carried through the soundproofing of the door.

"What the hell?" I murmured.

"You don't come out right now, I'm coming in after you!"

I pulled the door open a crack. Outside, there were muffled sounds of a struggle. Saliriel caught my wrist and pushed the door closed again, pressing the lock on the knob.

"Are you saying that Dorimiel bound him?" she hissed. "How?"

"That little Nephilim trinket you sent me after takes powers, as well as memories. How do you think?" I shot back.

Sal's nostrils flared as she considered this, but she didn't relinquish my wrist.

"*Zaquiel*," Lil roared, and the power she put behind

it crashed against me, making the insubstantial bits of me flare with silver fire.

"Someone get that woman under control!" Saliriel bellowed back, loud enough to make my ears ring. She didn't bother to open the door, just counted on her orders to carry through sheer volume. As soon as the words were out, she turned her attention back to me.

"If I help," she said, "I require an oath."

"I'm not swearing to anything," I said.

"We can't blithely barge in on another decimus of the Nephilim—especially not if he's armed with an Icon," she answered. "Dorimiel pretends his vessel is a pleasure boat, but he's on that lake for security. No one approaches without approval. It was risky enough the first time, getting discreetly within range so you could slip onboard through the Shadowside."

"Obviously you didn't stick around long enough to help me with an exit strategy," I grumbled.

"That wasn't part of the arrangement," she replied tersely, "but it was your plan, and it failed. This time, we do things my way."

"Not a chance."

More noise came from the main floor of the club. I thought I heard Remy yelling, but with the door closed, it was too muted to make out anything of substance.

"They're looking for you. They've already come to me for help on that point. It's a perfect opportunity. They'll let us on board if they believe I'm delivering you."

I didn't like it. "How do I know this isn't some trick to get me out there willingly?"

Sal tightened her grip on my wrist, and I had the sick

realization that she could crush bones if she wanted. She locked eyes with me.

"You want my help? This is the cost. You will follow my orders without question until we get you on board Dorimiel's vessel. Everything discussed back here—including the Eye—remains our secret. You don't breathe a word to another living being. Swear it to me."

"I don't trust you, Sal. Not as far as I can shot-put your implants," I snarled. "Even if you move against them once we're on board, how do I know you won't just grab the Eye, and use it on me?"

Something heavy slammed against the door, rattling the whole frame.

"Would you rather it stay in Dorimiel's hands?"

The door shook again, and someone twisted the handle. I still had my hand on it, and Sal closed her spindly fingers over mine, forcing me to hold it in place.

"Are you seriously using the lesser of two evils argument?"

"You don't remember our previous agreements," she hissed. "I assure you, this is not our first back-room deal."

Again—frustratingly—I couldn't dispute her. I ground my teeth while she ground my knuckles.

"You swear, then," I answered. "Swear you won't use it. Not on me. Not on Remy. Not on anyone."

"As a gesture of goodwill, I will swear not to use it on you," she allowed. "Others? No—I can't predict what circumstances may arise in these changing times, and I refuse to be hobbled in matters of survival. But I assure you," she purred, "it's not my intent to abuse the Eye. I want it for safekeeping."

"Bullshit," I spat.

"With the information that I have, I could go and seize it without you," she threatened. "You *must* swear that you'll keep it a secret. No one learns of it. Not even Remy."

I hesitated, uselessly trying to tug my hand out from under hers. Sal's grip was unyielding.

"I get why you want something that powerful in your arsenal, but why hide it from Remy? He's like Alfred to your Batman."

Sal leaned down so she was nose to nose with me—so close I could see the green striations in her otherwise yellow eyes.

"I don't have time to explain to you why it's so important," she hissed, "but I won't do anything without your oath. Secrecy, and you follow my lead."

Lil and Remy's voices rose and fell on the other side of the door, and I thought I heard the muffled roar of the lioness.

Another impact battered the frame.

Yellow fire flared in the depths of Saliriel's eyes.

"I could make things very difficult for you without the slightest inconvenience to me. Dorimiel's man left me ways to contact him. Should I call to inform him that you're here with me?"

I couldn't risk calling her bluff. What would they do to Lailah?

"I'd really prefer not to burn my bridges with you, Anakim," she said. "Now swear. On your strength and on your Name," she urged, "swear to keep this discussion a secret. You will not speak of the Eye to any living being except for me, and until we get you onto the boat, you will do as I say."

I closed my eyes. I drew a breath.

And I swore.

The words shuddered through me as they were pronounced, none more resonant than the syllables of my Name. The backwash of power stirred a pale strand of Saliriel's hair that had fallen free of her ponytail. The yellow fire of her eyes flashed, then faded as the last word left my lips.

Sal nodded once, almost imperceptibly, then made her own oath to exempt me from her use of the Eye. Finally, she relaxed her grip on my hand. I peeled my fingers away from the door handle, wincing as a tingling rush of feeling began to return. A moment later, the door flew open with such force, the hinges squealed. Sal neatly side-stepped it, and I danced hastily away.

Wild-eyed, with her red hair streaming, Lil burst into the room.

"What did you do, Zack?" she demanded. "I felt the ripples. That was an oath, wasn't it?"

Remiel stumbled after her, nursing a fresh cut above his brow.

"Decimus, I'm sorry," he started.

Sal fell back into character immediately, emitting a world-weary sigh

"I shouldn't need a full security detail to maintain control over just one woman," she pronounced.

Lil ignored them both, grabbing for me. She shook the front of my jacket.

"How could you be so stupid?" she said. "What did she make you swear?"

I glanced toward Remy where he lingered in the open doorway. I wasn't sure what Lil had hit him with, but the fact that it was still bleeding was impressive. There was no sign of the other two security guards, at least not from this vantage point. Lil shook me again, her fingers digging into my leather.

"Zaquiel?" She pronounced my name like it was a threat.

"Get off of me," I spat. "It wasn't anything you didn't already ask."

Lil opened her mouth to start yelling again, but I shoved her away, pushing past Remy, as well. He gave me a querulous look, but I couldn't meet his eyes. As I stomped toward the dance floor, I heard the throaty rumble of the lioness, even over the pulse of the electronica. She lay stretched across one of the fallen bouncers, her tail lashing her flanks. He wasn't moving.

"What the hell, Lil," I called. "Did you have to kill everyone?"

"Oh, shut up," she snarled. "I just knocked them out. They shouldn't have gotten in my way."

39

"You're not coming."

Sal faced off with the Lady of Beasts, arms crossed beneath her augmented D's. The bouncers had recovered from being thoroughly pounded, and were scrambling to clear the detritus left over from the fight. I leaned against the bullet-scarred bar, trying to escape everyone's notice. I didn't want anyone talking to me—it seemed the safest way to hold to the oath.

"Like *hell* I'm not," Lil hissed.

"I am not bringing a daughter of Lilith on board a Nephilim ship," Saliriel replied. "It would be considered insulting."

Daughter of Lilith? I nearly choked. Suddenly an awful lot about Lil made sense.

"You forget the part where we're going to kill that sonofabitch," Lil objected. "Who cares about insults?"

Saliriel's gaze flicked briefly to me. "Who said anything about killing?" she asked with an imperious lift of her pointed chin. "We're going to get his side of the story."

Even Remy sputtered at this statement. "But, Decimus, the photos, the article—all of Zaquiel's claims—"

"May be nothing more than the delusions of an addled Anakim," Saliriel replied. "Have you seen any of these jars for yourself? Held them in your hands, to verify what they contain? All I've seen is a photo. Photos can be faked," she added witheringly.

"I know he's a favored pet of yours, Remiel, but please remember, he's also claimed that our brother Dorimiel has harnessed cacodaimons to do his bidding. That alone places his credibility in question."

The rumbling growl of the lioness shivered the air as her fierce mistress stalked up to Sal. With threat vibrating through every molecule, Lil snarled at her.

"Don't feed me that bullshit, Salvatore. You know something rotten is going on, and you're hip-deep in it. You've known about Dorimiel's ship this entire time, and yet you said nothing."

"Oh, please." Saliriel waved off Lil's accusations with a lazy flounce of her wrist. "It's customary for a decimus to announce himself in another's territory. He was out there for a Halloween party—not really a threat, don't you agree?" With an ugly sneer, she added, "And you will address me as Saliriel, or I will kill you where you stand."

Lil's lips peeled back to show all her teeth.

"Try it."

The sharp scent of ozone crackled on the air as they locked eyes. Timorously, Remy spoke up.

"She has a point, Decimus."

Sal whirled on her underling, fury flashing in her

inhuman eyes. It was all an act, and I couldn't even raise my voice to object. I'd given my word.

"You dare to question me, Remiel?" Sal hissed.

Convulsively, he swallowed, dipping his head out of reflex. Even so, the long, thick braid held all his hair, providing him no cover for his conflicted expression. Then he drew upon some hidden well of courage.

"Zaquiel woke up on the shore of the lake," he said through gritted teeth. "You didn't think once to mention Dorimiel's presence on those waters."

Saliriel went still as a snake stalking a rodent.

"Are you implying that I have some involvement in this?" she asked in quiet tones.

He lifted his eyes to meet hers.

"I knew nothing about the ship."

"You didn't need to know," she snapped.

"Ha!" Lil scoffed. "That's how much she values you, Remington. Haven't I been saying it all along?"

Sal was playing an elaborate game of chess, to maneuver her pieces into the positions she wanted, and I was pretty sure she wanted Lil to come along. Except it couldn't look as if that was her goal. Had she demanded it, Lil would have refused her out of pure spite. I guessed my place in her gambit.

"Let her come," I said quietly. No lightning bolts struck me as I spoke, so I was on the right track.

"It has a voice," Sal purred. "Didn't I put you in your place, Anakim? I showed the courtesy to do it behind closed doors, but if you want me to embarrass you in front of everyone here, please, go on."

"If there's nothing to hide and Dorimiel's not

involved," I responded, "then it costs you nothing to bring Lil along."

Saliriel pivoted toward me. "On the contrary, it costs me quite a bit," she replied. "I run the risk of insulting another decimus. I can't expect you to understand the manners of civilized tribes, but—"

"I'll vouch for her," Remy offered.

Both Lil and Sal turned toward him.

He almost faltered beneath the combined weight of their gaze. Then he continued with a quiet fervor.

"I'll take responsibility for her presence," he insisted. "If this comes to nothing, then the insult can fall to me. You will remain blameless."

While Lil gawked openly, Saliriel made a show of considering it. Suddenly someone near the front of the club cleared their throat. The bouncers tensed, then relaxed as a trim woman of medium height stepped into view. She wore a smart pin-striped uniform complete with a chauffeur's hat.

"The car's ready," she announced.

"Thank you, Ava," Sal said. To NIN guy, she called, "Caleb, you're coming along. Contact Gerald and Asif and have them meet us at the marina. Ivan, you're in charge of the work crew here. I want these repairs finished tonight, understood?"

The bruiser in the bowling shirt grunted his acknowledgment.

Abruptly, Lil shoved past and headed toward the chauffeur.

"I'll be in the car," she said. "Make my night and try to stop me, Sal."

Remy's lips pressed into a fretful line as he tracked her progress across the room. The little redhead strode with purpose, heels clacking smartly on the freshly cleaned tiles. When Saliriel raised no objections, he ducked his head and followed Lil. Sal swept after him, her own heels punctuating each determined step.

"Well?" she called over her shoulder.

Chewing my silence, I brought up the rear.

Beyond the doors waited a sleek stretch limo—gun metal gray and pristinely waxed. The smartly dressed chauffeur held the door, and I squinted at her as I went past. She returned my speculative look, unruffled.

"Bring any zombies this time?" she asked.

I blinked, a little taken aback. After a moment, I placed her. It was Sal's slave—the one who had managed not to get shot. I fumbled for something to say

"Um, sorry," I said lamely. "Didn't recognize you."

"With clothes, you mean," she suggested archly. "Guess you weren't looking at my face, the last time we met."

Lil snorted. "I like her."

40

We rode to the marina in silence. Lil, Remy, and I perched tensely across from Sal and her goon Caleb. Everyone avoided eye contact with everyone else. Saliriel made things easy by staring out the heavily tinted windows, watching the cityscape glide by.

Lil's lioness was stretched across the floorboards at our feet. I could feel her as a warm pressure against my ankles, and if I looked just right, I could see the pale outline of her tawny, muscled form. I almost wanted to ask Lil about the beast, but knew that was a conversation for another day.

The marina was gated. When we approached the guard shack, Saliriel had Ava pull forward so she could roll down her window and speak to the guard herself. The guy at the gatehouse was an older fellow with pockmarked cheeks and a thick, graying mustache. Saliriel greeted him warmly, pitching forward in such a way that he got a lavish view of her enhanced cleavage.

"Sully," she cooed, pitching her voice a little softer

and higher than was usual. "They still have you out here all alone on these chilly nights?"

"Indeed they do, Miss Valkyne," he responded in a voice rough from years of coffee and cigarettes. At least those were a good bet, considering the stains on his teeth.

He actually doffed his hat for her. It was styled like an old sea captain's hat, complete with a little ship's wheel pinned to the front. His whole outfit—or uniform, rather—made him look like the escaped mascot of some obscure seafood restaurant. If he rang a ship's bell when we left him a tip, it would complete the effect.

"Well, I know it's late, but I need to go out," she chirped. "Early meeting."

Sully consulted a clipboard hung from a nail above his computer.

"Twice in one week? They really got you running around—but important people like you never seem to sleep," he observed, pretty shamelessly ogling the parts he found most important.

Sal fished something out of her purse, then leaned her cleavage even further toward Sully as she handed over an ID. She also folded a crisp bill of some undoubtedly high denomination beneath the plastic identification card, and let her fingers linger briefly on the guard's hand.

"Just so we're official," she purred.

He had the most besotted grin on his face as he took her ID, punched some numbers into an archaic computer, then handed the glossy little rectangle of plastic back to her. Somewhere in the midst of all that, the money disappeared. Like magic.

"Any time, day or night, Miss Valkyne," he said, doffing his hat again. "It's always a pleasure. You be careful on those waters. This late in the season, the lake gets tricky."

She responded with her most ingratiating smile—managing to hold her lip in just such a way that it covered the tips of her fangs. Not that Sully's eyes were anywhere near her face.

Once she was done, she rapped on the divider that separated us from the driver. Then she hit the button to roll up her window. The minute the tinted glass slipped back into place, the smile slid from her features and she squared her shoulders again, smoothing the front of her shirt.

"Nicely done," Lil observed.

Saliriel practically beamed. "To misquote an old associate of ours, 'You get more with a kind word and a nice rack than you can with just a kind word.'" Nodding politely in Lil's direction, she added, "I learned a great deal, watching how you operated back then."

"Good to know you were taking notes." They faced off with rigid smiles, their expressions mean-girl sweet. Even the bouncer shifted awkwardly in his seat, leaning ever so slightly away from our group. I couldn't really blame him.

In the tense silence that followed, Remy asked, "What did he mean, second time this week?"

Sal's smile faltered, but she recovered quickly.

"Oh, that," she said. "I got restless the other day. I thought a bit of sailing might soothe me."

As lying went, it was pretty weak.

Another play, then.

"But you didn't tell me," Remy objected.

"I don't answer to you, Remiel," she replied stiffly.

He pursed his lips, swallowing any further comment, and peered uneasily out the window as the limo pulled around to park. Lil wouldn't let it drop, though. She lunged forward with an almost hungry look.

"Didn't expect the gatehouse guy to bring it up, did you?" she taunted. "I knew you gave in too easily. So what's the real plan?"

"Always so suspicious," Saliriel said.

"You can change everything about your appearance, Sal, but you can't change what's underneath," Lil pressed. The lioness lifted her head, growling softly as its mistress grew more agitated. The air crackled electrically around the Lady of Beasts and it suddenly felt way too small in the limo. The vehicle came to a stop, but everyone kept sitting on the edge of their seats, each waiting for the other to do something.

Someone rapped their knuckles on the window closest to Saliriel. I jumped, tasting bitter adrenaline—but it was just the driver. A moment later, she opened the door.

"Asif and Gerald are already here, ma'am," she said, extending a hand and helping Saliriel out. "If it's all right with you, I'll head to the *Daisy Fay* and start getting her prepped for open waters."

"Of course," Sal responded. "Thank you, Ava."

I wasn't waiting a minute longer in the limo, and I sure as hell didn't need a chauffeur to help me out. I grabbed the door on my side and stepped into the lot. Lil and Remy followed suit. As did the lioness. She chucked her head into the backs of my knees as she went by. It seemed affectionate, but it was still damned creepy.

"Zack, isn't that yours?" Remy asked suddenly.

"What?" I responded. Then I realized he wasn't looking anywhere near the lioness. I tracked his gaze without really knowing what I was looking for. I didn't see much. It was off-season, so most of the boats were in storage, though one or two were still moored at the docks. Aside from the limo, the parking lot was nearly empty.

"That motorcycle over there," he said, gesturing, "near the retaining wall."

The bike he pointed at was a sleek, black Kawasaki. It was parked up against a far wall, and there was a pink slip pasted to the front.

"I guess it's mine. Maybe?" I replied, shrugging. "How should I know?"

Lil eyed Sal skeptically.

"An innocent little cruise?"

"All the bike proves is that our sibling has been stalking my yacht," Saliriel snapped from the other side of the limo. "Given his quirks lately, that's hardly the strangest thing he can be accused of."

I went over and took a closer look. According to the pink slip, it was an unauthorized vehicle and scheduled for towing. That figured, though I noted with interest that the slip recorded the date. Thursday—the day I turned up in the lake.

So I'd come to this marina willingly.

"Are you joining us or just standing there fondling your machine?" Saliriel called.

Grabbing the slip of paper, I pocketed it. It had a

number to call in case the vehicle was impounded. If it really was my bike, I wanted to come back for it—assuming I survived the impending confrontation.

I was beginning to have my doubts about that. Lil, Remy, and I weren't exactly an overwhelming force, and despite her reluctant cooperation, I had no reason to think that Saliriel would actually take our side if any fighting broke out—and there was bound to be fighting. Dorimiel wasn't going to hand over the Eye simply because Sal asked nicely.

Lil and the others were halfway down one of the docks. I turned to catch up, then paused when I heard the lioness chuff unhappily. Without even thinking about it, I relaxed my eyes, letting my vision cross more fully to the Shadowside so I could see what was bugging her.

Across from me, the lioness paced back and forth, her massive paws falling soundlessly against the gravel of the parking lot. She shimmered warmly in the shadows, her amber eyes like two yellow lanterns in the night. Those lambent eyes anxiously searched the waters of the lake—and I thought I saw fear reflected in their depths. I followed her gaze toward the docks and the rest of our party.

I immediately wished I hadn't.

The boats were insubstantial whispers of form floating upon a black sea. Only "sea" wasn't the right word, because that would imply some kind of substance—albeit an ever-shifting one. This was a yawning, gaping void, roiling black-on-black as far as the eye could see.

This was what Sal had meant about security. A boat was hard enough to approach physically—but on the

Shadowside, it would be nigh impossible.

Suddenly I realized I was trembling. There was a wind coming off the lake, deep-throated and chill, but I knew it wasn't the wind that left me feeling too frozen to take a single step.

Fragmented dream images rose unbidden in my mind—a chasm of shadows and endless flight, my wings burning from effort and the darkness below seeking to suck me in. A hole in my mind, and teeming horrors echoing that fresh and painful void, all eager to consume what was left of me.

These weren't nightmares. They were memories. I had thrown myself from the rail of a boat that floated even now somewhere in that formless, hungry sea, and flown desperately across the void.

"Are you coming, sibling?" Saliriel shouted impatiently. She might as well have been calling from the depths of a lightless well, inviting me to climb in.

With vision caught between the two halves of reality, I hesitated on the shore. My palms were sweating and my heart hammered so viciously in my chest that it made my ribs ache. The being from whom I'd fled—the one who had consumed my memory and bound my brothers—was still out there. Lailah was out there, too—and so was any hope for resolution.

If not victory, then at least vengeance.

"Zaquiel?" Remy called. Concern echoed in his voice.

So I put one foot in front of the other, and walked rigidly down the dock to Saliriel's private yacht. The lioness remained on the shore, pacing.

I didn't blame her one bit.

41

When we arrived at the slip, I had a vague feeling I'd seen the yacht before. Suddenly the message scribbled on the back of the business card made sense.

55 and Marginal—2

The marina was located at 55th and Marginal Road.

The yacht was shiny and new, or at least so well maintained that I couldn't tell the difference. Saliriel called it a Cantius, and the name on the side proclaimed her the *Daisy Fay*. The *Gatsby* reference fit Sal like an opera glove. The vessel looked to be forty feet long, maybe a little more, and seemed built for speed. There was a wheel room up top that also had a small entertainment area. All the fittings were rich wood or brushed chrome, and everything looked sleek, modern, and expensive.

Ava, the bondage pet who doubled as a limo driver, seemed also to be in charge of the boat. Multi-talented.

Already in the pilot house, she crisply called orders to the others—Asif and Gerald. Caleb hurried to join her. He helped with the mooring lines. No one bothered with life jackets.

Saliriel ushered us to a living space below, and while not exactly spacious, it was cozy in its way. The warm wood and brushed chrome themes repeated, with a beige leather wrap-around couch dominating the section. I spied a lavishly appointed double bed in the berth beyond. It felt more like a posh apartment, but I couldn't shake my unnerving perception of the lake.

I also couldn't stand in one place for very long.

"You'd best make yourselves comfortable," Saliriel said with a negligent wave in our collective direction. "Ava has the coordinates, but it may take as much as an hour to meet up with the *Scylla*."

"Seriously?" I said. "He named it the *Scylla*?"

Saliriel gave a haughty toss of her head. "Do you have a problem with that? He's a decimus. He can name his ship anything he wants. Why don't we ask the Lady of Beasts whether or not she still names all her cars after dead Sumerian heroes?"

Given the way Lil's eyes bored a hole through the floor, it was a good bet that the answer was yes.

I let it drop.

In a surreal twist, Sal began playing hostess, stepping over to the bar and offering us all drinks. The forty-year-old Scotch she withdrew from a cabinet under the bar probably seemed a little young to her. I wondered if she'd purchased the original bottle herself. Hell, for all I knew, she owned the distillery.

The boat began to move, and my thoughts fixated on the hungering darkness that moved of its own volition beneath my feet. Remy saw my expression and shot me a worried look. Lil was too busy watching Saliriel—I think she expected the Nephilim to put poison in the drinks.

I tried picturing the closed mental fist, tried clenching my actual fist until my knuckles ached. Nothing stopped the flood of images roiling through my mind. Flying, then falling, then sinking—all in darkness, pursued by the guilt. The agonizing memories mingled with psychic impressions until I couldn't separate one thing from another. Muttering excuses about feeling too warm, I stepped out onto the deck. At least there I could stare into the face of my fear.

Ava maneuvered the Cantius away from the marina, pointing us toward the black expanse of the lake. The sky was overcast, so not even the moon or the stars were visible to break up the monotony. Two lonely lights—one red, one green—marked the transition from the marina to the open waters. Beyond that, Erie was a light-drinking void stretched across the horizon.

Standing there, gripping the railing, I was sick with fear, but I couldn't look away. Once she was away from the marina, the *Daisy Fay* picked up speed until we were fairly skipping along the choppy waters. Spray from the lake speckled my face—or maybe that was the cold sweat I'd been working on since setting foot on the vessel.

"You won't be much help to anyone if you confront him like that."

My whole body jerked when Lil walked up next to me.

"There you go, proving my point," she added. "A little harder, and you'd go right over the railing."

"Not funny," I said through gritted teeth.

"None of this is funny," she allowed. She turned and leaned her back against the railing. "We're out-gunned and we're out-numbered. Sal has Remy drinking and reminiscing about old times down there, so I don't know if we'll be able to count on him once we arrive. Predictable. He never stays mad at her for long," she added bitterly. "And you—I know you cut some kind of deal with her. I felt the oath. That was the height of stupidity."

"It's not what you think."

"Of course it isn't," she said. The wind plucked at her hair, whipping strands of it across her face. "What did she do, extort you for the Eye?"

"No," I insisted. "All I promised was to keep—"

The words died in my throat. I gulped air and ran headlong into the power of the oath. Nothing had prepared me for this. When I tried speaking again, I got the same result. The message was right on the tip of my brain, but even the thoughts were slippery. A slow shiver of fear crept over me. Keeping my word wasn't a matter of choice.

"You should have known better, Zaquiel," she chided. "Words have power. Binding yourself to them can be crippling. Never swear anything lightly."

"Little late for that," I grumbled.

Lil shifted against the railing, lifting her face to the veiled sky. "So Sal knows about the Eye," she observed coolly.

"I, uh…" I stammered, but found myself up against the mental roadblock. So I cleared my throat, and opted for a different approach. "That thing—when you kissed me—to keep it from Remy. From the French book."

Lil pinched the bridge of her nose.

"I get it, Zack. You can stop. You sound like an idiot playing charades. Did you promise to give it to her?"

I didn't answer.

"That's something at least," Lil replied, "but she swore you to secrecy."

I still couldn't respond, and smacked my palms against the railing in frustration.

"Answer enough," Lil observed. She stepped closer, pitching her voice so I could barely hear it over the combined murmur of engine, wind, and waves. "If it's there—if he really has it—drop it to the bottom of the fucking lake. That thing should have stayed buried," she hissed. "And if you swore anything else to Sal, understand this—I am here for my sister, and I will kill *anyone* that gets in my way. You're not exempt, Anakim."

"Lil, we don't know who else is on that boat," I objected. "There could be other hostages—"

Lil cut me off with a curt gesture. "Everything on the *Scylla* needs to die, Zack," she said bluntly. "I'm not leaving a decimus of the Nephilim with any anchors." Her gray eyes went flat and cold. "Fuck Sal's diplomacy. Dorimiel kidnapped my sister. I'm going to kill him, and if the bloodsucker's going to pull his ever-living ass out of the fire, I want him to work for it. All the way across the water."

"Killing innocents," I said. "You don't have a problem with that?"

The steel of her eyes found its way to her voice. "Nothing

touched by the Nephilim remains innocent, Zack, and a week ago, you wouldn't have argued that with me."

We both fell silent, our thoughts as dark as the churning waters. Her jab at the person I used to be stung more than I cared to admit. I thought about the Eye and everything it had stolen from me.

"You think I could take it back?" I asked.

"You can't take back an oath, Einstein. The person you swore to has to release you," Lil responded.

I shook my head to show she didn't understand. I faltered, trying to find a way around what I had sworn. Fear thrilled through me at how difficult a prospect that was.

"No—you know… take it the way it was taken from me. Get my life back."

Lil's eyes widened. Her face shifted rapidly through expressions—comprehension, shock, fury.

"Don't you *dare*, Zack. Don't even think about it," she hissed. She raised a hand as if she intended to beat the thought out of me. I slapped it away angrily.

"Wouldn't you do it if you were in my place?" I demanded.

"Hell no," she growled. She balled her fists but kept them at her sides this time, muscles straining. "Don't go that route, Zack. Some weapons cut both ways." She turned abruptly and walked away, leaving me to brood in silence.

For a while all I could hear was the noise of the lake and the engine of the boat, punctuated by the roar of my own pulse thundering in my ears. Something empty throbbed over my heart—not with pain, but with absence.

42

"Is that a fucking gunboat?" I said as we headed toward a large metal hulk, floating low on the water. It had floodlights on sections both above and below the surface, and their combined luminescence made the ship appear unreal, like a mock-up on the set of a motion picture. Moisture in the night air reflected the ship's lights, surrounding them with a kind of misty halo which only helped to reinforce the pervasive sense of unreality.

Ava must have heard me.

"Asheville class. Ideal for these waters. Environmental Protection Agency has a bunch out here, especially with all the algal blooms and problems with the zebra mussels."

"To hell with the EPA," I responded. "It's a fucking *gunboat*!"

Saliriel came up from below as we made the approach. She peered at the distant vessel a moment. It was easily three times as long as the *Daisy Fay*.

"Always so dramatic." She sighed.

I nearly cackled at the irony.

"What does one of the Nephilim need with a Vietnam-era gunboat?" Lil demanded.

Saliriel shrugged philosophically. "Unless he has some interest in declaring war on Canada, I suspect he simply wanted the space."

Lil made a sour face and turned away.

Even I wasn't sold. "Oh, come on, Sal," I said.

"Size matters," she said with a smirk.

Ava cut our speed, easing the Cantius up to the side of the *Scylla*. There was activity on the gunboat's deck. I hovered at the railing, just staring across at the massive vessel. The sheer bulk of the ship kept my attention away from the dark, churning waters of the lake.

Saliriel stepped up to the wheel room with Ava and Caleb. She put Asif and Gerald to work making preparations for us to board the other vessel. Remy was still below. That left Lil with me.

"It's a lot bigger than I was expecting," she murmured.

"Still planning to kill everything?" I asked.

She shrugged. "I may need a distraction."

"That'll be easy," I mused. "They're not going to be happy to see me."

One of the figures on the *Scylla*'s deck seemed significantly taller than the others, with a familiar lithe and spindly build. Nephilim. There were reasons history referred to us as giants. Of all the "family" I had thus encountered, I measured in as the short one at six foot three.

"Here, hold my purse," Lil said suddenly. She didn't wait for a response, just shoved it at me.

I blinked down at her, mystified.

"The hell?"

As I held it loosely in one hand, she started pulling things out of her little bag of holding, stashing them on her person. With quick and practiced efficiency, she tucked the Derringer into the back of her waistband and slipped a tactical knife into the top of her boot. When she bent to adjust her pants leg, I noticed she already had another knife tucked into the top of the other one.

"What are you, a freaking ninja?"

She eyed me skeptically. "I like to be prepared. Speaking of which, take one of these," she added, digging into the pocket of her blazer and pulling out a tangle of charms. She unwound one from the mess. It was a bronze amulet stamped in the shape of a stylized sun.

I took it, and held it gingerly.

"Uh, thanks, I think," I said. "What's it do?"

"Kind of like a flash-bang. Snap the charm to activate it," she instructed. "It's just a one-shot. Face it away from you." I frowned at the gaudy little pendant, turning it around in my hand. MADE IN CHINA was stamped on the back.

"You've got to be kidding me," I muttered, but I shoved it in one of my pockets anyway.

Lil slipped another of the cheap little pendants around her neck. It appeared to be a pewter Mardi Gras mask. Purple, white, and green enamel glimmered brightly on its vaguely misshapen surface.

"Is that like the masking charm you threw on me the other night?" I asked.

"Something like that," she replied, then proceeded to untangle the remaining few charms, tucking each away in different pockets. She froze when Remy walked up to us, then quickly smoothed the lines of her suit jacket, managing to make it look like she was fussing with her clothes.

"I had no idea this was out here," he said, nodding toward the ship.

"I wonder what else Saliriel hasn't been telling you," Lil said, sneering nastily. "By the way, did you enjoy the drinks?"

"No sense turning down good Scotch," Remy replied defensively.

Lil muttered something unkind, which Remy chose to ignore.

"Unless Sal's plan is a game-changer, we're pretty well screwed," I said, gesturing toward the *Scylla*. "That's not a boat—it's a floating fortress."

The expression in Remy's unearthly blue eyes grew pensive as he studied the stark metal lines of the other vessel. He turned to Lil.

"Can you sense her?"

"What?" she asked sourly.

"Your sister," he persisted. "We should be close enough. Can you sense her?"

Lil's frown deepened as she peered over to the deck of the gunboat.

"No," she said, adding quickly, "it's hard to pick up on anything with all this water."

Remy made a thoughtful sound. More suspicious than ever, Lil twisted to make a study of him. Hurt and anger quarreled on her features.

"Sal fed you more bullshit than whiskey." It wasn't a question.

Remy didn't seek to deny it, I noted. Rigidly, they faced off with one another, Lil glowering and Remy bearing her challenge passively. Tension knit on the air between them until I couldn't stand it anymore.

"What's it mean if you can't sense her?" I asked.

Before Lil could respond, Remy said, "It might mean she's not here."

Lil shot him a withering look.

"What about dead?" I asked bluntly.

To my surprise, Lil just shook her head irritably. "No, dead would be easy. Once her spirit slipped free, she'd come to me on the Shadowside. It's the silence that's had me worried this whole time."

Kessiel's threat resounded in my mind—that they would bind Lailah even without the Stylus. I didn't want to think about that, but with the secrets Sal had me keeping, I couldn't hold onto more.

"Uh, Lil," I started, trying to figure out how to broach the subject.

"What?" She picked up on the change in my body language.

I hesitated. "She's immortal, right? Like my people?"

"We're nothing at all like your people," she responded, and I was suddenly thankful the lioness had remained on shore. Given how responsive the spirit-beast was to Lil's moods, she might have taken a chunk out of me right then and there.

I took a deep breath, and met her steely gaze.

"At the museum, before I killed him, Kessiel said something about binding Lailah."

Lil's eyes widened for an instant and then she lost it.

With a roar to rival the lioness, she threw herself on me, landing blow after blow. My leather biker jacket took the brunt of it, but she jammed the Beretta painfully into my ribs a few times. Still howling wordlessly, she tore her purse from my hands, began beating me with that—and the damned thing weighed a ton.

I threw my arms up, protecting myself half-heartedly.

"I could be wrong," I cried. "He was doing that whole monologue thing. You know the Nephilim."

That did nothing to placate her.

"Why didn't you say anything, you asshole!" she snarled. She had me up against the railing, my back arching uncomfortably over the dark waters. One push and I'd be in the lake. Terror welled up at the thought, and I twisted away.

She let me go.

"I wouldn't be able to sense her if they bound her," she huffed, "but you better hope they didn't take things that far." Her eyes were fierce as a hurricane.

Saliriel chose that moment to come down from the wheel room.

"And this is why I shall do all the talking, once we board the *Scylla*," she called. "Diplomacy isn't a strong suit for any of you."

Remy scowled a little, but didn't raise an objection.

"You seriously expect us to believe you're going to just parley him into a surrender?" Lil growled, still fuming. She pushed wind-blown strands of her wild hair back from her face, and glared defiantly at my towering sibling.

"Of course not," Saliriel snapped. "I'm going to

keep him talking until we can determine what's really going on."

"There's one problem, Sal," I said. "If I'm right about any of this, these people aren't going to be interested in talking. They want my fucking head on a platter—dissected for easy consumption."

"I have it under control," she responded. Yellow eyes flicking to mine, she added, "Just follow my lead."

"What the hell's that supposed to mean?" Lil demanded.

Instead of answering, Sal turned on her heel and strode over to where Asif and Caleb lashed the final rope between the two vessels, effectively mooring the Cantius to the anchored gunboat. The *Scylla* sat low on the water, but her deck still rose higher than that of the *Daisy Fay*. When the small party of workers on board the *Scylla* tossed down a walkway, I balked.

"We're crossing on that?"

It didn't look like much more than sections of wood and knotted rope. Caleb and Asif began fixing it to points on the Cantius without so much as a glance my way. I drew back with mounting dread.

"Marching order," Sal called. "Zaquiel, behind me. Remiel, stick close to him and be ready to restrain him should he attempt anything foolish."

"I—I would prefer not to, Decimus," Remiel replied.

"If I give you an order, Remiel," she said, biting off the end of each word, "you will follow it—as we've discussed."

"Discussed?" Lil asked suspiciously.

Saliriel talked right over her. "It's bad enough we've brought along a daughter of Lilith. I'll not risk further insults through the actions of one hot-headed Anakim. Stay behind him, Remiel, and be ready. You know how he gets."

Remy clenched his jaw, but lowered his head. His strained, "Yes, Decimus," barely carried over the shushing sounds of wind and water. While he glared unhappily at the tips of his shoes, Sal flicked her yellow-eyed gaze to me. Her look didn't linger, but it was enough. I felt the prickling power of the oath, and it was too late to back out. Too late for a lot of things.

"Where do I fit in your marching order?" Lil growled.

"You, my dear," Sal answered wryly. "Will bring up the rear."

Lil muttered angrily in some dead language, no doubt spewing curses on the lot of us. She whirled away from the railing, her barely contained fury burning a hole between my wings. Saliriel strode forward and, mutely, I fell into step behind her. Remy, more subdued than ever, hovered near my elbow. Lil was right—something had passed between him and Sal below decks, and it wasn't just some forty-year-old Scotch. How much had she told him of the plan? Not the Eye, that much was certain.

Maybe enough to get him to play along.

Can I even count on it being the same plan? The thought sped the staccato knocking of my pulse.

The reluctant Nephilim trudged miserably behind me. When I turned to check in with him, I couldn't find a single consoling word.

We filed to the newly rigged walkway, Asif tightening a final knot as we approached. Although it had handrails, the walkway looked neither sturdy nor safe. Saliriel stopped me as I hesitated at the edge. Water sucked and slapped in the narrow gulf between the two vessels. The rest of our party clustered behind me, Lil jostling Remy to peer toward the *Scylla*'s higher deck.

"Wait here while I deal with the greeting party," Sal instructed. She pointed to the very lip of the Cantius where the dark waters roiled in the gap below.

"Are you fucking kidding me?" I choked.

"It's not your place to argue," she reminded with a flash of fangs.

I seized the rails, white-knuckling as Saliriel pulled ahead with Caleb. The primly dressed Nephilim walked nimbly across the walkway, mincing in her heels. Rooted to the spot Sal had indicated, I effectively blocked the narrow passage between the vessels. Behind me, Lil shoved Remy till they both objected, but I couldn't budge—the oath bound too tightly.

Fucking hell.

On the deck of the *Scylla*, another Nephilim approached Saliriel. Flanked by two burly henchman-types, he stood at least six foot five. His short-cropped hair screamed *paramilitary*, and his cheekbones looked sharp enough to slice paper.

Saliriel glided toward him on her not-so-sensible shoes, launching into an elaborately rehearsed greeting. The other Nephilim dismissed the words impatiently, his hate-filled eyes lasering on me.

"What the hell are you thinking?" he growled to her.

The grin Sal offered him went as cheerful as a shark's. "Jubiel—you forget yourself. I am a decimus. You do not speak to me that way. Where is your master?" She held herself stiffly, telegraphing affront with every line of her body. Caleb moved closer beside her, a wary expression deepening the lines of his face.

Jubiel's name stirred scraps of memory. The red-rimmed taste of old fury rose hot in my throat. I averted my face to hide my expression, but kept him at the edge of my vision. Behind me, Lil murmured, but the fickle wind stole her words from my ears.

Jubiel ignored Sal's question, stabbing an accusing finger toward me. "He's dangerous. He should be wrapped in warded chains. Unconscious." Tension thrummed across his muscled upper body. The lines of a shoulder holster shone against the light windbreaker he wore.

"And yet here he is, delivered docile to your door—a feat which I doubt you could have accomplished yourself." Her voice rang with eerie clarity on the damp night air. She folded her lightly muscled arms across her chest, skimming the faces of his greeting party with a look both haughty and bored. "Dorimiel is the one who should welcome me aboard this vessel, not some gaggle of underlings. Where is he?"

"Busy," Jubiel spat.

Remy fidgeted anxiously at my shoulder, muttering, "He shouldn't speak to her that way."

Lil smacked him.

"She's up there double-crossing us and you're fretting over protocol?" Her next words were pitched for our ears alone. "This stinks, Zaquiel. If we start shooting now, I think we've got a chance. I know you've got a gun on you."

I didn't respond. The oath gave me no option. I knew Sal was playing someone, and I hoped to hell it wasn't me. A cold, hard knot clenched in the pit of my stomach. I had no way of knowing if I could trust the Nephilim in her latest gambit—the only oath I'd gotten from Sal involved not using the Eye on me.

Too late now.

"Why are you stalling?" Lil gritted.

She shoved her way between Remy and me, elbowing me in the kidney in the process. My grip tightened convulsively on the railings. I wanted to shout or run or pull the Beretta for one last blaze of glory, but all I could do was stand there, rigid and waiting. My throat closed around all questions and objections.

The panic of my thoughts flew to the precise wording of the oath.

Half this shit drops away once we get on the damned boat.

Cold comfort—Sal rooted me in place on the very lip of that transition. I shuddered at her reasons.

"That's not helping, Lilianna," Remy said.

"Screw this," she spat.

She snapped the charm at her throat. I felt more than heard the sound as it broke. A sudden backwash of power surged against my wings. I twisted to gawk behind me.

Lil was nowhere to be seen.

Sal's voice cut imperiously over the waters, triumphant in her argument with Jubiel. The other Nephilim nodded grudgingly, then leered in my direction. The smile he flashed was all fangs.

Fuck me running. Here it comes.

"Remiel!" Sal cried with thunderous authority. "Incapacitate the Anakim and bring him to me."

"What?" I choked, amazed the oath allowed me that much. "No!" Behind me, Remy loosed a stricken breath.

"I am so sorry, Zaquiel," he whispered.

He was still apologizing as he knocked me unconscious, the blur of his fist too swift to track.

43

The world returned in stages, each punctuated by the ache in my head. Rough hands seized my jaw, tilting my face till my neck kinked. Someone pried my right eye open, peering so closely that all I could see was an indistinct smear of shadow.

Everything swam.

They did the same with the other eye then released my jaw with a dissatisfied grunt. My chin dropped forward bonelessly, and only part of that was an act. The world spun, its axis fixed to a throbbing lump at the base of my skull. I'd been dumped into a chair. It had a hard back, all metal. Bolted to the floor. Loops of rope coiled from my ankles to my knees. The deep throb of machinery vibrated through the floor.

"I'd be happier if you took him below decks. We have cells where we keep the Anakim. Warded."

Jubiel. From the way his voice resounded, we were in a relatively small room. Both his voice and the mention of warded cells stirred unpleasant memories—bright stabs of guilt and desperate fury. His naming of my tribe incensed me, as well. I wasn't the first Anakim they'd held on this vessel.

Lailah's down there, too. I knew it with jangling certainty. With any luck, Lil had figured it out, as well.

"And I tell you again, he is *my* prisoner." Sal flung her words like ice chips. "I will not budge from this room until I speak with my fellow decimus. My bargain is for his ears, not yours."

Gentler fingers tested the ropes that bound my arms behind me. Remiel, most likely. Despite the dead-fish stink of Erie, I caught a whiff of his cologne.

I played possum and listened.

"Then you'd better get comfortable," Jubiel said. "My decimus will be a while. His work cannot be hurried."

There was a sudden change in the pitch of the machinery.

"What's he doing, exactly?" Saliriel sighed the words, as if she were bored. Her heels tapped a slow circuit through the room.

Jubiel snorted. He wasn't fooled.

"You can ask him yourself, once he's topside." With simpering sarcasm, he added, "I wouldn't want to speak above my rank."

"Far too late for that," Sal snapped.

A tense silence followed, the stretching seconds punctuated by that constant, rhythmic hum. I cracked a gummy eyelid. Sal stood with her spine straight, vibrating with pent-up fury. Her head came close to brushing the low ceiling. Jubiel lingered a few feet away, a defiant sneer twisting his lips. Caleb hulked against a corner, clenching and unclenching his fists. He liked this situation less than I did.

Jubiel's head swiveled to me.

"The bastard's awake. Can't you feel the change in his pulse?" Before anyone responded, he shot forward and struck me. Stars exploded and the world tumbled end over end. "Keep him unconscious," he snarled. "I need to check on something."

I was just getting my eyes to open when he popped me again.

"I don't think he broke anything." Remiel's voice was hushed.

"Let me take a look." Cool fingers touched the side of my face, testing bruises along my cheekbone and my jaw. It took me a moment to realize that delicate touch belonged to Sal. I jerked my head away with a snarl.

"Don't." The shape of the word opened my split lip. Spittle or blood traced a slow line down my chin, but at least I could talk. So much for the "follow-Sal's-lead" part of the oath. But we were on the damned boat.

I tested my freedom by thrashing in the ropes. Nothing bound my movements save the tight coils of hemp. Remy took a halting step back. The fabric of his neatly pressed slacks brushed my bound hands as he drew away.

"I'm so sorry, brother," he said miserably.

I didn't dignify it with a response. I'd heard it all before. Blearily, I forced my eyes to focus.

We were in a chart room. Streamers and swaths of

orange and black drapery had been tacked to all the walls with patterned duct tape. Crepe bats and toothy jack-o'-lanterns dangled from the ceiling. I blinked again, and Sal read the incredulity spreading across my battered features.

"I wasn't joking about the Halloween party," she said. Conveniently, that put them near Cleveland just days before the break-in. Like that was a coincidence.

"I guess this time they decided not to take any chances," I said. "Or do I have Remy to thank for the ropes along with the lump on the back of my head?"

His silence was answer enough.

Saliriel dropped her voice to a whisper. "To sell this kind of deception, Zaquiel, certain performances must be convincing." She stood, smoothing her skirts. "You've always needed a little help."

"Yeah?" I replied. I spat blood, aiming for her fashionable beige pumps. "Your boy Jubiel nearly 'helped' me into a concussion."

"He's not mine," she replied tersely. "He'd have more manners if he were mine." She sniffed, and with grandiose dignity found a crumpled napkin on a counter, using it to wipe away the blood.

"How shall we proceed?" Remy asked. He framed the words with barely any breath.

"Damn you, Remy," I growled, "when did you switch sides?"

"I haven't," he responded.

"It's hard to believe you when I'm tied to a chair," I said. "Let me up already." I twisted my wrists against the ropes. They wouldn't budge.

"Where do you plan to go? Both Jubiel and Dorimiel have anchors and agents all over this vessel," Sal responded. Without waiting for an answer, she strode to one of the windows—portholes—and peered out. With the edge of one sleeve, she wiped away a film of moisture, then cupped her hands for a better view of what lay beyond. "The man they had at the door isn't there any more," she observed. "We should get our stories straight before Jubiel comes back. We have a little time, I think. He appears to be occupied with something aft—they all are."

"We're missing Lilianna," Remiel reminded.

"She had the right idea," I grumbled. I tried the ropes again, cursing when no one lifted a finger to help me. Straining forward, I felt an angular weight pressed against my ribs.

No one had taken the gun.

As I tried to process that puzzling bit of information, the persistent, mechanical hum that had underscored all other sounds dropped away. My ears rang dully in its absence.

Immediately it was replaced by shrill and desperate keening. No one but me reacted. I pitched forward and only the ropes around my torso kept me from hitting floor. The horrid sound rose in volume, till the inside of my skull felt shredded by it.

"What the hell is that?" I managed.

Sal, Remy, and even Caleb regarded me with varying degrees of astonishment and confusion. I writhed, certain my ears were bleeding. Remy knelt to loosen some of the knots that were biting into me. Sal stopped him, motioning further for him to step away. She backed away herself, her calm mask crackling around the edges.

A concussion of power rushed abruptly from beneath the ship. It slammed me in a cold and oily wave. My cowl shredded away, and my vision bled to darkness. All the breath rushed from my lungs as thoroughly as if I'd been thrust face-first into a vacuum.

The effects lasted only an instant, then the power—whatever it was—sucked back upon itself. It threatened to pull me under with it. I slumped within my bonds, blinking a scrim of shadow from my vision. The shrill wail left a crushing silence in its wake. I couldn't even hear Remy as he bent and took me by the shoulders. Urgently, he shook me.

A shadow passed between us, close enough to touch. A man in faded jungle greens. I twitched my face away, but he passed through us with barely a whisper of his presence. Another phantom soldier bent at the table to my right. Ghosts? I opened my vision further to my otherworldly perceptions, and was startled at what I found.

The ship had seen some action—enough to leave a solid imprint on the Shadowside—and at the moment it felt like a single, gigantic crossing.

Remy asked what was wrong, but his words came slowly into focus. Wanted to know if I was OK, what was happening to me. I shook him off—or tried to. It wasn't easy with my hands still bound behind my back.

I ignored him.

"Hey, Sal," I called over his shoulder. "Fuck your plan."

Gulping a breath, I willed myself across the weakened barrier, and left my brother clutching empty ropes.

44

Red mist boiled around Sal and Remy as I made the transition. Before the blood-soul of the Nephilim obscured her features entirely, Saliriel flashed a knowing smile at me. She appeared intensely… pleased.

It wasn't the look I was expecting.

Remy's grip upon my abruptly empty bonds sent him tumbling backward to the floor. He raised his voice in dismay. Broken snippets of his words carried across to the shadowed realm in which I stood.

"…can't do that. Not… all this water!"

"…told you… find a way." Sal's smug satisfaction rang unmistakably.

The red-mist wings of my brother's Shadowside presence twitched as he got back to his feet. Not all his movements translated clearly, but I could still picture the way he fussed to straighten the lines of his suit jacket.

"…don't understand," he objected. "…not safe… over the lake." Whatever boundary stood between us stole half his words, but the worry was clear in his tone.

I could almost see the shape of the emotion agitating the crimson echo he'd become. Saliriel's blood-soul vibrated calmly, both brighter and denser than Remiel.

"...wasn't safe... this side," she answered. "...done it before... part of the plan." She turned as if that should be the end of it.

Bitterly, I wondered which plan, and how much of it she'd bothered to share with either of us. While I pondered Sal's intricate machinations, a phantom soldier flickered to life near my elbow. Reflexively, I stepped out of his way. The deck beneath my boot buckled startlingly. Swiftly, I found surer footing—but it wasn't easy.

Not every aspect of the old gunboat translated perfectly. Uneven portions of its gray-tone corpus appeared eaten away. The edges of those holes glimmered with a substance slick and black as a cacodaimon. I shuddered, supposing what that might mean. The soldier walked through me again with all the self-awareness of a video replay.

Picking my way across the uncertain flooring, I headed toward the door. Closed tight on the skinside, it sketched a filmy echo on the Shadowside. A current of repeated mortal passage flowed through it, weaker even than what I'd encountered at the museum. I still felt the eddies plucking at me. Lil was out there somewhere, searching for Lailah. It was high time I joined her.

As I passed between Saliriel and Remy, more broken conversation crossed the boundary.

"Again... his life at risk..." Remy swept a gesture, agitation painting swirls upon the air. He took a confrontational step nearer to Sal. "…play that card too freely… Providence—"

I halted, straining to make sense of Remy's words, even as I caught Sal's answer in frustratingly tiny scraps.

"…debt… he bargains… as freely." The gleaming crimson shadow tossed its head, an intimation of hair floating thin as spider webs. "…know… how he is."

"…too well," Remy assented. His wings slumped in weary resignation. Crossing the room, he bent to the memory of a window. "…do now?"

"…assuming… demon jars… few moments… Jubiel." It dropped in and out like a bad cell-phone connection, yet I took the Nephilim's name as my cue to get moving.

The oppressive weight of the Shadowside would quickly wear on me. Ghosting from the chart room, I emerged upon the *Scylla*'s open deck. Washed-out images of Vietnam-era soldiers wavered around me. At the far end of the vessel, a subtle splash of crimson stood out against all the muted grays.

Jubiel.

Other hazy echoes fluttered around him. They held hardly any substance. Then something collectively focused their attention. Whatever it was, I couldn't make it out, and I wasn't curious enough to waste a walk that far across the vessel. He had mentioned prison cells below decks. If Lailah was still on board, I was sure to find her there.

As I turned, something careened into my ankle. It tangled in my pants leg with an irritated hiss. With a string of curses, I studied the shadows pooling near my boots and saw—of all damned things—a weasel. Scratch that. It was a ferret. A sleek, squirmy little ferret with blonde fur and bright eyes. It was looking right at me. The minute it noticed that I was looking back, it did this weird, spastic maneuver, arching its spine and dancing from side to side while it chattered urgently.

Lil, I thought.

Almost as soon as I did, the chattering increased and the ferret—which was softly glowing in the Shadowside's perpetual twilight—bounced itself off my ankle again. Scrabbling, it snagged a bit of my pants leg in its teeth, and tugged.

So it wasn't just the lioness that could come out to play.

Lady of Beasts, indeed.

I followed the excitable creature as it led me toward a covered set of stairs built in the deck. They disappeared into the darker levels below. To my left, the formless waters of the lake stretched to the horizon, a thin memory of rusted railing between me and the yawning deep. Despite my fear—or perhaps because of it—I felt an irresistible urge to peer down into those dark waters. The ferret snarled and yanked on the hem of my jeans, fighting me every step of the way.

Ignoring the diminutive beast, I drifted toward the water like a comet caught in a black hole's gravity well. With my heart hammering a desperate rhythm, I dared to take a look.

The lake surged like oil and shadow, figures drifting in the lightless maw beneath. When we'd first arrived, Jubiel had promised Dorimiel would deal with us once he got topside. At the time, I'd taken that to mean his decimus was working below decks. One look over the railing proved that wasn't the case.

The bastard was beneath the gunboat—cavorting with the cacodaimons in the deep places of the lake. I didn't understand all of what I saw there, but instinct clamored that it was bad—catastrophically bad.

In the heart of Lake Erie, I saw a quivering hole from one space to the next, its edges shimmering with an *absence* of light. My eyes swam with its intensity. Things drifted around the edges, almost elegant in their hypnotic undulations. Cacodaimons. I tried not to consider how tiny they seemed as they floated near the fringes of what could only be some hellish crossing.

I staggered back from the rail with an inarticulate shout. The ferret made angry huffing noises and it nipped my ankle reproachfully with its tiny needle-teeth.

"Stupid, stupid," I muttered, hands pressed against my forehead as I sought to drive off the sickening vision. A queasy weakness shuddered through me in its wake. Once I trusted my legs again, I followed the ferret below decks, searching for a place where I could return unnoticed to the flesh-and-blood world.

The Shadowside here felt less than safe.

45

Emerging from the Shadowside at the bottom of the stairs, I stepped into an abattoir. Lil had made good on her promise of wholesale slaughter.

Corpses littered the narrow halls, most with their throats slit. The wounds gaped like grisly mouths caught in red and silent screams. The stain of recent death lingered oil-slick and shimmering to my psychic senses, so thick I felt I couldn't breathe. The foul smell didn't help.

Room after room revealed half-naked corpses flung across velvet pillows and silken drapes, all pulsing with echoes of their death throes. Orange and black streamers and grinning pumpkin shapes hung from the walls and ceilings, a surreal contrast to the brutality of the scene. Nearly a week had passed since Halloween, but down here, they'd still been partying. The Nephilim took their decadence seriously.

I stopped counting after a dozen dead, my horror and moral outrage numbed to something hard and cold that ached within my chest. Blood spread across glinting bits of confetti and shattered flutes of champagne. It was impossible not to walk in it, and I tried to ignore the tacky way my boots stuck to the floor, nearly tripping over one of the corpses as I rounded a corner. He was sprawled across the hallway, wearing nothing but a Harlequin mask and pair of leather pants. Blood smeared his face and chiseled abs, gelling in his tangled spill of dreads.

From what I could see of his face, he couldn't have been more than twenty.

Still prompted by my spirit guide, I followed the trail of carnage, and soon caught up with the lady herself. She crouched over a figure in the mess hall, driving what looked like an ice pick into the base of her skull. Wine bottles and party decorations, including half of an elaborate, multi-colored cake, were scattered around the room. The corpse—a dead woman with a long fall of black and purple hair—still had a smear of frosting at the edge of her lush, scarlet lips.

Lil wasn't expecting me.

I kicked a bottle as I ducked in through the door. Without looking in my direction, the Lady of Beasts produced a knife from nowhere, and sent it sailing at me.

The blade would have found its mark in my throat if not for the ferret. Insubstantial as it was, it let loose a hoarse squeak just as she let the blade fly. At the last possible moment she jerked her hand a little to the left, and the throwing knife went whistling past my ear. It struck the metal wall then skidded across the floor.

"Idiot!" she growled, eyes flashing.

"Glad to see you, too, Lil," I choked.

"What are you doing here?" she demanded. "You're supposed to keep him distracted." There was a hard, cold fury to her expression that I hoped wasn't intended for me.

"I want to help you find your sister," I replied. "I thought you sent your ferret to fetch me."

"Is that where she went?" Lil muttered, bending back to the corpse.

"We can search for Lailah together," I offered.

Lil's expression darkened, and she resumed stabbing the dead woman in the head.

"Go back up and do your job, flyboy," she replied. "From now on, I work alone."

The tiny creature scurried at her feet, somersaulting around and through the corpse, but Lil seemed determined not to notice.

"I'm not going back up there with Remy and Sal," I said, "and Dorimiel is plenty distracted. He's under the damned ship, communing with the cacodaimons." I pitched my voice low. "Didn't you feel that weird wave of power maybe ten minutes ago? I think he opened some kind of crossing for them."

"Crossing?" she echoed, her voice a low growl. "For the cacodaimons? That shouldn't be possible." The squirming ferret finally managed to catch her attention, and the hard look around Lil's eyes softened momentarily. Something passed between the two of them, and Lil's expression darkened again by rapid degrees.

"Mother's tears," she swore. "Dorimiel's really gone crazy." She opened her mouth to say something else—

but there was a clattering behind us, and back down the hall someone took a sharp inhalation of breath.

Instantly I stepped out of the open doorway, joining Lil on her side of the room.

“I thought everyone down here was dead,” I hissed.

“So did I,” came her whispered response.

She crouched among the tables and over-turned chairs, all the muscles in her body taut and thrumming. Her long hair was wild, a streak of blood on one cheek echoing the scarlet highlights glinting in its waves. I found myself staring. Lil possessed a deadly beauty which the gore and carnage seemed only to emphasize. My lips tingled where she’d kissed me only once, and thoughts extremely inappropriate to the situation began playing through my mind.

Gritting my teeth, I tried to shake the full-body flashback.

Fucking hormones.

Lil seemed blissfully unaware. Without taking her eyes from the open door, she wiped down the ice pick, stowing it in her purse. Then she scooped up the knife, holding it loosely at her side. Staring at her bloodstained hands, I discovered that she was wearing blue nitrile gloves under all the gore.

Raising two powder-blue fingers, she indicated her eyes, then pointed toward the hatchway. Balancing on the balls of her feet to avoid striking the floor with the heels of her boots, she moved toward the opening. Checking the hall, she gestured for me to follow.

But I didn’t share her grace and efficiency, and my footsteps sounded like drumbeats. I barely made it to the door before she gestured sharply, indicating that I should remain behind.

Fine by me. I wasn't cut out to be a ninja, anyway.

Stifled movement echoed down the hall again, but I wasn't certain where it was coming from. Peering, Lil searched for her prey. Something pale and low to the ground streaked from one doorway to the next, barely visible even to my keyed-up senses. Then it struck me—it was the ferret.

The little bugger was moving stealthily, exploring each darkened room that lined the hall and conveying some kind of message to its mistress. Shifting my perceptions, I discovered not one, but *two* ferrets casing the hall. Lil crouched patiently while they worked, not so much as a tremor moving through the muscles of her thighs.

One of them found something. Its chattering call ghosted to my ears. Lil reacted by pulling a small metal ball from a pocket, and chucking it through an open door.

The instant it left her hand, Lil crossed the hall and pressed herself flush against the wall beside another open doorway. She waited silently as a college-aged guy with thick round spectacles stepped out cautiously to investigate the source of the disturbance.

He was wearing what looked like a kimono, though he didn't have it belted. The front of it trailed open. He was naked underneath. He lofted a makeshift weapon—a champagne bottle, of all things. Blood covered the soles of his bare feet, staining the edges of the kimono. More blood coated the floor, and he nearly slipped in a thick pool of it.

The poor bastard looked terrified and half-stoned, and he moved like a man caught in a terrible dream. I almost called out to try and save him, but hesitated.

In that instant, Lil moved in for the kill. The knife flashed, almost too fast to follow. Kimono Guy stiffened, emitting a wet and gurgling noise that could have been a cry, except Lil had cut through his voice box. The guy was half a foot taller than her, but she knew just how to hold the body so the arterial spray arced fully away. She slowly lowered the twitching corpse to the floor, hovering watchfully as he bled out.

The two ghost-ferrets came tumbling out of the room, bounding nimbly past the freshly made corpse and racing each other down the hall. Lil watched them carefully for a few moments, then finally relaxed, giving me the all-clear.

"What the hell do you do for a living?" I muttered, still wary of raising my voice.

"I sell shoes," she replied, wiping a stray droplet of blood from her cheek. "Now ask me what I do in my spare time."

I took an involuntary step back.

"I don't think I want to."

Her grin only widened. "Smart boy."

That was when the ice pick came back out, and she knelt by the dead man, turning his head to one side. With swift, practiced precision, she stabbed it repeatedly into the soft depression at the base of his skull.

"What are you doing that for?" I asked, swallowing hard. "He's dead already."

"Cacodaimons," she responded, grunting. "Scramble

the brainstem and they can't ride the body. Didn't want to believe you. Didn't want to risk it, either." I watched for a few moments, then glanced nervously down the hall, alert for any more lurkers.

"I don't want to tell you how to do your job," I ventured, "but shouldn't we focus more on finding your sister? They've got to be keeping her somewhere down here."

She stabbed a little harder. The ice pick made unpleasant sucking sounds as she thrust it in and out.

"Lil?" I said.

"Fucking drop it, OK?" she said flatly. "They bound her. That's why I couldn't sense her. I found her body. She's been dead at least a day. I couldn't find the jar they stuck her in, but trust me, I *will* find it." There was no fear, no regret, just an adamantine certitude.

"I'm sorry, Lil," I managed.

"Be sorry if we don't find the jar he put her in," Lil growled, finally ceasing her mutilation of the corpse. The gore-streaked ice pick still in hand, she stood and rounded on me. She stabbed a blood-smeared finger at my chest. "Be sorry if he's dumped that jar at the bottom of the lake."

There was nothing I could say to that, so I kept my mouth shut. Guilt had a taste, and I could feel it clawing its way up the back of my throat. A day? Had they killed her before I got here the first time, or immediately after?

It was my fault, either way.

Lil wiped down the ice pick and stashed it again.

"I'm done here," she said. "It's time for the real fight. You want to be useful? There's a supply room with propane tanks. Minimal effort. Carry a few up with me, and we'll make the night glow."

"But we're on a damned *boat*," I objected as she started swiftly down one of the narrow corridors. "We have allies up there. Remy, and Sal—"

Lil snorted.

"If they get in my way, I'll blow them up" she called over her shoulder. "Sal I might even aim for."

46

Lil and I each retrieved two of the ball-shaped tanks, then moved topside. Using the shadows to our advantage, we scurried from the steps to a bank of machinery about halfway between the redecorated chart room and whatever occupied Jubiel and his goons.

They scurried around like ants with an anxiety disorder. A crane rose on that end of the ship, while the main thing that concerned them looked like a giant winch with coils of metal cable running to a carriage swinging out over the water. The cables—some as big around as my wrist—descended into the lake on the side opposite the *Daisy Fay*.

The anchor, maybe? I thought. If it was the anchor, though, they were pulling it up. A surge of noise and clatter erupted as they lifted something into the carriage, fixed it there, then maneuvered it onto the deck. It was big. Water sluiced from curving sides, shedding runnels of fine gray silt.

Not the anchor. Underneath the silt, the bullet-shaped

object looked like something straight from Captain Nemo's drafting table—all dark metal fittings and thick, curving glass.

"Is that a mini-sub?" Lil whispered. "Where the hell did he even get something like that?"

"Guess he wasn't just swimming down there," I offered. "Could Dorimiel open a crossing inside of that thing?"

She peered around the edge of our cover, then pulled back with a grimace.

"I don't even want to think about that."

Neither did I, but the black-on-black vision of cacodaimons swimming in the depths returned with sickening clarity.

"Head in the game, Zack," she reminded me with a jab. "I count six people on deck—seven if Dorimiel's inside of that thing—but I think I can handle it. I see a rack of diving tanks over by that winch. Fire and oxygen make for a hell of a party." She grabbed the propane tanks from me, set them down with the others, then gave me a shove in the direction of the cabin.

"Remember. You're the distraction. Go keep them busy."

"'Busy,' she says. While Sal and Remy hide out in the fucking chart room." I stifled a bitter laugh. "You got any suggestions for tangling with someone who makes Voldemort look like a pushover?"

"You'll come up with something," she responded, fiddling with the top of one of the tanks. She examined her work, then nodded to herself.

At the far end of the *Scylla*—'aft,' Sal had called it—Jubiel and the others rushed around, hosing off the mini-sub and securing it to the deck. Once they removed the carriage, a hatch opened on top, and Jubiel rolled a set of steps up to the side, fixing them firmly in place. Then he climbed up and reached into the vessel, offering his hand to help its occupant out.

I froze beside Lil.

The arm that emerged was covered to the elbow in blood. For a breathless instant, I hoped that something had gone horribly wrong down there. Then Dorimiel rose, covered in gore. He paused while still half in the mini-sub, plucking a gobbet of flesh casually from one curl of his hair. He regarded the bloody morsel with the air of a man picking out a leaf. He tossed it aside with as much care.

With a nod to his man Jubiel, Dormiel crawled from the hatch like a spider, thin and long-limbed. Under the gore his clothes were comically ordinary—a light olive polo shirt, a khaki tactical vest, a heavy gold watch that probably cost more than most cars. He reached back into the sub, bringing up the severed head of a young Asian man. He tossed this at Jubiel, grimacing as if the owner had done him some grievous personal insult by bleeding all over his clothes.

"Help me clean up this mess," the decimus said. He had a light baritone with hints of a British accent that carried sharply across the deck. The sound of that voice stirred echoes deep in my hindbrain. That empty ache above my heart twinged, and my palms were suddenly clammy with sweat. Choking waves of fear threatened my volition. Anger galloped swiftly on its heels, however, and I gladly embraced it.

Across the deck, Jubiel set aside the bloody head as if he handled mangled body parts all the time—and he probably did. Dorimiel hoisted himself further up, throwing a severed arm after the head.

"I don't understand it," he said, lips twisting in a sneer. "I feed the gate just like they ask me to, and it opens wider every time. All my little friends come through, but I still can't pass a damned thing across." He flung another chunk of dead flesh at Jubiel.

The Nephilim flunky blinked stupidly, as if trying to muster a response, but he was well out of his depth. He scrambled to collect the grisly body parts while the other henchmen stood around at mute attention. From their collective expressions, they were happy not to be in Jubiel's place. One of them produced a cloth for the decimus, holding it out so he could wipe his hands.

"I'm close, though. I know it," he said. He patted a bulging pocket in his tactical vest. "A few more tries, and I'll shove her through—like offal down a garbage chute. Then we'll see about the rest. No more endless war." He wadded up the bloodied rag, planted his hands on the railings, then slid down the metal stairs.

Jubiel jigged to get out of the way.

"Maybe they couldn't stand the taste of her," he offered. From his look, he was trying to be funny.

Dorimiel responded by throwing the blood-stained cloth in Jubiel's face. That confirmed it—behaving like a raging asshole was somewhere in the decimus handbook.

Beside me, Lil hissed, and I jumped.

"I'm going to make those two dance in the ropes of their intestines before I feed them their still-beating hearts."

She could have set off the propane tanks with the heated fury of her words. Hideous comprehension slithered through my brain—Dorimiel had been down there with Lailah. That bulge in his pocket had to be her jar, and he'd been trying to open a crossing.

To feed her bound spirit to the cacodaimons.

I felt beyond sick—and beyond angry.

"You said you had the Anarch?" Dorimiel said. "Where'd you put that meddling son of a bitch?" He drummed the fingers of one hand idly against the swell of Lailah's jar. That hand didn't look right. The fingers curled to talons, long and spindly at the tips. I'd never seen one of the Nephilim with a physical imperfection, and the sight of that gnarled limb raised my skin in gooseflesh.

"Saliriel brought him, but she won't turn him over to anyone but you," Jubiel replied sulkily. "I put them in the chart room. Karl's on the door."

"Hrmh," Dorimiel grunted. "I wonder what that scheming chameleon will want in exchange."

"That's your cue," Lil said, looking up from the propane tanks. When I was slow to respond, she hissed, "Dammit. *Move!*" Then she gave me a shove.

At the sound of my boot scuffing against the deck, Dorimiel's head snapped up. Eyes green as infection and backlit by their own unearthly light scanned the shadows of the *Scylla*. They settled for a moment near the place where we crouched, and though I knew Lil and I were well hidden, it felt as if that inhuman gaze bored straight into my soul.

Jubiel and the henchmen snapped to high alert, drawing their guns and covering every angle around their decimus.

"Shit," Lil swore.

"Guess it's time to be distracting," I breathed. I dashed for cover, heading away from Lil. Before I could think better of it, I pulled Kessiel's Beretta, flipped off the safety, and opened fire.

47

Chaos erupted on the deck. Dorimiel bellowed something in an ancient tongue, gathering dark power around his twisted hand. My nerves jangled unpleasantly at the sight—I could feel it, despite the distance.

My first few shots went wild as I crossed from Lil's position to a stack of wooden crates lashed to the deck. Two of Jubiel's thugs fired prematurely toward the sound of my gun. They didn't even come close. Then they sprinted for strategic positions behind pumps and hulking metal containers.

Jubiel clearly didn't care about getting shot. He stayed out in the open, running like a linebacker straight for my position.

"Zaquiel," Dorimiel called. "I know it's you. I can taste your fear, and I never forget a vintage." His smug voice carried the entire length of the ship. Like Jubiel, he seemed wholly unconcerned about the threat of bullets, remaining in the open near the housing for the sub.

Before he could spit out another witty bad-guy taunt,

I stood up from behind the crates, took a deep breath, then squeezed off shot after shot.

As much as I wanted to take down Dorimiel, I aimed for Jubiel first. He was the closest—and in another few moments he'd be on top of me. I aimed for the heart, and then the face. He went down in a spasm of limbs, his own gun clattering across the deck. I hadn't expected to take him out so quickly, but I wasn't going to question my luck.

Then Remy was shouting from the chart room. I couldn't really make out the words over the gunfire. Saliriel's voice was in there somewhere, as well. I thought I felt Lil rush past me, but one minute she was there, and the next she was gone. So was at least one of the propane tanks.

I slipped into this weird calm where everything slowed, and all my senses seemed hyper-real. I raised the gun away from Jubiel's crumpled form, aiming for Dorimiel where he still stood near the sub. Casings clattered to the deck at my feet as I planted three bullets in his upper body, trying not to hit the bulge in his pocket. I landed a fourth right between those poison-green eyes. His head rocked back and the force of the impacts staggered him.

He twisted and fell, head bouncing off the rolling metal stairs. One bullet might not fell a Nephilim, but a hail of them seemed to do the trick.

While the other goons returned fire, one rushed to his fallen master. Dorimiel lay still, but it was short-lived. I watched in horror as his twisted claw of a hand shot up and palmed the startled guy's face.

What I saw next made me stop shooting. Calm or no calm, all my muscles locked up with shock and disgust.

Dark energy coiled visibly around Dorimiel's fingers, skirling like smoke. The power thickened into inky black tendrils—one for each digit. The tendrils reached out to twine in the henchman's hair, while one caressed the side of his jaw with a disturbingly sensual gesture. Then, like living things in their own right, the ropes of dark energy stiffened and drove themselves deep into his flesh.

The man shrieked and jerked from the assault, and I couldn't help feeling sympathy pains. I knew what was happening.

It had happened to me.

Dorimiel dragged himself up by the big guy's head, the wound on his own face knitting like a time-elapsed film as he sucked his henchman dry. With a disdainful sneer the decimus drew his curling talons away, and the man slumped like a sack onto his side. His limbs flopped nervelessly. Thinner, wispy tendrils still trailed between the Nephilim's hand and the twitching man's face. Even at this distance, I could see the livid bruises imprinted on the guy's temple and forehead, like fingerprints done in the unforgiving black of pure void.

"Damn," I whispered tremulously.

Before I could react, Jubiel arose with a roar, leaping at me with his fangs bared. Another figure streaked across the deck, long hair streaming like an ebon plume. Remiel threw himself on his ill-mannered brother, and they grappled in a blur of limbs.

"You're insane," Saliriel scolded in her throaty contralto. "Racing across the deck like that." I jumped and my skin twitched. I hadn't even heard her move behind me. She grabbed me by the collar and pulled me down behind the crates while the rest of Dorimiel's thugs laid down suppression fire.

Remy and Jubiel kept fighting.

"Did you see that?" I choked. "What he did to that guy—did you see his fucking hand?"

"Shut up and keep your head down. Bullets can kill you, you know," Sal reminded. "Now where is the Lady of Beasts?"

A gurgling cry rose in the night. It cut off suddenly.

"Trent?" one of the goons called. No one responded.

"There's your answer," I hissed.

"Perfect," she said. Sal's smile was chilling.

Remy shrilled in pain. Ignoring Saliriel's words of caution, I poked my head up from behind the crates, trying to catch sight of my brother. Instead, I spied a stealthy figure scrambling up the side of the sub, working opposite from where Dorimiel still crouched on the deck.

Lil. Quick as a cat, she hoisted herself on top, propane tank in hand. Before anyone became wise to her, she dropped the tank neatly down the vessel's still-open hatch, then slammed it shut. A heartbeat later she sprang away, dropping and rolling toward our original cover.

Lil made James Bond seem like an amateur.

Dorimiel turned toward the reverberant sound of something dropping into his sub.

"Who's that?" Dorimiel demanded. "Petrov, Jackson, I want these intruders found and dealt with. Kill all but Zaquiel. I need what he still knows."

Even as he barked the commands, a second propane tank rolled across the deck in his direction. It crashed into the diving equipment near the base of the winch, like a dented, white bowling ball of doom.

One of the henchmen figured out what was going on. He leapt at Dorimiel, dragging the startled decimus down and away as the propane tank detonated. It was a little underwhelming as explosions go, but then it set off the oxygen tanks.

As promised, that was a party.

The blast knocked the sub from its housing and it listed to one side, slowly sliding toward the edge of the ship. The crane supporting the carriage over the lake sagged at half-mast, smoke and fire seething from its base. Thick steel cables twisted everywhere, frayed by the strength of the explosion. The heat from the fire started warping the deck, wood and metal groaning with a sound eerily reminiscent of a whale song.

Then a second explosion rocked the sub, this one coming from the inside. Somehow Lil had MacGyvered a delay on that propane tank. Fire blossomed bright orange and yellow against the thick glass windows. It set off a series of smaller explosions inside and, shuddering, the little vessel slid from the deck to crash into the dark waters below.

Oily smoke choked the whole aft of the *Scylla*, shot through with the red glow of the flames. Against that hellish backdrop, Dorimiel rose. His clothes were singed and half his face was a bubbled mask of reddened flesh. Loosing an inhuman cry of fury and pain, he shook his twisted claw.

"You cannot kill me so easily, Anakim. I've swallowed the power of more things than you can dream, and I have new brothers."

He spread his arms and loosed a chittering cry. Harsh and ululant by turns, that sound had no business erupting from a human throat—or in the case of the Nephilim, semi-human. Beside me, Saliriel swore in an ancient tongue, her normally mask-like features creased with revulsion. For once, the expression was genuine. She gripped my shoulder with such ferocity that I could feel her painted nails digging into my skin even through the thick leather of the biker jacket.

"Now do you believe me about the fucking cacodaimons?" I snarled.

Calls resounded across the waters of the lake, answering Dorimiel's eldritch cry. Another, more human shriek pierced the night, ending in a gurgling wheeze. Lil was still afoot, picking off henchmen one by one.

To our left, Remy howled in pain.

He and Jubiel tumbled into view from behind some enigmatic machinery. Jubiel had Remy pinned and it looked like he was trying to wrench my brother's head from his neck. Both of them were bloody, but Remy had clearly seen the worst of it.

"Remiel!" I cried, and I aimed the gun in their direction, fighting to get Jubiel in my sights. The bullet might only be a nuisance, but it could give my soft-spoken sibling a chance to regain his feet.

I pulled the trigger.

Nothing.

I'd emptied the entire magazine.

Saliriel slapped the useless gun from my hands. "Do not hurt what is mine!" she bellowed at Jubiel. Then she leapt at him in a streak of slender legs and platinum hair.

I was alone behind the crates when the first cacodaimon slithered over the side of the ship, black hood flaring and crimson eyes alight. A second swiftly followed, and then a third—and they each skittered to Dorimiel like obedient hounds. Smiling triumphantly through the smoke and gloom, the blood-streaked Nephilim whispered a guttural command.

At a flick of his fingers, the cacodaimons launched themselves at me.

48

With a shriek that sounded like fingernails on metal, the cacodaimons swarmed. I bellowed my name in defiance, blue-white power leaping swiftly to my hands.

Finally—a fight I could hope to win.

As the living shadows closed around, I slashed the air with blades of searing light. One of the creatures shrilled as I connected, and I pinned it against the deck, tearing viciously at its central mass. Clinging globules of dark scattered like blood across my vision as the thing writhed, and then dispersed, its rasping death cry echoing through the corridors of my mind.

Charging a second, I seized it in hands aglow with spirit-fire. It writhed and lashed, coiling its tail around my ankle. Stinging appendages sought to drag its gnashing maw closer to my face. I wrestled with it for several moments, spinning and twisting as I sought to keep it from getting those jagged teeth into me.

It worked to pull my legs out from under me. I kept my feet, planting them a shoulder-width apart, then drew back a hand to once again call the brilliant blade. With a thunderous cry, I drove the diamond-bright weapon of focused will straight into what served the thing for a heart. I dropped its writhing carcass to the deck, shaking out my tingling fingers as the shadow-thing dispersed.

Another of the creeping horrors hissed a challenge, swooping up and around in an attempt to dive behind me. It raked my wings with half a dozen of its scythe-like claws. Staggered, I let out a coughing cry of agony.

The cacodaimon took advantage of the lapse in my attention and made another scathing pass, whipping around to slam its toothsome jaw into the middle of my back. The armor of my leather protected me from the worst of it, but the impact sent me reeling. Waves of numbing cold shot through my shoulders and arms, so intense I couldn't even catch myself when I fell. I smacked my chin painfully on the deck and saw stars. The thing clung to my back, lacerating my wings and legs where the jacket provided no cover.

I started screaming.

For every jolt of bone-searing cold, I knew it sank another appendage into me. It would eat me if I couldn't get it off of me. I flailed uselessly, but couldn't seize hold of it. The angle was all wrong.

A fourth cacodaimon started circling.

I heard gunshots, more explosions.

I panicked, knowing Dorimiel had to be closing in, but I couldn't fight past the creeping numbness stealing the life from me.

Somewhere in the midst of the chill and the pain, I became aware of another chittering cry. For a minute, I thought it was yet another cacodaimon, coming to make a meal of me—but it didn't sound quite right. Looking wildly around, I spotted one of Lil's little beasts, doing some kind of angry ferret dance as it squeaked a challenge at the cacodaimon. Maybe it was trying to work up its courage before striking. Under less dire circumstances, it might have seemed comical.

As it was, I found myself staring, too muddled by pain to muster a coherent response.

Then the spirit-ferret launched itself at the cacodaimon on my back, a wriggling projectile of teeth and blonde fur. The sound of the little beast's war cry dredged a brief flash from childhood memory. A name—Rikki Tikki Tavi. That was a mongoose. This was a ferret, but the effect was the same.

With an angry hiss, the bold critter sank its teeth into the rubbery meat at the base of the cacodaimon's flaring hood. The tenacious little bugger was still clinging to that spot when the cacodaimon reared back, pulling half out of me. It shrieked and tried to shake the ferret off, unsuccessfully.

The misbegotten spawn of shadows didn't detach itself from my legs, but by then it didn't have to. It moved enough for me to throw my shoulders back and grab onto its central mass. Digging my fingers into the meat of the thing, I brought a nimbus of blue-white fire to my hands.

With a furious cry, I tore it away like the leech it was, whipping it around to face me. It scrabbled against the front of my jacket, seeking some kind of purchase, but before it could work its way around or through the leather, I intoned the syllables of my name, lashing out and sundering it at the core.

The ferret wisely dashed to safety at the last possible instant.

"Two down," I gasped, my head, wings, and legs throbbing. "No, three. How many more could be out there?"

I knelt for a few heartbeats, struggling to catch my breath. The fourth cacodaimon continued circling. I still didn't see Dorimiel anywhere, and that worried me.

A fifth squirming nightmare slunk onto the ship. It hugged the deck, skittering toward the man Dorimiel had eaten. The chitinous horror quested around the fallen man's form, moving sinuously along the curve of his shoulders and spine. For a minute, it looked for all the world like it was spooning him—then it slid right into his body, as if he were an empty suit of clothes.

The guy lumbered to his feet, shambling in a circle as the cacodaimon tested out his nerves. I wanted to be sick all over my boots, but there really wasn't time. Even as the not-quite-dead man staggered toward where Remy and Sal still struggled with Jubiel, the nearest creature slashed at me. I threw up my hands in defense, and it raised angry welts on my wrists and palms.

Two more were calling in the distance. I was already worn pretty thin—if those joined the fight it wasn't going to be pretty.

Where the hell is Lil? I wondered.

As I pinned the fourth cacodaimon to the deck and dragged my blades through its clammy flesh, the ferret shrieked a warning, then danced away in haste. I reacted a moment too late.

A vise-like hand seized the shoulder of my biker

jacket. Pallid green eyes agleam, Dorimiel lifted me bodily to my feet. He called power to his twisted hand, and I finally got to see what was wrong with it. His fingers were blackened and warped, the skin shrunk tight against the bones. Dark veins ran up his arm to the elbow, pulsing visibly against his discolored flesh. Each finger was tipped with a scythe-like claw. The shape was unnervingly familiar—alien, insectile—

"You ate one of them," I choked as he twisted me around to face him. "You ate a fucking cacodaimon."

Dorimiel loomed over me, easily as tall as Saliriel, if not a little taller. A wild light gleamed in his poisonous eyes, manic and completely unhinged. He gave a smile that made gooseflesh flee down my spine.

"He was a messenger. I misunderstood. I tried to destroy him, but he transformed me. It was glorious." Leering scant inches from my face, he hissed, "I'll make you a part of me, too, Anakim. Then you'll see."

He lifted his tainted hand, the darkness throbbing around his clawed fingers. An answering pulse leapt to life beneath the thin fabric of his shirt—red, not black. I didn't need to see the jewel to know it was the Eye. With his normal hand, he seized the front of my jacket, seeking to hold me in place as he prepared to feed.

I shouted my power, blue-white flames flaring round my hands and chasing away at least some of the cloying shadows. With the chill of his fingers just inches from my face, I slashed the blades with desperate fury.

He was ridiculously stronger than me. I managed to land a glancing blow, and at least I got him to let go of me, but his counterattack was swift and terrible. I found myself quickly on the defensive, and it was all I could to do keep him from laying his deadly hands on me.

"The last time you were here, you fought with equal fervor," he sneered, "but you know how well that ended." Landing a flurry of punches, he added, "Hand over the Stylus and reveal the jars. Make things easy on yourself."

"You have a fucked-up definition of easy," I snarled, fending off blow after blow.

"Tell me and I shall kill you quickly," he offered. "I'll rip it from you either way." Then he moved methodically forward, and I realized he was herding me—the lashed-down pile of crates was perhaps ten feet behind me.

I'd strayed pretty far in my struggles with the cacodaimons. Where before the crates had provided cover, now they were an obstacle against which he could pin me. I didn't like that idea. I intoned the resonate syllables of my name till the twin blades of power gleamed bright as magnesium.

Spitting curses in a language still strange to me, I dove forward, slashing viciously, but he sidestepped every blow.

"You have no hope to free them," he taunted. "Only I know the phrases that serve as lock and key. You'll never get them from me."

I drove my blades at him, but I was losing. Badly. The light that glimmered around the spirit-daggers sputtered, growing dim. I couldn't keep this up.

"Once I've emptied you, I'll bind the tatters of your soul with your lady," he threatened, patting a bulge in the pocket of his vest. "I had her screaming near the end."

He pressed forward, his tainted fingers grazing my cheek.

They stung with the same numbing cold of a cacodaimon's claws. He cackled wildly at my pained reaction.

"Last chance for a quick death, Anakim."

"My name," I bellowed with all the strength I had left, "is *Zaquiel*!"

I used the power of that Name to carry me forward in one last and desperate assault. I managed to connect this time, slamming my blades into his chest, but it seemed like all it did was knock the wind out of him. At least he stumbled backward. We grappled, but somehow I ended up on the losing end, pinned on the deck beneath him within sight of the crates. I wrestled weakly, working to get his back to them.

"You know what would be great about now?" I shouted desperately. "A little help here. Remy? Lil? Sal?"

The shadow-tainted Nephilim sneered nastily, exposing yellowed fangs. "Not so valiant now, are we?" He shifted his weight, pinning my legs with his knee even as I struggled to bring them up, kicking. Usually someone my size had height and reach to his advantage, but not against Dorimiel. He was close to a foot taller than me.

"You've earned your suffering," he promised. "You and all your tribe. I can bring an end to your atrocities. With my new and hungry brothers, we will feed you to the void."

His eyes bled briefly from green to black, and it was like staring into the pitiless vacuum of space. I fought to grab his wrists and at least keep his hands away, but between his superior strength and my growing exhaustion it was a token effort at best.

"Shut up and get it over with," I cried. My strength was spent.

His sneer broadened and he wrapped his hand around my throat. The black film on his eyes cleared, and they flared poison green again. I thought—ridiculously—that the color reminded me of pistachio ice cream. I cackled hysterically... then I felt his power burning coldly around his fingertips. Those inky tendrils took physical shape and slithered against my skin.

My laughter turned to screams.

The Eye pulsed above me, its power twining through the veins of darkness that ridged his arm. The pain quickly eclipsed all conscious thought, and I became a mute and unwilling witness to a parade of memories flashing with rapid-fire speed through my mind. Things I didn't even realize I still remembered—pictures from childhood, images of the museum, a weathered, ancient statue which, in that moment, I knew to be the true face of the Rephaim Terael.

That blinding power riffled through the files of my mind, upending everything. Each page or photograph flashed once, brilliantly, before crumbling to ash. Dorimiel drove images of the jars at me, returning again and again to memories that were linked with them.

The third line of the cipher flashed past—

Gandhi guards my brothers.

—but nothing useful followed it. The Nephilim's frustration shook the very pillars of my mind. Maybe it lasted only a minute. Maybe the space of a few heartbeats, but it was long enough.

Too long.

I made myself hoarse with screaming.

Then suddenly, it halted. My vision—red and ragged

around the edges—returned to the here-and-now. I saw the Nephilim above me, and fumbled for his name. Then behind him, another face. Fiercely beautiful. Russet hair spilling everywhere. And two eyes like thunder.

"I knew I could count on you for a distraction," Lil said.

Then she slit his throat all the way down to the bone.

49

Dorimiel's blood fountained over me—and with it, a backwash of memory. I choked on it even as snapshots of recollection popped like flashbulbs in my mind. They flew by in a rush, nothing in order, all too rapid to clearly identify. I lay there stunned for a moment, astounded simply by the fact that I *could* think.

Above me, Lil grappled with Dorimiel. The dancing flames that burned across the deck cast weird shadows on both of them, though maybe that was my still hazy vision. I wasn't a drooling idiot by any means, but it still felt like someone had introduced a blender to my brain.

Incredibly, Dorimiel still put up a fight. It was ghastly, especially from this perspective, because his neck had a wide and gaping smile which opened like a second mouth every time he struggled against Lil. He scrabbled with one hand, working to hold the edges of the wound shut. As he did so, I could see the lips of the laceration knitting.

Lil clung to his back like a red-haired fury, the ice pick

clenched between her teeth. She kept trying to get him into a hold so she could apply it properly. I wondered if thrusting it into the base of Dorimiel's brain would make a corpse of the shadow-tainted monster.

I didn't get a chance to find out. The minute he realized he might actually be losing, the decimus twisted nimbly out of Lil's grip, leaving her startled and still holding his singed and bloody tactical vest. Then he did something neither of us could have expected of a Nephilim.

He stepped through to the Shadowside.

"Bleeding Mother!" she swore.

"Lailah," I croaked, gesturing at the vest. "Upper right pocket."

Fury and relief vied upon her features as she retrieved the vessel holding Lailah's bound spirit—but it counted for nothing without the sigil's key.

I levered myself to my feet, feeling something slide heavily off the front of my jacket. It clattered onto the deck and I stared at it blankly for several heartbeats, hardly able to process what I was seeing. An amulet of thick and blood-smeared gold winked up at me, the leather thong that had fixed it round Dorimiel's neck sliced as cleanly as his throat.

The Eye of Nefer-Ka.

A chance. I had a chance to find the key that would release Lailah and my brothers—maybe even take back all that had been taken from me. I snatched up the icon. Lil's eyes widened the instant she saw it. She reached to take it from me.

"Sorry," I mouthed. Drawing on some reserve of strength I didn't even know I possessed, I turned from her—and plunged after Dorimiel through the other side of reality. I could hear her cursing behind me.

I regretted it almost immediately. This part of the ship wasn't solid at all. I nearly slipped through the spongy deck into a dark and yawning void.

"Shit shit *shit*," I gasped, struggling to get airborne. My wings still ached from the battle with the cacodaimon, but they held. I marveled at the sensation, spreading them wide and soaring on an updraft.

Struggling to orient myself, I gripped the Eye in one hand. The heavy gold amulet throbbed against my palm in time to a heartbeat—but not my own. I wracked my aggrieved brain for everything I had learned about the artifact. It devoured knowledge and power—I'd experienced that first-hand. It had been crafted by the primus of the Nephilim, but anyone could tap into it. Both Terael and Saliriel had mentioned that there would be a price, though.

A blood price.

Even as I thought it, the central tail of the Eye of Nefer-Ka shifted in my hand. The narrow, wedge-shaped gold of the amulet wasn't firmly attached. I tugged on it, following instinct, and the tail revealed itself to be a sheath. A small sliver of bright metal glinted in the twilight of the Shadowside. A hidden blade.

I hesitated for a moment, then slashed across my open palm. Blood welled up, a shocking shade of crimson in the gray of this shadowed realm. I pressed the amulet to the wound, slipping the sheath back on the blade.

The red stone central to the Eye flared and, for a moment, my entire arm went numb. The pulse of the icon abruptly ceased. I held my breath, coasting on the currents above the Shadowside wreck of the *Scylla*. Needling points of sensation blossomed around the edges of the wound, as if the back of the amulet had sprouted teeth, and they were biting hungrily into me.

With a sudden wave of heat that washed all the way up to my elbow, the throbbing beat started up again, this time tuned to the rhythm of my own racing heart. Sensation returned to my hand by degrees, and with it a sense of strange whispers in the back of my mind.

I didn't like that part at all.

But there wasn't much to lose.

I clenched my hand around the Eye, and searched the shifting darkness for my quarry. A roiling figure of crimson mist, shot through with ebon veins, scudded above the hungry waves—the blood-soul of the Nephilim. Once I spotted him, he was hard to miss.

Just as using the Eye on a cacodaimon had infected him with its twisted darkness, no doubt it was my life and memories that had given him the ability to cross over—but that didn't mean he belonged on the Shadowside. I was the native here, and with luck that gave me the advantage. I needed it, because I was battered, weary, and what I was about to attempt seemed a little insane.

Maybe more than a little. "Here goes nothing," I muttered to myself, tucking my wings for the dive.

I crashed into Dorimiel at what felt like ninety miles an hour. For an instant, I was worried I would just ghost right through him, but the whirling scarlet cloud had both substance and weight. He reacted immediately, countless eyes snapping open across the twisting expanse of him. Each of them retained that same pale green iris so remarkable in the flesh. They glared at me menacingly, then pseudopods of black and red veins whipped out from the main mass, twining around me.

We twisted in mid-air, wrestling. I could feel him scrabbling at my mind, trying to draw power, but I had the Eye now. As we tangled, I thrust my hand forward, and used it.

My hand passed *into* the central mass of him and I could feel his essence down to the last syllable of his Name. Images blossomed in my mind. We whirled together over the void-like waters. At the same time, I was pulled into a labyrinth all twisted over with black, throbbing vines. Some of the walls were crumbling, and whole sections were choked with cloying shadows.

I was inside the construct of his mind.

Choosing the first corridor, I barreled down it, and everywhere I turned there rose chiseled faces. Beneath the faces, there were names—but not the ones I'd come here seeking.

Pressing deeper, I avoided contact with the walls. Those writhing black veins were a sickness, and I wanted no part of them. They chewed at the substance of the labyrinth—the cacodaimon taint was even now unmaking him. He'd been unraveling in body and mind the instant he'd had the audacity to thrust the Eye at one of those horrors and try to make it a part of himself.

At the thought, I saw the memory. A party onboard the *Scylla*. Late summer? Hard to tell. Someone on deck complaining of feeling sick. Peering across the

Shadowside to see the dark shape hovering over her, slowly worming its way into her drug-addled brain. Grappling with the horror, exulting in the ability to seize a spirit with the swallowed skills of collective Anakim. Drunk on stolen power—intent on stealing more.

I shied away from the rest of that memory. I didn't want to know what it felt like to taste the absence of reason that was the Unmakers.

We continued to spin in the empty air above the dark waters, fighting mind-to-mind as the images flashed by with the speed of thought. Not fast enough, though. We were still in the Shadowside.

Borrowed time.

"Where's the key for Lailah?" I bellowed through his mind. "How do I release the ones you've bound?"

Voices gibbered—and they were all Dorimiel, underscored by a surging wave of insectile chittering that rose and fell like the cycling of cicadas. I heard expletives, imperatives, whispered names.

I clung to one that I sought—*Anakesiel.*

Turning a corner. I encountered a door. Huge and graven, the lines of his face emerged from the stone, carved on a cyclopean scale. I seized the handle, dragging it open. Memories spilled forth as vividly as if I'd lived them myself. I staggered beneath the flood, striving to control the rush of information. There was too much.

Hunted. We're being hunted. In a carriage riding through the Alps. Someone across from him—*Tashiel*—I knew the name instantly. Tash recounted an attack. A group of Nephilim. It was 1833.

A memory far older—so old my brain spasmed

around the truth of it. A wind-swept mountain. A great stone table, the tribes gathered round. Faces of the other primae. The reverberant sound of the oath. Each setting his icon upon the table as he swore to bury the power. Anak pulling a smooth, carved stylus from his robe, reluctant to part with it. Feeling how it was perfectly weighted to his hand.

He laid it beside the Eye.

The 1800s again. Imprisoned. Delirious. Pain and thirst and fever. Dorimiel's face twisted with fury.

Where did you bury it? Tell me and I'll let you die.

A clay jar, freshly fired. Dorimiel presenting it with a look of triumph. In his hand, a stylus—*the* Stylus.

I doubt you even know what this is anymore, but I promise to keep it safe for you, Anarch. You and all your tribe.

I blinked, and the labyrinth scattered. I grappled with the ugly pulsing thing that was the decimus on this side of reality. The rubine glow of the Eye lit him from within.

"I already know about the icon," I shouted. "Give me the words that open the seals, dammit!"

Dorimiel shuddered in my grasp. Half the green eyes dotting his form rolled up to show the whites. Shadows spilled across the sclera. The veins of black rippled through him, spreading little tendrils. Maybe using the Eye on him had hastened the decay—or maybe the Eye had been the only thing keeping him together. Either way, he was losing the battle with the taint of the cacodaimon.

I dove back into the collapsing architecture of his mind. The walls around me buckled, the black taint like hungry vines pulling ruins back into the jungle. More twists and turns as I frantically searched.

Arriving at a crossroads, I felt the foundations of his mind deteriorating. Black rot twisted and the nearest wall nearly tumbled down on me. Desperate, gibbering, the decimus threw galvanizing images to throw me off the chase—the pillaged temple, scattered bodies. My face from his perspective, features twisted with hate.

We killed everyone.

We made him watch.

He and I had dropped perilously close to the face of the waters. He was trying to distract me so he could drag me down with him. I pounded furiously with my wings, trying to pull us free from the sucking current. Muscles across my back—ones I didn't even know I possessed—burned with the effort.

Dorimiel screamed with fear and rage. I felt more than heard his voice. One last chance. With the Eye glowing fiercely in time to my thudding pulse, I launched my mind at his. I saw a corridor that was all tumblers and gears. Light spilled through keyholes, shimmering with sigils. I heard Names, phrases. Lailah. Haniel. Countless others. They rang like music, chiming on the wind. I almost had them—then Dorimiel shoved a final image at me.

The portal bearing my face.

All my memories were locked in that vault. I could take the phrases, or reclaim what he'd stolen from me.

Choose, Anakim. Loyalty or self-preservation. Prove you are no different from me.

A tremor shook the labyrinth of his mind. More

crumbling destruction. The last shreds of reason unraveled. There was no more time.

I made my choice.

With the final scintillating shard of knowledge, I fled the maze before it collapsed.

Dorimiel was screaming. Black veins consumed his form, whipping out from a central lesion boiling with rot. His cries grew shriller and shriller until anything like a human voice was lost in a harsh cicada buzz. Revolted, I flung him away from me.

An answering cry echoed from below. Then another, and another.

A crashing wave of darkness leapt up from the water, comprised entirely of living, shrieking shadows. They moved in a swarm like a colony of hellish insects, their red eyes gleaming with ferocious intent. Dorimiel's tainted blood-soul pushed and pulled against itself, the last few tendrils of crimson seeking to crawl away on the air to escape the swarm—but his black veins reached like countless hands, greeting his new brethren.

I strained furiously with my wings, pushing away even as the cacodaimons swarmed the Nephilim like an army of hungry ants. Tendrils of bright red and pale emerald eyes peeked out from the writhing mass of chitinous black, struggling with a bitter desperation. His cries of agony echoed across the bleak landscape of the Shadowside.

More of them were already speeding after me. Trembling with effort and weary to the bone, I flew as fast and as far as my wings could carry me. My strength was quickly waning, and in fact, I was amazed it had taken me this far. In a few moments, I wouldn't need a swarm of cacodaimons to drag me into the abyss. I was going to drop like a stone.

Then they were on me, more of them than I could count, their taloned appendages frigid and grasping. Stinging points of cold erupted all over my legs, arms, and wings. Wordless panic filled my mind as I started falling.

At the last possible instant, I remembered Lil's little charm. With the nerveless fingers of my free hand, I dug it out of my pocket, turning it to face the swarm of cacodaimons. I snapped it with a cry, and a burst of light like the stored brilliance of half a dozen sunsets flooded forth. It was warm and pure and golden and wholly alien to this portion of the Shadowside. The cacodaimons shrieked in agony, many of them just disintegrating in the wash of light.

She must have known.

I felt myself slipping from their grasp, and then I was tumbling away. In the midst of a terribly swift descent, I made a last-ditch effort to thrust myself back to the skinside. If I crashed into the lake on the flesh-and-blood side, at least it would just be water and not a direct pipeline to the abyss.

I felt the familiar tearing sensation, and I could see the sickly red light of a fire in the distance. The *Scylla* was still burning. I tumbled end over end for what seemed like an eternity. Finally, I plunged with bone-jarring force into the icy water.

Bulleting below the surface, I kicked and clawed at the choking waves. Everything was black, and I couldn't tell which direction was up. My lungs burned and I fought to blink the darkness from my eyes. Every direction I turned there was water. Water and no air.

I stopped fighting, and the numbing cold swallowed me whole. With my last shred of awareness, I felt the bloody Eye slip from my grasp.

50

Someone shone a light into my eyes. With a groan, I batted them away.

"Welcome back," a cheery voice said. Blearily, I tried to focus on the owner. She had a pleasant face with warm, coffee-colored skin. Her thick braids of dark hair were pulled together in a kind of ponytail with a ruffled blue band that matched her scrubs.

Great. A hospital.

"What day is it?" I croaked. Anything else I might have asked was lost to a coughing fit. My throat and lungs felt raw. My voice sounded worse. She held a glass of water with a straw out to me, and I drank. That helped.

"It's Tuesday morning, Sunshine," she replied, setting the water aside. "Now lay back, I need to check a few things out."

"Tuesday?" I murmured. I couldn't recall what day it was supposed to be, but that didn't sound right. I went to rub my face, only to realize that my hand was bandaged up, and there was an IV taped to the back of it. I scowled, picking at the medical tape until she nudged my fingers away.

"None of that," she scolded lightly.

The doctor or nurse—I really couldn't tell which from her outfit—bustled around, poking at monitors and clipping some weird little doohickey to my middle finger.

"What's that do?" I asked, then the hacking started again.

"It tells me how much oxygen you're getting," she replied. "Oxygen's important for brain function."

Something in the way she said it niggled at me.

"Is there something wrong with my brain function?" I asked. All my words came out thickly, like my tongue was carved from wood. I ran it across the back of my teeth. They felt disgusting.

The woman met my eyes and I spied the evasion immediately. Trying to sound casual, she responded.

"Why don't you tell me your name, sir?"

I started to say *Zaquiel*, but stopped myself.

Everything crashed back in a violent rush. I struggled not to react to the memories of breathless panic—Dorimiel, cacodaimons, and plummeting through the darkness into choking, frigid waters. My pupils must have dilated or something, because her penciled brows furrowed as she studied me.

"Your name?" she prompted.

"Zachary Westland," I replied, trying to seem calm and rational and probably sounding nothing at all like either of those things. I gripped the rail of the hospital bed so fiercely I snapped something off of her little oxygen-reader thingy. I winced as it emitted a series of angry beeps, then held it up to her, muttering, "Sorry."

"It's fine, Mr. Westland," she said gently. "You've been through a lot over the past week. Do you know where you are at the moment?"

"Hospital," I quipped. If I was being a smart ass, that meant I was OK, right?

The nurse didn't seem to share my belief in the restorative powers of humor. She pressed her full lips together disapprovingly.

"Aside from the hospital."

"Cleveland," I replied. "At least, that's where I should be. I'm still in Cleveland, right?"

"How much do you remember about what happened to you?" she pursued, working hard to keep her tone neutral. I noticed she wasn't exactly answering me.

"Not a whole lot," I told her. It was mostly the truth.

She frowned. "I'm going to check some of your charts again. Are you feeling up for a visitor?"

I shrugged. "Sure."

The nurse—at least I was pretty sure she was a nurse—grabbed a clipboard and headed out of the room. I heard her speaking in hushed tones with someone out in the hall. A moment later, the door creaked a little as whoever it was entered. I looked up, expecting to see Lil or maybe Remy. Instead I was greeted by a uniformed police officer.

I almost bolted, though I hardly knew where I thought I would go in a damned hospital room.

"Hey, Zack," he said soothingly. "It's me, Bobby. Good to see you awake finally. You had us pretty worried."

I recognized the name from my answering machine.

His badge expanded that name to Officer Bobby Park, with the Cleveland PD.

"Bobby," I echoed. Nevertheless, it stirred no memories.

He nodded—two rapid dips of his chin. They made the gelled spikes of his black hair quiver. He pulled one of the chairs closer to my hospital bed and, moving a brightly colored fedora to the side, perched on the edge of it. I knew who the hat belonged to, and I wasn't exactly happy to see it there. The trim little officer misinterpreted my expression.

"You don't remember me?" he asked.

A note in his voice made me study him more carefully. He was a young man, Asian descent, probably not more than mid-twenties. Deep lines of worry scored his round features. He dug restless fingers into the knees of his uniform. Tendons ridged the backs of his hands from gripping the fabric so tightly. I searched his face again, hoping for some flash of recognition.

Nothing.

"Sorry," I said.

Something like pain touched his features. How well did I know this guy?

"They said that might happen—the doctors," he amended. "Not your fault." Then he mustered a smile of sorts. "Can I get you anything? How you feeling?"

"Like I got run over by something with its own ZIP code," I responded.

His smile widened at this, the edges of his eyes crinkling. The laugh-lines vanished in the next instant, eaten up by his worry.

"Still got your sense of humor." He pulled out a

digital recorder, holding it up significantly. "You up for some questions? I mean, if you remember anything. We need to piece together events from last week."

I sat up straighter in the hospital bed. Tape around my mid-section let me know my ribs had recently taken a beating. I took a shallow breath. It ended in a fit of coughing. Bobby set the recorder aside and held out the cup of water.

"We can do it another time," he offered.

I took a drink through the straw and cleared my throat. Sometime between the *Scylla* and now, I'd been gargling razors.

"Do I have a choice in the matter?"

Bobby's brows shot up. "No! Geez, Zack. Nothing like that. You're not a suspect or anything. I got that covered. Maybe you don't remember, but you can trust me."

I started to ask what he meant by that, though thanks to the answering message, I had some ideas. Before I could speak, however, Remy's clipped and accented voice interrupted us.

"Excuse me, but what are you doing badgering my brother," the Nephilim said, "when he has only just regained consciousness?"

He stood in the doorway, dressed in a spectacular suit of vivid goldenrod wool that only he could pull off and look dapper, rather than ridiculous. He drew himself up to his full six foot four, glowering at the police officer with an imperious expression that he'd undoubtedly learned from Sal.

"Um," Bobby offered, squirming beneath Remy's unearthly blue gaze. He recovered quickly enough, jumping to his feet and extending a hand politely. It was a sight, because Bobby came up approximately to Remy's shoulder. "I'm sorry. I didn't even know Zack had a brother. He never said anything. I thought all his family lived in Kenosha."

"Half brother," I said quickly.

"Blood's still blood," Remiel said with a knowing expression.

"I didn't know. There's nothing in the records," Bobby persisted, but it was less a challenge than it was an apology. Still holding his hand out to Remy, he said, "I'm Officer Bobby Park."

"Remy Broussard," Remiel said with a polite nod of his head. He delicately clasped the officer's hand in his own.

"Well, Mr. Broussard," Bobby responded quickly, "I'm working Zack's case, along with several other very capable officers. He's in good hands. I promise you, we will find the people who did this."

"I'm sure you will make your very best effort," Remy replied evenly. He held the young officer's gaze, also maintaining a grip on the young man's hand. For a moment, Bobby seemed strangely captivated. Pointedly, Remy said, "I think you've forgotten something."

"Oh, sure," Bobby said, blinking. He looked a little dazed. A moment later, he announced, "I forgot something. I'll have to come back later." The little guy vacated the room in such a rush that he ran off without collecting his digital recorder. I reached over and made certain it was turned off.

"Pretty sure what you just did there was illegal,"

I said, eyeing the Nephilim. I didn't know he could whammy people like that.

"I have no idea what you're talking about," Remy responded.

"Suuure," I said, drawing it out.

He looked as if he expected something more from me. I didn't give it to him. Once the silence between us had drawn out to something surpassing awkward, Remy swept toward the chair and recovered his hat. He didn't sit, but instead stood, picking imagined lint from the cloth.

I stared at the ceiling tiles.

"Are you well?" he ventured.

"I feel like hammered horseshit. No thanks to you."

"Still upset about that." It wasn't a question.

"You think? You knocked my ass out and tied me to a chair."

Another spate of dry coughing stole some of my vehemence. Remy spied the cup of water and held it out to me. I glared at the proffered drink. I wasn't about to let him feed it to me. I tore it from his hand, sending the straw spinning. Remy's expression went opaque, and he settled into the chair. He watched me for a long while, neither of us saying anything.

"She told me I would have to do it," he said at length.

"And you obeyed her blindly." I slammed the cup onto the nightstand. Water splashed in the process.

Remy's fingers crimped the brim of his fedora. He caught himself before crushing it entirely. Pale lips tugging in a frown, he set the hat aside.

"Never blindly," he objected.

I scoffed. My thoughts leapt guiltily to my back-room deal with his decimus. There were things she kept from him—and things she'd maneuvered me into keeping from him. Secrets within secrets. It couldn't have been the first time.

"Then you don't know Sal."

"I know her quite well," he replied. "Better, perhaps, than anyone." His voice was remote, and his eyes held an echo of that distance. I wondered how many years unspooled in his internal vision. It didn't soften me to him.

"I thought you took some kind of oath to look out for me." Even to my ears, it sounded petulant.

"My actions on the *Daisy Fay* served that oath," he answered. "They got you on board the *Scylla* without an immediate altercation. I didn't agree with Sal when she first proposed that course, but once Jubiel started talking, I recognized her wisdom. At the time, it was the safest way."

"So you hit me on the head for my own good. That's convenient."

He flinched as if I'd thrown acid. Lacing his fingers tightly in the absence of the fedora, he said, "I suppose I should be grateful you recall enough to be this angry."

"Sure, change the subject." I shifted among the pillows, angling my back to him. My left hand got tangled in the IV. The cut beneath the bandages throbbed dully, a grim memento of what I'd fed the Eye.

Which reminded me thunderously about the Stylus. My pulse and blood pressure spiked so swiftly, a couple of the monitors I was hooked up to vented irritable beeps. I bolted upright. Remy's unearthly blue eyes flicked from the monitors to me, filled with unvoiced questions.

"Where's my leather jacket?" I asked.

Remy's brows went up slightly.

"With everything you've been through you're worried about that old thing?" he responded.

"Where is it?" I insisted.

"Lil took it when she dragged you from the water. She has a tracking spell on you—did you know that?"

I couldn't have cared less about her tracking spell right then, though I suspected it had four legs and sharp teeth.

"What did she do with my *fucking* jacket?" I came close to shouting it.

"Calm yourself or the nurse will be in here," he said. His voice was a quiet contrast to my own. "You had something important in it?"

Only the fucking icon of the Anakim primus. I chewed my cheeks and forced myself to breathe steadily. Remy was right—if I didn't calm down, I was going to send the machines into fits. Could Lil have known about the Stylus? She wouldn't have just tossed the jacket without searching it. She'd probably hoped to find the Eye, but that was at the bottom of Lake Erie.

Perhaps they both were.

The rush of thoughts sped my pulse again. Remy watched me avidly from the chair at my bedside. I wondered how much he really knew—or suspected. I couldn't even ask him about the Eye—Sal had made certain of that—and I didn't dare make mention of the Stylus.

"Was it the demon jars?" he ventured. "They weren't on board the *Scylla*."

"I never found them," I said curtly.

Remy settled back in the chair, adopting a falsely casual pose. He clung to it too stiffly. Silence stretched between us, heavy with the weight of our secrets.

"I wish that you could trust me." He sighed.

I felt a stab of guilt and fervently wished the same, but I couldn't trust him any more than he trusted me.

"Tell me what I need to know," I said. "That cop's going to come back eventually."

"Terrorism," Remy replied. "The museum heist, the explosive sinking of the *Scylla*, all of it. You and Dr. Ganjavi discovered information being smuggled in forged artifacts, and you were both taken hostage last Monday for your pains. Something went wrong with the security cameras throughout the museum, so nothing exists to dispute those claims."

"By 'something,' you mean the local Rephaim," I suggested.

Remy gave a little roll to one shoulder.

"Presumably. Given some of Dorimiel's global connections, and the origins of the artifacts in question, it wasn't difficult to steer the authorities in that direction. Low hanging fruit, really." He flipped a wrist distastefully. "You can choose to remember all of it or only parts. You stopped breathing long enough out on the lake to provide a workable argument for brain damage."

"Brain damage," I said flatly.

"Is there a better explanation?"

I considered, wanting to argue, but it covered all the bases.

"The Rockefeller Park shooting…"

"A misunderstanding, and already handled. When they came for you and Dr. Ganjavi, you fled on foot. They chased you down to one of the park's Cultural Gardens. You were defending yourself. Simple, really."

I sighed, picking at the tape on my IV.

"I don't suppose anyone found my Kimber."

Remy shook his head.

There was a sound at the door and we both froze, waiting to see who—if anyone—came in. It turned out to be the nurse again. She must have seen a lot of Remy over the past few days, because she gave him a warm, familiar grin, her perfect, even teeth very white in contrast with her skin.

"You've got about fifteen minutes, Mr. Broussard. We don't want you wearing him out now that he's awake."

"Thank you, Ms. Jeffreys," he responded with a dazzling smile, flirting with an ease that amazed me.

"I'll be watching the clock now," she said, then she ducked back out, shutting the door behind her. Remy watched it for a few moments, and I got the distinct impression that he was listening to her as she walked away. I couldn't hear anything but the noise of the ventilation and the various monitors that were attached to me.

Finally, my sibling turned back my way, a peculiar mix of curiosity, anxiety, and hesitation playing across his pale features.

"What now?" I asked.

He drew a deep breath.

"I need to know what really happened with Dorimiel."

I looked away, far too conscious of all the things I couldn't say.

"I know Sal well enough to understand that there are things you will not—or cannot—tell me," he began delicately.

I lifted my brows, regarding him differently in that moment than I had before. In true Remy fashion, he didn't come right out and say it, but he knew as well as Lil did that Sal had oathed me. He'd been with Sal a very long time. I wondered how many oaths he himself carried.

"Go on."

Remy fussed with his cufflinks. "I suspect I know what you can't talk about. I'm not really stupid, or unobservant," he explained. "I've simply made choices for where my loyalties lie, and those loyalties often demand a certain manner of... discretion." He shifted in the hospital chair, dark hair swinging forward to hide his expression. When he raised his face again, his cerulean eyes gleamed with an emotion I couldn't name. Hoarsely, he whispered, "I saw what he did with the cacodaimons. While you were passed out, Jubiel made terrible claims. Tell me he is gone, Zaquiel. I have no desire to go to war again."

I didn't dare ask what Jubiel had told him, lest I give my own secrets away—though I wondered now if all of it were pretense. How long had we played this game?

"The cacodaimons got him," I breathed. "He thought he controlled them, but they were eating him up from within. They turned on him in the end."

"So he *is* gone?" Remy inquired. "Truly ended?"

I uncurled my fingers from the railings of the bed. I couldn't remember grabbing them, but my knuckles ached from the way I'd been hanging on.

"If being chewed to pieces by a swarm of unmakers is truly an end for one of us, then yeah—he's gone."

"Good," he said. "We may avoid war for a little while longer."

I flashed back to the four lost jars and all the names marked MISSING in my secret files. Two hundred years with my tribe disappearing. Someone else had to have known. I let loose a breath I didn't realize I'd been holding.

"I think it's already here."

EPILOGUE

After a few weeks, I got cleared to return to work. The doctors and neurologists at the hospital did everything they could to sort out my memory loss, seeking explanations for why I retained foundational knowledge like language and learned skills, but not more personal details like faces, names, and life events.

Eventually they put me through rigorous occupational therapy to teach me a variety of mnemonic skills for moving unconscious recollections into consciousness, citing trauma in addition to brain damage. I endured it, knowing there was little any of it would do for my particular issue, but it couldn't hurt to try.

My occupational therapist kept telling me lightly, "brains are funny things," as a kind of excuse for why none of her techniques worked. I wanted to tell her that demented, soul-sucking vampires were funnier, but knew she wouldn't get the joke.

Due to extensive water damage—imagine that—my

office wasn't ready by the time I was back at work. With effusive apologies, administration set me up in a part of the basement most staffers referred to as the dungeon. It wasn't much more than a furnished storeroom, and it was so far off the beaten path that no one but me was ever down there—which suited me just fine.

Museum staff threw me a party when I first got back, and I found myself surrounded by cheerful faces and sympathetic colleagues—few of whom I recognized. It was pretty awkward all around. Several tried offering condolences about Lailah. Apparently our workplace romance hadn't exactly been discreet. After a few surly dismissals on my part, they learned to avoid the topic and anything connected to it.

"Brain damage" is a dirty word among intellectuals, and loss of memory function is probably the worst kind. No one ever questioned my ability to do my job, because it was clear I recalled enough for that—even though I wasn't always sure *why* I knew certain things. Yet for every friendly face I failed to recognize, I caught more hushed whispers of pity behind my back. I'm not even sure most of them realized that they started to avoid me, but that was fine. I was definitely avoiding them.

I wanted nobody's pity.

I just wanted to do my job.

Of course, the most important part of that job had nothing to do with what the museum paid me to do, and the relative isolation of my office meant that I could discuss my work with the resident Rephaim without worrying about being overheard.

"I don't get it," I complained as I hunched over the

messy collection of papers and notes spread across my desk. "The cipher says *Gandhi guards my brothers*. I've looked everywhere around this museum, widening the circle each time. No plaques, no paintings, not even graffiti with Gandhi's name. Not on the grounds or anywhere. I can't figure out what I was trying to point myself to."

In this my sight is little help, diminished in this place and time.

Terael's regret was a palpable thing vibrating in my mind.

"Yeah, I know," I replied wearily. "Neither of us are what we used to be—but life goes on, right?" I rubbed my jaw, scowling at the maps of Wade Park, Rockefeller Park, and the rest of University Circle. "Kind of wish Saliriel's people hadn't been so efficient at making things disappear. My bet is that the police photos from the shooting are the key."

My left hand throbbed, and I idly massaged the scar angled across the palm. The cut hadn't been deep—they hadn't even bothered to stitch it at the hospital—but the healed wound often itched and tingled. Every once in a while, my pulse thudded along the scar.

I was really hoping I'd nicked a nerve.

Shoving the discomfort to the back of my brain, I focused on the maps again.

A sore subject it is, I know, but can naught be dredged from memory?

"Everything I have is after the fact." I sighed, too resigned to the loss to really get upset at the reminder.

The oracle-box of sound and sight can reveal nothing more?

"Even that reel of footage from the park has disappeared," I complained. "Did I mention thorough?" But he had me thinking back to that night in the Pub n' Sub, where I'd seen the police sketch of my face. Almost on reflex, I started doing one of the memory exercises the therapists had drilled into me, imagining myself back in the moment, building everything one sense at a time.

Country music.

Fryer grease.

Bare feet on the tiled floor, still raw from walking a couple miles with no shoes. Little lines marching up the television screen. The police sketch itself, followed by footage of the park—a bronze statue almost the same color as the naked branches of the trees in the background.

There was something about the statue that made it strange to see it standing so near to the scene of a shooting. A scene connected with violence. I fluttered my eyes as if dreaming, willing myself to see.

"I'm a fucking idiot," I said, smacking a palm against my forehead. "It's a statue. The Cultural Gardens run all the way through Rockefeller Park. There's *got* to be a section for India."

I brought up the browser on my computer and did a search for the Cleveland Cultural Gardens. The India Garden was a relatively new addition, and its central piece was a statue of one of the most famous sons of that country—Mahatma Gandhi. I scrolled through the images on the web page, stopping at one galvanizing photograph. It was the statue from the newscast.

"This is it. I'm sure of it," I said excitedly. "How the hell did I not think of this?" I grabbed my new jacket off the hook and zipped myself into the stiff leather.

And when you see our brothers' safe return, how long before you set them free?

I faltered as I buckled the bottom strap across my waist.

"Uh, about that..." I hedged. Terael didn't think anything specifically, but I could feel the expectation as he waited for my explanation. I knew he couldn't read my thoughts—not directly, not unless I allowed it—but still, I struggled to fight back the flood of images that arose from distant memory.

The Anakim Primus and other members of my tribe attacking Dorimiel's temple. The wholesale slaughter. The look on my face—all our faces—as seen from the Nephilim's perspective.

"Terael?" I asked, speaking to the empty air as had become my habit of late.

Yes, my sibling?

"Did you know Anakesiel at all?"

When last we heard the music, brother, all seven hundred and seventy-seven touched heart and mind together in glorious song. However, he added with a reflex of sorrow, *much time has passed since then, and many things have changed.*

"Seven hundred and seventy-seven. That's a lot of big egos on a little planet," I mused. Casting aside the flood of questions this inspired, I asked, "What was he like here, Terael? Once we couldn't hear the music any longer."

Moody, as sometimes so are you, my brother.

"Moody how?" I pressed, fidgeting with the bottom strap of the jacket. The buckle was different from the jacket now lost to me, made of a cheaper metal. This one didn't fit right through the shoulders, either, and it certainly didn't feel like armor. I missed the old one.

He angered at our errors, for he felt we lost our way.

"So what did he do about that—all that anger?" I inquired, visions of Judge Dredd dancing in my mind. "Forget it. I'll sort it out eventually. For now, I've got a date with Gandhi."

It was about a mile to that part of the Cultural Gardens through Rockefeller Park, and I walked the whole way. The air was crisp and chill, and white holiday lights were strung on all the trees. They glittered against the faint dusting of snow. The statue of Gandhi came into view, striding eternally across the base of the memorial. I walked circles around the gaunt figure, certain I'd found the answer to the cipher.

I still almost missed the jars, even though they were right in front of me. I kept instinctively checking around the base, expecting to find a hole or something. There was no hole, yet it felt as if the jars were just beyond my reach.

Then I stopped thinking like a mortal, and squinted across to the Shadowside. That was the key. The statue was one of the relatively newer ones in the Cultural Gardens, and on the Shadowside, it wasn't really there. Not yet, at least. A dim and murky outline hovered above the base, slowly gaining substance as time and peoples' perceptions cemented the object into whatever substance made up this side of reality. Thoughts, maybe. Or dreams. Deeper questions I could explore at a later date.

There was a crossing a little way off, by the monument of Confucius. I headed back there then stepped across, launching myself into the air. The sensation of living flight never got old. I flew the short distance back to the Gandhi statue. Then I waited for the faint echo of its base to flicker and fade. Four fist-sized objects were tucked inside. The spells of binding made them as solid on this side as any other. I slipped them into the front of my new biker jacket, cradling their chilly weight against my chest. Then I stepped back into the flesh-and-blood world.

Lil was waiting for me.

"Holy shit, lady!" I cried.

"Hello to you, too, Zack," she said wryly. She was wearing a sable driving coat over a smart navy-blue dress that ended at her knees. Sleek black boots, polished to a high gloss hugged her legs from mid-calf down. The whole ensemble had a vintage feel, and she wore it like a '50s pin-up girl.

"How do you keep doing that?" I complained.

"Doing what?" she purred, amusement dancing in her bright gray eyes.

"Randomly finding me. I didn't see any of your little friends around, and trust me, I've learned to watch for them."

Her mirth erupted as rich, ironic laughter. It echoed through the park.

"Come on, Zack. By now you should know. I have my ways."

I leaned against the statue of Gandhi and folded my arms lightly over my chest, trying to obscure the shape of the jars tucked into my jacket.

"No one's seen you since the *Scylla*. I thought you went back to Joliet," I said guardedly.

"I did," she replied. Slipping a hand into one of the pockets of the fur coat, she withdrew a jar of her own. Pointedly, she held it up in the faded light of the evening. "But we have some unfinished business, you and I."

My chest grew tight with the bitter absence of memory. Her name rode on the plume of my breath.

"Lailah."

"You didn't think I'd let you shirk your responsibility to her, did you?" Lil responded.

At first I couldn't answer. My throat felt too choked with the echo of loss. I stared past Lil at the tall, straight maples and twisted sycamores edging Doan Creek across the parkway.

"You do know how to free her, don't you?" Lil prompted.

"I got the sigil-phrases from Dorimiel, but I don't exactly remember how they work," I admitted.

"Looks like you have a couple of subjects you could experiment on," she suggested. She eyed my jacket with a knowing gleam.

I squirmed under her thundercloud gaze.

"I'm not sure that's such a good idea."

"Experimenting on them?" she wondered.

"No," I said flatly. "Letting them back out." There was a flash of shock on her face before her smug and sultry demeanor slipped back into place.

"Really?" she said, brushing back a long, russet strand teased loose by the wind.

With a shrug, I explained. "I'm not so sure they're blameless. I don't know if any of us really are."

With a thoughtful noise, she slipped her free hand into the front of her coat. It was pretty clear where that hand was going. I tried to be polite enough not to stare. Of course, I failed. She withdrew something I took initially to be an antique cigarette holder—the kind you might expect Marlene Dietrich to tote around.

Idly, Lil twirled the object through dexterous fingers.

"I guess you might be ready for me to give this back," she mused.

I did a double take at the thin length of pale bone.

"That's the Stylus," I gasped.

"You've got a keen grasp of the obvious, Zack." She waggled the Icon in my direction. I made a sudden grab for it. Nimbly, Lil danced back, boots crunching on the snow. "I don't really want your tribe's precious toy," she said, "but if I hand it over, it's going to come with some conditions."

"Oaths again?" I asked sourly.

She tapped the Stylus against her full, red lips while she thought.

"Maybe not," she allowed.

"What? You actually trust me with something like that?" I scoffed.

She pinned me with her steely gaze. "I think it's a good sign that you don't trust yourself."

A chill came over me that had little connection with the frozen winter landscape. I hugged myself, the shape of four rough earthenware jars pressing hard against my ribs. My stupid scar throbbed again.

"Shall we go somewhere to talk about it?" she inquired.

"Do I have a choice in the matter?"

"Not really," she said, and she laughed, lifting Lailah's jar like she was leading a toast. "You're stuck with us, flyboy." She hit a button on her key fob, and the engine of the Sebring growled to life. "I'm driving," she announced—in case there was any question about it.

My old leather jacket waited for me on the seat.

ACKNOWLEDGMENTS

While the writer shapes the story, it takes the effort of many people to get a book from manuscript to publication. Each job is an essential part of the finished product and without the hard work and support of a number of dedicated people, this book would never have made it to your hands. Allow me to spill a little ink here to show my thanks.

First, I offer deep gratitude to Lucienne Diver of the Knight Agency for having faith in the series and being a diligent advocate for my books. Thanks also to all the good people at Titan – Steve Saffel, Natalie Laverick, Miranda Jewess, Nick Landau, Vivian Cheung, Laura Price, Paul Gill, Selina Juneja, and Julia Lloyd. Steve, especially – your editing style was exactly what I needed. I'm thrilled that we click on the series, and I can't wait to dive into the next installment of Zack's adventures.

For words of encouragement as I developed the series, I have to thank Jim, Laurell, and Quinn. You each helped more than you probably realize. And I can't forget all my Shadow Syndicate friends – Zoë, Vissy, Saibere, Rokes, Quenn, Justin, Halk, Ergenekon, Duende, Daspien, Buck, Abri and everyone else – thank you for helping the stories come to life over the years.

For research tips, I want to thank tour guide Chad and everyone else who helped out on the USS *Hornet*, Aaron Hammon for 3 am questions about ballistics and Ohio criminal law, Elyria Little for web development and insights into Hebrew, and Merticus Stevens for giving me access to his copy of the *Celestial Hierarchy*. Finally, I have to thank Cat Mason – artist, guildie, and friend – for lending her incredible talent to all my Shadowside extras on the website.

Thank you, all.

ABOUT THE AUTHOR

Michelle Belanger is most widely recognized for her work on television's *Paranormal State,* where she explored abandoned prisons and haunted houses while blindfolded and in high heels. A leading authority on psychic and supernatural topics, her non-fiction research has led to more than two dozen books such as *The Dictionary of Demons*, *Walking the Twilight Path*, and *The Psychic Vampire Codex*, and has been sourced in television shows, university courses, and numerous publications around the world.

She has worked as a media liaison for fringe communities, performed with gothic and metal bands, lectured on vampires at colleges across North America, and designed immersive live action role-playing games (RPGs) for companies such as Wizards of the Coast. Her research on the Watcher Angels has led to both a Tarot deck and the album *Blood of Angels*. She has appeared on CNN, A&E, Fox News, Reelz, and the History Channel.

Michelle resides near Cleveland, Ohio in a house

with three cats, a few friendly spirits, and a library of more than four thousand books. More information can be found at

www.michellebelanger.com.